THE CULT OF ANICK

Book One

L.E. Brooks

Blueflight Press, LLC

2024

Avelina

The Cult of Anick: Book One

Published by Blueflight Press LLC, PO Box 652, Bettendorf, IA 52722.

www.blueflightpress.com

Cover design by Rebecca Frank

Book design and interior illustrations by Leo Hartas

ISBN: 978-1-962922-01-2 (paperback)

ISBN: 978-1-962922-00-5 (ebook)

ISBN: 978-1-962922-02-9 (audiobook)

For my ducklings. Someday you'll be old enough to read this.
Still don't. Just know that everything I do is for you.

Beware!

This novel contains:

- Intentional POV & verb tense switches . . . gasp! I know. I'm as mad about it as my editor was, as you will be and as my beta readers were.
- Themes of LGBTQ+ acceptance, diversity, and feminism. If this bullet point is more disturbing to you than the first one, then you are *definitely* in the wrong place.
- An open door sex scene. This is an *adult* fantasy novel with a romance. Some might even call it a romantasy. I love made-up genres, don't you?
- A black and white map. A color map, glossary, magical system index, and more fun stuff can be found at www.brooksbooks.net or scan this QR code:

IRONWOOD FOREST
Noble River
OXEN FIELDS
GROVES FARM
Neesee River
Caravan Trail
THE WALL
GREY DISTRICT
(Wall Slums)
AETOS PALACE
GROVES TRADERS
NEESEE
EBOROS ESTATE
Bridgestone
CENTRAL DISTRICT
WEST BRIDGE
EAST BRIDGE
BAY of MARCH
Mines
GALE RIDGE MOUNTAINS
DOWNTOWN NEESEE
RIVER DISTRICT
Neesee River
SCHOOL of NOBLE ARTS (SONA)
Caravan Trail
Meriweather Sea
SEAL BEACH
THE RHOYA
Standing Bridgestone
AARON'S COTTAGE
O'FELD COMMERCIAL DOCKS
Caravan Trail
Jarring Weed Grove
OARDOO FIELDS
O'FELD FARM
O'FELD HOMESTEAD
Bridgestone
Priscilla Bay
VILLAGE of SEAGRAL
MOORE FARM
Shadow Caves
MERIMO ISLAND
N
W
E
S
The Province of
SOUTHERN
GALE

Chapter One

Once upon a time in the Kingdom of Hartha, there was a girl named Linorra Dragonrider. She was a smart girl, but young and naive. She believed that the world she lived in was all there was, and that she was the master of that world. She never thought that anything difficult or terrible would ever happen to her. She was wrong.

I don't remember much from the day of my accident, but I remember Rogue barking furiously. He was somewhere in the woods, running farther and farther away as I lay on the rocky trail, facing a sky as brilliant and blue as a Steller's jay. I squinted up at the brightness, tracking that very bird as it flew toward the sun. Its wings beat a hectic *hwa-hwa-hwa* as it fled, as spooked as my horse had been. The silky, gold-tipped grass around me waved from the gust it kicked up as if to say "Farewell, little bird." Its silvery black head was all that stood out against the sky before it disappeared entirely.

I awoke to a sharp stabbing in the right side of my chest. My throat and lungs burned each time I sucked in a breath, which was difficult, given the tube in my throat. It was like trying to breathe through a straw. My right wrist throbbed with pain, but I couldn't see it clearly through the goop in my eyes. My hands, hot and sweaty, were stuffed into puffy white mittens. The rest of me was freezing, especially my feet.

Sunlight streamed into the room from a window on my left, brightening the sterile white room into something incongruently cheerful. My mother stood in front of the window, facing away from me. She pushed a suction cup against the glass to attach the crystal prism that usually hung in our kitchen window. It caught the light and scattered colors around the room. The rainbow cut across the white walls like a scalpel.

I tried to speak, then remembered the tube. Mom heard me stir and turned to face me. I reached out to her, and she smiled but didn't come closer. A pretty, red-haired nurse in blue scrubs was on my right, leaning over me to wipe the ointment from around my eyes.

"Avelina, you're waking up from sedation," said the nurse. Her voice was gentle and clear, but a little too loud, as if she were used to talking exclusively to elderly people. "We're gonna try to get that breathing tube out, okay?"

I nodded. I didn't care about the tube nearly as much as getting those disgusting mitts off my hands so I could scratch my face.

"Can you pick your head up off the pillow?" she asked, and I did. "Good! I think you're ready, you just need to wake up a little more, okay? Are you in pain?"

I nodded again, thinking, *What a dumb question.*

"Okay, I'm gonna keep a little bit of pain medicine going for you, but not too much. I'll come back in a bit and check on you." Quietly to my mom, she added, "You can go stand next to her. It's okay. It's good for her to see a familiar face while she wakes up."

"Thank you," she responded. The nurse scuttled through the large sliding glass door to the right of my bed.

My mother, Giana, wore dark jeans and a green T-shirt that had a picture of her own bay horse, Gem. It was her lucky T-shirt, the one she'd designed for the family business, Silverstone Stables. It was rumpled and had a coffee stain on the bottom. Dark circles showed prominently below her hazel eyes, and loose strands of straight black hair hung from a messy bun perched high on her head. Somehow, she managed to make it work.

My father used to call her a timeless beauty. With smooth, caramel skin that never progressed past the fine lines at the corners of her eyes, her age was always difficult to pinpoint. We were roughly the same height, but that's where the similarity ended. I have fair skin and my hair is a chestnut brown that turns auburn when I get too much sun.

Plus, I have a dimple in just one cheek that makes my face asymmetrical when I smile. Dad used to call *me* a genetic anomaly, but he swore it wasn't because of the dimple.

"Time for you to wake up, lazy bones," Mom said as she walked to the foot of my bed. It was the same thing she used to say to me when I was a kid. She pulled out some soft woolen socks and tugged them onto my feet.

I motioned to the walls around me with my mitted hands, trying to ask where I was and what had happened. She had no idea what I was trying to say.

"Dad will be back in a minute. He always steps out two minutes before people come in to say important things. I'm sure the doctor will be here before he gets back from the bathroom." She must have been nervous because that was a lot of talking for her. A chunky jade and malachite ring adorned her left index finger, and she absentmindedly rubbed the stones with the thumb of her right hand.

I gave up on communicating and closed my eyes. A few minutes passed and my mom let me rest. She was good like that.

The nurse eventually returned, followed by a dark-skinned physician, who leaned over me to press a stethoscope against my chest. The doctor smelled strongly of lemon, like the scent of the cleaning products that I hoped the hospital used. She peered down her long nose at me, nodded her head, then walked back out without a word, nearly bumping into my father, Alberto. The nurse remained behind and gathered a few supplies, pulling out a blue paper mat the size of a dinner napkin to lay on my chest.

"What I miss?" my dad asked. Mom rolled her eyes. He chuckled and sat down in a boxy chair pushed into the corner of the room.

Another woman, the respiratory therapist, I believe, came to stand across the bed from the nurse. She fiddled with the breathing tube, did something with an empty syringe, then pulled off the stickers that held the tube onto my face.

"Okay, one, two, three!" the therapist said enthusiastically and yanked the tube out, as if pulling a foot-long plastic tube out of someone's throat was the most natural thing in the world.

I coughed violently as she set the monstrous thing on the paper mat and wrapped it up to be thrown away. Every cough sent lightning into my ribs and out through my back. I gasped for air while the disconnected ventilator dinged insistently. The respiratory therapist sucked foamy slime out of my mouth with a suction wand thingy while the nurse slipped oxygen tubing around my ears and into my nose.

"Good job, Avelina," the nurse said as she untied the mittens, tossing them into the garbage. "Cough that stuff up. Don't try to talk right away. Your throat will be irritated from the breathing tube, but your oxygen levels are good. I'll come back in a couple minutes, okay?" She got her own stethoscope out, listened to my lungs again, then left the room with the respiratory therapist.

My dad stood up and walked over to the foot of the bed. "Look at you!" he said in that Spanish accent everyone loved. "You are a survivor!" He smiled his usual genuine smile, but his eyes were red, and his face had a few days' growth of patchy beard.

My father was a proud Spaniard, from Málaga, but his grandmother, who helped raise him, was from Scotland. He used to say that explained our mutual blue eyes as well as his impeccable English. He was about five-nine with shoes on but was always a giant in my mind, one of those inexplicably likable people who could put you at ease immediately, no matter what was happening. He smiled down at me, then at my mom. I could see his bald spot shining with sweat despite the cold room.

Mom glided over to stand next to him, and he wrapped an arm around her waist. She leaned on him a little, staring at the fat tube jutting out of my right rib cage, just under my armpit. She didn't say anything, reverting to her usual MO.

"You were asleep for three days. Can you believe it?" Dad asked.

"My back can," I croaked as I stretched out. Even at the age of twenty-six, three days in a hospital bed took its toll. "My chest hurts right in the middle."

"Well, Fanny trampled you," he said, "and, uh, you died for a minute."

My eyes snapped to his face. "I *died*?"

"Just for, like, a minute. Your lung collapsed, and your windpipe got cut off, then you died. Your heart stopped, but the doctor says your brain is fine. They put that tube in your chest, did CPR, and brought you back. Cool, huh?"

I stared at him, then glanced over at my mom, giving her my famous *What the hell?* expression. She shrugged.

"Drew came to visit you yesterday," she said.

I focused on my woolly feet. Drew was my ex-girlfriend, an artist, and my first and only real relationship and heartbreak. She had been my college roommate for two years and was the first girl I ever kissed. We broke up the day after graduation when Drew confessed that she'd been accepted to the master's program at CalArts. I offered to follow her there, but she said we needed a clean break. I hadn't taken it well.

Now, two years after finishing that degree, she was trying to reestablish a relationship and had been texting me almost every day. I had moved back home to work for my parents at Silverstone Stables, wanting desperately to build some semblance of an adult life. I wasn't interested in dredging up the past. At least, I didn't think I was.

I pretended that my mom hadn't mentioned Drew. I needed to shoot the elephant in the room. I took a semi-deep breath, coughed until my face turned pink, then asked, "Did you find Rogue?"

Nobody said anything for what seemed like forever. A blood pressure cuff on my left upper arm inflated and deflated of its own accord. I waited, coughing a few more times and looking back and forth between my parents.

Finally, my dad said, "Rogue never came out of the woods, Lina. We searched for him, but . . . he's gone." The stab I felt was worse than my chest tube.

Rogue was my dog, but that tiny noun is grossly inadequate for describing what he really was to me. He meandered into my life when I was fifteen, when I had just begun figuring out who I was and what I wanted to be.

We weren't exactly sure what he was either. Rogue looked like a pharaoh hound, except huge. The vet said that he was about four times bigger than normal, so he couldn't possibly be a purebred pharaoh hound. She had recommended a DNA test, but my dad said that was a hilarious waste of money and refused.

Rogue had a rich auburn coat everywhere except for a white patch on the left side of his face in the shape of a handprint. His eyes were a deep amber that followed everyone around the room, missing nothing. He had these adorably huge Dumbo ears that stood straight up and turned pink when he got excited or nervous.

When he first came to us as a stray, Rogue never wanted to leave the house. He would just throw himself on the ground and go limp when we tried to make him go outside to do his business.

My mom said he had abandonment issues, but that stinker knew exactly what he was doing. My dad had to pick up his ninety-pound body and carry him out. Since he wasn't fully grown yet and eventually got up to a hundred ninety pounds, that was not a winning strategy.

One day, about a month after we found him, he followed me into the bathroom. When I pulled my pants down and sat on the toilet, Rogue tensed, and his ears turned bright pink. Then he walked in a little circle and lay down, facing away from me. It was the funniest damned thing I'd ever seen. I laughed for literally days after that, and every time I did, his ears would turn pink again.

After that, Rogue used the toilet. Yes, I'm serious. He would wait for everyone to get busy, then run in there. Based on the mess, it must have taken him a couple tries to figure out how to get his butt in the right place, but he did it. That is how I learned that my dog was brilliant, and I treated him more like a person than a pet.

For ten years, Rogue was my best friend. I talked to him about everything, including the secret stuff. He was there every time I had a bad day, which could be fairly often. I used to talk to him when I was alone in my room, telling him about what frustrations or exciting events had happened. He was the first one to hear that I had a girlfriend, a full six months before I told my parents.

He was there, whining, when I left for college, and he was there when I came home for every break. He had gone missing a couple of times during the school year. My mom said he was out searching for me, which sounded like nonsense. Then again, he hadn't disappeared since I came back to start working for my parents.

I couldn't believe he was gone. I wouldn't believe it. My throat tightened in that burning way that precedes crying, and I squeezed my eyes closed.

"I'll search for him when I get home," I said, my voice breaking.

My mom didn't meet my eyes, but my dad asked, "Lina, do you remember what you told us when we found you?"

I shook my head. I remembered that little bird, the bright sky, Rogue barking, and . . . something else. The barking had stopped suddenly when I heard it. What was it? *A man's voice*, I thought. *No, that must have been my dad when he got to me.*

"You said that a white wolf had spooked Fantasma," he said and waited for me to put together the pieces.

I was still clamping down on the emotion burning in my throat, and speaking would have broken the tenuous hold I had on my grief.

"Baby," Mom said, "Rogue was more than ten years old. That's ancient for a dog his size. You remember our shar-pei, Molly, don't you? She only lived to be ten, and Rogue was three or four times her size."

Is, I thought. *Not was.*

"He saved me," I whispered, choking on the words. A tear escaped my right eye. I moved to wipe it away but forgot about my wrist. A lightning bolt flew up my forearm to my elbow and I winced. A few more tears slipped out, running down both my cheeks.

My parents glanced at each other, making vague gestures and facial expressions that indicated a silent continuation of a previous disagreement. They were always talking to each other like that. My dad sighed, saying, "Okay, we can search for him again when you get home."

I guess my mom won.

I nodded and closed my eyes. The nurse, Tarah, came in and helped me maneuver my chest tube so that I could lie on my left side. The pain in my chest was excruciating, but at least I got to blame that for my crying. She said chest tubes hurt like a son of a bitch and that I would feel a lot better when it came out.

Nevertheless, she offered me some pain medicine, to which I responded, "Yes, give me all the drugs." That made her laugh, and we were friends after that. She pushed something into my IV, then bundled me up in a stack of heated blankets.

My mom handed me my favorite book, *The Crystal Key*, then my parents left. It's actually children's fiction, too short to be called a novel or even a novella, but something about it has always been so relaxing to me. When I was fifteen, my mother got me a signed copy from the author, Violet Atticus. I had been reading it once a year ever since. I always liked to read it when I was sick or depressed. It made me feel like I was hanging out with an old friend.

The story is about a young woman named Linorra Dragonrider, who finds a magical key that opens doors to other worlds. She uses the key to search the universe for the lost dragons of Hartha. When an evil queen kidnaps a man she believes to be her future husband and demands his life in exchange for the key, Linorra must decide between love and the safety of all the lands.

It's a simple story, but I've always identified with the girl, not only because her name is similar to mine, but also because she had to learn how to trust herself and be brave in the face of ignorance, deception, and fear.

I read until the light coming through the window dimmed to the point that I had to choose between turning on the overhead light or turning over to go to sleep. I asked Tarah to stick the book in my pack and resolved to start calling people in the morning to help me find my Rogue.

Chapter Two

The name Dragonrider was old, and though the last of the dragons had disappeared more than a hundred years before, Linorra could feel in her very soul that she was meant to have one. She dreamed about finding new lands where dragons still ruled the skies, and she searched for evidence that they still existed somewhere hidden and unknown. One day, she found it.

I was in the hospital for about a week, which was great because if I had stayed any longer, the food would've killed me. The doctors and nurses all said that I was lucky to be alive given how I'd arrived. They were surprised at how quickly I recovered, but I've always been a crazy-fast healer. My collapsed lung reinflated, and they took that horrible chest tube out. My right wrist was broken, but it didn't need surgery, just a hard plastic splint.

My mother offered to pay for the search party by cooking for everyone, which anyone within fifty miles would tell you was a great deal. I had spent the last few days calling everyone I knew to come help.

I called my best friend, Marti Jermez, who enlisted her husband, Milo, and he brought his twin brothers, who I'd never met. I also asked another friend, Spirit, a new age hippie who believed in healing crystals. She was kind of an oddball but was also one of those people you could always count on for steadfast moral support.

I purposely did *not* call Drew. I wasn't mad. I swear. I just wasn't in the mood for drama. Marti called her, though. Did I mention Marti was a sneaky bitch? That girl always found a way to get what she wanted. At five-two, she was like a teacup wolverine with bright red claws and lipstick to match. She wasn't great with moral support, but she was incredible when you needed someone on your team to keep the others in line.

We all met at the stables, which was about a forty-five-minute drive from Eureka, California. It was Fourth of July weekend, so we turned the hunt into an occasion. Though it wasn't terribly hot, we couldn't do any kind of fireworks due to a fire ban. So, we all just wore red, white, and blue and let Ray Charles and Lee Greenwood do the rest.

I chose to wear my favorite running pants, which were a light iridescent blue, and a crimson tank top with a denim button-down over top for a cool walk through the woods. To complete the ensemble, I wore my running shoes, white Giants hat, and pink smartwatch.

Since we were in the middle of the foggy season, we decided to wait for some of the fog to burn off. In that part of the state, a dense fog took over the forest in the early afternoon and usually burned off by the middle of the next morning. It made for a beautiful, eerie walk in the woods, but it wasn't exactly optimal for finding a lost dog.

At about noon, after some sausage-stuffed mushrooms and toasted ravioli, my parents saddled the horses and took off to ride the trails. I was too broken to ride Fantasma, my own dapple-gray Andalusian, not to mention traumatized by my accident, so I planned to hike on foot with my friends.

My hiking pack, a blue REI co-op, had been my de facto purse since I'd been working at the stables, so I had a lot of random junk in it. The bag was stuffed and disorganized as always, but I wasn't in the mood to sift. I added water, bear spray, a remote GPS, and a few other things. Marti insisted that I bring a collar and leash, though I hadn't needed it for Rogue in ages. But as Milo always used to say, *when Marti insists, you can't resist.*

We set out on our hike, scanning the forest for evidence of my Rogue, alive or otherwise.

In the redwoods, the forest floor was a thick tangle of ferns and other brush, so you couldn't just walk through it. We stuck to a smaller footpath through the property that was probably an animal trail at one point. It was the trail that Rogue and I always took when going out for a walk. Drew stayed close to me.

"I heard you have paintings displayed in a few galleries," I said.

Drew beamed, her enormous brown eyes alight with pride. She had always been cute, but she had a new quiet confidence. She tucked a lock of curly brown hair behind her ear and caught my eye, trying to hold it.

"Yes, it's very exciting," she said. "I have one painting in LA, two in San Francisco, and one up in Seattle. All oil on canvas. Nothing fantastically inventive like some of my classmates, but people seem to like my work. I hope so. I have pretty intense loans to pay off. I've applied to be an art teacher at a couple different high schools."

"Local?" I asked.

"One is," she said, glancing down, then back up at me. I nodded noncommittally.

The dark side of my personality—the one I had long ago nicknamed Evil Lina, or Evilina—saw right through Drew's innocent act. *She's fishing. She wants you to say that you hope she'll take that one. It's kind of pathetic.*

"Well, I'm very happy for you," I lied. "I'm glad you're doing well."

"Thanks," Drew said. "So, you're working at your parents' stables?"

"Yeah, for the last three years. I'm basically their office bitch."

"Oh, so they hired Evilina?" Drew suggested.

I laughed. "They sure did. Anyway, I arrange the group rides and guest room scheduling, and I do the advertising and books. I might start doing it for a few other places too. I'm good at that kind of thing, taking details and organizing them. I was getting ready to take some pictures for our website when I had my . . . ya know." I waved my splint at her.

"Hey, can I sign that?" she asked, pointing to the splint.

"Not unless you've got that label maker on you." It was an old inside joke, and Drew laughed. She had a nice laugh, soft and genuine. It made my heart do little somersaults, which led to a strange pain in my chest. I stopped walking, holding my chest with my uninjured hand.

"Are you okay?" Drew came up close and placed her hand on my back. I could smell her lavender shampoo. It was all familiar and effortless, yet the sensation of her touch made my fists clench involuntarily. It would have been very easy to slip back into a relationship with her, especially since it had been a year since I had even kissed anyone, but the memory of the night we broke up stuck in my mind like those spiky hitchhiker seeds that get stuck on your clothes. I became acutely aware that the tightness in my throat was back, and I swallowed it aggressively.

"I'm fine," I said, "just a little sore. I should probably concentrate on our search."

"Sure," she said, stepping back. A frown crept onto her face, but I couldn't deal with that right now. I had goals, and I didn't want to get sidetracked. I needed to find Rogue.

We walked for several hours, chatting idly. Marti left me alone with Drew, walking with Milo at a comfortable distance, not even trying to hide her smug expression. Freaking Marti, I swear. I would get her for this.

The Jermez twins flanked Spirit, saying anything to make her laugh. They were quietly competing for Spirit's attention, and she gave it to them, though I doubted she could tell the difference between the two. Aside from the fact that one had long black hair and the other short, they were otherwise indistinguishable.

Spirit didn't seem to mind, though. She flashed a bright white smile at the short-haired twin and giggled, toying idly with a lock of her white-blond hair. I wondered if that would later turn into something weird and wonderful. If it did, I wanted to be a part of it. Chuckling at them under my breath made my ribs hurt, and I grabbed my side, groaning. Everyone stopped to stare at me.

"I'm fine," I said in my most exasperated voice, then I took a calming breath. *Inhale. Exhale.*

I loved the subtle aroma of the redwoods. It had a faint woodiness, but also a hint of something sweet and spicy, mixed with damp earth. To me, it smelled like freedom, a feeling echoed in the birdsong that rushed out in a chorus so high above your head that you couldn't tell exactly where it was coming from.

Rogue and I used to go in there sometimes, find a little clearing, and lie down on the mattress of needles, gazing jealously up at that distant reality at the top of the trees. Their otherworldly height made the forest feel spacious in some ways, and yet the canopy would be so thick that both light and sound sometimes struggled to penetrate all the way down, making you feel like you were tucked into a cozy, echoey cavern.

That was my place with Rogue. To be there without him felt two-dimensional, like I was looking at a photo of the forest rather than seeing, feeling, and smelling its true depth. It was a beautiful walk, but hollow.

We gained elevation, sometimes hopping over small streams or winding around the steep side of a hill. At about three o'clock, Marti shouted, "Hey, what's that?" She pointed to a clump of something rank and gooey in front of an otherwise lovely patch of white coral bells.

As I approached, Marti stepped into my path. "Let Milo go first. It will make him feel useful." Marti was about four inches shorter than me, but that fact made no difference when I needed to get my own way. There was no getting past Marti when she made up her mind about something.

"No!" Milo said, gagging. "That's Thomas the Tank Engine you're thinking of. I don't give a shit about being useful. And I can smell it from here." He coughed and covered his nose with his sleeve. So much for love conquers all.

"Milo!" Marti shouted, using her mom voice. Marti didn't have any kids that I was aware of, yet she had a solid mom voice that made you want to immediately apologize for whatever it was you had done. We called it her "mommytone" voice. Ya know, instead of monotone? She liked to use it whenever I made stupid dad jokes, which I admit is one of my favorite things.

"I'll do it," Spirit said, rolling her eyes.

Marti pressed her bright red lips together in a tight line. She flicked her black hair over her shoulder and shifted from foot to foot, cracking every knuckle in her right hand. I lifted my palms in acquiescence.

Spirit heroically advanced on the pile of goo. She found a stick and poked it. "I don't think this is a dog. And even if it is, the rib cage is pretty small. Rogue is a big boy."

I liked how Spirit used the present tense. Rogue *is*. Damn right. I unclenched my jaw.

Marti let me pass, and I walked over to see for myself. "Not a dog," I said. "Probably a fawn."

The image of a white wolf forced its way into my thoughts. It had been huge, much bigger than I ever imagined a wolf would be. What the hell was a white wolf doing in this grove anyway? The redwoods weren't even wolf country, let alone home to a giant white one. Black bears, yes. And coyotes. Not wolves.

"Let's turn back," I said. "The fog is rolling in again, and I don't think he would have run this far anyway." Nobody in the group moved or said anything for a minute. It was like a little impromptu moment of silence.

No. Rogue isn't gone. He's out here somewhere. I felt my chest tightening beneath the weight of that silence, and I had to close my eyes and focus on my breath.

I lifted my hand to my heart, a habit I'd acquired as a child. Sometimes I would imagine a friend laying a hand over mine as I stood there. For a long time, imaginary friends were all I had, but I often thought I could actually feel a hand there. I felt that now, and when I opened my eyes, I expected to see Drew's hand over mine.

It wasn't.

"Come on," Drew said, taking my other hand. "Maybe your parents found him."

"Maybe your mom is cooking those spicy chuck burgers," said Milo. "That'll make him come running. Let's go find out!" He set off, power walking back the way we came. Marti eyed me, then followed behind.

Spirit turned to me. "Lina, I know you don't believe in the same things I do, but I know Rogue is alive. It might sound bizarre, but I bonded with him, too, the night you and I met." Behind her, the twins gave each other a look. "I would definitely know if he were gone forever. You will see him again. I have a strong feeling about it." She smiled brilliantly at me, shot Drew what appeared to be a genuine smile, but which I knew to be annoyance masked by polite civility, and turned to go.

The long-haired twin leaned to put his arm around her, saying, "You're such a good friend." The other twin pinched the back of his arm and he hopped away, chuckling.

Okay, confession time. I couldn't actually remember the twins' names. I forgot their names one second after Milo told me because I was so distracted by trying to detect a difference between them. They weren't exactly the same, but other than the length of their hair, I couldn't put my finger on exactly what the difference between them was. I could've asked Marti their names, but she would've laughed in my face and announced my faux pas to everyone. I kept hoping someone would mention them casually in conversation so that I could pretend I hadn't forgotten. Sadly, that's not uncommon for me.

Drew still had my hand and pulled me gently in the right direction. I followed, but I glanced back down at the unfortunate fawn one more time, shivering. The fog actively rolled in around us. It would soon be too thick to see beyond the trail.

I turned to follow my friends back toward home but jumped when something behind me cracked loudly. I spun, eyes searching left and right. My chest ached again from my pounding heart. I just knew that the big bad wolf was about to leap out of the fog and get me. I backed away from where the sound had emanated and almost ran over Drew.

"What is it?" she asked.

"I . . . nothing." I gave a nervous little laugh. "I'm just paranoid. I thought I heard something. Let's catch up to the others."

We'd only taken one step down the trail when I heard a woman's laugh, soft and incorporeal. I spun back around, my heart racing.

I've never really believed in ghosts or the afterlife. Technically, I'm agnostic, but the way I see it, if all those people who believed in the gods of Olympus were wrong, then why are we so sure that all other religions aren't just as wrong? It's all just mythology to me, but when I heard that woman's laughter, I thought for sure that I had made a grave error in judgment.

I backed away again, my adrenaline surging. It could have been an echo from one of my friends, but I didn't think so.

"Drew, do you hear that?" I whispered.

"Yeah, it sounds like a ghost laughing," she replied, her mouth hanging open in disbelief. Drew was even more of a skeptic than I was, but this was undeniable. The laughing got louder. We looked at each other, eyes wide, then turned and ran.

Sticks and leaves crunched under our feet as we ran down the narrow trail. Small animals skittered out from under bushes and bolted up trees.

We caught up with Milo, then snaked around him and kept on running. I turned back every few minutes to glance behind me, but there was nothing there except my friends, for whom, I'm embarrassed to say, I had no intention of waiting.

When the rest of the group saw us running, they turned back to see what we ran from, but I knew there was nothing visible from the trail. They yelled questions after us that I couldn't make out. I just screamed over my shoulder, "Ghost!"

Chapter Three

The old woman had long silver-streaked black hair that reached down to her knees and was braided into a splendid plait. Her very presence vibrated with magic such that Linorra could feel it from across the musty room.

"Are you a witch?" Linorra asked.

"I am," the witch said. "What are you?"

"Nothing," Linorra said. "I'm just a girl."

"Just a girl?" the witch asked. "That's a funny thing to say, but I suppose I know why you said it. I've thought that myself once or twice."

"You?" Linorra asked, astonished. "Haven't you always had your magic?"

"Yes," the witch said. "I have."

It was downhill most of the way back to the stables, and we made it in less than half the time it had taken to walk out. We didn't run *all* the way back. I was in good shape, but I had just gotten out of the hospital, and I was still broken in two places.

We ran until we couldn't run anymore, then we walked, discussing what Drew and I heard. Then someone would hear a sound behind us, and we would run again. By the time we made it back, we were all exhausted and sweaty. The creepy weirdness in the woods was smothered by intense physical exertion, and our ghost discussion had turned into half the group believing and the other half laughing hysterically. Nobody had seen any sign of Rogue.

As the sun set, we all shuffled into the screened-in porch at my parents' house and collapsed onto the couches. The porch had an oversized stone fireplace and seating for bed and breakfast guests.

Four guest rooms were accessible from the porch, none of which were fancy, but they were clean and had comfortable beds. Only the room at the farthest end of the porch was occupied. A twentysomething girl traveling alone, the guest in that room was pretty in a Snow White kind of way and could have lured away one of the Jermez twins, but she had yet to emerge since checking in.

We had the porch all to ourselves, so we tucked in for a night of merriment that would inevitably end with my friends crashing in the guest rooms.

My mom had, indeed, made her spicy chuck burgers and paired them with scalloped potatoes, corn on the cob, and a keg. Yes, a keg. My parents were thrifty, and a keg was cheaper than individual bottles of beer—not to mention better for the environment, as Spirit enthusiastically noted. Plus, it's just fun to drink out of a red Solo cup. I mean, come on. What's better than a keg party with friends? Nothing, that's who.

My parents left us to it, retreating into the house once their friends left. We all sat together on the outdoor couches, which were arranged around a large wicker coffee table with a glass top. We had our red cups, which had been drained and refilled multiple times. Our paper plates—which had been piled with food beyond the confines of societal norms—lay empty in front of each one of us, except Spirit, who was vegan and hadn't needed a plate for her one piece of watermelon.

Milo had eaten two giant burgers to make up for what he called her obvious error, and he was on his eighth beer at least. He'd been laughing loudly at us for the past five hours and showed no signs of stopping anytime soon. I was sure he was trying to memorize every detail of the night so he could tell the story for years to come. I doubted he would remember any of it.

"You didn't see a ghost," Marti said.

"I didn't say I *saw* a ghost," I corrected. "I *heard* laughing that wasn't attached to a person. You guys had all walked away already, and Drew heard it, too, dammit!"

"I did hear it," Drew squeaked, "and it was the weirdest thing in the history of ever. I was so scared!" Her eyes were wide as she spoke, but they danced, and a small smile played on her lips. It was dangerously adorable.

Milo laughed again. Marti smiled, too, her eyes rarely leaving Milo. She appeared uncommonly relaxed, though she had stopped drinking after the first beer in case she needed to manage her husband.

"I believe you, Lina," Spirit chimed in.

"So do I," said the twins at the same time.

Milo rolled his eyes and Marti laughed out loud. "You guys are so pathetic. Especially you, Juan," she said.

Finally, I thought. "Yeah, Juan," I said.

Milo and Marti both burst out laughing. Marti said, "You see? I told you she didn't remember their names!" This, of course, made everyone laugh.

"Freaking Marti, I swear!" I said, exasperated. I wasn't actually mad that she had tricked me into revealing my secret mental impairment. Everyone already knew about it anyway. However, I *was* still irritated that she'd called Drew.

"I can't believe you fell for that again," Marti said, still laughing.

"I'm sorry," I said to the twins. "Can you guys please just tell me your names again?"

"And shoe size," interjected Milo.

"Never mind. I'm getting another beer. Anyone?" I asked. A chorus of agreement followed. "Everyone. Got it," I said. I got up and walked toward the keg, giving Marti a little side-eye as I passed. She glanced at me, then back at Milo, shrugging. I had no room to judge. I was a little wobbly myself as I walked to the keg.

The door squeaked open, and my mom came through it, holding a bottle. "Does anyone want port?" Another chorus of merry agreement resounded. Even Marti sat up with interest.

"Everyone. Got it," she said. "I'll get the port glasses." She walked over to the outdoor bar to fetch them. She had a weird obsession with using the proper dishes and utensils for things, as if she were entertaining royalty and didn't want to appear uncouth. I wondered if her fancy glassware would survive the night. I didn't care either way. I hate port.

Another door squeaked. I glanced up, expecting my dad, but a guest door opened, and Snow White walked out. She smiled crookedly at me, but it didn't touch her eyes, which were a luminous blue-green color. They didn't seem like human eyes but more like the kind of monster eyes you might see coming out of the darkness on a vintage episode of *Scooby Doo*.

I tried to return her smile, but it was stiff. "Are you finding everything okay?" I asked. She nodded. "Are you interested in dinner? My mother is famous for her cooking."

"Yes, thank you," she said. "I should eat something." She had an unusually deep voice, and something close to a standard American or maybe Canadian accent, but I couldn't quite place it. She was several inches taller than me with well-muscled shoulders and a lean frame. She looked me up and down, one corner of her mouth twitching. Something amused her, apparently, and I had no desire to know what.

I turned away, avoiding her intense gaze, and got her a plate. It was tricky to maneuver the tongs with my splinted extremity, but I managed. She didn't offer to help, despite my obvious injury. I had to stop loading food before the plate got too heavy to hold with just my left hand. I walked over to her, holding out the plate.

"Would you like to eat out here or in your room?" I asked, hiding my annoyance.

"It's a lovely night. I think I'll eat out here," she said, her crooked smile poised to jump right off her face and bite me.

I looked away from her, out past the screens toward the trees. It was getting late, and the fog had fully consumed the property. It was cool, but not cold, and there was very little wind. A symphony of frogs and toads out in the grove reminded me of summers with Rogue when I was in school. It really was a perfect night, but the fun of the evening hadn't relieved my profound sense of loss.

"You're right," I said. "It's a beautiful night. Sit anywhere you like."

The guest settled at a table in the corner of the porch and picked up her burger. I pointed a fake little smile at her and turned to go back to my group, but before I could escape, she coughed loudly. I turned back to find her spitting out the burger.

"What's wrong?" I asked.

"Nothing, it's just a little spicy for me," she said, coughing again.

I did my best to hide my incredulity. The burgers weren't that spicy. It was mostly paprika. "I'm sorry. Can I get you something else?" I asked.

"No. I will eat the . . . um . . ."

"Potatoes?" I supplied.

"Yes," she said, picking up the corn.

Huh. Maybe she's from Quebec. "Okay, I'll be over here if you need anything."

"I don't mean to be rude," she said quickly, before I could leave. "We eat very little spice where I'm from."

"Oh? Where is that?"

"Neesee," she said, her crooked smile returning.

I looked at the ceiling, trying to rack my brain. "Is that in Canada?"

She paused, furrowing her brow, then said, "No, much farther away than that, but I have a feeling you will like it there."

"Would," I corrected. "*Would* like it there."

Her smirk returned and she said, "Maybe I should go back to my room. I'll need my rest tonight." With that, she rose and walked out, shutting the door softly behind her. I didn't hear the click of a bolt. Her food sat on the table, untouched except for that one bite.

"What a psycho," I said out loud.

"Lina!" my mother hissed. I did a slow-motion turn to find my mother giving me a stern expression. "Be nice to my guests."

"Sorry," I said, chagrined. Mom nodded, then she went back into the house, taking the platters with her.

I headed over to where I had been sitting earlier and plopped back down next to Drew.

"What is it?" Drew asked, her eyes narrowed.

"I just talked to our guest, and she is super weird."

"Weird how?" Drew asked. That's what I always liked about Drew. She was always on my side. Ya know, until she wasn't.

"I don't know," I mumbled, glancing down at my feet. "Oh, I forgot to get my beer."

"Here," Drew said, holding up a small glass. "I got you this port."

I wrinkled my nose. "It's kind of an elderly person's drink, don't you think?"

Drew rolled her eyes. "Just take it, judgy."

I took the glass but didn't drink, then glanced over at our friends, who had all drifted into smaller units. Milo seemed like he was about to pass out and just wanted to hump something before that happened. He whispered to Marti, who giggled unexpectedly. They got up, stumbled into the closest guest room without saying good night and closed the door. I heard the bolt turn, then I heard Milo's boisterous laugh, then nothing.

Spirit and I gave each other a look and we both smirked. The twins were still in competition for her attention, and she appeared weary of the game. I stood, preparing to rescue her, but Drew took my hand, holding me back. I looked down at her and she stared back at me very directly. I could almost read her mind. She wanted me alone and she was done waiting. I sat back down, resigned, then glanced up at Spirit.

Spirit glanced from me to Drew and seemed to come to a decision. She took the hand of the long-haired twin, giving him the come hither, and walked toward the last guest room. He jumped up, triumphant. The other twin sagged into his chair and groaned. When Spirit got to the doorway, she turned around and said, "Hey, Bobby, aren't you coming?" Bobby stared blankly at her for a second, then jumped up and practically skipped after her. Spirit and I made eye contact before she shut the door, and I felt suddenly flushed.

Drew seemed perturbed. "I don't even want one," she whispered, "let alone two. And brothers? That's more than a bit ick, for me." I stared after the trio, thinking how very, very wrong she was.

If Drew weren't here, you could be skipping over there yourself, Evilina thought. I had a lot of pent-up energy after more than a year of celibacy, and I wanted to expend it over there in that other room, not over here with Drew.

I was being presented with a chance to get back together with Drew, and all I could think about was knocking on Spirit's door. It wouldn't be the first time, let's be honest, though never with so many participants at once. It turned me on just thinking about following those three into the room. I mean, who wouldn't love a foursome? Nobody, that's what.

Actually, maybe Drew.

I looked over at her, trying very hard to keep my face relaxed so she couldn't see how annoyed I was by her presence. I'd missed her, but I'd gotten used to missing her. I'd made peace with it and had moved on to bigger and better things. Or at least a wider variety of things. It would be a sacrifice to go there with her again. I'd have to leave behind a side of myself that I had come to love.

I set the glass of port down on the coffee table, stood, and said, "Bobby, huh? I never would have guessed that name in a million years." Drew laughed her nice, soft laugh and gripped my hand firmly.

A lead weight lay in the pit of my stomach. How do you reject someone who might love you when you yourself know exactly how much that sucks? You just do it, I guess.

"Lina," she said. "I just want you to know that I never stopped loving you. I know I said we needed a clean break, but—"

"Drew," I interrupted, but as I glanced out past the porch screen again, searching for the words, I saw it. At the end of our gravel driveway, maybe twenty yards away from the porch, was a sign that read "Silverstone Stables." Even though it wasn't very far away, I could hardly see it through the fog. A light hung over the sign, illuminating it at night and creating a spotlight on the ground.

In that spotlight stood Rogue.

I sucked in a breath. "Rogue!" I looked around the room wildly for my hiking pack. It still had the leash in it. I saw it sitting on the porch bar, grabbed it with my good hand, and burst through the porch door without a second thought. It made a loud slapping sound as it closed behind me.

"Lina!" Drew shouted.

"Go get my dad!" I screamed. I never found out if she did it. I ran toward Rogue. I kept my eyes on him, as if losing sight of him would make him vanish again. I got to within ten yards of him before he bolted.

I guess I'm going to need that leash after all.

Before he tore down the road, he'd been silently staring at me, like he'd waited for me to see him so that I could follow. He kept a little distance ahead of me on the driveway, then turned down a footpath to the right, straight into the woods. He wasn't running full tilt but just fast enough that I could keep him in sight without catching him.

"Rogue!" I shouted again. Between the fog, which was thicker than usual, and the dark, I couldn't see a damned thing. I didn't care. I had to get to him.

I cried as I ran, letting the branches scrape and slap my face, confused about what was happening. Just as I began to despair of ever catching him, nature decided to make me its bitch and created a nice hole for me to step in.

To be fair, I was still a little drunk, which is absolutely the only reason why I twisted my ankle and tumbled to the ground like a cheerleader in a 1980s slasher movie.

I still held the pack in my left hand, and so I thoughtlessly thrust out my injured right hand. When I landed, I heard a disturbing *crack* as the weakly supported injury took the brunt of the impact, likely splitting even farther down the bone. Pain blinded me for a good ten seconds, shooting up my arm all the way to my shoulder. I dropped the pack and instinctively pulled the injury to my chest, screeching and curling up like a roly-poly.

When the initial pain subsided and became a merely nauseating throb, I uncurled and looked up. Rogue had stopped within a few feet of me, waiting. I heard him whine. His amber eyes, always so impossibly aware, glowed in the darkness.

"Rogue, what are you doing?" I pleaded, still clutching my wrist to my chest. He didn't move. I managed to get the pack and pull it all the way onto my back, then used my good arm to get up, limping a little on my now-sprained ankle. Tears streamed down my face from both pain and frustration.

"I can't run after you anymore, Rogue. Please just come home." He stared at me, motionless. His eyes flicked past me, over my shoulder, then back to my face. His ears were bright pink.

I listened for voices coming after me from the house, but I heard nothing. It was dead silent. Even the frogs and toads had stopped singing.

"Please, Rogue. What do you want?"

Then, as if in answer, a swarm of light blue fireflies appeared between us and flew around in a little circle.

No, not fireflies, my brain informed me. *Not the right color. Flecks of light.*

They were an aqua color and ethereal, like swirling bits of dust that you might see floating in a beam of afternoon sunshine. It was beautiful, but my brain couldn't process what I saw.

The lights swirled until the circle became a sphere, then it made a loud and unexpected whooshing sound. I jolted back and stared, transfixed.

The sphere slowly expanded, the pinpoints of light becoming brighter and more numerous until it was essentially a raging ball of blue fire.

It was so bright that it lit up the surrounding area, coloring everything with a peculiar blue sheen, as if we were in an ice cave instead of the middle of a forest. The light cut a tunnel through the fog, and I recognized a familiar clearing.

I squinted and used my good hand to shade my eyes. Below the sphere, set into the ground, was a stone with a large *X* carved into it. I knew this place. It was my treasure spot from a childhood game.

"*X* marks the spot," I said to myself, remembering the last time I was here.

Finally coming to my senses, I backed up and looked around for Rogue. I stumbled backward, just barely keeping myself from falling again. A pain shot up to my knee from my sprained ankle, but I gritted my teeth and ignored it.

The light expanded slowly enough that I had no trouble escaping, even in my condition. When it reached about the size of a small car, it stopped.

I searched my pockets for my phone to take a video. I couldn't find it. After some fumbling, I finally remembered that it was stuck in my bra. I pulled it out, but the screen wouldn't work because it was covered with sweat. I wiped it on my shirt and hopped back a couple feet so I could get the whole sphere in the frame.

I bumped into something. I expected a tree, but when I looked over my shoulder, I saw a woman with a crooked smile and red lips. I flinched away from her.

"Lina," she said in her husky voice. "It really is a beautiful night, isn't it?" She laughed, and I would have recognized that laugh anywhere.

"You're the ghost," I said, my heart pounding.

She laughed again. It gave me a chill despite the ball of fire not six feet from me. I wanted to back away from her, but I also didn't want to be incinerated. I was trapped. "Who are you? What do you want?"

Psycho Snow White pursed her lips, then shrugged. "My name is Seleca, but that's not important. You and I may get to know each other at some point, but for now, I'm just a girl searching for her *dog*, like you." She said the word "dog" like it was a great insult. Rogue, having navigated around the ball of fire, walked between us and sat down, glancing up at me and then back down as if ashamed.

"Who's a good boy?" she said, smiling. He growled for a brief moment, then quieted. I had never heard him growl before. I looked from him to the woman and back again, trying to comprehend what was happening, but I couldn't. I was experiencing an abrupt dissolution of my reality.

Psycho Snow White stepped toward Rogue, crouching down to slip her hand under his rib cage. She picked up his giant body with one arm as if he were a stuffed animal. Rogue whined loudly, but he didn't struggle. He turned his head, and for a split second, I saw the skin around his eyes ripple like the surface of a pond. Then she threw him into the ball of fire.

I screamed. I'm not proud of it. I don't think of myself as a person who screams stupidly and falls down, but I had done both of those things in the last two minutes. *You are such a cliché*, Evilina thought.

"Don't worry. He'll be fine," she said, walking toward me. I got the definite feeling that she stalked me now. The closer she got to me, the bigger she looked. I had never been in a fight before, and I had absolutely no instincts for it. Plus, I was injured, okay? I didn't have a prayer.

Her interaction with Rogue had given me an out, and I turned to run, but she caught me easily from behind, wrapping her arms around *my* rib cage. I convulsed, my broken ribs screaming, but she hung on, dragging me toward the blue fireball.

"Have a nice trip," she said. "I'll catch up with you later." Then, she tossed me in.

Chapter Four

Linorra cracked the door open, looking out. The first thing she noticed was the smell of roses. Beyond the door was a lovely garden with giant yellow flowers she didn't recognize. They were as tall as her castle and as wide as a drawbridge. She pulled the key out of the doorknob and watched it transform back to its original shape, then dropped it into her coin purse and tied it shut, pushing the door all the way open to step through. Somewhere in the distance, a deep roar vibrated through the air, straight through her body. She steeled herself and closed the door behind her.

The blue light engulfed me, seeping into my flesh and dissolving my skin like acid. I squeezed my eyes against the light, but it had a crushing physical presence that penetrated through my eyelids, directly into my brain. My skin bubbled, melting away from the muscles and bones.

I had an instant to ponder that before all coherent thought was banished by pain. My entire being, every inch of skin, every organ, every bit of real estate inside my body and spirit, lit up with what could only be described as agony.

I think I screamed, but I couldn't hear myself. All I could hear was a ringing in my ears so loud that my whole body vibrated with it, making me feel like I would rip apart from the inside out.

Out of nowhere, a terrible anguish struck me, a deep self-loathing I couldn't explain or sufficiently justify until, in a moment of horrifying clarity, I realized that so much of me had burned away that I could see my own soul.

And it wasn't good.

Evilina, who had always lurked in the back of my mind, was actually my truest self. I was not only capable of carrying out evil deeds, but I thoroughly enjoyed them. I was that person in the movie theater who laughed at the wrong times, like when everyone else is fighting tears. I was that person who saw horrific news stories and shrugged. I was that person who was the last to know everything because I didn't much care about what happened to other people.

I wasn't all bad, of course. I loved my parents and my friends, but I had spent an inordinate amount of time thinking about myself. I was selfish and spiteful. Was I really even that close to my friends? I'd been essentially friendless until my twenties, and when I finally did make friends, I always kept them at enough of a distance that I would emotionally survive it when they inevitably realized they'd made a mistake. I really only had one friend I hadn't slept with, and Marti was arguably a bigger bitch than me.

If I was being honest, my best friend was a dog, and even he had abandoned me.

In that moment, I didn't think so much as know, irrefutably, that I had earned this pain, and I was now in Hell, as was only right and just. Despair filled me, but I couldn't cry. I only trembled, rigidly braced against the pain as I floated, weightless, useless, and appropriately forgotten in that merciless light.

I lost all sense of time, but at some point, I regained an awareness of my physical body and realized that I was waking up. The pain was gone, leaving behind a blissful numbness. Whatever I had been before had surely been burned away.

Good riddance.

I still squinted my eyes against the piercing light, but it had turned into a cool presence that was ecstasy by comparison. I relaxed, reveling in the sweet absence of sensation. I stretched out my arms and legs experimentally, but I couldn't feel my injured wrist, ankle, or anything else.

I could sort of feel them. I feared that my moment of respite would soon end, and I mentally braced myself against it. Unlike the initial experience of intense pain, however, I now had a dull throbbing that started in my chest and gradually spread outward. The stronger it got, the more I understood that this was not pain. It was *pleasure.*

It was as if a devoted lover embraced me, gently massaging away all the pain in my body. Having come face-to-face with the worst part of myself, I surrendered to my fate. Shockingly, the despair that had consumed me was replaced by unqualified acceptance. The throbbing in my chest traveled down the length of my arms and legs, pushing out a joyful warmth.

Hesitantly, as if addicted to the feelings, I released the fear and anguish that had skulked in the background of my psyche for years, terrorizing me and simultaneously tricking me into ignoring its presence.

The gentle throbbing built to a crescendo of emotional and sensory pleasure, transforming into something resembling physical pleasure. It was like waking up to the smells of sizzling bacon and baking bread on Christmas and then finding out that someone had gifted you an industrial-strength vibrator. Every physically or emotionally gratifying feeling I'd ever experienced mixed together like a warm broth and soaked into my body and spirit.

I had never really believed in Heaven, and if I did, I was pretty sure that Evilina and I wouldn't be making an appearance there, but this place came close. Tears spilled down my cheeks as a surge of profound relief flooded my entire being. I screamed out my excitement, only to realize that this place still blocked all sound. *Maybe I was wrong*, I thought, as the pleasure reached a terrifyingly intense climax. *I do belong here.* The feeling pulsed through me over and over until I thought I might overdose on it.

Finally, the sensation ceased just as abruptly as the pain had begun and I drifted limply in the silent aqua-blue light. The ringing in my ears subsided. All was calm and still. I took a deep breath in and out, wondering idly how I could breathe at all in this strange place, and let myself relax completely. I'd dozed off when the whooshing sound started again, first as a low grumble and quickly escalating to a roar, and then I fell a few feet through the air, landing with a soft squish onto wet grass. I had the uncomfortable impression that I had just been flushed down a toilet, or maybe out of a birth canal.

A cold, misty rain drifted in from the side instead of from above, cooling my face and arms. The return of scents and sounds overwhelmed my senses. I opened my eyes to look around, but my light-assaulted eyes could now see nothing except blackness and a fading afterimage. I closed my eyes again and just lay there, shivering.

Low, muted thunder rumbled somewhere in the far distance. Leaves rustled in the wind, mixing with the rhythmic pattering of rain on the ground to my left. The familiar scent of redwood trees wafted into my nose, quickly replaced by dog breath and a disgusting, all too familiar tongue licking my face.

I opened my eyes again, squinting. My sight adjusted, and I could just barely make out Rogue's form in the dim moonlight. I tried to push him away from my face, but I was too weak. He eventually stopped to snuggle his huge body into the space between my knees and chest, half sitting on me, and sticking his wet nose under my chin. I managed to flop an arm up over him, but it was an absurdly strenuous effort.

"Where are we, Rogue?" I asked. He made his little dog groaning sound, then licked my neck. I squeezed him, grateful for his warmth. "I missed you, too, buddy," I whispered. I was uncomfortable, but for the first time since my accident, my heart didn't ache.

After a few minutes, my eyes adjusted fully to the dark and I noticed, with shock, where the dim light came from. It wasn't moonlight. It was *me*. The arm I'd placed over Rogue glowed faintly with the same light that I had seen in the . . . whatever it was.

A portal.

"Maybe I'm in the nether," I mumbled, laughing weakly to myself. "I better get some glowstone while I'm down here." I was glad no one was around to witness my pathetic attempt at *Minecraft* humor.

I looked at my arm again. The glow was fading, taking my vision with it. I closed my eyes again, thinking I would just rest for a few minutes.

I'm not sure how long I lay there, but when I opened my eyes, the rain had stopped. The first hint of sunlight cast a faintly golden glow over an expanse of meadow and forest. The air smelled of pine and damp earth and was saturated with the moisture of last night's rain.

Rogue was gone.

I lifted my head and, though still weak, it was more like weakness after a long run. I stood up and was only a little dizzy. The straps to the splint were loose, and I yanked it off with little effort. I found my pack, which had landed nearby on the ground, and picked it up with my right hand to test it out. There was no pain.

Okay, just a bit of S&M and I'm all fixed up, I guess.

I unzipped the bag and stuffed the splint in there, then peered down at myself. My clothes were muddy but intact. I didn't know how it hadn't all been burned away. My hat was gone, which meant I had some auburn highlights to look forward to, but at least I wasn't stark naked. I also noted, with relief, that I was no longer glowing.

I turned in a circle to survey my surroundings. To my right, a sheer cliff face shot up into the sky, hanging over me just enough to block the worst of the rain. Otherwise, I was surrounded by shoulder-high grass, topped by feathery seeds. The spot where I had been lying left a perfectly circular patch of muddy grass that was sheared down to the ground, bits strewn everywhere.

Did I really sleep in the mud all night? I really need to quit drinking.

It was foggy, but I could see a grove of redwoods across a small meadow. Wildflowers, somehow delicate and also larger than I had ever seen, poked their heads above the tall grass here and there in a vibrant eruption of yellow and purple.

A large, flat stone leaned against the cliff face. It had an *X* carved into it, similar to the one I knew, but standing upright.

X marks the spot.

I stared at it for a moment, thinking that I had better remember where this place was. Then I backed away from the stone to see a mountain rising behind it. My heart skipped a beat, and I nearly stumbled backward. This snow-capped mountain was enormous. My parents' stables were in the foothills of Klamath, nowhere near a peak like this one. I squinted at it and rubbed my eyes.

Yep, still there. Where the hell am I?

I searched for my phone but didn't see it anywhere. I patted my bra. Nope. I searched in the tall grass around the circle, finding nothing, then gave up. At least I had my watch.

I heard barking and glanced up to see Rogue trotting toward me on a footpath through the redwoods, followed by a man in strange clothing. I felt a brief moment of relief at seeing Rogue and possibly even getting help from someone who might know where the hell I was, but my hopes were dashed when I saw him scowling in my direction as if he envisioned imminent violence. My heart rate spiked. Even worse, despite his expression of wrath, he was still uncomfortably handsome, which always makes me uneasy. Especially when I look like an avalanche victim.

As always, when coming across an unknown man with no one around to help me, I performed a quick rape threat assessment, or RTA, as Marti used to call it. This man seemed to be in his late twenties, maybe early thirties. He appeared healthy and clean, like he took good care of himself. That was a good sign. He wore his dark brown hair tied at the nape of his neck, and his beard was trimmed and well-kept. His clothing was super weird, though. A dark brown tunic hung to his knees and was belted with what looked like red snakeskin, paired with knee-high boots of the same material. On second thought, perhaps my muddy, disheveled appearance was in my best interest.

Rogue obviously knew him and trusted him. That was a very good sign. As he got closer to me, though, I noticed how massive he was, at least a foot taller than me and twice as wide. He reminded me of a bear. That wasn't good or bad by itself, but could be very, very bad if combined with a bad RTA.

I decided to trust Rogue's judgment. The man had already seen me, despite the tall grass. I could have run away, I suppose. I was pretty fast, and I could run for hours. Then I remembered that I had bear spray tied with a quick-release strap on the outside of my pack.

"Trust, but verify," I whispered to myself. I found the canister and yanked it loose. The little orange safety clip was still intact. I decided to risk it and left it that way. The pair came out of the redwoods, wading into the grass. Rogue must have sped up when he saw me because a swish of grass blades outpaced Bear Guy.

"Rogue!" the man shouted in a deep voice. "Get back here!" He had the same strange accent Psycho Snow White had, like he was North American but from some region I had never visited.

The man held some kind of metal weapon. It looked a bit like a crossbow but much smaller and narrower. He lifted it up to point at my head. Suddenly, my bear spray seemed rather naive and stupid.

Rogue ignored him, jumping up and almost knocking me over. He planted both front paws on my shoulders and licked my face. He also blocked any shot that Bear Guy might have had since, standing on his hind legs, he was as tall as I was. Bear Guy knew Rogue somehow, so he wouldn't shoot through him to get to me, or so I nervously hoped.

I was glad to see that Rogue had not run away again, and I smiled despite my possibly desperate situation. I felt weird about it, though. Obviously, my Rogue had not only been *my* Rogue. His name fit him better than I had ever understood. I hugged him anyway as I tried to remember where we'd gotten his name from.

Bear Guy closed the distance between us, scrutinizing our little reunion. Now that he was closer, I could see that his eyes were an extraordinary shade of ice blue that contrasted sharply with his bronze skin and dark brown hair. He was even more attractive up close but exuded a menacing energy that beamed out of his hard eyes.

"Rogue!" he called again.

"Excuse me?" I said. "This is *my* dog. See this collar?" It came out a little angrier than I meant it to, but his sharp attention and overpowering presence had me flustered. I pointed to the metal tag. "I'm the one who had this made for him," I said. "It's literally got my name on the other side." The man's eyes widened, bringing my attention back to their unusual color. They were magnificent. I barreled on. "*I* named him. He's *my* dog, and I will hug him when and where I want to."

I finished my rant and then, not wanting to be a complete Marti-level bitch, I said, "Thanks for your concern, though. Now, please stop pointing that little toy at me and tell me which way the road is so I can get home." I probably failed on the not-being-a-bitch thing, but I had just spent a whole day searching for Rogue, and I wasn't about to relinquish custody.

Bear Guy stared at me for a long moment, then down at Rogue, then back at me again. He didn't lower his weapon. "Avelina Silva?" he asked.

"Yeah," I said, taken aback that he knew my name. He must have gotten it from the dog tag, but it still unsettled me. "You wanna see a driver's license?" The man knit his eyebrows together but didn't respond.

I rolled my eyes, slid Rogue's paws off my shoulders, and turned to walk away. It was a calculated risk. I wasn't going to overcome his ranged weapon with my bear spray, and if this man wanted to assault me, there was very little I could do about it.

"Come on, Rogue," I said, hiking down the hill away from Bear Guy. Rogue followed on my heels. I wanted to get his leash out, but I was afraid that Bear Guy might get spooked and shoot me out of an abundance of caution.

"Stop!" he commanded. I almost stopped just from the sheer force of his authority but overcame it just in time. I had a point to make, and if he was gonna shoot me, then he was gonna shoot me. Talking to him while I was in Marti mode wasn't going to help my case. After the intense emotional roller coaster I'd been on for the last twenty-four hours, I wasn't taking any shit from some random dude with a toy crossbow.

"Bite me," I said over my shoulder and kept walking.

He sighed. "Wait. Please."

I stopped, turning to give him side-eye. He still had his weapon up. I gestured to it with an open hand, giving him my famous *What the hell?* look. He pressed his lips into a flat line, but he put it down.

"Who are you?" he demanded.

"Um, I'm Avelina. We just covered that. Like, twenty seconds ago." *Okay, Evilina, seriously. Rein it in.* I squeezed my eyes shut to banish my evil twin, then I clenched my fists, took a deep breath, and opened my eyes to face Bear Guy squarely.

"Let me start over. I'm Lina. I live over there." I pointed up at the mountain, then I stopped, glancing around. "Or maybe it's that way," I said, pointing in the exact opposite direction, down the hill. "Um, which way is the road again?"

Bear Guy wrinkled his brow, ticking up one corner of his mouth. I wasn't sure if it was a small smile or utter contempt. He pointed down the hill and said with feigned patience, "Well, no one lives in that direction for about fifty kilometers." He turned to point up at the mountain. "And no one lives in *that* direction for at least a thousand kilometers, which is good because they would be eaten by ridge wolves. Or mountain bears, I suppose."

My stomach dropped. I ignored, for the moment, his strange use of metric units and focused on the fact that if what he said were true, then I was nowhere near home.

Because you went through a portal, idiot.

"Wait, did you just say wolves?" I asked. He nodded. "And are these wolves white, by any chance?" I asked.

"Of course," he said, giving me his own version of the *What the hell?* look. "What other color would a wolf be?" He dropped his eyes to my muddy clothes as if trying to decide if I were crazy. By the expression on his face, his conclusion was not in my favor.

"Oh, okay," I said, growing irritated. "You're right. I'm the strange one here, but let me ask you a question. If you had to choose, would you rather fight Medusa or release the Kraken?"

Rogue coughed. I looked down at him, smirking. "I know, right? Who is this guy?"

"I don't know who the Kraken is," said Bear Guy, "but if we don't get out of this clearing soon, we'll both be fighting. The wolves have likely smelled us already." He turned toward the mountain, then said under his breath, "Especially you."

I fingered the cap on my bear spray. Bear Guy obviously wasn't my biggest fan. But how did he even know I would be here? He knew Rogue well enough to have seen my name on his collar. Did he really just follow Rogue, not knowing where the dog would lead him? That seemed unlikely.

Maybe he knows about portals. Find out what he knows.

"Where did you come from?" he asked.

Well, that was convenient.

"Over there," I said, pointing to the *X* stone. "I just sort of fell out of the sky, I guess." I laughed nervously. He narrowed his eyes but said nothing.

He knows something. Pry it out of him. Evilina's demands were more insistent than usual. In fact, that didn't even sound like something she would say.

My own confusing thoughts distracted me just long enough for Bear Guy to sigh and march away. His ponytail whipped up behind him as he moved through the tall grass. Rogue gave me his best *What's for dinner?* look, then trotted off behind him. Bear Guy didn't even ask us to follow. He just expected it.

"Well, can you at least tell me your name?" I called after him.

"Aaron," he shouted over his shoulder. He didn't turn back. I sighed and hurried after him. At least I still had my running shoes on.

Chapter Five

The dragon peered at Linorra from behind the stone cottage. He wasn't as large as some dragons, but to her, he was as big as a mountain. His scales were a beautiful rainbow of colors, and his eyes glowed like embers. Fine tendrils of smoke escaped his nostrils, and his talons were black and wickedly sharp. He didn't quite fit behind the cottage, but he continued to hide all the same. Linorra approached him with caution, holding her hands up as a sign of friendship.

We hiked for a couple of hours downhill, away from the mountain. It was a fairly typical jog for me, but I was exhausted from the previous night's journey and had trouble keeping up.

I tried to memorize our path. If I could get back to the portal and figure out how to activate it, I might be able to jump back in and ride home. Had Psycho Snow White opened the portal to this place or was it spontaneous? Even if she hadn't activated it, she knew it was safe to travel through, so she must have knowledge of it. If there was knowledge to be had, then I could get it somehow.

And if we ever see her again, we're going to bear spray the crap out of her, Evilina thought. I growled a little, in complete agreement with her for once. Since going through the portal, my evil alter ego lived so close to the surface that I could no longer separate our thoughts.

I might need to become her to get myself out of this mess. A shiver of foreboding swept through me at the thought. *God, what would happen if I couldn't get rid of her afterward?*

The farther we went, the more certain I was that I was somewhere *else*. The trees looked the same, but the terrain was different. It was rockier, with less underbrush, making it easier to hike without a path. The air was a little crisper than it should be, with less fog, although that was changing as we lost altitude. I pulled out the GPS that I had randomly stuffed into my pack before setting out to look for Rogue, but it wasn't getting a signal.

The mountains at our backs were way too big and way too snowy. As we walked away from them, the ground leveled out and giant ferns grew in clusters at the bottoms of the redwood trees. Small forest creatures scuffled noisily beneath the feathery leaves but didn't show themselves.

I heard no birdsong. The lack of an avian choir in the background set my teeth on edge. My mind flashed to the memory of a Steller's jay soaring over my broken body, its deep blue wings and black head supernaturally vibrant. I wondered if I would ever see that exquisite bird again.

We came through a large grove of trees and made our way across another grassy glade. The grass was taller than I was used to, reaching up to the height of my shoulders and fanning out at the top in a bouquet of fluffy wheat-colored seeds.

More than once I saw what looked to be a grasshopper, but instead of green, it was yellow with brown stripes and, shockingly, was the size of a rabbit. Rogue darted into the grass chasing the thing and it shot out like a champagne cork. I must have squeaked because Aaron looked over his shoulder and glared at me. When he saw my stunned expression, his face morphed into something like mystified annoyance.

"Sorry," I said, lowering my eyes. *Sheesh. Can't a girl be surprised by gigantic prehistoric insects around here? It's not like I screamed and ran.*

Other than occasional glimpses of discontent, Aaron did his best to ignore me. We hopped over two streams, one of which was rather robust and had a giant log stretched across it. A nearby stump looked like it had been struck by lightning and was charred to a craggy spike.

Just as I reached the other side of the log on the far bank, I heard that same scuffling noise I'd heard in the ferns before, now coming from underneath me. I hurried my steps to pass the sound, then was appalled to see a hairy green spider the size of a housecat scuttle from underneath the log only a foot behind me. It moved with lightning speed, then stopped dead in the middle and reared up on his hind legs as if to bar my passage back across the log. Before I could register what I was looking at, it spit something in my direction.

I threw my arm up and jerked away in time for the substance to hit my elbow and the right side of my button-down shirt instead of my face. It sizzled as I hastily scrambled away from the spider, yelping in surprise and almost tumbling off the log. I stared back, ready to sprint away if it came after me, but when I felt a stinging through the sleeve of my shirt, I tore it off in a panic, forgetting all else.

Luckily, the spider did not follow. It only dashed underneath, presumably to continue its supporting role as troll under a bridge. Still looking behind me, I smacked into Aaron, who had turned back to see what had happened. He grabbed my shoulders and held me still.

Already jumpy, I instinctively pulled away, but his grip was like a steel vise, and his hands were so hot that I thought the spider venom was burning me again. Once my brain caught up to the fact that it was Aaron who'd grabbed me and not a monster, I stopped struggling and stared up at him. That's when I noticed it wasn't just his hands that were putting off heat. His whole body radiated a heat that even a person in the throes of a high fever couldn't manage. Whatever this man was, he wasn't like any human I'd ever met.

Aaron glared at me, his ice-blue eyes flashing. He shook his head as if I were an unruly child who needed discipline.

"You make too much noise," he growled. "Walk quieter."

His attitude was really starting to get under my skin. I gave him a withering glare, but he didn't notice. He just released me, glanced down at my newly uncovered tank top, and turned back to walk again.

"Okay," I muttered to myself, "I guess we can talk about that fucking acid-spitting troll spider later. No biggie. I see those all the time." *Asshole.* I kicked a rock, and it hit him in the back of a leather boot. "Oops, sorry," I said. Yes, I tower above all others in my maturity.

He glowered at me over his shoulder, then continued onward. What was I doing following this dude? I mean, I was in the middle of nowhere, on a strange planet or in another dimension or something, with a giant, super-mean bear guy who might crossbow me to death at any time. That's if the troll spiders didn't get me first. I had to be demented to follow this man. And I had just kicked a rock at him. The whole thing was just so preposterous. Thinking about it made me giggle.

What's next, little green men? I squinted up at the sky as I walked. *Nothing would surprise me right now.*

I bet they have enormous cockroaches here, Evilina commented.

A violent shiver ran through me. "Gah!" I hate cockroaches more than anything in the universe.

Aaron stopped abruptly and faced me. I was still looking up and almost ran into him again. He towered over me, unamused. I backed up and bit my lips together to keep from giggling. Rogue looked up at him, his tongue stuck out to the side in a doggy smile.

Aaron looked down at the dog and sighed. "What have you gotten me into?"

Huh?

Aaron looked like he was about to scold me again but then froze, looking up over my shoulder. A sudden, intense heat, even hotter than before, flowed off him and hit me in the face. I flinched away from it and tried to back up, but Aaron grabbed my upper arm, pulled me toward him, and dragged us both to the ground. I landed on top of his arm, which wound around me and pulled me against him. Our chests pressed together.

For a panicked second, I thought I had miscalculated my RTA, but he wasn't even paying attention to me. He was craning his neck to see through the grass. He looked at me, saw that I understood the situation, and loosened his grip. I gently pulled his hand from my forearm.

When I touched his hand directly, an aggressive shiver ran through me, followed by a dizzying rush of heat. I had the uncomfortable feeling of piping hot water flowing through my body. It started in my chest, moved into my arms, then streamed out through my hands to my fingertips. Shocked, my hand clamped down of its own accord, and a flood of emotion struck without warning.

Fear and hope coursed through me in equal measure, followed by confusion, loneliness, resentment, and a dozen other emotions I could barely identify. They were like my feelings, but more insistent than anything I'd ever felt and so fierce that they threatened to sear the inside of my skull. My vision swam, and I sucked in a breath, then released a pathetic whimper.

Aaron jerked his hand away, and the feeling abruptly vanished. He stared at me, his ice-blue eyes so wide that the color absorbed my whole attention as I stared back, panting as if I had just run a race. He leaned back cautiously, his face reflecting what I knew but didn't want to believe. Those feelings weren't mine. They were *his*. Something inside me had latched onto him and rushed in. I had connected to him and felt his emotions, and what I found was mostly pain.

I blinked away a tear, swallowing hard. His eyes searched mine, though I couldn't guess what he looked for. I knew he was afraid of something out there, but the bulk of his torment was old. He was a man who had endured something terrible, had stayed the course, and now felt a hesitant hope which balanced precariously atop years and years of grief.

"*So* much grief," I whispered before I could stop myself. His blue eyes glistened for a moment then went flat. "I'm sorry," I said and averted my eyes. I didn't know what I apologized for, but it felt crucial. Embarrassed, I pulled away from him, and he let me.

Rogue whined, but he wasn't paying attention to us. I glanced back at Aaron for direction. His gaze dropped to my mouth, then quickly away. He stretched to see through the grass, but whatever he'd seen must have vanished because he stood, silently scanning the clearing.

"Come on, we're almost there," he said. "We need to hurry before the fog completely blocks our ability to see him."

"See who?" I asked.

Aaron walked past where I still lay on the ground, hesitated, then backtracked to stand above me. "The dragon," he said. Then, warily, he held his hand out to me. Heat still radiated from him, but it was more subdued than before.

I considered his hand for a moment, indecisive, then shuddered and sat up without his help. I hugged myself across my stomach to steady my nerves. I wanted to be brave, but I just wasn't. It was all too much. I was lost and at the mercy of a stranger. I had no choice but to follow him, but I didn't know where we were going. For all I knew, he could be leading me to his murder cabin, where Kathy Bates waited to break my ankles. I was feeling some kind of weird super-empathy crap. God only knew what the hell that was. And now, dragons.

My throat tightened. I squeezed my eyes shut. *I shouldn't let this guy see me cry.*

Rogue pressed himself against my shoulder, and I opened my eyes to see him scrutinizing me like a worried older brother. My vision was blurry, but no tears fell as I reached up to scratch the back of his neck. I steadied my breath.

You can do this. At least there's no cockroaches.

I ground my teeth and took Aaron's hand. There was no rush of feeling this time. Instead, I got only the impression of confusion with something buried beneath that. Distrust, for sure. Very loud distrust. And shame, maybe?

Huh.

He nodded. "Maybe you won't be completely useless," he said and turned away again.

Wow, this guy really is a dick.

I huffed out another breath and followed him. Rogue trotted closely next to me, his tongue sticking out the side of his mouth and his tail wagging, as happy as a kid on Christmas. I scowled down at him.

"What are you so freaking happy about?" I asked.

I swear, he made a sound like, "Ri ron't row." Despite everything, it made me laugh. My Roogy-Roo. At least I had him.

Aaron turned his head back to glance at Rogue. His blue eyes crinkled a little at the corners.

Now we're getting somewhere, Evilina and I thought.

That's when the dragon struck. It appeared above Aaron's head like a Klingon warship, which is a pretty apt comparison given that it looked more like a pterodactyl than the standard mythical dragon I had expected.

Its flight had been completely silent, but Aaron had somehow sensed the creature. He jumped backward and fell hard. His stumble was all that kept the thing from plucking out his larynx as it dive-bombed him. Aaron threw his arms up, but the dragon was too fast and clipped his forehead with one talon. Rogue jumped back, too, knocking into me so hard that I was thrown backward. Rogue stood over me, growling viciously at the creature.

The dragon swooped over Aaron, landing between us. Smoke rose from its nostrils. Its eyes, focused on Rogue, were as big as my fist and glowed a bright orange red. It was a mass of sinewy crimson as it stalked the snarling dog, his long tail whipping back and forth like an agitated lion. It didn't have any teeth that I could see, but its beak didn't look like it needed any. I was fairly certain that if the thing got to me, it could crunch my head off like a Blow Pop. As it approached, it opened its beak and made a coughing sound reminiscent of someone trying to start a lawn mower.

"Holy shit!" I gasped, scrambling to get up and run away. Rogue didn't allow it. He crouched over me, pinning me down. It was a good thing. The creature's throat exploded with a wet *thwack*, and it crumpled to the ground, rolling a couple of times before flopping down a few feet away, still thrashing.

Rogue and I were sprayed with scalding hot blood as it convulsed. The blood spattered my face and I screeched, wiping it off desperately with my bare hands. The dragon flailed weakly a few more times, then went still.

For a moment, all was quiet except for the thudding of my heart. Then, for the first time since I arrived, a bird chirped somewhere in the distance. Rogue finally stepped off me and cautiously circled the thing. I wobbled into a sitting position, shaking violently and hyperventilating.

I had tried so hard not to cry, and I had really done well considering the circumstances, but I couldn't hold it in anymore. Crying isn't always about being distraught. Sometimes crying is just a generic way of releasing stress. I cry when I'm upset, sure, but I also cry when I'm pissed off and, apparently, when I'm attacked by a dragon.

Aaron walked up to the creature cautiously, holding a scrap of cloth to his forehead. Blood dripped into his right eye, down his cheek, past his chin, and into his previously well-kept beard. The front of his tunic displayed a sizable splotch of it, as well. His brow furrowed, and the corners of his mouth pulled down.

"That was my last bolt," he grumbled, crouching down by the thing. "Dragons."

When Aaron had called it a dragon earlier, I had imagined something very different from this birdlike animal. It was about the size of a horse with a body covered in red iridescent scales and a bright orange crest that ran from the back of its head all the way down to its tail. Its wings were covered in multicolored feathers and ended in a single hooked talon. It was gorgeous, other than the pool of dark red rapidly expanding beneath its head.

That had been an amazing shot, especially with an eye full of blood.

Aaron noticed the state I was in and rose from his crouching position. He walked over to me, peering down, once again reminding me of how massive he was.

"Are you hurt?" he asked.

My face stung like it had been splashed with spider spit and a little had gotten in my eyes. My vision had blurred momentarily, but it was already clearing. I brushed away my tears and willed myself to stop crying. "I'm fine," I lied, wiping snot from my nose with my muddy tank top. I wasn't sure if that was better or worse. "Why was its blood so hot?"

"It vomits fire," he said simply. "Its whole body is hot. That's why I used my last bolt on it. It was about to cook you for dinner."

I nodded, my face tight. "Makes sense," I said, getting to my feet.

"It's been stalking us since before Rogue and I found you. They're pretty easy to kill if you can get them before they vomit on you. Especially if they're small like this one." His face was more or less neutral, but those wrinkles at the corners of his eyes had reappeared.

I narrowed mine. "You think this is funny!" I accused.

A small smile finally invaded his face, and he said, "Well, it's my turn." It was slightly disturbing to see him smirking with a face smattered with blood, but I was too annoyed to care. "You really are from over *there*, aren't you?" he asked.

"Over *there*? Why? Because if I was from over *here*, then fire-vomit would be normal?" I asked, gesturing to the downed dragon.

"Yes. At least, outside of Neesee it is," he said, watching my face. I wondered what he was looking for.

"Neesee," I repeated. "That girl said she was from Neesee."

"What girl?" he asked, narrowing his eyes.

I shrugged because, as always, I had forgotten her damned name. "She was taller than me with black hair to here." I motioned to my neck. "She had very, very red lips and stupid yellow pants." He nodded as I spoke. "In my head, her name is Psycho Snow White," I added.

"Did she have a man with her?" he asked.

I shook my head. "No, but she didn't need any help. She picked me up and threw me into the . . . the . . ." I felt ridiculous saying the word "portal" out loud. Portals are not real. I looked over at the dragon. It was possible I needed to reevaluate my belief system.

"Bridge," Aaron said. My eyes flicked back to him. He was no longer smiling. "That's what they call it."

"Bridge? Do you know how to use it?" I asked, almost whispering the question.

He didn't answer right away. He reached up to my chin, turning my head to examine my cheek. His skin was rough, but his touch was surprisingly gentle. I could *feel* him through the contact and was struck, once again, by a feeling of grief. The subtle whiff of hope I had sensed earlier was gone, fallen from its perch. "No," he said finally. "I was hoping that you could help me with that."

I clenched my jaw, pulling my face out of his hand. He lowered his arm, frowning.

"Is that why you're helping me?" I asked.

He sighed loudly, then turned and stalked over to the dragon, bending down to pick it up. "Not exactly," he said.

I was about to push further into this line of questioning, but at the sight of Aaron heaving the giant creature up by its tail and slugging it over his back, I couldn't help but squeal, "Holy crap! That thing must weigh half a ton! How in the hell are you lifting it?"

He turned back to me, a vertical line splitting the space between his eyebrows, right next to the gash above his right eye. "It's only two-fifty, maybe less," he said.

"Two hundred and fifty pounds is heavy."

"Pounds? What are pounds? No, two hundred fifty kilos."

I lifted one eyebrow. "I have no idea what that means."

Aaron shrugged, then turned away. Blood trailed behind him from the dragon's pierced neck, dribbling a circle of dark red dots. A few clumps of nearly black, clotted blood squished out.

I wrinkled my nose. "Bleck," I said. "It's basically a big dead bird, isn't it?"

He snorted. "You're in no position to judge."

I looked down at myself. I was covered in dried mud, blood, and snot. My hair was absolutely disgusting, as were my hands. I'm pretty sure I had smears of mud across my face, intermingled with second-degree burns. I looked like an extra from a bad zombie movie. I groaned, wondering if they had showers in this world. Aaron was already walking away.

"What are you planning to do with that thing?" I asked, hurrying after him.

"I wasted a bolt on it," he said. "The least it can do is provide us with a meal. Come on, my cottage is just over the next hill."

I looked down at Rogue. He had his doggy smile back on, but I noticed that his whole face and chest were covered in dragon blood. His nose looked raw.

"Oh my Roogy-Roo, are you okay?" I bent down to examine him more closely. His fur had protected his chest and some of his face, but he had burns around his eyes and nose and inside his giant Dumbo ears. "Oh, Rogue, does it hurt, buddy? When we get to where we're going, I'll clean you up and put some ointment on your face, okay?" He wagged his tail. It seemed like I was more upset by the burns than he was.

I stuck out my lower lip, kissed the top of Rogue's head, then stood back up. Aaron had paused to watch our little interaction. He had a strange look on his face.

"What?" I asked.

He shook his head, which I understood to mean "nothing," then he continued walking.

The dragon's dead eyes, having lost their vermilion glow, stared up at me dully from behind him, daring me to follow.

Chapter Six

"Dragon," Linorra said. "Please don't be afraid." She could sense what he felt, for that was her greatest gift.

"I am not afraid of a sprite like you," the dragon said.

"I am not a sprite," Linorra said, giggling. "I'm just a girl, and I want to be your friend."

Aaron's cottage was well hidden. It was tucked between two fallen redwood logs, which, even lying sideways, rose above the roof. The logs were covered in several of those giant, fluffy ferns, which I had dubbed "spider ferns." To my dismay, the roof of the cottage was equally covered in spider ferns, though I heard none of the telltale rustling. The back of the cottage butted up against a half dozen bushy evergreens. It was effectively invisible on three sides and the top, and the small front yard was surrounded by tall bushes. I would have walked right past if he hadn't pointed it out.

The cottage was made of wood and gray cobblestone with two small windows on either side of the front door. Underneath one window were rounds waiting to be split for firewood, neatly stacked and organized by size. A few pieces of split firewood rested on top. A large metal basin was pushed up against the front of the cottage with several wicked-looking hooks protruding from the stone above. In the yard, there was a firepit, dug into the ground and edged with more stone.

Aaron dropped the dragon carcass next to the firepit and stopped to listen. We stood silently for an endless minute, then Aaron snapped his fingers at Rogue, motioning him forward. Rogue ghosted between the cottage and one of the giant logs, disappearing around the back, then appeared again on the other side. He trotted back up to Aaron and sat at his feet.

The big man peered down at the dog, then up at the cottage, finally stepping toward it. In his right hand, he gripped a knife with a wooden handle and a serrated blade about ten inches long. It looked small in his hand. He held it out in front of him as he walked toward the front door. I moved to follow him, but he waved me back, shaking his head.

I stood there, useless, wondering what fresh horror I was about to witness. Rogue stayed with me. I couldn't imagine anyone finding this place, and I questioned, again, why Aaron helped me. He had dodged that inquiry earlier.

How did he know that I wouldn't attack him while his back was turned, or that I wouldn't report his location to someone? Based on the painstaking camouflage he'd arranged, he was clearly hiding. If there was such a thing as a murder cabin, this would be it. I worried I was making a huge mistake.

Aaron opened the front door. It wasn't locked, but it also didn't look like the doorknob had a keyhole. Perhaps it could only be barred from within. I looked behind me, unsure of which was more unsafe, the house or standing outside of it.

I scowled down at the dragon's corpse. "We're going to cook *you*, not the other way around," I mumbled.

Rogue sniffed the dragon carcass. Psycho Snow White had also known my dog. She had been looking for him. What did that mean? Could she locate Rogue somehow? I considered telling Aaron that in case she followed us, but what if he was working with her?

I sighed. If I wanted to make it out of this mess and go home, I would need help, which meant I had to trust someone. Thus far, Aaron had kept me alive. In the absence of a viable alternative, I decided I could trust him a little longer.

Finally, Aaron's deep voice called from inside the cottage, "Okay." Rogue sneezed at one of the dragon's feathers, then headed for the door. He passed Aaron, who walked out the front door toward me with rope in his hands. His eyes were trained on me, almost glowing with intensity.

My heart skipped a beat as I backed up, panicking. I didn't think I could outrun Aaron from this proximity, but I certainly wouldn't let him tie me up without a struggle.

"It's not for you," Aaron said, rolling his eyes. "It's for the dragon. I have to hang it to butcher it. *Rhoya*, woman, get a hold of yourself. You're all over the place. First you giggle like an underling, then you scream and cry. You're worse than me."

I stared at him, shaking, and feeling very foolish, especially given the "just trust him" speech I had given myself ten seconds earlier. I covered my face with my hands, trying to calm down. "I'm sorry," I said. "I just . . . I don't know you. I still don't understand why I'm here or why you're helping me. Who are you? How did you even know I would be out there?"

I had been planning to deviously extract that information through charm and guile. Instead, I made the very sensible choice to just blurt out my questions. Hopefully he would still make me dinner.

"I told you my name," he said.

"That's not what I'm asking, and you know it." I exhaled in frustration, then decided to try his brilliant tactic from earlier. "Please," I said, softening my voice.

He didn't answer. He just crouched down to tie the dragon's hind legs together tightly, then he hauled it over to the front of the cottage. He attached the rope to one of the hooks, letting the creature dangle by its feet, head down, its meaty tail flopping over the top. The metal basin sat underneath to catch blood, or entrails—or whatever.

Ew.

Rogue had reappeared from inside the cottage and plopped down, right in the doorway. He watched Aaron work.

"Aaron, I need to get home. I can't do that without information. Please, I need your help."

Aaron pulled out the serrated knife again. He made a shallow vertical slit from the dragon's groin, continuing past the belly, and farther down to the neck where his crossbow bolt had killed the thing. He took a deep breath and said, "I knew someone would be there. I knew your name, that you would be from over *there*. I knew that a dog with your name on his collar would lead me to you. That is all." He faced away from me as he worked and spoke, his voice quavering ever so slightly.

"How did you know all that?" I asked.

He continued butchering the dragon, his movements certain and efficient but jerky, as if he were taking his frustration out on the carcass. I waited in silence for him to answer, watching him slide his knife under the skin at the tail. He peeled the hide back a few inches on each side of the cut, then worked inch by inch to tug it away. When he finished, he murmured, "My mother told me before she disappeared. She's . . . a seer, a precog."

Rogue made a strange coughing noise. I barely registered it. "She's a psychic?" I asked incredulously.

He rounded on me, his face red. He exuded that same *What the hell?* look I had seen earlier. I thought I had exclusive rights to that look, but he wore it like he'd invented it.

"Why can't you understand simple things?" he demanded. "She's a reservoir for the Precognition fragment."

"Great, that clears things up. Thanks. Oh, by the way, what the hell is that?"

Aaron snorted derisively. "Precognition? Or *fragments*?" He asked the question as if the answer should be obvious and was intended to insult me.

I sighed. "Either one." *Jerk.*

Aaron blinked, staring at me. Then, as if all my stupidity finally made sense to him, he whispered to himself, "Doesn't know about fragments."

I blew out a breath. "Of course, I do. Just stick a subject in that sentence and it'll fix it right up." Aaron gave me the *look* again. What can I say? Grammar humor isn't for everyone. Or anyone, really.

He closed his eyes, shaking his head as he turned back to the dragon. He finished peeling the skin away from the incision, then he reached into the carcass and yanked open the sternum, producing a loud *crack*. The sound made me cringe, and a wave of nausea struck me. He reached inside the dragon, sliced out the windpipe, and tossed it in the basin.

"I'm gonna vomit," I mumbled. That made me think about the dragon's fire-vomit, and I giggled again. "Wow, you're right. I *am* all over the place. What is wrong with me?"

"A perfectly constructed question," he commented.

I narrowed my eyes. *Is he using grammar humor against me? This man is more formidable than I thought. And more educated. He isn't just some mountain man with a penchant for belted tunics.*

"Huh," I said.

He chuckled softly. "It's my turn to ask a question."

"Okay," I said. "Shoot."

"Earlier, when we were"—he paused for a moment—"eh, on the ground. Did you feel something? From me?"

I resisted the urge to make a sex joke. That might send the wrong message. "Yes. Heat, then—"

"So much grief," he finished.

"Yes."

He turned to face me, his hands dripping red and black fluid. "That was your fragment. Fragments are slivers of power. They are broken, fragmented, into different forms, just like light breaks into different colors. Together, they are the force that holds together our physical reality. At least, that's what they teach in school." Aaron raised his eyebrows and shrugged as if he weren't convinced.

"In order to harness the power of a fragment, you must have a reservoir for that fragment, an internal container that lets you store the power. Everyone has a reservoir, though the depth and type vary. Most people have a lesser reservoir, too small to willfully exert any kind of physical effect, but on rare occasions, someone might have a greater reservoir. A greater reservoir is an unusually deep container that allows you to wield the fragment as power. It is said that people don't just *have* reservoirs, but that we *are* them, like our minds and bodies are imbued with the quality of whatever fragment they contain, for better or worse."

Aaron paused, thinking. This was the most he'd said since we'd met. I stared, entranced. His voice was like silk that I wanted to rub against my cheek. He was thoughtful and eloquent and used fancy words like "imbued." Now that he was communicating and not looking at me like I was a complete idiot, he was positively captivating.

Uh oh. I tore my eyes away from him just as he looked at me with an intense stare that penetrated down into my soul.

"You are a greater reservoir for the Connection fragment," he continued. "It lets you feel people's emotions and communicate with them through touch. It's one of the rarer ones, but not unheard of. There is at least one other greater connector in Neesee." His face reddened again, then momentarily twisted into something like pure hatred, but he recovered quickly, relaxing back into a neutral expression.

I shook my head, clearing the trance he had just put me under, then tried to digest what he was actually saying. What kind of insane magical thinking was this? And yet, I *had* sensed him.

"Have you ever experienced anything like that before?" he asked.

I shook my head. "No. I've always been sensitive to people's emotions, I guess, but nothing like that. It shocked the hell out of me."

"Yes," he said, nodding. "I remember my first time. It was disturbing. Of course, I was fifteen when it happened."

"You have this ability too?" I asked.

"No, mine is different," he said, then he turned back to his work again without elaborating. Another touchy subject, I presumed. He had a lot of those.

Rogue rolled over in the doorway and whined a little.

"Okay, my turn," I said. Aaron didn't answer, but he didn't argue either. He just pulled open the dragon's stomach cavity as he had the sternum and tugged out organs and intestines. He didn't use his knife for this part. I supposed that it might be bad to poke a hole in the poop shoot.

The intestines slid down into the basin and then hung, caught at one end inside the carcass. Aaron cut the end free from the outside, carving a hole in the creature's butt, and the intestines fell with a *splat*.

Aaron sniffed and then turned back to me. "Ask your question," he said.

"Okay," I said. I wanted to look away, but I just couldn't. Blood dripped freely into the basin, and it occurred to me that Spirit might have a point with the whole vegan thing. "Why would your mother have a vision about me?"

He shrugged. "Not a vision. It's more like a very accurate prediction. The future is always mutable." He sounded like he was quoting a textbook. Maybe he was.

"What does that have to do with me?" I asked, my frustration bubbling up again.

"I don't know," he said, grabbing a rag that had been hanging from another hook and wiping his hands. He retrieved the split firewood and stacked it in the firepit, presumably to make a cooking fire.

I wondered if he would start rubbing sticks together. He finished stacking the wood, then he stood, staring at his work, as if trying to decide something.

He raised narrowed eyes to me, then said, "Why don't you go get cleaned up. There is a bath in the back of the cottage with a privacy screen. I won't disturb you. You can wear one of my shirts while we wash your . . . uh . . ." He looked at my blue pants but didn't finish the sentence. Either he changed his mind about promising to save my clothes or he didn't know what pants were.

"There is a water spigot over the tub. Try not to waste it. The rains won't come for a few more weeks."

I nodded. "Okay, thanks." That did sound like a good idea, although I doubted the water would be warm. Beggars can't be choosers, though, and I definitely fit that description. I turned to go, but then curiosity got the better of me. "How are you going to light the fire?" I asked.

He snorted. "You can't let anything go, can you?"

"Endearing, isn't it?" I answered, grinning. "It's my best feature."

"I doubt it." He sighed. "Come, I might as well show you."

He might have been complimenting me, but it just as easily could've been an insult. I decided to assume the former and walked up to stand beside him. He crouched close to the firepit, and I did the same.

I noticed for the first time, squatting there next to him, that he smelled amazing. It wasn't cologne, but a sort of non-BO man smell. A little musky, a little sweet, a little sweaty, but not in a gross way. It was that, mixed with spearmint and a hint of blood. Even the blood smell didn't bother me. It only added a strangely seductive tanginess.

Jesus. What is wrong with me? Now I'm turned on by the smell of blood*? I need a psychiatrist. Any minute now I'm going to wake up in a straitjacket.*

I wanted to ask him how he managed that amazing scent when I was such a disaster, but I reminded myself not to get sidetracked by sniffing the man I'd believed would kill me only three minutes ago.

Aaron stuffed one large log underneath the firewood in a way that would smother any attempt to start a fire. He reached out and touched the edge of that log, then took a deep breath in and out. For a split second, a flash of bright vermilion light streaked through his hand, beginning at his wrist and moving down through his fingers. It was so fast that if I'd blinked, I would have missed it. When the glow reached the log, it burst into flames. It startled me, and I fell back on my butt with a little yelp. I stared at the fire, then at Aaron. His lips quirked up at the corners.

"That's your fragment," I said.

"Yes," he said. "Evocation."

"God . . . that is so much cooler than mine."

He gave me the *look* again.

"For god's sake, what is it this time?" I asked, throwing my hands up.

"Your words make no sense. Who is this deity you keep talking about?"

I laughed. "You don't know who I mean when I say the word 'god'? That's . . . okay, no, that's a long conversation. We should handle that another time. I need to go burn these clothes." I was rambling, but my proximity to him made me nervous.

"The fire didn't frighten you?" Aaron asked the question quietly, in a way that made me think the answer was important.

"Should it?" I asked.

He stared into the fire, frowning again, and shrugged.

So much grief, I thought.

I let the silence just *be* for a minute. I suspected he needed that space. After another minute, I asked, "Why are you out here, Aaron?"

He smiled a little. "That's a long conversation. We should handle that another time."

I laughed. "Touché. Well then, I guess I have some scrubbing to do. Hey, can you heat up water?"

Chapter Seven

"Syndeth is my name," said the dragon hesitantly. "I am small for a dragon, I know, but I am big for a human."

Linorra laughed, believing that Syndeth jested. "Yes," she said, "you would be a big human indeed. It's a good thing you were made a dragon instead."

An oil lantern with an ornate bulb of frosted glass and delicately etched flowers lit the inside of the cottage. The single small room was otherwise barren. A cot in the back corner sat opposite the bath. Above the cot, a ladder secured to the wall led up to a trapdoor in the ceiling. Next to the front door stood a wooden counter with a ceramic basin and a few knives and utensils, neatly arranged. On the other side of the door, a workbench with metal tools and an unfinished project awaited the return of attentive hands.

Everything in the cottage was practical, with a clear use. There were no books, pictures, or decorations of any kind. The lantern was the most decorative thing in the cottage. The place had the feeling of a bunker rather than a home, but it was also organized and impeccably clean. Aaron, it appeared, was a neatnik. I rubbed my palms together, smiling.

Enter Hurricane Lina.

A trifold room divider stood next to the bath. I stretched it out, watching Aaron turn the spigot on to fill the tub. He could heat up water, but he avoided my gaze as he did it. I wasn't sure if he was ashamed of his ability, or if the intimacy of helping me draw a bath and then giving me his own shirt to wear made him uncomfortable. Regardless, I was grateful.

While Aaron finished heating the bathwater, I found a wooden bowl on the counter and dunked it in to gather water for cleaning Rogue. I rinsed the blood out of Rogue's fur but decided to let him dry before applying the antibiotic ointment that I hoped was still in my first aid kit, tucked somewhere in my pack. Rogue shook, spraying me, then followed me back inside.

After the day I'd had, the hot water was a revelation, even though the "bath" was just a barrel. He only had bar soap so hard that it didn't release much soap at all, but it smelled like spearmint, which explained a fraction of his signature scent. I used it to wash myself and my clothes. *All* my clothes, which left me in a bit of an undergarment situation, but I thought it best to take advantage of the opportunity to get clean while I had it.

I draped my wet clothes over the side of the tub, dried myself off with what was essentially a washcloth, then donned Aaron's shirt, which he'd laid out for me. The shirt was white and reached just past my knees. It smelled like him. The odd thing about the garment was that it didn't have any seams or stitches, as if the cloth had been woven directly into the shape of a shirt. When Aaron saw me, he blinked a couple of times but said nothing. Very wise.

While I'd been scrubbing, Aaron had skinned and deboned the dragon. Then he finished butchering it and cooked the "best pieces," which included the liver for some reason, in a large, wok-like pan that sat directly in the fire. He cooked it with a broth that he'd stored in a ceramic jar, then cooked some of the scraps from the basin and tossed them in a bowl for Rogue, who devoured them.

Rogue licked his bowl clean and flopped down by the door again. He appeared relaxed, but his amber eyes were alert as always, following me around the room as I finished snooping, then sat down with Aaron to eat. The meat was chewy and tasted like whitefish, except pungent, like goat's milk. It reminded me of the time I vacationed in Florida and ate alligator. It was weird but good, making the whole fire-vomit thing seem well worth the trouble.

It had taken Aaron hours to prepare the meal, and by the time we finished eating, it was nearly dark. Fog had invaded the garden, and it was so dense that I couldn't see the bushes out front. It felt safe, as if the fog knew we were trying to hide and wanted to help.

Aaron set my wet clothing aside and carried the tub outside to empty. Though I had seen him lift the dragon, I still couldn't believe it when he lifted a tub full of water.

When he came back inside, he locked the door behind him. He had to duck to get through the doorway, and his head was mere inches from the cottage ceiling. I confirmed that the door could only be barred from the inside, and Aaron closed not just one but three separate locking mechanisms on it. I wondered, again, why he was hiding.

"Thank you for the meal," I said, looking around. We sat at a wooden table that looked handmade. There was only one chair, which I sat in. Aaron sat on a wooden chest that also looked handmade. I had the impression that it was his normal seat anyway. "I can't believe I just ate something that tried to kill me."

Aaron smiled. "That's nearly all there is to eat around here. Dragon is a common meal for me."

"Now there's something you don't hear every day," I said, peering down at what I now realized were dragon-skin boots. "At least *I* don't. You live out here in the forest all by yourself?"

He nodded. "You are the first to visit."

"No kidding," I said, looking around the barren room.

Aaron stood to gather the wooden bowls, taking them over to the counter. I watched as he placed them into the basin there, rinsed them with water from a jug, then used a rag and the same soap from the bath to clean them.

Aaron had changed out of his bloody tunic while I wasn't looking. He wore another one that looked almost the same but in a slightly darker brown. He must have changed while I was in the bath, though I never heard him. It made me wonder what else he could have been doing in silence while I bathed. The image of him changing on the other side of the screen invaded my thoughts. Once again, I had to tell myself not to get distracted.

He's so big. I wonder if the kickstand matches the bike.

I heard an odd laughing in my mind, and I bit my lips together to keep from laughing out loud. *Shut the hell up*, I told Evilina. I had a goal, and I needed to stay focused in order to accomplish it. On the other hand, there was something about Aaron rescuing me from a painful death, cooking me dinner, and then doing dishes afterward that was especially endearing. The whole thing was like a bad blind date that had turned wildly around.

Aaron finished the chore and turned to regard me. His eyes reflected the lamplight like a cat. I stared at them for a second too long.

"What is it?" he asked.

"Your eyes are different from mine," I said. "Can you see in the dark?"

He nodded. "Pretty well. You can't?"

I shook my head. "No." *That would be so cool!*

I wasn't sure what to say next, so I continued looking around the room. The cot had a thin bedroll that didn't look very comfortable. He saw me looking and said, "I have a second bedroll that I take out on longer journeys. I will sleep on that. You can take the cot. I will put the screen in front of it if you wish."

"Okay, thank you."

An awkward silence loomed, and I contemplated the best way to say good night without being rude. Normally, around this time, I would brush my teeth and fall asleep to whatever fantasy novel I had next on my TBR. I didn't have a toothbrush, which would be a problem, but I did have my favorite book. The thought of curling up with that book and a flashlight sounded like a dream.

Aaron broke the silence. "Your face was burned, but it looks fine now," he said.

I touched my face. He was right. "Must not have actually been burned," I said.

"It was," he insisted, "and now you're healed." He was trying to tell me something, but I wasn't sure what it was.

"Aaron," I said.

"Yes?"

His voice was soft and deep. I shivered, a fuzzy emotion running through me. I had been avoiding analyzing my situation for the sake of stability, but for the first time since I'd been there, I allowed myself to think about my parents and the rest of my friends. I wondered what they had done when I never came back from the woods. Had they assumed the worst? Had my friends formed another search party, this one a little less of an actual party?

They were probably still out there right now. My dad would have called his friends in the Forest Service. My mom would be out on Gem, searching the trails. Marti would be falling apart, and Milo would be consoling her. Spirit would know that I was fine.

Spirit, I thought. Thinking her name tugged at something in my brain. Spirit had known that Rogue was okay. She had *known*, and she had told me that right before we heard the ghost. And that ghost had been Psycho Snow White. I had a terrible realization. What if Spirit's knowledge somehow made her a target? My heart skipped a beat as I followed that line of thought. What if Psycho Snow White went back to murder my entire family just for the fun of it? If Aaron's mother was a psychic seer or whatever, wouldn't she have predicted that?

"Can you tell me more about the Precognition fragment?" I asked.

"I don't know that much about it since they don't teach it in school. My mother just said that she could see cause and effect more clearly than others. She said it was like being very, very good at Daggers and Dragons. She could see a hundred moves ahead, but if someone changed their mind about something, then the future would change.

"Fortunately, she's very good at predicting what people will do in certain situations or how the environment will affect the outcome. She's quite gifted, but it also gives her terrible headaches. At least, it did when I saw her last. She could barely function. That's why they went over *there*."

I ignored the Daggers and Dragons comment, assuming the game must be something like chess. "They? Who's they?" I asked.

"Both my parents and my younger sister."

"How old were you?"

"Fifteen," he said.

"The same year you discovered your reservoir," I remarked. He didn't respond but continued looking at the ground. I could see that the subject was painful for him, but I needed to know. "How would going to Earth help your mother?"

"Earth is under a Protection matrix, and all fragments are blunted there. Most people never know they have access. That's probably why you didn't know about yours. My mother is from Earth, so she knew her abilities would be limited there and, presumably, so would the side effects."

I only understood about half of what he'd said. He noticed my confusion and clarified, "Each known world emanates a different fragment. The planet itself may be its source, but they don't know for sure. The fragment radiating from each world has a dominant presence on that planet, a matrix, and the people who live there tend to be reservoirs for that fragment. Monash emanates the Transformation fragment, so there are many transformers here. Our economy revolves around the use of it. Earth emanates the Protection fragment, which acts as a sort of shield for the whole planet, blocking reservoirs from filling. In the case of my mother, it keeps her sane."

"If she's from Earth, I could understand wanting to go back there, but why didn't they take you with them?" I immediately regretted asking the question. I hadn't meant to mention that particular subject, but sometimes things just slip out without permission. Like pee when you laugh too hard.

Aaron kept his eyes downcast, his expression haunted.

"I'm sorry," I said. "I just met you today. I shouldn't be asking personal questions." I shook my head at my own idiocy. "I'll just . . ." I rose from my chair to walk toward the cot.

"It's okay," he said in a voice so soft that I had to strain to hear him. "She warned me you would." I turned back to face him, but he didn't meet my eyes.

"What do you mean?" I asked.

"My mother knew someone would come," he said. "That's why they left me here. She said that I needed to help you and that you would be the key to helping me find my way back to my family."

"Oh," I said, taken aback. I didn't know what to say to that. His mother had predicted my arrival in their world, hadn't known who I would be, and left her only son behind to help me? That was insane. And wrong.

"How long have you been waiting for me?" I asked. I didn't want to hurt him further, but I felt like I needed to know what I was getting into. And also, selfishly, I wanted to know how old he was.

He took a measured breath and said, "Sixteen years."

He's thirty-one. Jesus. Sixteen years—no wonder he was so pissed.

"You must absolutely hate me," I whispered. I shook my head, bewildered. "I'm so sorry, Aaron."

He still didn't look at me. His eyes were red, and his face looked like anger and sorrow warred for dominance. I wanted to hug him. I had been away from my family for less than a day and it already hurt. I couldn't imagine being separated for so long, alone and trying to survive, never knowing if you would ever see them again. And it was all because of me.

And yet, he still cooked for you and helped you draw a bath.

"I'll do what I can," I said. I didn't know how I would do it, but I would figure out how to help this man.

He nodded, recovering himself a little. "What is it like over there?"

I smiled, grateful for a change of subject. "There's good and bad. We have a lot of inventions, like this watch. See?" I pressed the side button and the screen lit up, casting a glow in the dim lamplight.

His eyes widened and he drew closer to look.

"What is it?" he asked.

"It's a smartwatch. It connects to your phone but . . ." How do you explain a smartwatch? Or a phone? Especially when you're not even sure how they actually work? "Uh, it lights up," I said.

"Useful," he said, stepping back again to lean against the counter.

"I guess," I said, turning away from him. I stepped over to where my pack lay on the table. "There are too many people there," I continued as I unzipped my pack. The sound of the zipper startled him, and I laughed, then quickly zipped up and down to make the sound. This whole thing with showing him modern technology would be fun. I dug through the bag to look for the first aid kit. I still needed the ointment for Rogue, and there might be something in there I could use for my teeth.

"There are very few places where you won't find people roaming around. The cities are huge, with millions of people, and they make a lot of garbage and use a lot of water. In fact, we're sort of in the middle of a slow-motion apocalypse. The air is so polluted that the entire planet is heating up."

Aaron stared at me blankly.

"Let's go there anyway," I said cheerfully. "It's not that bad yet, and I can't live without electricity and indoor plumbing. Or french fries."

"Do you live in one of these enormous cities?" he asked.

"No, I live with my parents in a forest like this one. I love it there. We have horses. Do you have those here?"

He frowned, shaking his head.

I found the kit, but when I pulled it out, a replacement head for my electric toothbrush fell onto the table. "Yes!" I squealed. "I forgot this was in here." I clutched the tiny thing to my chest like it was made of solid gold.

I looked over at Aaron excitedly. He had the *look*, but I didn't care. "It's a toothbrush," I said, holding it up for him to see. "It cleans your teeth."

He raised one eyebrow, unimpressed. "We have those here too," he said.

"Oh." *Well, that was anticlimactic.* "Do you have any toothpaste?"

For the next hour, I talked Aaron's ear off, and he asked questions. The awkwardness from earlier had lessened, and he wanted to see what else was in my bag. He tried a granola bar, which he said he liked but didn't finish. I showed him a steel water bottle, which he thought was ingenious and then spent five minutes screwing and unscrewing the top. I had two of them, both orange with a Giants logo, so I gave him one, and it seemed to make him happy, though it was hard to tell.

We got about halfway through the pack when he noticed that my watch had a photo on it. He had never seen a photo before and stared at it for several minutes, taking my hand to hold the watch up to his face. I showed him how to scroll, and though his face gave away very little, the contact showed me new emotions from him, like wonder and excitement.

He looked at pictures of my life. My friends, my car, the places I had traveled over *there*. England, Scotland, France, Spain, Italy, Greece, and so on. He saw a picture of my parents, which made him frown. I let him look for a moment, feeling his longing.

"When we find your parents, I'll take a picture of you with them, just like this," I said. He nodded but didn't say anything.

Then, I showed him pictures of Fantasma. "That's a horse," I said. "They're beautiful animals, about the size of that 'small' dragon." I made air quotes around the word "small" like a nerd. "Which makes sense because Fantasma also tried to kill me." The memory gave me a chill. "I should have eaten *her* afterward." Aaron nodded again, not realizing it was a joke.

"Anyway," I continued, suppressing a giggle, "we ride them all over the forest. My favorite thing in the world is to grab my pack and go ride for hours and be alone with the trees. Alone except for Rogue, that is. There are a lot of similarities to here, actually," I said. "The trees are the same." I thought about that for a moment.

Why are the trees the same? In fact, why are the people the same? Almost the same, except for the eyes. The language is nearly identical, with a slightly different accent. That can't be a coincidence. I thought about the white wolf that had appeared in our forest. I stopped speaking for a minute, lost in thought.

"Aaron, do bridges occur spontaneously?" I looked up to see him staring at me with those reflective blue eyes. He still held my hand.

In that brief moment, I realized something. You know how they say that women decide quickly whether or not they would sleep with someone? Well, I can't speak for my entire gender since I'm far from average in my tastes and behaviors, but I can tell you that, for me, it's pretty much true. I was attracted to Aaron from the beginning, but the uniquely bizarre circumstances caused me to be wary and act like a frightened doe. Now that I had calmed down and Aaron was so close, holding my hand, gazing at me with those incredible eyes, and smelling like a goddamn pheromone factory, it was undeniable. This gorgeous man was a big fat hell yeah.

You've been here one day, idiot. Stay focused.

Aaron looked back down, letting go of my hand. Right before he let go, I registered something like the shame I'd sensed in him earlier. It was muffled, as if buried.

"Bridges do spontaneously appear," he said, "but it's rare."

I had forgotten what we were talking about and had to snap my attention back. *Bridges, right.* Maybe the worlds were more closely linked than I thought. If I just stood by that *X*, would I eventually be sucked up into a portal? Would it hurt like it had before or was that a one-time deal?

I gave Aaron a sideways glance, then looked over at Rogue. He lounged by the door, staring at us. I opened the first aid kit, found the antibiotic ointment, and took it over to Rogue. I crouched next to the smelly furball to dab his burns. They were still visible, and he winced but let me apply the ointment. When I was finished, I walked back over to the table and slumped down in the chair.

"I'm exhausted," I said honestly.

He nodded. "We should sleep. We'll walk to the farm tomorrow."

"The farm?" I asked, sticking the little toothbrush head into a side pocket so I could easily retrieve it. The rest of the bag was a mess that something that small could get lost in.

"Yes, the O'Feld farm. Jorin O'Feld is my uncle by marriage but was sort of a second father to me after my parents . . . Anyway, he might know something useful. And I need to resupply. I'm out of bolts, and I'm almost out of oil. Jorin and Terik, my cousin, resupply me from the farm two or three times per year."

"Okay," I said, absorbing the flustering knowledge that I would soon meet multiple members of Aaron's family. "Can I ask one last thing?"

He nodded.

"How come I don't have access to the Protection fragment if I'm from Earth?"

"Not everyone does," he said, pausing, "but you might have it and not know since you're from over *there*." He looked at my face again, his eyes searching where my burns had been, and got a look on his face that I couldn't decipher.

"What is it?" I asked.

"Well, there is a way to find out," he said. He couldn't meet my eyes.

"How?" I asked, not sure if I wanted to know the answer.

"Well, the Protection fragment has two sides to it. Shielding and . . . healing." His eyes quickly flicked over my body. It was unclear if he was checking for signs of healing or if he was just plain checking me out.

"Uh-huh. Where are you going with this, Bear Guy?" I asked, parking my fists on my hips, and narrowing my eyes exaggeratedly.

He wrinkled his brow. "Bear Guy?" he asked, finally looking at me directly.

"Yeah, cuz you're as big as a bear and I thought about spraying you with my bear spray when I first saw you. But that was before you saved me from a dragon, cooked me dinner, and informed me that I ruined your whole life. That earned you a reprieve from the bear spray."

"Bear spray?" His brow deepened further, and my attention shifted back to the gash over his right eye. It wasn't bleeding anymore, but it looked angry. Redness had spread from the wound to the surrounding skin. I still had the antibiotic ointment in my hand. I opened the first aid kit again and rummaged through, looking for iodine and a cotton ball.

"Never mind," I said, pulling out the iodine and bandages. "Just finish your thought."

He ignored my suggestion, watching me unscrew the iodine bottle and flip it upside down with the cotton ball on top. "I am nowhere near as big as a bear," he said. His denial was precious, and a smile spread over my face. "I am not big at all," he said. "You are as tiny as a fledgling oardoo."

"What the hell is an oardoo? Wait, no, we're getting off topic again. Go back to the healing thing. But hold still, I'm gonna clean your wound." I ripped open the bandage, squeezing antibiotic ointment onto the center to use after I cleaned the wound.

"Healing," he said, looking at the orange cotton ball dubiously, "is a very helpful skill, but it's frowned upon."

"Why?" I asked, then interjected, "This might sting." I lifted myself up onto my tippy toes to reach his face, but he bent his head forward so I could reach him, and I relaxed down. I dabbed his wound with the cotton ball, and he winced but didn't move. I waved at the cut so it would dry.

He took a big breath as if he were about to deliver devastating news and said, "It's frowned upon because it feels . . ."

He looked so uncomfortable as I waved at his face that I thought I knew the answer to my earlier question. His emotion then, as now, was embarrassment—not pain—so . . . he felt deep shame surrounding pleasure? *It had definitely been the bath that had unnerved him, not me discovering his ability*, I decided. *And I think he likes me.*

Was this a world of extreme sexual repression? Because that's basically Hell, especially for someone like me. I'm not exactly known for my immaculate chastity. Marti had once called me her most favorite miscreant. I was beginning to wonder if I had, for real, died in the portal and gone to actual Hell. That made me think of what had happened after all that pain: That had definitely *not* been Hell. Quite the opposite.

Then an idea bloomed in my mind. I had exited that bridge with all my injuries healed. I had thrown aside my wrist brace, and my chest and ankle were completely fine. What if that was connected to the pleasure at the end of my bridge experience?

My mouth dropped open. "Oh my gosh. I think I know why," I said, then I stretched the bandage over his wound, pressing the adhesive sides to his forehead. He let me, and as I touched him, I sensed his relief at not having to explain it.

So, to be mean, I patted his forehead and said, "Because it feels like sex."

Aaron squeezed his eyes shut and groaned. He pulled away from me and covered his face with his hands. It was both sad and adorable and I couldn't help but laugh. It made me wonder if this enormous thirty-one-year-old man was a virgin. He had been out here alone all this time, supposedly waiting for me, never meeting anyone else, and living in a world where sex is frowned upon?

Yeah, Evilina thought, *he might be a virgin. And this is definitely Hell. And holy crap! And, uh, maybe the IUD would be enough protection for us to—*

"I should turn in," I said. "I'm sure I'll have plenty of time to . . . try the healing thing. Ya know, if what I just did doesn't work." I gave my handiwork one more look, and then I turned and walked over to the table. I haphazardly stuffed my belongings back inside my bag and headed over to the cot, setting my pack on the floor and flopping myself down. I'm pretty sure he stared after me, but I didn't look.

A second or two later, he walked over to the privacy screen and dragged it in front of the cot. I wondered why he even had a privacy screen if he was alone out here. It looked old and was painted with little yellow flowers. Maybe it had been his mother's.

"Aaron," I said before he finished pulling the screen over. He looked at me from around the side but didn't answer. "Thanks for . . . rescuing me."

"Welcome," he said, one corner of his mouth ticking up. Then he pulled the screen a little more, blocking my view of him.

I exhaled and gave myself a stern lecture about how it was not my job to fix this man's problems. He was lonely, and I was there and convenient. If this were Earth, he'd seriously have been way out of my league. I'm not hideous or anything, but I'm no Spirit, who performed this amazing magic trick where, upon entering a room, she made everyone else disappear. The thought of her made my heart ache a little.

A quiet *clink* came from the other side of the screen, then the light went out. I heard Aaron rolling out the second bedroll onto the floor. I looked at my watch. It said 10:30 p.m. I reached down to my pack and grabbed the little toothbrush head out of the side pocket. Aaron had never heard of toothpaste, but he did give me a few semi-dried spearmint leaves to chew. I figured it was probably better to save them for the morning, so I pulled my water bottle out of the bag to use instead. I scrubbed my teeth as I lay there, listening to Aaron breathe.

The bedroll was surprisingly comfortable, like a thin memory foam mattress. This world was full of surprises, it seemed. I finished scrubbing my teeth, then leaned down to tuck the toothbrush head back into the side pocket.

A minute later, I heard Rogue sneaking toward me. He jumped up onto the cot and snuggled his huge body in, half beside me, half on top of me. I thought that I would have a hard time sleeping in this strange world, but Rogue made it almost normal.

His head rested close to mine, and he stretched to lick my face. As he did, I got a powerful emotion from him and I jerked back, surprised. It was pure love. I'd never sensed anything like that from him before, but this feeling was so clear that it left no room for doubt about who he belonged to. I hadn't realized how worried I'd been about Rogue's loyalty until relief flooded through me. This was *my* Rogue.

"I love you, too, Roogy-Roo," I whispered, smiling at him in the dark.

As I drifted to sleep, one last thought kept running through my mind: Psycho Snow White knew Rogue somehow, and she was the key to getting the information I needed. Maybe he could lead me to her. Maybe I could figure out how to communicate that to him through Connection. I would have to think on it.

Chapter Eight

"I'm sorry, Syndeth," Linorra said in alarm. "I did not mean to upset you. It's just that you are so brilliant and beautiful, I would not think to compare you to a human. You're the loveliest dragon I've ever seen. Why, you are made with every color in the rainbow, and you gleam with a magnificent shine." Linorra did not bother to tell Syndeth that he was only the second dragon that she'd seen. That did not matter. She could not imagine a more stunning creature.

When I awoke, a blanket covered me that was made of the same material as Aaron's shirt, but thicker. It was too dark to see. I pressed the side button on my watch, and it glowed enough for me to spot Rogue curled up at the foot of the cot.

I'm a belly-sleeper, and drool dripped out of my mouth at the corner. I wiped it away with the back of my hand. *That must have been cute when Aaron placed the blanket over me.* Then I realized that my borrowed shirt was hiked up over my bare hip in a way that would have been comically indecent with no blanket covering me. I hoped he didn't see anything. Then I remembered his cat eyes and groaned.

I sat up and swung my legs over the side of the cot and waited, listening. I didn't hear anything.

"Rogue," I said, "I think we're both going to have to pee outside this morning." I didn't hear any snickering. "And maybe poop too," I said a little louder. Nothing. Maybe Aaron was already up and outside.

I stood and peeked around the other side of the privacy screen, then lifted my watch and pressed the side button again. The glow was enough to show me that Aaron wasn't there anymore. My watch said 3:11 a.m.

The light went out, and I pushed the button again to find my pack, but nothing happened. *Ugh.* The watch was dead.

I turned and reached down, feeling for my pack. I found it by touch and dug out the flashlight, which I used to find and retrieve my clothes from the side of the tub, where Aaron had replaced them after dumping the water. They were still somewhat damp, but I could live with it. I changed back into them behind the privacy screen, then rolled up Aaron's shirt and stuffed it into the pack. I didn't think he would mind if I borrowed it for a few more days.

I had a gross taste in my mouth, so I grabbed a spearmint leaf and chewed on it while I put on my socks and shoes. I'd have to find something better for my teeth, eventually.

I felt oddly comforted by the sensation of wearing shoes. They were trail runners, a little stiffer, heavier, and more durable than my road shoes. I had taken to wearing them when I began training for my ultramarathon, and the solid weight on my foot somehow made my entire body feel more durable.

I took my watch off and stuffed it into the pack. Then, using the flashlight, I looked around to make sure I wasn't forgetting anything. I sat down next to Rogue and mentally prepared myself to leave the relative safety of the cottage to go look for Aaron.

After a minute, I stood and moved as silently as possible toward the front door, navigating around the table and chair. Rogue followed closely behind me. The door wasn't barred, so I grabbed the knob and turned it. It must have been recently oiled because it didn't make a sound.

The first thing I noticed when I cracked the door open was the aroma of the redwoods. The forest here had that same scent that I loved. It smelled like home, which was comforting, despite the memory of yesterday's dragon attack.

It was dark outside, too, but I got the impression that the sun was about to rise somewhere behind the trees. It felt too early for that, but I supposed if we were at a high enough latitude, it could rise this soon during the summer. Then again, this world might have a completely different size and rotation than Earth. Who knew if it even *was* summer?

I pushed the door open, but hesitated, hovering in the doorway. I didn't see anyone or anything outside, so I listened for a minute while Rogue waited next to me. I glanced down at him, then motioned ahead just as I had seen Aaron do the day before. He darted around me, trotting out the door to the left, then around the house and back up to the right, as he had done when we first arrived. Then he sat still, gazing up at me.

"Okay," I whispered and stepped out of the doorway.

"That was well done," Aaron said from above my head. I about jumped a foot out of my durable shoes. He laughed quietly from the roof.

"Rude," I said, turning around to scowl up at him. He laughed again. My adrenaline screamed at me to do something drastic, but I didn't know what it was. Perhaps Evilina would tell me later.

"Have you been waiting up there just so you could scare me to death?" I asked.

"No," he said, "that was just a side benefit. I always come up here for the early morning watch. I can see you were paying attention yesterday, but next time, don't forget to look up."

"Great, thanks for the tip. Say, did you climb up that ladder that was right above my head while I slept on the cot?" I asked.

"There's another way up from out here," he said, gazing down at me.

That wasn't a no.

"Okay then. Now what?" I asked.

"Now, we start walking. It's safer in the dark. I'll meet you inside so we can pack up." I suspected that he still silently laughed at me, but it was too dark to tell. His voice gave away nothing.

"Actually, I need to make a pit stop before that," I said. Aaron looked at me blankly. I guess they didn't have race car–related euphemisms in this world.

"Oh, for heaven's sake, Aaron. Just give me a minute alone, would you? Rogue and I have to go water a tree." That did the trick. He made that same hilarious groaning noise from yesterday, did a literal facepalm, then turned to head toward the trapdoor.

Yeah, that's what you get, you big bully. You're lucky I didn't talk about fertilizing the tree too.

I glanced down at Rogue. "Where's the bathroom around here, Rogue?" He looked at me for a second, huffed out a breath, then disappeared around the back of the cottage. That dog was always pee shy. Weirdo. I laughed softly to myself, then followed him to what turned out to be an outhouse behind the cottage.

By the time we made it back inside, Aaron had relit the oil lamp and set it on the table. He had attached both bedrolls to his own rucksack and now knelt in front of his wooden chest, digging through it. He'd donned a leather utility vest that had multiple sheaths, and he was attaching every knife he had to it.

"Expecting trouble?" I asked.

He shrugged. "I'm out of bolts," he said from the floor. I walked to stand next to him, looking over his shoulder into the chest. Everything in there was neatly organized and perfectly stacked. Rogue walked over to look in, too, nudging my hand with his head.

"Can't you throw fireballs or something?" I asked, scratching behind Rogue's ears.

Aaron gave me the *look* again. I was beginning to think it was his default setting. "That would be convenient, but no. I can burn someone with a touch"—he paused for a second, frowning deeply—"or set the ground where they stand on fire, but it doesn't work over distances and it's difficult to manage quickly."

"That's unfortunate," I said. I looked around for what else I might pack in my bag but didn't see anything obvious. "Maybe you could make little flammable balls, set those on fire and throw them."

He stopped to think. "That's not a bad idea."

"Really? Well, maybe I won't be completely useless," I said. I walked back over to the table and set my pack down. I spotted a little wooden bowl and grabbed it to put Rogue's water in while on the road, then glanced back at Aaron. He glowered down into the chest from his kneeling position, his mouth forming a taut line.

"I was rude to you yesterday," he said. "I apologize. I have no excuse."

I gaped at him, surprised by his blunt apology. When I saw that he was serious, I felt a surge of affection for him. Anyone who apologizes outright like that always elicits a feeling of protectiveness from me because an honest apology is a show of vulnerability. It's a request for acceptance, an experience that I could definitely relate to.

"It's okay, Aaron," I said. "I was just kidding. I'd be bird food if you hadn't come to get me."

Aaron stared at me, still on his knees. I looked right back at him, and an understanding passed between us. From that moment on, we would try to trust each other. Given his history, I could see how that might be difficult for him. I had an intense urge to hug him again. I ignored it, and the moment passed. *Whew.*

He went back to searching through the chest, and I stuffed the little bowl into my pack. It barely fit. I picked up the oil lamp and carried it over to Aaron, holding it over the chest.

"Do you want me to carry anything else?" I asked.

"Are you sure you can fit anything else into that disorganized mess you call a pack?"

"What? I know exactly where everything is in this pack! I just don't know exactly *what* is in the pack. And it's a good thing, too, because otherwise . . ." My voice trailed off.

I was going to say that he'd benefitted from my random first aid kit, but then I looked at the gash that I'd supposedly tended to. With the light so close, I could now see that it actually looked quite bad.

"Holy crap, Aaron! This is terrible. Your eye is completely bloodshot," I said. I held the lamp at a better angle, and he lifted his hand to shade his eyes. "Hold still," I said sternly, batting his hand aside. I stepped in closer to remove the bandage, and I saw him wince again. The skin around it was so swollen that it looked like a giant welt. I carefully peeled the bandage off, releasing a putrid smell that made me gag. The edges of the wound were black, and the center was filled with yellow pus.

"Holy shit, Aaron. We have to get you some help with this wound. It's so much worse than yesterday." I coughed at the foul odor.

He waved the light away from his face again. "I've been scratched before. Dragon talons are poisonous, and they can kill, but I am protected. I always heal from everything."

"What does that even mean? This is not healing, Aaron, this is spreading. At least let me clean it again. It stinks, and if it keeps turning black and spreading out, you'll lose your eye and maybe worse."

Aaron sighed. "Fine, but if what you say is true, then it probably needs a real healer." He looked at me obliquely, letting me draw my own conclusions.

I hesitated, thinking about what the implications of that would be. I was bonding with him, sure, but this was a pretty big step beyond friendly teasing. My experience in the portal was still fresh in my mind, and I knew that if this healing was anything like that, then I might as well just sleep with him now and get it over with.

"I don't know how," I said finally.

Aaron reached up tentatively and touched my cheek where a burn should have been. His fingers were warm, and I instinctively closed my eyes for a moment in response to the sensation. A thrill ran through me, and I wasn't sure if it came from me or him. "I know you can do this because you already healed yourself," he said softly. "Look at Rogue's face. He is still burned, but your face is . . ." He searched for the right word.

"Beautiful? Enchanting? The very essence of perfection?" I suggested. I tried and failed to keep a straight face.

"You make everything into a joke," he said, shaking his head.

I shrugged. "Get used to it. It only gets worse the longer you know me."

He huffed a breath out. "I guess I have no choice."

"There's always a choice," I said seriously.

He paused, thinking about that. "I've never healed anyone myself," he said, "but I know the theory, and it's not dissimilar to what I do. I'll guide you the best I can." He stared at me much as he had the night before when he had inadvertently held onto my hand, his eyes penetrating straight through my emotional defenses.

"Okay," I said, "but you better sit down for this. Ya know, in case it works. I'd hate for you to pass out and crack your head. That could start a vicious cycle."

He hesitated for a second, just like I had, then stood and took off his blade-bedazzled vest. He replaced the chest lid and sat on top of it, ignoring the chair.

"Are you sure?" I asked.

He paused, then nodded.

"Okay," I said. "That looked like consent to me. What do I do first?"

"First you have to picture what you want. This will guide the flow of Protection from your reservoir. The Protection fragment works to halt or reverse forces of change and decay. The body has a stable state that it prefers to be in, and Protection forces that state into existence or prevents it from diverging in the first place. It is the complementary fragment to my own, which is a force of change."

"You and I are opposites?"

"Not exactly. The Absorption fragment is the true opposite of Protection. They repel each other. Protection and Evocation are complementary and work together. You also have access to Connection, which will let you sense what you need to heal. I'm honestly not sure how this will work, since I've never heard of anyone having both greater Connection and greater Protection." He grimaced for a moment, then said, "Not naturally, anyway."

"How do you know I have this greater Protection thingy?" I asked, gliding past the last comment.

"Because I have lesser Protection, and I know what it feels like. I can sense it in you, in fact. It gives us a sort of resonance, but lesser Protection doesn't speed up the healing process at all. It only ensures that it meanders in the correct direction. Your face was burned badly enough that it would have left scars on most people, but today you're healed."

"That's what you meant when you said that you were protected?"

He nodded. "Yes. Protection helps you heal, and it shields you from needing to be healed in the first place."

"Okay, so I have to what? Imagine healing you?"

"Not exactly. Imagine that I'm already healed. Picture the end result, then direct your fragment to work toward that result. You won't have to know how, it will just happen, the way that your body knows how to use the air when you breathe."

He took my hand and I felt him immediately. The pain above his eye was sharp, and I felt it as if it were my own. Then, without warning, the memory of his night flashed through me like a shiver, showing me what he had been trying to hide.

The pain above his eye was difficult to ignore, but he'd been scratched many times before and always overcame it. He knew how to endure pain, but this time it felt different. The dragon's talon had dug far too deep into him, and its poison had gotten into his blood. His body was spending too much effort to purge it from his system for him to also prevent his skin from dissolving and sloughing away.

He had been worrying about it but not saying anything. He hadn't slept all night. He'd spent a few hours listening to me breathe and feeling an annoying jealousy of Rogue. Then he got up, gaped at my legs and half-uncovered bare ass, laid a blanket on me, and climbed up to the roof. He was exhausted. His fatigue had left his mental defenses weakened, allowing me to get all of that from him in a split second.

I sucked in a breath and yanked my hand away. The pain and memory vanished. I stared at him in shock. I had felt far more than his emotions this time. I had seen right into his mind and spied on his memories. I had physically felt his pain. I lifted a hand to my forehead, rubbing at the tingling skin above my own eye.

"Why didn't you say anything?" I asked.

Aaron swallowed. "It's not your job to solve all of my problems," he said.

I nodded, though his response was infuriating, despite me having already had that same thought. I ground my teeth, wondering if he had picked that phrase out of my brain in the same way I had just seen his memories. If so, had he also heard me debating the ethics of sleeping with him? I felt my face flush.

"But if I can help you," I said, "there's no reason not to, and every reason to do it. I need your help to get home just as much as you need mine. Probably more so, and you can't help me if you're exhausted and blind in one eye."

He didn't respond but took a big breath as if trying to calm himself.

"Can I try again?" I asked. "I didn't even get to the healing part."

He nodded. This time I took his hand, bracing myself for the pain. It stabbed me again and I winced but held on. The skin around the wound burned, and the vision in his right eye was blurry. The wound itself was numb, which made me worry that it might be too late.

I marveled at how Aaron already felt familiar to me after less than a day. So familiar, in fact, that I was comfortable lecturing him like a child. Maybe that was the resonance that he had been talking about. I had to ask myself if I was actually interested or if this was just a coincidental relationship between us. I had just met him yesterday, and now I was going to touch him in a way that felt like sex?

Yep, I thought, and despite his literal groaning at the prospect, he was voluntarily holding my hand, so he couldn't have been too opposed.

I glanced over at Rogue. He had rolled over to face the door, as if he were too embarrassed to watch. I took a big breath and delved in deeper. He was more apprehensive than scared, but he was also more open to me than he had been yesterday. The grief was still there, but our conversation about his family had helped. He wasn't quite as alone as he had been.

That was rather heartwarming, and I smiled. He smiled, too, and I realized, with amazement, that Connection was, indeed, a two-way street. I felt him, and he felt me. We had created a space there together, where we were inside each other's most private joy, fear, and shame. It was frighteningly intimate.

Aaron was filled with a yearning I knew well. It wasn't just a physical need but a deep desire to be connected, a desire which, when unmet, humiliates you with its deprivation.

I went through an entire childhood with no friends. In college, Drew had been my sole social support until she ended things. I met Marti at a bar in Trinidad the night after my breakup, and I'd tried to drink myself to death. Marti says she drove me home, but I don't remember any of it. She probably saved my life. Even more incredible, she became my first female friend.

Aaron breathed in and out, and I did the same. His scent filled my nose and then permeated the rest of me, seeping into the dark corners that I preferred to keep hidden from everyone, even myself.

There was something else there, too, that was similar to what I had previously experienced as heat, except this time my mind interpreted it as a scent. It smelled like him but more vivid.

It reminded me of the night that Drew and I kissed for the first time. It was our junior year at San Francisco State, and we had been in the living room of our tiny college apartment. I scrolled on my phone while she studied for a test on the American Civil War. I was in the class, too, but had calculated that I only needed a D on the test to keep my A in the class, so I wasn't about to waste time studying when I could instead watch an endless stream of fifteen-second videos.

She was frustrated at trying to remember dates and names of supposedly important people. I made a joke about where I thought Robert E. Lee could stick his musket. She laughed, and then, in a moment of impulsivity, blurted out that she had something to tell me but she was scared that I wouldn't want to be her friend anymore.

I told her not to be an idiot and that she could tell me anything. Then she stepped out of the closet right into my arms. I embraced her, then I kissed her, and a thousand near misses culminated in a life-changing blur of revelation and sweat and long-awaited relief. I remembered what the bedsheets smelled like afterward. That was what this scent reminded me of. It was desire, one that had never before had a viable outlet.

My body reacted to it, and Aaron sensed it. His hand tightened on mine, and he struggled to keep himself from pulling me toward him. If I were going to find this ability to reach into someone and heal them in a way that felt like pure pleasure, it would have to be in this realm somewhere.

I braced myself and threw my awareness into his desire as fully as I could, trying to go deeper. There was a barrier that I couldn't break through, an old wall that had hardened with time and fear. I pushed against it, but it was as solid as the mountain, unbreakable. He truly was protected.

What if it isn't a wall but a door? One that is barred from within.

Instead of pushing, I knocked. I whispered, both mentally and aloud, "Can I come in?"

The question echoed in both of our minds. Nothing happened for a moment, but I could sense Aaron warring with himself over the answer to that dangerous question.

Yes won, and the door cracked. My awareness flooded into him, and I was assaulted by an explosion of information and sensation. Aaron sucked in a breath, and his eyes flew open to lock with mine. I wobbled on my feet a little and he grabbed my arm with his free hand to steady me.

I had only *thought* that I could feel him before. Now, I wasn't just inside him. I *was* him, and he was me. I felt his lips part as if they were my own lips. I saw his memories, and he saw mine. I felt his desire, and he felt the same from me. I felt him getting an erection as if it were my own. That was an eye-opener, let me tell you. Jesus. I felt a sharp, deeply ingrained shame that the unmasking of those urges caused him to feel.

What is this? I asked. *Where is this shame coming from? This doesn't make any sense.*

I forgot about what I was supposed to be doing and swam through his thoughts and memories about where this erroneous belief originated. What I discovered was deeply unsettling. Men in golden capes, a dagger with a golden handle, a council sitting at a high table, burning houses, a room full of students with various injuries, a young girl being dragged away by a man in a black hat, a belt hanging on the back of a door, a secret room filled with banned books. Something called the Ministry.

What is the Ministry? I asked. I had already suspected that this was a conservative society, but this went far beyond that. Every single person was indoctrinated to believe that purity came from pain and that sexual desire was shameful and wrong. They had to get permission to have sex from their Ministry leader, even for the purpose of having children. They literally needed a fucking permit.

Holy shit. This is so much worse than I thought. This entire world is controlled by a cult. The whole godforsaken planet.

I sensed Aaron's confusion at my certainty in this, and he rejected it at first. He came from one of the more rebellious families in the region, so he wasn't as anchored in the dogma of the Ministry as some, but when it came down to it, he couldn't entirely escape the brainwashing of his own culture. But then, just like I had done, he immersed himself in the memories of my life.

My family was the opposite of conservative. We didn't go to church. My mother educated me about sex at the age of seven. She put me on the pill when I was fifteen and took me to get an IUD when I was seventeen. I had sex for the first time later that year, and my mother bought the condoms. My parents were so open that they hadn't batted an eye when I had asked if my friends could all stay in the guest rooms together. This was normal and expected. I sometimes underestimate how much their way of thinking influenced me, but my parents, and my mother especially, taught me that absolute freedom of mind and body is the most natural and *right* way to be.

Talk about seeing things from someone else's perspective. Imagine believing in something your whole life, with your whole spirit, only to learn beyond a shadow of a doubt that you had been duped. There was something happening in this world that I didn't understand yet, a force trying to exert control over everything and everyone. It wasn't right or just. Everything about it was deeply wrong.

It doesn't have to be this way, he thought.

It's not this way. Not for me.

I became aware of a pressure that started at the base of Aaron's spine and pushed upward like a geyser. He grew unnaturally hot and shook violently.

Rage, I thought, watching in spellbound dismay as Aaron's memory flicked through all the ways the Ministry had ruined his life. They were the real reason his family had left him behind. They were the reason he had to hide in the woods like a criminal. He had always resented the Ministry, but he had also believed them when they called him a traitor. He had spent years running, feeling deeply conflicted about his rebellion.

It had all been a lie.

I thought for a moment that he might accidentally set me on fire. Reluctantly, I withdrew from him again, extinguishing our shared mental experience. I knew I didn't need to heal his anger and resentment. I only needed to exist there with him in that room. Again, I felt an overwhelming urge to hug him. This time, I gave in. I leaned forward and wrapped my arms around his shoulders.

He returned the embrace, hugging me so hard that I feared being crushed by his unnatural strength. He pulled me onto his lap, and I let him. I held him there until he stopped shaking, soaking up the heat radiating from his body. The intimacy would have frightened me a day ago. Now, it felt completely natural. I had never become so close with someone as quickly as I had with this man over the last day. I knew him now, and he knew me. I felt for him. More than that, I could feel my priorities shifting for him.

Aaron released me from the hug, allowing me to breathe again. Neither of us smiled as we stared at each other, taking in the change to our situation that I knew we both felt. Whatever we were before, whatever we thought we were, that was over now.

His eyes were exceptionally pale, a beautifully bright shade of blue that was almost clear. His pupils were huge. He looked down at my mouth and then back up at my eyes again. I knew I would let him kiss me, but I wasn't ready yet, mostly because I found the wound above his eyebrow to be revolting and I didn't want to put my face anywhere near it.

"Can I try one last time?" I asked.

He licked his lips, then nodded. I had my arms around him already, so I reached up with one hand and rested it on the back of his neck, opening up my awareness to him again. He bowed his head a little, his face nearly resting against my own neck. He let me in readily this time, and I closed my eyes to concentrate on finding the wound above his eye with that awareness.

It was all but impossible. Attempting to comprehend the internal mechanisms of his body was like standing in a crowded auditorium, struggling to understand someone shouting from the opposite end in a language I didn't know. There was so much information to sift through, and I didn't know what to do with any of it. On top of that, everything was fuzzy, as if I were looking at it through smudged glasses. My heart sank as I grasped that this was beyond me. Aaron sensed my disappointment, and he squeezed me a little, lifting his face away from my neck to look at me.

It's okay, he thought to me. I jerked in surprise. Unlike a moment ago, when I had gotten emotions, images, and jumbled memories, his thoughts were now spoken words, as clear and loud as his real voice. It was super weird. He laughed inside our minds, and although his face barely registered a smile, I could feel his laughter shaking my bones.

You did it to me again, you big bully, I thought to him.

His eyes crinkled at the corners, and he laughed at me again, even harder this time. *Get used to it, it will only get worse the longer you know me.*

Oh, shut up, stop copying me and let me work, I thought to him.

His face finally cracked into a grin. It was the first full, broad smile I had ever seen on his face, and it made my heart sing. His expression, normally so closed and stoic, opened as wide to me as his mind had, a fresh joy warming his features like a newly lit hearth in a cold room. I had no choice but to grin back at him.

After so many years of isolation, Aaron was overwhelmed by the sudden insertion of a woman into his life. A *tiny* woman, even smaller than his mother, which he didn't think was possible. A gorgeous woman who liked him and who was considering sleeping with him.

Godammit, I thought. *You heard that?* I covered my eyes with one hand and felt my cheeks heating up again.

"Well, shit," I said out loud. I am generally very open about sex, but that thought was meant to be private.

He buried his face in my neck again, partly to hide his laughter and partly to breathe in my scent. The experience of smelling my own scent through him was disorienting, but to feel him revel in it was thrilling.

I'm so lucky you had that barrel yesterday, I thought. I laughed, and he laughed with me. I shook my head in an attempt to release the embarrassment. It sort of worked.

I decided that instead of trying to find the injury mentally, I would just physically look at the wound. I pushed myself away from him a little so I could look at it properly, then I imagined pressing healed skin on top of the injury like a bandage. Something connected there, like a magnet attaching to a refrigerator. I got the impression that the actual imagery I used didn't matter as much as the effort to press my intention into the wound. So, I pushed.

It was a little bit like blowing up a balloon but with a muscle my brain wasn't accustomed to controlling. It was a massive effort to continue, and a pressure accumulated behind my eyes. After a few seconds, I felt a pressure in my chest as well.

Aaron sensed my struggle and thought, *You can stop.*

No! I'm a marathoner, dammit. I keep going when I'm tired.

It made me dizzy, but I pushed even harder. Aaron tensed, then closed his eyes and released a deep, guttural moan, letting his head rock back. The sound—I swear—made my uterus twitch, and my heart suddenly raced. Heat rushed to my pelvis and my body begged me to wrap myself around him. I resisted, instead concentrating on pushing Protection with all my strength. I was doing it!

The blackened skin at the edges of the wound shriveled up and fell off, revealing pink, shiny skin underneath. A quiet fizzing sound came from the wound itself. It bubbled as if I had poured hydrogen peroxide on it. The pus dripped out of the wound, down into his eyebrow. It was absolutely disgusting, but I could feel the intense pleasure it gave him as if it were my own.

Our thoughts intertwined, flowing back and forth simultaneously, such that I struggled to distinguish mine from his. Our attention was brought back down to his erection, and we noticed the way I sat pressed against him at an odd angle.

So much for not wrapping myself around him. What a shame. I readjusted myself so that I straddled him, a much more comfortable position for both of us.

Thank you, he thought, and his hands slid down from the small of my back to my waist, then down to my hips. His hands moving over me made me shiver and lose my concentration for a moment. He gripped me a little harder and pulled me toward him. The juxtaposition of sexual tension against the horrifying process of wound healing was so ludicrous that I laughed.

He knew why I laughed, but the intense pleasure made it hard for him to think about anything except lifting me up by my ass, kicking the chair out of the way, and carrying me over to the cot so he could tear my damp clothes off. He narrowly contained the impulse, but the image kept circling and spinning in his mind like a Tilt-a-Whirl.

He growled in frustration, then pulled me into a tight hug to try to make the spinning stop, burying his face in my neck again, inhaling me. Then he opened his mouth and tasted my skin. I let him, a little sigh escaping my lips. His mouth was feverishly hot, and I closed my eyes to just feel it. To him, my skin was silky and cool against his lips, and salty on his tongue. He imagined his mouth moving around the rest of my body, and I knew he would not be able to withstand the urge much longer.

His shame and embarrassment were unraveling. *But what will replace it*? we asked. *Love? No.* As much as that idea appealed, this was not about love. This was about freedom. It was about exulting in the exquisite pain and pleasure of *being*.

My skin tingled all over and my vision blurred. *I should stop*, I thought. *You'll be okay now. I should definitely stop.* I didn't stop. I pushed Protection into him as hard as I could. He clenched his jaw and let out a sort of grunting whine, then his hands went from my hips down to my butt and he squeezed.

The room started to spin, and I closed my eyes against it. Aaron was about to kiss me when he sensed the change. With extreme effort, he pulled his face away to look at me. His grip loosened a little.

"Lina, stop," he said.

At least, that's what I think he said. I'm not entirely sure because I passed out. Aaron caught me before I fell. I heard him say my name, but it sounded far away. I couldn't respond.

When I came back, he still held me on his lap, keeping me from falling. His face was tense, and he was drenched in sweat.

"Lina," he said again. He relaxed when I opened my eyes and looked at him. "You okay?" he asked.

"Yeah. I just . . . I healed you. It was *really* hard." He didn't even smile at the joke. He stared at my face. "What is it?" I asked.

He shook his head and whispered, "You're glowing."

I held my hand up to my face and stared. "Again?" He didn't respond. After a few seconds, the glow faded and I said, "I'm okay."

He released a breath. "Okay," he said, then he kissed my forehead and hugged me. I suppose he was too euphoric to worry about a little thing like involuntary bioluminescence.

Something did worry him, though. He felt a new, rather intense affection for me. It made him uncomfortable because it came with a new kind of fear, the kind you feel when you have something precious that you're scared of losing. He wasn't sure if he liked this new feeling.

I sighed. *Relax, it'll probably go away when the euphoria wears off.* His skittish apprehension annoyed me, and he could feel it. I sat back, releasing Connection. The withdrawal felt like a blast of cold air.

I avoided his searching gaze by looking back up at his wound. It wasn't fully healed, but he was out of danger. I saw a healthy, glistening pink in the center of the wound, and all the red and black was gone, although it was still swollen. He also still had a disgusting glob of goop in his eyebrow, and I wrinkled my nose.

I slid off his lap and stumbled woozily over to my pack to retrieve the first aid kit again. I followed the same routine I had the day before, cleaning his wound with iodine, letting it dry, then covering it with ointment and a bandage. I wiped the goop out of his eyebrow with the other side of the cotton ball and asked, "So, how was that?"

"That was . . ." He sighed. "I have no words." He let out a short laugh and wiped the back of one hand across his sweaty brow.

"Yeah?" I asked, my smile returning. "It felt like it was supposed to?"

"I wouldn't know," he answered, his face regaining its stoic mask. "I've never been healed before. People like me don't go to healers unless they're dying. Sometimes not even then."

"Oh," I said, confused. I wasn't sure if I should explore the "people like me" comment. "That was fun except for that part at the end. That's the second time I've glowed like that since I've been here. I did it after I crossed the bridge too." I thought about that night. "I can't believe it was only a day ago that I was at my parents' stables drinking beer."

"What is beer?" he asked.

I looked at him blankly. "Good lord, please tell me you're kidding. No sex or beer on this planet? That is completely unacceptable." My head swam. "Anyway. I'm sorry I couldn't finish the job."

"You did more than enough," he said. "Don't give so much. You'll hurt yourself."

I laughed out loud. "Oh, Aaron, I shouldn't tell you this, but ordering me not to do something is the perfect way to ensure that I *continue* doing something."

He didn't say anything; he just lifted his hand to stroke my one dimple with his thumb, then gently pulled me back into his lap and kissed me.

He tasted like spearmint, and I hoped to all that was holy in the universe that I did too. He hugged me to his warm body, wrapping his arms around my back and enveloping me in his scent. A low growl rumbled in his chest that made me think he held back. I leaned into him, clutched the sides of his tunic, and pulled him closer. His hand came to the back of my head, and he kissed me harder, his tongue exploring the inside of my mouth. His other hand slipped under the back of my shirt and brushed the skin of my lower back.

"Your skin is so soft," he whispered, pressing his hot palm against my back and running it up the length of my spine. I let out a soft moan that made him chuckle quietly. "You like that?"

"Yes," I said. "I like everything about you." As soon as the words were out of my mouth, I froze, dreading what would undoubtedly be the return of Aaron's earlier reluctance. *Stupid big mouth.*

He sighed, brushing his lips softly against mine. "And I could kiss you for days," he said, pulling away, "but we've already missed our chance to walk in full darkness. If we don't leave now, we'll hit the oardoo fields at high heat, and we'll have to wait at the edge of the forest until nightfall."

I nodded, trying to ignore the nagging feeling that I had just ruined something. *It doesn't matter*, I told myself. *You're not here to add another name to the mile-long list of people who have realized how strange you are and have decided you aren't worth the trouble. Your goal hasn't changed. Get home.* It wasn't as simple as that, though, and I knew it. Aaron had gotten under my skin—deeper, actually—and he wouldn't be that easy to shake off.

I sighed, wondering what time it was. I guessed four thirtyish. It was a weird time to kiss someone for the first time. "Okay. Well, my bag is packed," I said. "I don't know what's taking you so long."

Aaron raised one eyebrow but didn't respond.

"How long will it take to walk there?" I asked.

"About eight hours."

That was probably about twenty-five miles. "On Earth, we could do that in a car in less than an hour," I said. This time, he raised both of his eyebrows.

I smiled. "Inventions, I'm telling you. We've got a ton of 'em. I can't wait to show you." *Especially the one currently lodged in my uterus. Oh crap, I really need to stop thinking things like that. He might hear me.* He smiled at me, oblivious for now, but then his smile faded.

"Lina, I feel like I'm waking up from a nightmare, but I need you to remember that when we get to the farm, everyone there will still be living in that nightmare. They won't understand."

"Okay, what do you want me to do?"

"You can't tell anyone that you healed me. You can't tell anyone that we slept in the same room."

"We didn't," I reminded him.

He smirked. Evidently, smiling was easier for him now that we'd mind-melded. "That's true," he said, "but we shouldn't even be in the same room together without an escort."

"Yes, we should," I said.

He paused. "These people are my family, but there are limits. You mustn't try to convince them of anything while you're there. In fact, talk as little as possible. There are definitely oardoo tenders that would report us to the Ministry if they found out you and I are . . . uh . . .”

Watching him struggle with labels was amusing, especially after he’d basically just told me to keep my big mouth shut. Granted, I did have a big mouth, but being instructed to “talk as little as possible” was insulting. I can be cool. Usually.

He sighed. “I would leave you here if I had rations for you.” He shook his head. “I never believed you’d actually be there.”

“Aaron, it’s okay. Your mother was right about me being there, so maybe she’s right about the next part too. It’ll be okay.”

He nodded, but it was more of an acknowledgment than an agreement. I had a feeling we would struggle hard before the end. I would need Aaron on my side. I just hoped that, whatever we were, it would be enough to get me home.

Chapter Nine

Linorra felt a mysterious yearning as she read the poem, so delicately etched into the wooden box. She could feel the crystal key within thrumming with power.

Aaron cracked the front door open, looking out cautiously. He listened for a full minute but didn't hear anything. He sent Rogue out ahead, as usual, then he opened the door wide and looked out, up, and all around. When he stepped out of the doorway, he turned around to look at the spot where he'd surprised me earlier, then continued out into the garden.

I followed behind, noting that if he walked at his normal speed, then this would be a bit of a jog for me. I was exhausted, having spent a ton of energy learning to heal, but I had been running two marathons a year since I was eighteen and had been training for an ultramarathon, so I knew how to keep going when I was tired. Just put one blistered foot in front of the other.

As I closed the door behind me, Aaron checked to make sure I followed. He looked even more exhausted than I felt, though I doubted he would admit it. It was still dark out, but he had me carry the oil lantern so I could see where I stepped. He set out at a brisk pace, which did require me to jog, but he noticed and slowed down for me. I followed behind, trailing him like a lost puppy.

As I walked, the scent of the redwoods was a balm to me, my link to home. Along with Rogue, of course, who stayed close to me, nearly rubbing against my legs as I walked. With him trotting at my side, looking up at me with those amber eyes, I felt almost safe, like we were on one of our usual hikes.

"Aaron, how do you know Rogue?" I asked. I couldn't believe I hadn't asked that yet.

"He showed up about seven years ago," he said. "I never knew from where. He would just come out of the Rhoya." Aaron looked at me over his shoulder again, and, noticing my bewilderment, he translated, "The trees." His explanation did nothing to relieve my confusion as I had previously thought "Rhoya" was a swear word.

"He would stay for a few months, then disappear." He chuckled. "I almost shot him the first time he appeared. I thought he might be a spy for *her*."

"Who?"

"Eve Aetos, the Holy Mother. She's the leader of all the Rhoyal Diocese of Monash, and they worship her as a goddess."

And now "Rhoya" refers to the Ministry? These people need a thesaurus. "I thought you didn't believe in a god here," I said, shaking my head.

"We don't. There is only the goddess. They say she was born a mortal, but her spirit was so pure that she ascended to godhood and is now immortal. I've never seen her, but she controls everything and everyone from her palace in Neesee. Her daughter, Seleca, is her second. I believe that is the woman you called Psycho Snow White."

"That's who you're hiding from?"

"Yes, and now so are you, I think," he said.

"Why?" I asked.

"Many reasons, but the main one is that Eve wants my reservoir."

"She *what*? She can steal your fragment?"

"She can steal your *reservoir*," he corrected. "That is how she really became who she is, not by some kind of ascension. Eve is a greater reservoir for the Absorption fragment. She can absorb any reservoir other than Protection, and she is always looking for the ones that she doesn't have yet, which includes both Connection and Evocation. If she finds us, she'll try to kill us and take those two reservoirs. Unless she does us all a favor and steals Seleca's Connection. She's the only other one I know of who has that reservoir."

"If she kills you, she can steal it?"

"Protection prevents her from absorbing it while you're alive, but yes, it can be done at the moment of death, even if you're protected. Or, if you voluntarily let her past your Protection it can also be done. Seleca has absorbed more than one reservoir that way. She tried to do that to me when I was sixteen. I'm the only one I know of who has Evocation. I didn't even know it existed until I accidentally burned down my father's barn. My mother had to explain it to me. It runs in the family, I guess."

"But why do they need so many reservoirs? What is the goal?" I asked.

He shrugged. "I don't know. She already controls all of Monash. She doesn't need any more power."

Ask him more about Rogue.

The thought popped into my head out of nowhere, almost like it didn't belong to me, but I wasn't touching Aaron, so I figured Evilina was just doing her strange insistent questioning thing again. She would try to use the information for our sole benefit, I was sure.

"So, Rogue just showed up unexpectedly?" I asked. "Why didn't you shoot him?"

Aaron shrugged. "I thought about it, but I remembered my mother saying something about a dog girl, so I waited. He sat in front of my cottage door for twelve hours before I finally let him in. Even greater transformers have a limit. For most, that limit is less than an hour. The most gifted struggle with two or three. It has something to do with losing the ability to think clearly, and they say there's a kind of irresistible urge to go back to your normal body that becomes painful after a while. They call it withdrawing."

"What's a transformer?" I asked.

"It's someone who can transform themselves and the objects around them. Some can turn themselves into animals, although it's said to be one of the hardest fragments to master."

"So, shapeshifting," I said, "only they can do it to others too? That's creepy."

"No, not to other living things," he said, "only to themselves and nonliving objects, like that shirt you wore yesterday. Transformers can take the raw material and transform it into a fine garment. It takes practice, though, like any skilled trade."

"Oh, that's why your shirt didn't have any seams," I said. "It was transformed, not sewn. That's amazing."

"Yes," he said, turning to look at me over his shoulder. He had a small smile on his face, looked at my legs, then turned forward again. "Did you bring that shirt?"

I knit my eyebrows together but didn't answer. "So, you let Rogue into your cottage, but how did he get to Monash? And why did he go back and forth?"

Aaron didn't have an answer for that. I looked down at Rogue. He was practically clinging to me as we walked. "I saw his skin ripple right before Psycho Snow White threw me onto the bridge," I said.

Aaron shrugged. "Reservoirs are not limited to people. A dragon's fire is a kind of Evocation, not unlike mine. That's how I always know when they're stalking me."

"Resonance."

"Yes," he confirmed, "and the oardoo use a kind of Transformation during their melding season."

"What's an oardoo?" I asked.

"It's a large bird that runs instead of flies. My uncle sells their feathers at the Harvest Festival every autumn. They're extremely valuable. Once per year, when they enter the melding season, they release all their feathers and grow new ones in just a few minutes. It's quite a sight." He laughed, thinking about it.

"Melding season?" I asked.

"Hmm, that's hard to explain. It would be easier to show you, although melding season just ended. Maybe next year."

"We'll be gone by then."

Aaron didn't respond right away, but after a moment, he said, "I hope you're right."

For the next few hours, we walked in silence. The only sound was the echo of birdsong bouncing off the redwood canopy.

The forest looked so much like home, but there were some clear differences. I knew our trees well, and I knew the feeling of hiking among them. These trees were slightly farther apart and taller. Though my forest had trees reaching greater than three hundred feet, most were shorter than that due to logging. The majority of the trees near the stables were less than a hundred years old. This forest looked to be all old growth, and most appeared to have reached their height potential. It was glorious, but it also made me sad for my own forest. It must have looked like this before humans left their irksome mark.

Another difference was the ground itself. It was rockier, and there were more glades interspersed within the forest. Within some of the glades were hot springs with red crystals growing around the edges. I suggested a swim, but Aaron told me that the pools were deadly and that if I went in the water or touched the crystals, I'd likely die within a few days. Maybe I was protected enough to prevent it, but it was better to play it safe.

After we had walked for about four hours, Aaron selected a place to rest that was hidden between some bushes. I plopped down on a small log with a groan and closed my eyes. Rogue sat down right on top of my feet. Despite the foot warmer, it felt good to rest. My feet ached and I was developing a blister.

You're not protected from everything, I guess. Remember that.

The thought struck me as odd. My mind had just put the word *you* and *I* into the same sentence while thinking about myself. I'd been having weird thoughts like that since crossing the bridge. Maybe it had been the mind-meld with Aaron, or maybe it was just time for a snack. I pulled out a granola bar and offered it to Aaron.

"No, thank you," he said, sitting down on my right to dig in his own pack. He pulled out his now-favorite orange water bottle.

"Ya know, you could just tell me the truth," I said. "I'm not going to be upset because you don't like my granola bars."

He gave me a wan smile. "I don't dislike them, it's just that they are so sweet. What are those dark brown bits?"

I stared at him in disbelief. "Chocolate," I said. "You've never had chocolate? No beer, no sex, and no chocolate. What kind of a crazy world is this?"

He shrugged.

"Okay, tell me this. Have you ever heard of coffee? 'Cause I think you could use some." I thought I might cry when he shook his head. As far as I was concerned, this was worse news than the worldwide cult-induced brainwashing.

Aaron pulled out a cloth and unfolded it to reveal strips of dried meat. *Dragon jerky*, I assumed. *What kind of a badass do you have to be to keep dragon jerky in your knapsack?*

Rogue sat up with interest, paying attention to Aaron for the first time since we'd set out that morning. Aaron offered me a piece, but I waved it away, so he tossed it to Rogue as I poured water into the wooden bowl for the dog.

"Aaron, I just realized I don't know your last name. Do you have family names here?"

He closed his eyes for a second, then reached out to put his arm around my shoulders in a side hug. "I'm sorry," he said, pulling me close. "I should have thought of that. It's Atticus."

I contemplated his apology, pondering why he considered it necessary. Our morning encounter was likely the first time he'd ever had that kind of contact with someone. It made sense that he normally would've offered his full name before diving into something so intimate. Had I known what to expect, and had Aaron's health not been in danger, I certainly wouldn't have let him look inside me so deeply after knowing him for only a day.

In truth, I'd never shown myself to someone like that, not even to people I slept with. The closest I'd ever come was with Drew, and she'd left me behind without a backwards glance—until it was too late. I'd promised myself that I'd never be in that position again.

Then something tickled my brain. *Atticus.* "Oh, that's the same last name as the author of *The Crystal Key*," I said.

"What's that?"

"A book," I said, unzipping the front pocket of my pack. I pulled it out and handed it to him.

He set down his meal and stared at the book hard. He removed his arm from around my shoulders, then frantically flipped through the pages, finally getting to the inside of the back cover. He stared at it and lifted his hand to his mouth, his pale eyes glistening.

"Aaron, what is it?"

Aaron stared mutely at the book, his face flushing. Tentatively, I lifted my hand to rest on his shoulder. I didn't delve, just touched him. He looked up as if he'd forgotten I was there.

"What's wrong?" I asked.

"My mother wrote this," he said. He held the inside cover up for me to see and pointed at the picture of a handsome woman with steel-gray hair. I knew the picture well. "This is her," he said.

"Whoa! That's your mom? That is so random."

No, I thought. *His mother set us up on this crazy blind date. She might have intended for Aaron to have this book.*

"What's it about?" Aaron asked.

"It's about a girl who travels to another world to find a dragon," I said. I was about to say more, but the words stuck in my throat.

I face-palmed. *How did I not see this before?*

Aaron looked at me with wide eyes. "It's about us! There must be a message in here," he said. "The names of all the characters are unfamiliar, but the girl's name is similar to yours, and the name Anick, of course."

"Who is Anick?" I asked.

He almost gave me the *look* but stopped himself. "Oh, of course you wouldn't know. He was Eve's bondmate and Seleca's father."

"Bondmate? What is that?"

"Well, my mother is from Earth and she used to say the word 'husband,' so you might know that word?" He looked at me to confirm and I nodded. "That term always made my father laugh because 'husbandry' is what they call the breeding of oxen at the Groves farm, northwest of here. Then my mother would tell him that that's why she said it." Aaron gave me a fleeting smile, which quickly turned sad.

"Anyway," he continued, "the Ministry teaches that Anick was a great leader who saved the entire world from destruction through noble sacrifice. The Noble Six are the six fragments that he thought were the most useful to a civilized society. He outlawed the use of any others. Our family archives show that the Ministry's history is all a lie and that he was actually a monster who enslaved and murdered thousands of people. He was like Seleca, except worse. They say he was a thousand years old, but he was killed about a century ago."

"He's the one who turned this entire world into a cult," I said.

Aaron paused. "If a cult is when a single person controls everyone on the planet with fear and violence, then yes."

"They don't usually get that big, but . . . wait, Seleca is a hundred years old?"

"At least," he said absently. "Regular healing extends your lifespan."

Say what? My eyes widened as I thought through the implications. When Aaron said Anick was a thousand years old, I'd assumed it was just a legend. But what if it wasn't? *I heal myself every second of every day. Am I immortal now? Holy crap. I mean, holy fucking shit.*

My hands went up to my mouth in shock, but Aaron was too immersed in the book to notice. I looked down at Rogue. He stared at me as if he knew exactly what I was thinking, then snuggled up to me and rested his face on my lap.

Was this a big deal? I didn't want to interrupt Aaron's literary excavation to ask him. I sat there for a long time, scratching Rogue's head and thinking.

Aaron searched for something, perhaps some kind of sign that his mother knew he would eventually read her book. He found it on page thirty-three, a poem I'd always considered odd. It was the only poem in the book and didn't quite fit the story, as if it were stuck in as an afterthought.

In the queen's garden, there is a key that opens up our destiny.
Covered in mud and blood, it pleads the wisdom of dishonor.
It helps you face your enemy and searches out what seems empty,
But if you wait, and don't misread, you may avoid a slaughter.
It dreams of time beyond the trees and sounds the call to mutiny
Because it cannot help but lead the horses to the water.
For though we may not all agree, our hearts are longing to be free
And so, we'll follow, fight and bleed until death weighs upon her.
Then through the rubble and debris the saplings grow in twos and threes
From stone to stone, their shade of creed expanding ever broader.
And so, my dragon, use the key; and in time, I'll have with me
The only thing I'll ever need, my husband, son, and daughter.

Aaron read the poem. Then he read the poem again. Then again and again.

"And so, my dragon, use the key," he said finally to himself.

"Yes, it's the poem written on the box where the girl finds the crystal key. Her family name is Dragonrider. Do you think *you* are the dragon from the poem?"

"That's what she's called me since I was a small child," he said. "It's a message from her. It has to be."

"She wrote something inside the front cover where she signed it," I said.

He raised his eyebrows, opening the front cover to look inside. It read: *Time for Jo.*

"My mom said it was probably a coffee joke, but I never got it. Does it mean anything to you?"

"She used to call my uncle that," Aaron said, looking up at me.

"Well then, I guess you probably have some questions to ask him," I said.

He nodded his head. "I certainly do."

Chapter Ten

The dragon laid his body flat on the ground so Linorra could climb onto his back. Linorra's words had moved him, and he now believed, as she did, that he was meant to fly with her to the far reaches of the universe. He could feel her excitement, and she could feel his. They were connected, now, by a force that neither could understand.

Aaron decided we'd missed our window to cross the oardoo fields during the day because one of us had short legs that moved like a silken goat. I wasn't sure what that was, but he assured me they were beautiful creatures, if a bit lazy.

"Oh, how kind of you," I said. "Please, Aaron, don't be afraid to say what's on your mind."

Aaron chuckled. "Let's go," he said, slipping on his pack.

Before we could take two steps out on the trail, however, he stopped short, motioning me to stay hidden. I crouched like a frog between two evergreens.

I didn't know if he'd seen a person or a predator, but if he said hide, then I would hide. Rogue, ever observant, slinked over to stand just behind me, pressing his body against mine. It was comforting, but I didn't know how helpful that would be if I needed to get up and run but instead tripped over his big body.

Aaron silently pulled two knives from his vest, one of which was longer than my forearm, then he crouched down in front of me, listening. The air around him heated up, and I leaned away from him and into Rogue. My heart pounded loudly in my ears as I watched him for signs that I needed to run. After a moment, his knives glowed a reddish orange, as if they had been pulled from a forge. He glanced at my surprised expression and gave me a little smirk.

I shook my head, looking down at the ground. It was covered in soft pine needles that smelled faintly of citrus, and I rolled one of them between my fingers to calm myself down, accidentally crushing it. When I touched the ground to pick up a new one, I got a flash of something like what I'd felt from Aaron, but fainter. I poked my fingers into the ground to touch the soil beneath the pine needles, and the feeling strengthened, revealing wary excitement and bloodlust.

Carefully, I touched the back of Aaron's arm. He turned to look at my face, questioning, but then saw what I was doing. I searched for the emotion again, found it, then passed it through Connection to Aaron, similar to what I had done with my Protection fragment. His eyes widened, then darted left to right and back again, trying to make sense of the feeling.

I broke contact with him, then pointed out beyond our hiding spot. He nodded, then shook his head in awe. Through Connection, I had sensed not only what that person or creature felt, but also *where* they were while feeling it. I could sense their movement. *Don't I have to be touching skin directly to feel that?* Perhaps the thing was barefoot. An animal then?

There was no way to know what was out there, but it wasn't friendly. I reached for the emotion again. It grew more distant, passing us. Then, it stopped. I could feel surprise and a growing excitement. Whatever it was had sensed me.

Oh, crap. Lina, get ready to throw up a shield!

A shield? It was that weird, insistent voice again, and so loud that it was as if I shared mental space with Aaron. Was that even me thinking that?

I had no time to figure it out. My Connection fragment shoved back against me so hard that I physically fell backward, but Rogue pressed against my back, keeping me from falling to the ground. I grabbed Aaron's arm again, both to steady myself and to jump into that shared mental space. Aaron sensed my fear and let me connect deep enough to allow telepathy.

It knows we're here, I thought. *It sensed me. I'm sorry.*

He looked at me, eyes wide, then thought, *Seleca*.

Aaron was terrified, much more so than he had been during the dragon attack. *I don't know if I can protect you, Lina. You have to run. I'll hold her off. Go!*

I stared at him, uncertain. I couldn't just leave him there. He wanted to be noble, but it felt wrong.

Go, Lina!

I'm not going anywhere, I thought to him. *Tell me how to shield. There's no time to argue, Aaron.*

I . . . he closed his eyes, racking his brain. *I think it's the same as healing but directed inward. Seleca can invade your mind by force, even with Protection. She could turn me against you. Please, just run. I couldn't live with myself if I hurt you.*

I saw his memory then, buried as deep as a corpse and haunting him every day. I experienced the whole thing at once, as if time didn't exist. It shot through me like a lightning bolt, only more painful.

He was in the school dormitory with his roommate, Ellis, who practiced Transformation by twisting metal ingots into rings and crossbow bolts. Ellis was only moderately talented but aimed to join the Metalworkers Guild. His future was bright.

Aaron lounged on his cot, reading a book. Sixteen years old now, he'd been hiding his Evocation for about a year and never practiced in front of others, especially not inside.

His roommate's little brother, Ward, came in to watch Ellis practice. Ward was a brand-new underling and had only been there for a few weeks, so he was still in the honeymoon phase and eager to learn. His Transformation reservoir had manifested earlier than anyone had ever seen. He would be a powerful fragmentor, but right now he was just a cute kid with auburn hair, skinny as a sapling.

He looked like a miniature version of his brother, who was also a redhead, except Ward was energetic and friendly where Ellis was quiet and reserved. Aaron was fond of the boy and spent a few nights tutoring him in beginning fragment theory. He couldn't do more than that because, as far as anyone knew, Aaron had no greater reservoir and would soon be forced to leave the school.

Aaron just wanted to finish his general studies so he could apply for a scribing apprenticeship with the Caravan Traders. He had always been among the best in reading and writing. No one cared, since he had no greater reservoir, but he would need an income while he waited for the supposed "dog girl," if that ever happened.

A few minutes later, the door to the dormitory opened and Seleca slinked in without knocking. The three boys stopped what they were doing, shocked, then knelt before her, eyes lowered, as was required.

This was the Holy Daughter, the offspring of the goddess Eve, pure and perfect in every way, and more beautiful than the stars in the sky. Though he knew it was wrong, Aaron had fantasized about her more than once, about what her blue-green eyes would look like underneath him as he took her. Never mind that she was the most powerful fragmentor alive and could kill him with a flick of her wrist. She *would* kill him if she knew his thoughts and he would deserve it.

Seleca didn't say anything at first, just walked around the boys as if selecting an animal to slaughter for dinner. She wore her usual yellow pants and blue shirt, not that anyone looked up to notice. Her boots scuffed the ground, making a soft noise. Ward, only eleven years old, giggled. He didn't understand the danger they were in.

Seleca stopped to look at the boy, then glided over to stand next to Aaron. Without a word, she placed her hand on his shoulder, sliding it up to his neck to poke her fingers inside the collar of his shirt. Aaron jumped at the sudden touch, fighting to remain still. His skin tingled, and he felt himself becoming aroused but remained frozen, hoping to conceal it.

She tried to force her way into him using Connection, but he was protected, and she couldn't get in deeper than superficial feelings. She could feel his arousal, though, and she made a sighing sound that only amplified the feeling. She laughed, then said in a husky voice, "Knock, knock. Let me in and maybe later I'll return the favor."

Though he sweated and his hands shook, Aaron didn't open the door because he knew what Seleca would find in there. A moment of weakness and he'd undoubtedly end up as her next Absorption victim.

She let out a disappointed whine. "Oh. I guess I'll just have to huff and puff and blow the door down." He felt a sharp pinprick at the corners of his mind. He thought to himself, *How bad could it be? Just let her in. It will be fine. She likes me.* The image of Seleca pushing him down on his back and mounting him right there in his room flooded his mind. He imagined her pulling up his tunic and pressing her red lips into his stomach while he ran his fingers through her silky black hair, gently pressing her to go lower. He didn't know if the fantasy was his or hers, but his resolve wavered.

Then she was inside him, digging aggressively into his mind. He lost his balance and fell to the ground. Seleca's invasive manner always sucked the vitality out of people she connected with, Protection or none, and her Projection trance kept him from fighting back. She knelt over him, smiling, her hand now wrapped around his neck.

She spent several minutes looking at his life, searching for his secrets, and then she found it: his Evocation reservoir. He felt her shock for the briefest moment, and the interruption in the flow of Projection was enough to allow him to slam the door closed. She strained against his wall, but it took a tremendous amount of energy to push past someone's defenses, and she couldn't get back in using the same trick.

She squeezed his neck so hard that he thought his windpipe would be crushed. Then she whispered in his ear, "You have something I want, boy. How lucky for you that you will get to please me so thoroughly when you give it to me. I have been looking for that reservoir for a very long time."

She released him, and he coughed harshly.

"Ward, come," Seleca said, standing up. The boy looked up at her, likely surprised that she knew his name. He popped up from the ground, scooted toward her, knelt back down, and bowed his head. "What a good boy," she said. "You may go, Ellis."

Ellis hesitated, looking at his brother with wide eyes, then rose and left the room.

"Now, Aaron, I want you to sit up." Aaron was groggy but did as he was told. He had already defied Seleca by not letting her back in. He had seen her strangle a girl nearly to death who had done almost the same thing. The girl was twelve. He shook just thinking about it, and, to his amazement, imagined escaping. He had seen people cry and beg for forgiveness, but they never tried to escape. That would be wrong. The goddess would never forgive that.

"Put your hand on Ward's face," she said. The boy looked up in alarm. Aaron didn't move. Seleca, growing impatient, grabbed Ward roughly by the scruff of his neck. His eyes widened, then they rolled back in his head and closed, his body going limp. Seleca held him up like a rag doll, his face turned toward Aaron.

"Put your hand on his face," she hissed, "or I'm going to crush his tiny little skull."

Aaron did it, but a dark and disillusioned loathing blossomed in his mind, and his fantasy turned from sexual to violent. The Holy Daughter, flawless and beyond reproach, had a body that would burn brighter than his father's barn if he wished it.

No. That would be wrong. I'm wrong. I should just run. He couldn't believe his own thoughts. What was wrong with him? He shook his head, trying to clear it.

Seleca laid her hand on top of Aaron's, smiling, and said, "Now, let's see what you can do."

The only thing Aaron remembered beyond that was the sound of Ward's screams.

I looked into Aaron's eyes, seeing the exposed pain and hatred he had for this monster. *She made you burn him,* I thought. *It wasn't your fault.*

The knives he held glowed so brightly I feared they were in danger of melting. He looked at me, incensed but pleading.

I gave up on trying to hide from Seleca. "Aaron," I said, "whatever happens, *I* will heal. I will not leave you. We'll face her together. That's how we win. It's the *only* way we win."

He squeezed his eyes closed, and I heard the handle of one of his knives crack. He opened his eyes again, took a deep breath, and stood up. I stood beside him.

Somewhere beyond the bushes, I heard that creepy ghost voice. "Avelina," Psycho Snow White said. "I can feel you in there. I see you've learned how to use your reservoir. That's good. There's no need to be frightened. You did what you were supposed to do. You drew the dragon out of his lair. Now it's time to come with me. You have been chosen for a greater purpose. Come with me now."

Aaron looked at me, his eyes wide. I could see the wheels turning. I shook my head fiercely. "I'm with *you*, Aaron," I whispered. "With *you*." He relaxed a little, but I could feel the distrust radiating from him again.

Shit. This is not the time for that, I thought. I could hear Seleca getting closer and it would be worse to be attacked while backed into a corner. I touched Aaron's arm. *You can trust me, Aaron. If you trust in your mother's predictions, then trust me. Can you do that?* He hesitated, then nodded. *Good, then we should just step out to face her. It's still two against one.*

No, he thought. *There's a dragon out there too. I can feel him.*

I gazed at him, letting him make the decision. We stood motionless for a moment, and then Aaron nodded his head. I released Connection, and we set our packs down behind the trees and walked out to face her.

"There you are," said Seleca. She smiled her crooked little smile but shifted her weight back and forth restlessly between her bare feet.

Bare feet. She was reaching out to feel us through the ground.

Behind her, silently perched on another fallen log, was a dragon, this one nearly twice as big as the last. Its glowing orange eyes fixed on Aaron, perhaps sensing him the way Aaron could.

"How lovely to see you again, Aaron. You know, my previous offer is still open to you. We don't have to be enemies. My bed comes from Earth. It feels like sleeping on a cloud. Come to me, and all will be forgiven. I didn't even like that man you murdered on your way out. You showed me that you could be one of us, Aaron. Come with me." Seleca held out her hand to Aaron, beckoning him as if she spoke to a treasured lover.

Aaron growled low in his chest like an animal, then the handle of his knife creaked again. I wondered where Rogue was. Hiding under a tree? I hoped so.

Lina, she doesn't know about your Protection reservoir. Listen to me, you have to start forming a shield.

"What?" I asked aloud. I wasn't touching Aaron anymore, so the words hadn't come from him. Was this a real voice in my head? Maybe the use of Connection had caused me to start hallucinating. This was not the best time to be going crazy. I needed to concentrate on the enemy.

Seleca must have thought my question was directed at her. "I've got five of the six Nobles," she said, "and thanks to your lovely friend, Spirit, I've got all but two of the Unspeakables. You and your new lover have the only ones I still need. Come, there's no reason for this to turn into a war. Why don't you just let me take it, and I'll let you steal away with your latest conquest."

No, Lina! It's me, Spirit. Please, I'm real. You have to listen.

"Spirit?"

Seleca smiled, still thinking I spoke to her. "Yes, she was understandably exhausted. It's too bad about the twins, though. They were lovely."

My heart dropped into my stomach. "You killed them," I whispered. "You killed Spirit."

Now, Lina! The shield!

For an endless moment, shock and grief paralyzed me. Spirit was dead? I couldn't wrap my head around it.

Spirit, I thought. *It can't be.* My eyes welled with tears.

Lina! a stern voice barked. *Shield now. Cry later. Or join me over here. Your choice!*

I didn't know if I was losing my mind or if the voice was real. What I did know was that Spirit had always had an eerie way of predicting the future, and she'd changed her own name to Spirit. I had never thought much of that choice, but it made an insane kind of sense now. Spirit must have had Precognition, like Aaron's mother. Seleca had discovered this on our walk through the woods and killed her to steal it. Somehow, Spirit had predicted her own death, and now her ghost shouted instructions into my mind like a pissed-off drill sergeant.

I feared that this was some kind of stress-induced psychiatric episode, but in my crazed state, I had to assume Seleca told the truth about murdering my friends. Based on that assumption, I made the sanest choice I could think of. I listened to the voice in my head.

"What do I do?" I asked.

Place your hand on your heart, and push Protection into yourself, thought Spirit.

I pushed my grief aside and did as I was told just as Seleca turned to her dragon and placed a hand on its wing. The dragon made a strange warbling noise and launched itself into the air, kicking up a gust of wind that whipped up Seleca's hair and clothes. Then, the dragon disappeared, blinking out of existence as if it had been a hologram.

I closed my eyes to concentrate, directing my intention into my own body. My chest vibrated, tightening painfully. Then a sharp pain exploded in my rib cage. I grunted, pushing the fragment out like a mother giving birth. The sensation ceased when the force expanded beyond my body, and I opened my eyes to discover a sphere of aqua-blue light growing around me, much like the entrance to the bridge had that first night. The difference now was that I was both the source and the destination. I glowed with that same soft, calming blue, and little firefly specks of multicolored lights sparked out of different parts of my body and were captured in a stream that swirled within the sphere.

The colors were a strange combination of green, magenta, blood-red, and aqua, and they all had a different texture and consistency. The green streaked around the sphere in squiggly lines, as if it were a vine sending out new shoots into the air around us, then disappearing like the tail of a green comet. The magenta lights looked like a tight swarm of flies, trailing smoke as they flew around. The red lights resembled a roiling sea of blood caught in a whirlpool.

The aqua lights were more solid than the rest, like they were actually aquamarine crystals appearing and disappearing in the air, reflecting a bright blue-green light that created a halo around all the other colors. I only controlled the aqua-blue lights, however. The others were pulled forward as if sucked into an energetic circulatory system.

Other than the bridge, this was my first time seeing fragments directly and, despite my terror and anguish, I gasped in wonder at the beauty of their power. Previously, my own reservoirs had been no more than an idea, but now I had visual evidence. I had glowed, sure, but this was far beyond that. I could no longer deny what I saw or banish it to the back of my mind to deal with later. Fragments were real. I was powerful, and here was proof.

As quick as lightning, exhilaration struck down my terror and I nearly laughed out loud.

Encouraged, I pushed the Protection fragment out of my chest, observing that the task of maintaining the sphere was easy. Whereas healing Aaron had felt like blowing up a balloon, this was more like blowing a bubble through a bubble wand. It barely required any force, but rather a delicate touch that could burst if I was too aggressive.

The sphere expanded out from me and bumped into Aaron, who stared up at the sky, holding his knife ready. He hadn't noticed my Protection sphere, though I didn't see how he could have missed the bright swirl of colors. The shield pushed him away from me, and he would be trapped outside of it. I couldn't have that.

I stretched out experimentally and found that I could reach my hand through the shield, so I grabbed his wrist and pulled him into the sphere with me. His eyes widened and darted all around, apparently now able to see what I saw from inside the shield.

"No!" Seleca screamed, her eyes widening as she caught on to what was happening. Spirit was right. Seleca hadn't known I was protected. She'd known about my Connection reservoir but not this.

The sphere wrapped around Aaron's chest as Seleca pulled a weapon out of a deep pocket in her voluminous yellow pants. It was a gun. In fact, if I wasn't mistaken, it was my father's navy Glock 17, the gun he taught me to shoot with. That weapon was the real threat. The dragon had just been a distraction.

I concentrated on bringing up the shield faster to expand around our entire bodies, praying it could stop bullets, but it wouldn't be fast enough. A manic grin spread over Seleca's face as she aimed her weapon at my head. Apparently, I was the juicier target, or maybe she still had other plans for Aaron.

Just as I had that thought, Rogue scrambled out from under the tree, directly behind Seleca. He lunged at her as she pulled the trigger, biting her right in the ass. Her arm jerked to the side as Rogue barreled into her, causing her to miss her shot. He weighed more than her and knocked her off-balance, but she was strong. She shook him off and kicked him in the face, shoving him back. Then she pointed the gun and fired three shots.

Rogue fell and did not get up again.

I screamed, just as I had the first time I thought she'd killed my dog by throwing him onto the bridge to Monash, and the emotion almost burst the delicate shield.

Aaron sheathed his knives and wrapped his arms around me.

"Steady," he said. The heat radiating from his body should have been intense enough to burn me. Instead, it sank into me, feeding the shield. I watched as a new color joined the spectral lights. It was a brilliant vermilion and looked less like points of light than it did a streak of orange and red flame, surging around the sphere and engulfing us.

Seleca turned back toward us and fired, but it was too late. Rogue had bought us the time we needed, and the shield expanded around us, locking us into a protective bubble. The impact of the bullets on my shield sounded like a metal bat banging on something an inch from my head. The vibrations were so painfully strong that I almost lost my hold on the shield, but Aaron tightened his grip around me, and we held.

The bullets must have ricocheted off the shield and hit the dragon because a split second later its corpse crashed into us from above. The weight and momentum were too great, and Aaron and I were both knocked viciously to the ground. Aaron's protective embrace never wavered, and together we withstood the impact, maintaining the shield.

The silence that stretched after the attack lay over us like a woolen blanket. My heart still galloped in my chest, and my ears rang. I panted hard, trying not to weep and failing miserably. She had killed Spirit. She had killed Rogue. She had my father's Glock, which meant she might have killed everyone else at the house, too. It was all too much.

Aaron held me for a moment, and then he whispered, "Lina, we have to get up. Come on."

The dragon's body had fallen on top of us but then slid off the shield like it was an oil slick. I looked around but didn't see Seleca. Fury bubbled up from my heart and out into the shield, and rage tears surged down my face as a fire exploded inside me. I needed to see Seleca's face dented and covered in blood.

Aaron got his feet under him and pulled me up. I didn't feel tired at all from holding the shield, but Aaron looked like the effort of getting up had drained him. He was unsteady and leaned on me a little. I didn't want to risk him collapsing and accidentally falling outside of the protective sphere, so I held onto him, focusing my intention on separating his fragment from mine. I imagined myself flicking off a light switch, closing the link between our two fragment reservoirs.

His energy contribution dwindled, and the fiery vermilion lights in the shield flickered and went out, leaving the original swirl of green, aqua, magenta, and that strange blood-red. Aaron regained some strength, and some of my rage drained away along with the Evocation fragment, though it didn't stop entirely.

Aaron peered down at me and nodded, then we looked in every direction. Seleca was nowhere to be seen. I squatted down, touching the soil with my fingers in an attempt to locate her. My own shield blocked the attempt. I looked back in the direction that Seleca had stood and saw Rogue sprawled on the ground.

"Let's go to him," I said.

Aaron nodded. We walked toward my friend, holding hands. I looked down at Rogue, tears dripping down my cheeks. It was hard to tell where the bullets had landed because his body was a mass of blood and fur. His eyes were closed. I wondered how long it had taken him to die. Did he suffer? Did Spirit suffer? A sob broke from my chest.

"Rogue, I'm sorry," I said, my voice breaking.

Rogue cracked his eyes open a sliver at my voice, lifted his head to look at me, then slumped back down. Aaron and I both jerked in surprise.

"Rogue!" I yelled. "Aaron, I can heal him." I prepared to release the shield so I could grab him.

"Wait," barked Aaron, searching over one shoulder, then the other. "She could be hiding under a Reflection veil, like the dragon, waiting for you to bring the shield down so she can shoot us with her crossbow."

I had no time to correct him. "The shield is too big now. I can't reach him. Can you reach through the shield and pull him in?"

"I don't know," he said. Aaron reached his hand out, but it pressed against the shield from the inside and couldn't penetrate through.

"We can move without ripping up the ground. Maybe we could just walk over him." We tried, and again, the shield bumped up against Rogue. Sweat dripped down my forehead, and I wiped it away with a shaky hand. "I have to bring the shield down before it's too late," I said, my voice rising almost to a squeak.

"Bring my reservoir back into the shield," he said and pulled me close, hugging me. His heat radiated out again, but it was much more subdued, as if the fragment itself was depleted. I hugged him back, tightly, concentrating my intention on bringing the heat into my body. His scent filled my nose, and I breathed him in greedily. He bent his head over mine, doing the same. We stood there together for several seconds before I accepted that it wasn't working.

"Look at me," he said. His hand came to my jaw, and he angled my face up toward his. His dark brown beard was a little longer and scruffier than yesterday. His hair had come loose from the tie and was now tangled and matted with sweat. I pushed it away from his eyes. They were a nearly translucent blue and reflected the light more than they should. I looked into those eyes and he into mine, feeling heat stirring beneath his skin.

I didn't think, I just wanted to pull that heat inside me. The heat *wanted* to be inside me, so it came. The swirl of colors shifted to add Aaron's bright vermilion. He exhaled slowly, then released all but my hand, bending down to grab Rogue by the scruff of his neck and pulling him into the sphere.

I closed my eyes briefly, relief washing over me. Aaron had guessed that if we connected in that way that brought his Evocation into my shield, he would be able to permeate the barrier. Aaron's ability to stay calm in an emergency would save Rogue, provided I could heal him.

"Can I even do this while holding a shield?" I asked.

"No," said Seleca from behind us, "you can't." I whipped my head around to see her holding the gun on us. "And you also can't hold that shield forever. Eventually, your reservoir will run out of fragment, and the shield will fall. It's too late. Your dog is dead, and you're about to join him."

Chapter Eleven

Syndeth's launch into the sky was so jarring that Linorra would have tumbled off if not for the horns protruding from his neck and spine. She held fast to him, bracing herself against the wind tugging at her cloak.

"Good thing these horns are here to hold onto," she said, "and they aren't too sharp."

"Those aren't horns," the dragon said. "Those are my memories. They grow every time I make a new one. I think I can feel one coming on even now."

My fury at the sight of Seleca flared like a newly lit match. She had killed my friends and had tried to kill my dog. The irrational temptation to lower my shield and attack her was nearly irresistible. She stared back at me with the same fury, as if what I had done to protect Aaron and myself from the same fate was an abhorrent sin.

She's trying to delay you, Spirit thought. *Ignore her. Try the healing.*

Aaron jerked, looking around. This was the first time he was connected to me while Spirit communicated. Since I'd been listening to her, her voice had grown more distinct, sounding like her real voice instead of my own thoughts, as I had earlier thought they were. He looked at me with wide eyes.

"How?" I asked Spirit.

Kneel over him and place your hand on him somewhere where there is bare skin.

I did as instructed, taking his massive paw in mine. I touched the pad of his foot with my thumb. It was cold.

Spirit cursed. *He's already left his body and is trying to cross the death bridge. You'll have to call to him before he gets too far away.*

"What do you mean? Are you saying that I can bring him back from the dead?" I squeaked the question out, panicking. "What in the hell is happening? Can I heal a body back from death?" The idea sent a shiver down my spine, and I felt very unsure of whether I should be doing this—was it wrong for me to make a decision like this?

I looked to Aaron for direction, but he was as confused as I was. "I've never heard of such a thing," he said.

Spirit hesitated. *He's already stepped away from us. Call to him. If he comes, then it will be okay to heal him. If he continues across the bridge, that's his choice. Just try.*

I nodded. "Okay."

Okay, Spirit thought to me, *to call him, think about your favorite memory of him.*

I closed my eyes. Just like it had with Aaron, my own memory flashed through me in one piece.

It was my sixteenth birthday, but I couldn't have a party because I knew nobody would come. It's not really a party when it's just you and your parents. My social troubles weighed on me, and I wanted to be alone. In fact, I wanted to go into those woods and never come out.

I never had trouble attracting boys, but friends were a different matter entirely. Back then, I thought there was something wrong with me. No matter how nice, accepting, funny, attractive, or any other good thing I tried to be, I just couldn't make any close friends. People weren't outright cruel to me, they just ignored or avoided me, as if they could sense some otherness that they found unconsciously unsettling. I just needed to accept the fact that if I wanted to keep living, I would have to do it alone. I never spoke that thought out loud, but somehow Rogue always knew when I felt depressed.

I stuffed my pack with some food and a blanket and set off to spend my birthday with my best and only friend. Rogue pressed against my legs as we walked. He did that a lot, but that day, it was even more pronounced than usual. We walked for a while until we found a sunny clearing that I knew well.

On the ground lay a flat stone, about the size of a single mattress, with an *X* carved into it. On top of the stone sat a small gift that looked like it might contain a piece of jewelry. It was wrapped in pink wrapping paper with a pattern of multicolored butterflies and a miniature purple bow. I recognized the paper. The gift was from my mother. I had always been drawn to that spot. I was calmer and happier when I was there. My mom knew that.

"*X* marks the spot," I said, smiling down at what I hoped was a tiny treasure.

I picked up the gift, then laid my blanket on top of the *X*, set my bag down, and sat on the blanket. Rogue sat next to me.

"What do you think's in it, Roogy-Roo?" I asked. He looked at me, panting a little, his tongue stuck out to one side. His tail thumped the ground rhythmically.

I decided that, before I opened the gift, I would sing "Happy Birthday" to myself. I was glad no one else was around, I told myself, so that I could do this. I sang loudly, getting halfway through the first line when Rogue shocked me with a burst of howling. I stopped in the middle of a word and stared at him. He looked back at me as if to say "What?"

I laughed, then started again, and again he howled, singing with me. When the song was over, he howled one more time as if to say "Cha, cha, cha. Ooh la la. Eat a lotta pizza." I laughed again, harder this time. He was just so cute. I couldn't take it. He barked once, which is the most he ever did.

"Fine, I'll open it," I said, ripping the paper from the package. Inside the box was a car key.

Aaron squeezed my hand, bringing me back to myself. I looked up at him, realizing that he had seen the memory with me. He didn't know what a car key was, but he could feel my excitement when I saw it. I smiled at him briefly, then bowed my head.

Okay, now reach into that memory and pull him out.

Aaron made a choking sound. "That is disturbing," he said.

I shushed him. "What do you mean?" I asked.

Picture him in that memory, then look at him in the memory as if he's really there. Call to him from the memory. Make him look at you. Then imagine yourself physically reaching into the memory and pulling him out. Quickly, Lina, you have only seconds.

I did as she instructed and felt a vague movement inside my brain. Another reservoir that I hadn't noticed yet hid in the background like a ghost. I looked hard at Rogue in the memory and saw him look in my mind's direction. He barked once, and I understood him. He was saying my name.

Rogue, come back!

He barked again, but he sounded farther away this time. Calling to him wasn't working.

Rogue! I didn't know what this new reservoir was that I felt stirring, but it pulsed when I called Rogue's name, almost an echo. I imagined taking a handful of fragment out of that reservoir, shoving my hand into the memory, and throwing it around Rogue like a net.

It clung to him like a spiderweb. I pulled on the net, dragging him out of that memory with all my strength. He didn't struggle, allowing himself to flow out of the memory into my physical body.

Good, Lina! You've got him. Now use Protection to heal his body. Quickly!

I followed her directions again, drawing on my experience in healing Aaron. Through Connection, I felt that Rogue's heart had stopped, but it had only been a minute or two and there was still time to get it going again. I pushed Protection into him as hard as I could, straining until my pulse pounded in my ears.

Aaron, help her!

Aaron jumped again, looking around. He cringed, then shook his head like a wet dog and knelt behind me. He wrapped me in his arms again, lending me what little strength he had left. My dizziness lessened but didn't disappear. He kissed the back of my head, reassuring me, but he shook, as if on the edge of collapse. Right then, I could feel that exhaustion in my bones. My whole body trembled with it.

Seleca circled the shield now, watching with wide eyes. I kept pushing. It was like trying to push a car that had stalled in the road. It was hard to move at first, but once it got going, it rolled a little easier. As I did, Rogue's spirit flowed into his body along with Protection fragment.

Once he got a grip on his body, he pulled the rest of himself in, causing a current that dragged Protection fragment along with it. Within seconds, I lost control over the flow. It gushed out of me like a wellspring, and I glowed so brightly that I started to heat up. It was as if I was in the portal again, feeling that excruciating light, except it came from me now. Pain stabbed me in the heart as the energy poured out of an energetic whirlpool in the center of my body.

Aaron tensed, then fell forward on top of me, losing consciousness. Somehow, I held on to his hand to prevent him from falling out of the shield, but his Evocation fragment vanished from the swirl of colors. That's when I noticed that the shield itself was weakening, the colors *all* fading, as if Protection was being sucked out of it to flow into Rogue. What had previously been easy became an overwhelming task.

I redoubled my effort to hold it, gasping from the strain. My chest pain grew sharper and spread down my left arm to my pinkie, then across my back, up my neck and into my jaw and eyes. I cried out, but there was no one left to help me. I was alone with my enemy, and my defenses were about to crumble.

Seleca stopped to kneel beside us with her hands pressed against the shield, her mouth twisted into a snarl. Never before had I seen someone look at me with such pure hatred.

"I tried to warn you," she said. "Your shield is about to fall. When it does, I'll kill you with your father's gun, just like I did to your girlfriend."

Her comment was like a slap in the face, and a wave of rage rushed through my body. "I don't think so, Seleca," I said through clenched teeth. "I'm going to hold this shield until Rogue comes back to bite you in the ass again."

Seleca's face contorted with fury. She screamed her wrath out at me, then opened fire. It was the best response I could've hoped for, and I laughed. The gun clicked empty, and she banged the butt of it against the shield repeatedly. The vibrations from her blows hit me in the center of my chest, adding to the excruciating pain of healing Rogue.

Though I gasped, Evilina couldn't help herself. "You were right, bitch," I said. "I *do* like it here."

With that, the pain ebbed, then vanished. I looked down at Rogue expectantly. Only, Rogue was no longer Rogue. In his place, lying face down, was an unconscious man. I stared at him, confused. His long, slender fingers were interlaced with mine.

"Rogue?" I whispered.

Seleca had stopped raving and watched me intently, breathing hard.

"His name isn't Rogue," she said, that unsettling smirk returning to her face. "It never was. I want to thank you for healing my most useful asset. I'll just leave him to kill you while I go take care of your parents. I was going to let them live, but now I realize that was a mistake. You don't deserve mercy."

Seleca held out her hand, and a sphere of fluorescent orange-yellow lights appeared and expanded. As the bridge opened, she said "After that, I'll find Aaron's mother. I have a complaint to make about her little book." The light of pure fragment radiating from the bridge entrance engulfed Seleca, and she disappeared.

Chapter Twelve

Syndeth curled his tail around Linorra, shielding her from the misty rain with his warm body. He flattened the scales at the narrow end of his tail to make a smooth pillow for her head. Though she was just a little thing, she had such a big heart, a heart that let him connect to the world around him in vivid sound and color. Their bond let him feel her exhilaration and joy when they were in the air together in a way he never felt when he flew alone. With her astride his broad shoulders, the world was more real and beautiful.

A deep, cold fear erupted in my chest. I released the shield, and it dissipated just like the portal had. My mind raced.

"Spirit," I called. This was the first time I had called to her on purpose. "Spirit, I need you." The words felt like a prayer.

I'm here, Lina.

"Seleca is going to kill my parents. Is there anything you can do?"

I don't know. I will go to them.

"Thank you."

Then, she was gone. I was getting a feel for her presence, and I wondered if hearing was all there would ever be. My poor Spirit. My friend. She had been one of those people who, when you meet them, you feel like you've known them forever. I had so few people like that in my life, and now she was dead because of me. I didn't know how I could get over this.

Aaron opened his eyes slowly, then bolted upright as if waking up from a nightmare. "What happened?" he asked.

I felt numb, so all I could do was state the situation plainly. "I pissed Seleca off and she vowed to kill both of our families. Then, she opened a bridge and disappeared. I sent Spirit after her. Oh, and . . ." I pointed at Rogue, or whoever it was.

Aaron looked at the naked man, then, having had a second to follow the logic to its conclusion, he stood and pulled out his giant knife again. The man looked like he would be tall and thin if standing, even taller than Aaron, although it looked like Aaron had about a hundred pounds of muscle on the guy. This man was so tall and skinny that he looked like he had been stretched on a medieval torture device.

"Rogue," I said, because I didn't know what else to call him. "Rogue, wake up." The man stirred, then stretched out on the ground just like a dog, rolling over and exposing himself without shame or embarrassment. He had coppery-auburn hair, the same color Rogue's fur had been, and the left half of his face had a nasty scar in the shape of a handprint. I knew immediately who it was.

"Ward," I said.

He opened his eyes and looked at me. He smiled brightly, looking relieved, then his eyebrows squeezed together, and he looked at his own hands. His eyes widened, and he sat up quickly, backing away from us. He didn't get up, though, but stayed on his hands and knees. Then, as if giving up, he slumped down to the ground and lay there, motionless, as if the life I had forced back into his body had unexpectedly drained out again.

Aaron and I looked at each other uncertainly. It didn't seem like this man planned to kill anyone. He looked like he had been so beaten down by life that he wanted to give up. In fact, he looked like he already had. Tentatively, I placed my hand on the ground, digging my fingers into the dirt, and sought him out. What I found there broke my heart. Anguish, dejection, humiliation, hopelessness. Even feeling a shadow of his despair through Connection was painful.

"Why did you bring me back?" he asked.

I got up to move toward him, but Aaron stopped me, stepping in my way. "Lina, don't. You don't know what he'll do. He's been spying for *her* all this time." Aaron stared at his ex-roommate's little brother in horror, the blood draining from his face.

"He won't hurt me, Aaron. Maybe Rogue has been Ward in disguise this whole time, but I *felt* him, and what I found there was love. He couldn't possibly have faked that. Seleca was lying. He could never hurt me. Please, I need to talk to him. Alone."

Aaron didn't move. He glanced at me and then back at Ward, an unsettling look creeping over his face. I stepped in close to him and raised my hand to his cheek, connecting. His eyes flicked to me, then softened. He placed his hand over mine. He was understandably worried but also jealous, something he had experienced before but not in a long time. Rogue had been with me for more than ten years and supposedly loved me. He'd slept in my bed, practically on top of me, and he was a man the whole time? How could Aaron compete with that kind of closeness when he'd known me for less than two days?

In answer, I lifted myself up on my toes, tilting my face as close to his as I could, and I pressed my body into him. He leaned forward and kissed me, much harder than earlier that morning, like he wanted to claim me.

My appearance in the Rhoya at the foot of the mountains had led to the worst and best two days of his life, but now it all unraveled before his eyes. Our near-death experience at the hands of his childhood monster had shaken him to his breaking point, and the family he'd been waiting all these years to find could be in danger. He doubted Seleca could find his mother since it's nearly impossible to sneak up on a precog, but it might be possible now that Seleca had acquired Precognition herself. Additionally, his uncle Jorin, as well as his cousin, Terik, were probably in danger, since they were easy to locate on the farm.

Aaron had never felt like he needed someone at his side, so it surprised him how much the idea of having to compete for my affection troubled him. My choice to stand by him at that critical moment when Seleca first found us had meant more to him than either of us had realized. He was attached now, for better or worse, and he worried that I would vanish like everyone else in his life. He didn't know if he could handle that on top of everything else.

Through Connection, I let Aaron feel that I shared his affection as well as his unexpected attachment. I let him take comfort in my lips and in the feel of my body pressed to his. I needed it as much as he did. If we had been alone and not in danger, and not in a hurry to figure out how to get back to Earth so that our families weren't slaughtered, then we might have—*wait. Slaughtered. That word was in the poem.*

Yes, Lina, the poem, Spirit thought.

Aaron heard her, too, and jerked his face away from me. "Ugh. I hope you find a way to block her at some point. There will be times when I won't want an audience."

I laughed a little, though the dire situation tried desperately to smother my sense of humor. "I'll work on it," I said.

He looked down at me, still debating. Aaron liked to think things through, and he needed time for that. I let him think while I questioned Spirit.

"What did you find, Spirit?" I asked.

Seleca is at your house, but it's empty. There's police tape everywhere from my murder. Nobody's around. Even the horses are gone.

"Thank you," I said, exhaling. "Could you please follow her and report back when you have something?"

Okay. You only need to call my name and I'll be there.

"Spirit," I said, my throat tightening. "I'm sorry I got you into this. It's my fault you're dead. If you hadn't been at the stables trying to help me, this wouldn't have happened to you. Now here you are, trying to help me again. I'm so sorry. I love you, my friend."

Spirit somehow conveyed a sad smile. I'm not sure how, but I knew it was there. Then, her presence retreated. She didn't seem angry about her own death, but I knew that if I dwelt on it, I would be overwhelmed by guilt. I didn't have that many friends to begin with. I wondered how long it would be before Seleca started to pick off the rest of them out of spite.

I can't think about that right now. I have to just keep going.

I steadied my breath, then turned to Aaron. "Everyone is safe for now. Seleca's waiting at my house for someone to show up. Hopefully, no one will." Aaron puffed out a breath and nodded. "I need to talk to Ward. He might know something that can help us. Please. I need you to trust me."

He sighed. "Fine. I'll get the packs." He wrinkled his nose as he said it, then turned and walked back to where we had hidden our bags. He looked over his shoulder several times as he went, then paused to stare for a long minute before disappearing behind the trees.

I sighed and turned to face my friend. He still lay on the ground, facing away from me, and curled into a fetal position, which looked very odd on his long body. I approached him slowly, trying not to frighten him. Then I knelt behind him and placed a hand on his bare shoulder. He jumped a little but then relaxed.

"I have a shirt you can wear," I said. Aaron grumbled from behind the trees. *He heard that? Huh. Super eyes and ears, I guess.*

Ward's shoulders rose a little with a deep breath and sank again with his exhalation. I lifted my hand to his head and stroked his hair. I could only see the burned part of his face. His eyes were squeezed shut.

"I brought you back because I love you," I whispered. Through Connection, I could feel his heart breaking at the thought that I still loved him. He didn't think he deserved it. I leaned over him and placed my cheek on his shoulder. "I don't know what's going on, Ward. I need you to explain it to me. I need *you*. Please don't leave me."

I was laying it on a little thick, but he needed it. He heard me, but he didn't have the will to respond. I sent all our years of affection and love through our Connection link. I thought about that birthday memory again, and the time I taught him what a bathroom was, which made so much more sense now. I thought about our walks through the woods, all our naps, and all the times he lay there listening to me complain about this thing or that thing, all the while unable to share his own story, his own pain and trauma.

I loved him so much it hurt. His use of Transformation to alter his body did not change that. It was little more than a minor detail to me. I sent that to him as strongly as I could, then closed my eyes and waited.

A minute passed, then two, then something touched my hair. I opened my eyes and saw him looking at me, his hand raised to my head. He brushed a strand of hair across my forehead and held it, rolling it between his fingers. I held my breath and kept as still as possible, looking back at him. His eyes were bloodshot, but they were that same intense amber I knew and loved. This was still my friend.

"I'll take that shirt," he said, his voice cracking.

I sat up and nodded. "Okay," I said, smiling. "Good."

Before I could get up to fetch it for him, he said, "She lied, you know."

I stopped. "About what?"

"She knows I would never hurt you. She tried to make me do it. She uses Projection to make people do what she wants." He shivered. "She made me do a lot of things, but she couldn't make me do that."

"Ward, why didn't you tell me? I would've helped you."

"I know," he said, "but I couldn't."

"Why not?"

He clenched his jaw and squeezed his eyes shut, swallowing hard. "She did things to me." He breathed in and out, struggling to get the words out. "She tortured me until I mastered Transformation." He touched the burned side of his face. "She chose that dog form. She said it made sense for someone like me. Then, when she saw that I had fully transformed into Rogue, she absorbed my reservoir, and I couldn't change back." Silent tears spilled down his cheeks from his closed eyes. "She said she wouldn't let me transform back until she got what she wanted from you."

"What does she want?" I asked.

He opened his eyes and sat up, wiping the tears away with the back of his hand. Aaron walked toward us with the packs.

"You died in your accident," Ward said.

"Yes," I confirmed. "But only for a few seconds."

"Well, you came back with a new reservoir, one that you can only get by dying and coming back. Even then, it rarely works. You have to have a combination of rare reservoirs, a combination that you have. That's why they sent me to you."

Goose bumps prickled up my arms. "I can hear ghosts now." My thoughts drifted to Spirit, but the guilt hit me again and I pushed her out of my mind.

"You can do more than that," he said, nodding. "You can summon them, make them do things, spy on people. And, if conditions are right—"

"I can bring them back from the dead," I finished.

"Yes, like you just did to me. It's an exceedingly rare reservoir. Unheard of, really. And it's something that Eve desperately wants."

"Why?" I asked.

Aaron swore. "She wants to bring back Anick," he said.

Ward bowed his head. "Yes. She couldn't have healed me the way you did today, so she's more limited, but there are ways around that. She could do it. She could bring him back."

"Lina, we have to go," Aaron said. "We're wasting time here. The fog is rolling back in."

I looked up at him, nodding. "Yes, you're right. Ward, we have to get to Jorin's farm. We believe he may know something that could help us."

Actually, we didn't know whether he could help us or not, but Violet's book indicated that we should start our search there. I hoped we weren't misinterpreting the text. I dug in my pack, pulling out the shirt I'd borrowed, but Aaron stopped me.

"Not that one," he said. I looked up at him, confused. He shrugged, then dug out a tunic for Ward and handed it to him. Ward slipped the tunic over his head and stood. He was a foot taller than Aaron.

Holy crap, I thought as I looked way up at Ward's face. *Aaron was right. He isn't big at all. Not compared to Ward, anyway. This is the land of giants.*

Ward didn't have a belt, and the tunic only reached to mid-thigh. He looked like Ebenezer Scrooge in his sleeping gown.

Aaron had to look up at him too. "You grew," he said, his face impassive.

"You didn't," Ward replied, his voice teasing.

Aaron pulled up one side of his mouth and rolled his eyes, then walked toward the dead dragon, presumably to collect our next meal. Over his shoulder, he said, "I hope the brambles in the oardoo fields don't hurt your feet. Too bad I don't have any boots to give you."

Ward met my eyes, sighed, then bent down and picked up Aaron's pack, strapping it to his own back so Aaron could carry the massive dragon.

"Here we go," I mumbled to myself. Both men looked at me at that. I rolled my eyes. *Stupid super hearing.* I put my pack on and turned to wait for Aaron and his bloody dragon.

Chapter Thirteen

Linorra watched Syndeth fly away with a heavy heart. She could not understand why he didn't want to be her friend anymore. The sun reflected off his scales in bright blue, crimson, and gold, like handfuls stolen from a treasure chest and flung wide. "Go, my treasure," she said to the sky. "Be free."

We walked for about two hours. Or, rather, the big and tall men did. I had to jog to match their pace. Aaron hurried now, impatiently looking back to see if I kept up. I did, sort of, but I carried the oil lamp, and it was hard to do that and jog at the same time.

"How old are you really, Ward?" I asked, wanting to distract myself from the growing concern I had over Aaron's new attitude.

Ward had to think about it. "We don't celebrate birthdays on Monash, but I think I had just turned fifteen when I came to you."

"Twenty-six, then, same as me," I said. "*We* celebrated your birthday, sort of. We used the date we found you."

He smiled back at me. "That's true."

"But we only gave you bones and chew toys," I said.

"And a cake that one time," he said.

"Oh, yeah! I forgot about the cheesecake. I had one piece and then you scarfed down the rest so fast that you got it inside your nose, and you couldn't stop sneezing."

"Yeah, and then you laughed so hard that you dropped your piece on the ground, and I ate that too."

"Ha, that's right! You gained a lot of weight that first year before I learned to stop giving you so much people food."

"You never stopped doing that," he said.

I laughed. "Yeah, that's true. You loved—"

"French fries!" we said together.

"Earth has amazing food," Ward said. "I'm going to miss that."

"Why? Aren't you coming back?"

There was a pregnant pause. Aaron grumbled under his breath again, but I only have normal hearing and couldn't tell what he said. I heard a loud *crack* and guessed that it was one of the dragon's leg bones breaking in his grip.

Me and my big freaking mouth. "Do you have family here, Ward?" I asked.

Ward sighed. "I'm not sure," he said. His voice was low, almost desolate, making me think that something might have happened to them.

Seleca.

Aaron didn't contribute to the conversation, but he stopped grumbling. I decided to change the subject.

"Ward, what is the ghost fragment called?"

"Conjuration," he said.

Ew, that's a dumb name. "Okay," I said, "but didn't you say that I needed a combination of fragments to get it? How could they have suspected I would gain Conjuration when Seleca didn't know about my Protection? My only other one is Connection."

"And Absorption, like Seleca," he responded.

I stopped in my tracks. So did Aaron. Ward almost ran into him but stopped in time, turning around to look at me.

"You didn't know that?" he asked.

I shook my head, then looked at Aaron. "Will that help us?" I asked.

Aaron's eyebrows squeezed together. "Yes, if it's true."

Ward shrugged. "Seleca said a person must have both greater Connection and Absorption at the time of death to acquire Conjuration. They can then be brought back with Protection, but the spirit of the one coming back has to decide to reenter their body. It can't be forced unless a conjurer is standing by to push them back in like you did to me." Ward's face was neutral as he stated this, but his choice of words left me with the impression that he was conflicted about his own return.

"I've never heard of someone having both Absorption and Protection," Aaron countered. "I thought that combination was impossible because those two fragments repel each other, but if it's true, then you could possibly gain enough power to defy the Ministry."

Aaron and I stared at each other for a moment, then he started walking again. Ward and I followed, but I refused to jog anymore. I wasn't tired, just grumpy and sick of arranging myself around the needs of others. I fell behind and the men finally had to slow down to my pace, which gave me a feeling of vindictive satisfaction.

I dug a granola bar out of my pack as I walked, guessing that maybe I was hangry because Aaron's attitude was starting to aggravate me. "Absorption is the one where you steal other people's powers, right? How do you know I have that?" I asked with my mouth full.

"I heard Seleca talking about it with *her*," he said.

"Eve?" I clarified, wondering why a supposed goddess would concern herself with me. One would think somebody that powerful could handle her own necromancy. *Or Conjuration. Whatever.* I sighed. *This whole thing is so ridiculous. Eve isn't a goddess. She's probably just some schmuck behind a curtain, demanding we pay no attention. But if she's no goddess, then how did she know which reservoirs I had?*

"Yes. Eve," Ward said. "Hey, do you have another one of those?" He motioned to the granola bar. I dug one out for him but paused for a second to wonder if he should be eating chocolate. Laughing at myself, I handed it over.

"You heard Eve talking about my reservoirs?" I asked.

Ward nodded. "After Seleca trapped me in the dog form, she kept me in a cage for a few days in her room while I went through the worst of the withdrawals." He looked at me to confirm that I understood withdrawals occur when you stay transformed for too long. Satisfied, he continued. "I thought I would die, but it eventually went away. I heard Seleca get instructions from Eve, and then she took me to you. I was supposed to watch for signs of those two fragments and report on it when she came to me." He wouldn't meet my eyes as he spoke.

"She broke into the house every few months while you were sleeping," he continued, "and then she would break into my mind and see what I had learned. It was never what she wanted. She commanded me to force you to absorb Conjuration by putting you in danger, but I wouldn't do it, no matter what she did to me. She got more and more angry and would kick me so hard I thought I would die. But, as time went on, she lost interest and showed up less. She went a year without showing herself at one point. I hoped she'd forgotten about me."

"But she came back," I said.

Ward nodded. "When you went to college, she came for me with a new assignment."

"Aaron," I guessed. "She sent you to him. That's why you disappeared."

"Yes," Ward said. "She figured out where he was hiding and that you were linked to him, so I was supposed to spy on you and find out how."

"How did she know we were linked?" Aaron asked over his shoulder. I hadn't known he was listening to our conversation.

"Your mother's book," I said, the pieces falling together. "Your mother wrote that I was meant to find you." I looked at Aaron, a shadow of suspicion growing. He was dangerous and may have been one of the only people who'd ever thwarted the Ministry. "Seleca probably thought she could use me against you, but the book must have tricked her somehow because she didn't know about my Protection. She said before leaving that she wanted to find your mother to complain."

"She thought that, as soon as she got you here," Ward continued, "she would wait to see what happened with you and Aaron, then try to take both of your reservoirs in one move. She didn't know that you could protect not only yourself but him as well." He smiled. "She must be livid," he said. I smiled back at him, feeling smug.

"What did she mean when she said, 'someone like you' should be in a dog's body?" I asked.

Ward didn't answer for a minute, but then he stopped walking and turned those piercing amber eyes on me. "Because I'm like you," he murmured.

I looked at him, trying to figure out what he meant. Then I got it. Ward was queer, like me. "Dog" must be the derogatory term they use here. "Oh, you mean you're . . ."

He nodded, peeking over his shoulder at Aaron, who had continued walking without us. He looked down at the ground, his body tense. I took his posture to mean that he assumed Aaron would be homophobic. I hoped that wasn't true, for both our sakes.

I stepped in close to him and whispered, "Exactly like me?"

He shook his head, indicating he was gay, not bisexual.

"I take it that's not very well accepted around here," I said.

Ward released a bitter laugh. "That's putting it mildly," he said, then drew a thumb across his throat.

"Oh," I said, giving Aaron my own sidelong glance. This could potentially be a huge problem.

I looked up at Ward and decided that we both needed a hug, so I held out my arms to him. He obliged me, though we both knew Aaron wouldn't like it. It was weird hugging someone so much taller than me, but his warmth was comforting. I missed Rogue, but Ward was still my best friend. He knew me better than anyone.

"When I came to your family," Ward said, "that was the first time I'd ever heard that it was okay. I was trapped in that dog body, but you made me feel like at least I wasn't broken."

I looked up at him, feeling his gratitude, and smiled. "I'm glad. Because you're not. You just started out in the wrong place. You belong on Earth, Ward. I mean, we'll have to special order all your clothes and you won't fit in cars or beds, but I think we could make it work."

He smiled, nodding, then turned to start walking again. I hooked my arm up into his and walked beside him, almost like old times. "If Seleca trapped you in the dog body, then why are you back to your real body?" I asked.

Ward thought for a moment, his mouth pinched. "Probably because you healed me. You freed me, Lina."

"I wish I would have known earlier," I said.

"I don't," said Ward. "That was my home. Now I can't go back. Even if I go back to Earth, I don't think your parents will want a giant stranger in their house."

I lifted my hand to my forehead. Yet another problem to solve. The list was getting long, but this one would be a priority. I took Ward's hand and squeezed it.

"We'll figure it out," I said.

We walked that way for a minute. I thought about how he used to walk so close to me through the woods that we were practically touching. I wasn't as deeply inside his mind as I'd been with Aaron, so I couldn't send thoughts to him, but I could feel his anxiety very clearly. Underneath that, though, was a solid foundation of love, and I reflected that love back to him.

He squeezed my hand, then let go abruptly when he saw Aaron turn around to look at us. I understood Ward's trepidation. Aaron was scary for a short dude, especially while hauling a giant dead animal that weighed more than he did. I wasn't sure if he saw us holding hands, but we made eye contact. His expression was blank, but his eyes were heated, furious. He turned forward again without comment.

I could only guess at Aaron's psychology, but I knew that he'd been isolated since his family had all but abandoned him to the mercy of Seleca, a literal psychopath. I guessed he anticipated nothing more than the same as he'd always had, plus a good dose of kicking himself for hoping otherwise. Ward coming back right at this moment may have even felt like poetic justice to him given their shared history.

Yeah, that sounded right.

Then again, I could have been projecting. Lord knows I'd had my share of loneliness. I could just be hoping that Aaron cared for me when in fact he preferred to be alone. It's not like we'd known each other for that long. He was probably thinking about what he wanted for dinner, and happy that Ward had come along to distract me so he could finally get a minute to himself.

But no, I could feel that wasn't true. Curiously, he was jealous. Nobody had ever been jealous over me before. It was simultaneously flattering and annoying, and holding Ward's hand in front of him definitely wouldn't help. On the other hand, was I supposed to ignore my dear friend, who was in the middle of a personal crisis, in order to take care of Aaron? I groaned in frustration, the back-and-forth logic making me dizzy. The two men looked at me. I didn't know who to look at, so I looked down at the ground in front of me and kept walking.

It was dusk by the time we made it to the edge of the forest. Aaron stopped and surveyed the oardoo fields. They were bordered by a very mundane wooden fence that looked much like the ones I had seen in the American countryside. The only difference was that these were taller, reaching maybe six feet high. Aaron could see over them, but all I could see were violet flowers poking up and over the slats as if trying to escape.

The flowers were so fragrant I could smell them from our position a hundred yards away, even over the pungent odor of dead dragon. It reminded me of lilacs, and I had a vivid memory of the house in Eureka where we lived before my parents moved us outside of town, to the stables. My mother had a potted lilac in the front entryway that smelled like that. She planted it in the yard before we sold the property, and when we drove by the house the next year, it wasn't there anymore.

I sighed. These random memories were making me homesick. Maybe I wasn't hangry, just tired and sad.

Aaron stopped to listen before walking out into the open. A dirt trail butted up against the outside of the fence. Grass growing down the center of the trail had recently been flattened, presumably by a wagon or a cart, but I didn't hear anything except wind rustling through the grass and the trees. A heaviness in the air weighed on my every breath, reminding me of Eureka in early autumn. It felt like a storm was coming, making me sleepy, and I sorely wished for a shower and a comfortable bed. My own bed.

"How long does it take to cross the fields?" I asked.

"An hour if it goes well," Aaron answered. "The oardoo make a lot of noise when they see intruders coming into their fields, and then they run back to the stalls and ring a bell. If that happened, it would prompt the flock tenders to come looking, and we would have to hide until they gave up. It is known that Jorin is my uncle, and there are bound to be spies among the seasonal workers. If any of the tenders are spies, it wouldn't be long before Eve's minions came looking for me."

"Uh, huh," I said, "and what's an oardoo again?"

Ward chuckled.

Aaron did not. Although he was once fond of Ward as a boy, he was obviously far from amused by his presence now. *Add it to the list of problems, I guess.*

"An oardoo is a large running bird," Aaron said, clearly annoyed at repeating himself. "It has a blue head and legs and is covered in white feathers everywhere else. My uncle raises them for the feathers, which are worth a great deal. The bedrolls are made with them."

"Oh," I said. "I was wondering what that was. And they can ring bells?"

"Yes," Aaron said. "Jorin has a large oardoo bell by the house. They are trained to run and tap on it when there's danger."

"They eat that purple plant on the other side of the fence," Ward said, smiling. "I'd recognize that smell anywhere. It's jarring weed."

"What's that?"

He grinned. "It's just like that stuff you smoked in high school and thought your parents didn't know."

"What? They knew about that?"

Ward laughed. It made my heart happy to see it, and I smiled back at him.

"Are you serious? You're not exactly the Black Widow."

"Quiet," snapped Aaron, dropping the dragon at his feet. "I need to listen."

I sighed. Ward was still silently laughing, and I was glad, but I also knew we needed to get serious.

"Maybe I can help," I said. I stuck my fingers into the ground, questing out with Connection. I sensed Ward behind me, still depressed but putting on a brave face for my benefit. I felt Aaron, whose anxiety was so sharp I could have cut my brain on it. That was it.

"Spirit," I called.

I'm here, Lina.

I jumped in surprise because it sounded like she stood right beside me, like if I closed my eyes, I could reach out and touch her. Instead, I grabbed Aaron's hand so he could listen through Connection. His hand was hot, and standing close to him felt like standing next to a literal fire. He kept his gaze averted and his expression closed, but he let me connect to him. He wanted to listen in, but he was also pissed.

"Any news?" I asked, looking at Aaron. He wouldn't look back at me.

Seleca waited at your house for several hours and turned on the TV as if she had done that before. Then she got angry and now you don't have a television. Or windows.

I sighed. "That's better than no parents," I said. "What else?"

When I left her, she was digging through drawers looking for something to burn the house down. There's nothing I can do.

"We're insured," I said. "Hopefully it won't burn the whole state down." *So much for that comfortable bed*, I thought, feeling a pang of homesickness. Aaron finally squeezed my hand back and I looked up at him.

"Why did I have to taunt her?" I whispered. "Note to self: don't purposely piss off the psychopath. Spirit, would you check to see if there's anyone around to see us climb the fence?"

"Or any oardoo to reveal our presence," added Aaron.

What's an oardoo? Spirit asked.

"Blue-headed ostrich," I said, suppressing a laugh.

Oh. Okay. No, there's no one.

"You're done already? That was less than a second," I said.

Time means nothing over here. Or very little, anyway.

I blinked at that. "Okay, go back to Psycho Snow White and let me know what happens. I want to know if she gives up and goes looking for Aaron's family."

Okay.

Then, Spirit was gone again. I was getting used to this ghost-whispering business. Conjuration was a dumb name, though. I would have to come up with something better than that. *Necromancy? Ew, no. Keep thinking*, I thought.

Aaron gave me the *look*.

"What?" I asked.

"Is that really relevant right now?" he asked.

"Hey, I've got to amuse myself somehow or you might have to see Evilina more and more often."

Ward coughed, suppressing a laugh. "None of us want that. Trust me," he said.

The comment annoyed Aaron, which is when I realized that I hadn't explained Evilina to him yet. He felt like he was stuck on the outside of an inside joke. He pulled his hand away, but I hung on. "Stop," I said. He blinked at me. "You have to stop."

"Stop what?" he snapped. Heat rolled off him like someone had opened an oven.

I scooted closer, craned my neck up to look him right in the eye, and gave him my best *Give me a freaking break* face.

He looked back at me, his jaw clenched, intimidating in its savage anger. I waited, stubbornly refusing to back down. *Impossible man. I never had this trouble with Drew.*

Aaron's face darkened. *Well, maybe you should go back to him then.*

I felt my eyes widen and my jaw drop. I hadn't meant to send that errant thought about Drew to him, but his response was needlessly spiteful. This conversation was going off the rails. I needed to get back on track.

I need you, Aaron. I also need Ward—my friend, *Ward. Don't make me choose.*

Why not? he thought, his eyes flashing. *Because you would choose him? Your* friend *betrayed you. He betrayed us both, but you told him you love him and you're acting like everything's fine. It's not fine.*

His stupid, freaking super hearing had picked up what I'd *whispered* to Ward. *That's what you're mad about? He's my oldest friend. I do love him. And he was trapped, Aaron. He didn't choose it.*

There's always a choice, remember? I guess you've made yours. He yanked his hand away, leaving me with an unexpected stabbing pain in my chest.

I stepped back from him, doubling over. The words themselves hadn't been that harsh, but the delivery had been absolutely venomous, and I had received them with my Connection link wide open and my Protection down. I grabbed my chest like I was having a heart attack. If I had been looking at myself from the outside, I would have called myself a drama queen, but this was real pain, not just an emotional response. Something about the interaction had caused a kind of energy blowback that had physically struck me. It was like Aaron had severed our Connection link, which then snapped back like a rubber band, smacking me right in my heart.

What the hell was that? I thought.

Ward flew to me. "Lina," he said, surprised as I was by the sudden turn of events. He wrapped his arm around my chest, supporting me. "What is happening?"

I shook my head. "I'm not sure." I hyperventilated for a few more seconds, letting tears stream down my face, but Ward's warmth and concern comforted me, and the pain dissipated after a minute. When I stood back up, my nose was running. I wiped it with the back of my hand, then noticed that it was streaked with red.

"For fuck's sake," I mumbled, pinching my nose. It was a good thing my shirt was red. I glanced at Aaron, expecting remorse, but his face was stony.

I could have pointed out that he'd burned Ward's freaking face off without a choice and that he had now done whatever *that* was, but instead, I looked down and said, "Spirit says the way is clear. We can climb the fence. I'll follow you if you still want me to."

He didn't move, and I didn't look at him. I didn't have the energy to continue the conversation and simultaneously keep my shit together. *I was wrong about him*, I thought, shaking my head. *He told me yesterday that he had a hard time regulating emotion, but I didn't listen.*

I stood there, waiting, not knowing what to do next. I couldn't believe the man I'd bonded with so strongly only that morning, who I'd been convinced would protect me from harm, was now someone I needed to keep a distance from lest he hurt me himself.

Don't cry yet. Wait until you're alone. Inhale. Exhale. I turned away from Aaron, swallowing a growing lump in my throat.

Aaron hesitated, then picked up the dragon and walked toward the fence without a word.

Ward handed me a cloth for my face, and I pressed it to my nose. I looked at what he had handed me and saw that it was Aaron's white shirt. He must have pulled it out of my bag. I gave Ward a wry look, but he just shrugged, smirking. Then, he took my hand, and we walked toward the fence like that, Aaron's opinion be damned.

Chapter Fourteen

Linorra crumpled to the stone floor, the arrow lodged snugly within her breast. She closed her eyes and let her body relax, knowing she would not be able to overcome her fate this time. If only she had the chance to speak with Syndeth one last time. She would tell him she loved him.

Climbing the fence wasn't that hard, but I had to wait for my nose to stop bleeding. I was learning the hard way that fragment use comes with a price, even the seemingly innocuous ones like Connection. The link had physically hurt me, and I didn't know how or why. It was so goddamn frustrating. There was no one to teach me, so I had to blunder around like an idiot.

When we reached the other side of the fence, Ward broke off a twig of jarring weed and gave it to me.

"Keep this under your nose while we walk," he said. "It will make you feel better."

He was right. I inhaled the jarring weed for the next hour while we walked through the fields. The scent was soothing and somehow helped me think more clearly, though it exacerbated my drowsiness. The longer I had it in my face, the more I realized that the smell alone had some kind of psychoactive effect. I started to feel like I was on the outside of my life, looking in, calming down to the point of nearly dissociating from my situation.

I asked myself deep, philosophical questions that I would later completely forget, and I stumbled a few times, forgetting to pay attention to my body.

In short, the plant got me high. I chuckled when this fact finally occurred to me, and I wondered if I could grow the stuff on Earth if I brought home clippings. *I could make a fortune. Evilina, queenpin of the Pacific Northwest.* I covered my mouth, trying to suppress my giggle, but looked up when I heard Ward laughing under his breath. He knew exactly what was happening, as always.

As night came on, I found it harder and harder to see where I stepped. The men, with their superior Monashi vision, didn't have any such problem. Ward took my hand again. He knew that I had stupid, useless Earth eyes and took it upon himself to guide me, which made sense given that it was Ward who'd drugged me to begin with.

Spirit, are you there? I called. I wanted to ask her opinion of my predicament and doing so while high as hell on jarring weed felt like the perfect opportunity.

I'm here, Lina.

I need you to help me figure out what to do. I feel lost. Aaron probably hadn't meant to hurt me, but it doesn't change the fact that he did just that. Maybe he doesn't understand friendship between people of the opposite sex. Maybe, in this world, that isn't a thing. I shouldn't just stomp off like a thirteen-year-old. I should give him a chance to apologize, shouldn't I?

Spirit sighed. *He didn't anticipate what happened to you, but he knew you were hurt. He could have apologized right after it happened, but he didn't. He just stood there while you bled.*

I sighed heavily. *That's true, but he was caught off guard.* Even to me, that argument sounded like making excuses for an abusive partner. One that didn't act like he cared if I made excuses for him or not. *I need him to help me get home*, I reasoned. *I should at least be civil, right?*

"Look," Ward said, pulling me out of my thoughts. He pointed directly above us.

I followed his gaze, and what I saw made my jaw drop. There were two moons. One was similar in size and color to Earth's moon on a clear night, bright white with specks of gray, but it had a paper-thin ring around it. The other moon appeared smaller, or perhaps farther away, and was a deep cinnamon red. The stars beyond were so bright that it was like the moons resided in their own personal constellation. I stopped dead in my tracks, paralyzed with wonder.

"They call them the Ancestors," Ward said. "Heshia, the shining mother, with her fine white circlet of purest quartz, bonded to Ishkar, the brooding lord of thunder. Right now, he watches her from afar as she blesses her children with light, but once every twelve years, he grows jealous and comes for her. Before he takes her, black clouds fill the sky to block our view, and Lord Ishkar's thunder deafens our ears so that we may not hear. But her children know what befalls her, and the sky weeps so many tears that the sea swallows the land."

I tore my eyes from the miraculous sight to regard Ward. His eyes were turned skyward, a sad smile playing on the unscarred half of his face while the other half was paralyzed. "Did you miss your home while you were away, Ward?" I asked.

Ward inhaled and exhaled, squinting his eyes a little in contemplation. He rested one arm across my shoulders but didn't take his eyes from the Ancestors. "You were my home, Lina."

I smiled, a warmth spreading through my chest, then looked back up at the moons as I stretched an arm around Ward's hips, squeezing him a little in a side hug. I stared up at the sky, shaking my head and wondering if I was the only person from Earth who'd ever seen the two moons of Monash. This one experience alone would have made the whole trip worthwhile. It was like the very cosmos reminded me to be patient because this was a whole different world.

I'll try, I thought. *No promises.*

"What's wrong?" Ward asked.

I thought he spoke to me, but when I looked at him, I realized the question had been directed at Aaron. I had been so absorbed in my own thoughts that I hadn't noticed Aaron looking warily into the dark. I needed to pay better attention and keep my head together. I couldn't depend on the men to keep me safe, especially now. That thought sent a shiver through me, and I let the sweet-smelling flowers drop to the ground.

Aaron dropped the dragon and stretched his back. "There are always at least a few birds that come out into the field to nest, but I haven't seen a single one. It's too quiet. Lina, can you send Spirit to go look ahead?"

"Okay," I said. "What is she looking for?"

"My uncle's house is just ahead. See those trees?"

A group of deciduous trees about two hundred yards ahead looked like they surrounded a building. The moons reflected off waxy leaves.

"Have her go to the house and see if anyone is there."

"Okay," I said.

Spirit.

I'm on it, she said.

The moons left an afterimage on my eyes, and a faint light emanated from the same direction as her voice. The image wasn't fading, though. It was there, but it also wasn't there.

The image winked out for a split second, then reappeared.

Yes, it's safe, she said. *No one is there.*

I blinked. *What am I seeing?*

It's me, Spirit thought. *You're starting to see me.*

"Well?" Aaron asked, his voice subdued.

A feeling overwhelmed me that was at once excitement and also trepidation. "She says there's no one there," I said absently, looking at the splotch of white light a few feet away. It was starting to look misty, as if materializing into something more substantial.

Aaron shook his head. "Goddess help us," he said.

"Any updates from the house?" Ward asked.

I squinted harder at the hazy form of Spirit, as if that would clear my vision.

I'm sorry, Lina, Spirit thought. *Seleca burned your house to the ground, then left to go look for Aaron's family.*

A lead weight dropped from my heart into my stomach, and I put my hands over my eyes, taking a deep breath. A hand touched my shoulder, and I looked up to see Ward peering down at me, his brows drawn together.

"She burned the house down," I said. He winced and then his whole face reddened. He pulled me into a hug. My throat burned as I struggled not to cry. I mostly succeeded. Only one tear escaped. That house had been my home for sixteen years and it had been Ward's home for almost as long. We would need to grieve for that life, but we didn't have time right now.

Ward released me from the hug and looked down at me, squeezing one shoulder. "It'll be okay," he said. "It's just a house. Everyone is safe, right?"

I nodded. "For now," I said. "Although we don't know where they went. God only knows what they did with the horses." I peered at Aaron. I'm sure he'd heard me say my house burned down, but he ignored us. I shook my head. I wasn't sure if I should tell him about the second part of that message right now. I felt heavy from trying to guard everyone's emotions while suppressing my own. You can only carry the weight of other people's needs so far before you have to drop it like ballast from an overloaded ship.

"Okay, thank you, Spirit," I said, trying to move on. "Can you still follow her?"

Yes, I could find that thing anywhere. I just have to follow the smell.

"Is that a metaphor?" I asked.

Not really. She has a spiritual stench. The other spirits avoid her.

"The others?" I asked.

Yes, there are many others who haven't crossed the death bridge, Spirit thought.

I wanted to ask her more, but afterlife research rated as a low priority just then.

"Thank you, Spirit. Keep me updated," I said, yawning.

She didn't say goodbye this time, just disappeared. It was comforting to know that I could call her back anytime. Conjuration was different from the other reservoirs. It didn't feel like using a fragment at all but more like making a wish. It was no effort whatsoever, like I could do it in my sleep, which I might have to since the jarring weed was still in full effect. I yawned again.

I should send Spirit to go check on Marti and Milo, I thought. *They lost the twins. They must be devastated.* My friends were all suffering because of me. It was all my fault. The whole thing made me so tired. We were all tired, I knew, but I was drowsy enough that I felt like I could lie right there on the ground. That sounded like such a great idea. *Just leave it all behind.* I yawned again and closed my eyes.

"Lina," Aaron said, his voice sounding far away. "Lina, open your eyes." He held me, but I didn't know why. Had he hurt me again? "She won't wake up," he said, his voice panicked.

But I am awake, I said. *I'm right . . .* I opened my eyes and looked down at myself in Aaron's arms. *This isn't right.*

Call yourself back, a deep voice said. I glanced up and saw a giant towering over Aaron. He strongly resembled Aaron, actually, except tall and slender like Ward, with pale skin. He had Aaron's ice-blue eyes, but they were missing something indefinable.

Life, I thought. *Huh.* I knew I should be surprised, maybe even upset, but I felt too relaxed and calm. I didn't want to go back to the pain and misery. I wanted to stay here forever.

You have very little time, the man said. *You must call yourself back into your body.*

That doesn't even make sense, I thought.

It doesn't need to make sense, the man retorted. *Just do it. A portion of your spirit is still seated inside your body. When you say your own name, that part of you will wrench the rest back in.*

I sighed. This was so unfair. I just got here. And this ghost man smelled so good, like jarring weed. I snorted. *Jarring weed. Such a weird name for a plant.*

Do it now, Lina, said the ghost giant urgently. His voice was even deeper than Aaron's, and he spoke with absolute authority. His eyes darted all around, then he looked over his shoulder as if we were children about to get caught opening presents before Christmas.

Fine, I said, sticking out my bottom lip. *Lina*, I said, as if calling a dog. *Here, Lina, Lina, Lina. Come back to your body, Lina.* I recalled a vintage episode of *Sesame Street* where Ernie called fish into a boat, and I giggled. I love old television shows. "Here, Lina, Lina, Lina," I said again in my best Ernie voice.

I heard the ghost giant sigh, and then I felt a gentle tugging as if an invisible cord attached the top of my ghost head to my real head. I accepted the inevitable, said goodbye to my new friend Bert, and pulled myself back in. I was then violently wrenched back into my body. If I had been in my body while that happened, I would have broken my neck.

My eyes flew open, and I sucked a deep breath in, then coughed. I was on the ground. Aaron held my upper body in his lap. It was the ICU all over again, except dirtier. The moons spun in the sky above Aaron's head, as if they, too, had been worried about me.

I squeezed my eyes shut until the dizziness passed, feeling Aaron's hot breath on my face. "That was so messed up," I said. Aaron had a death grip on my hand as if he'd been trying to connect with me. Once I came back to myself, the superficial link reestablished itself of its own accord.

"What happened?" Aaron asked. "One minute you were fine, and the next, you just fell over." His concern for me was evident, and he was actively trying to pull me into a deeper link and succeeding somehow. I thought dimly that I would need to get better control over my powers if I was going to face Seleca again.

"I think my spirit drifted out of my body," I said. "It felt great. I didn't want to come back, but the ghost giant made me."

"What giant?" Aaron asked.

I shook my head. "I don't know, Aaron." Now that I was alive again, calling the ghost giant "Bert" seemed utterly ridiculous. Ward and I made eye contact. Once he saw that I was okay, he shuffled toward the house and turned his back on us, looking at the trees. He hugged himself as the wind picked up, rustling the leaves.

Through our Connection link, I felt that Aaron wasn't angry anymore, except at himself. He felt desperate but fought to keep it together. He had a strong suspicion about what we might find when we got to the house, as it was something he'd feared for years. He also believed that I was secretly in love with Ward and was confused about it, so he braced himself for that disappointment as well. He had convinced himself that getting attached wasn't worth the risk. He would inevitably end up alone again once I realized how dangerous his life was. He just needed to accept his isolation and focus on the task at hand. That logic, however, completely fell apart when I collapsed, especially since Ward stepped aside and let him take over.

Aaron, you idiot, I thought to him. On the other hand, I knew exactly what it felt like to say that to myself. In fact, I had once used almost that exact same logic. I sighed. *We're both idiots.*

Aaron hugged me too hard, burying his face in my neck. He still smelled like himself, but also faintly of BO and dead animal. He needed a bath as badly as I did. The man was a mess, and the idea that he was just as imperfect as I was made my heart swell with affection. I couldn't hold on to even a sliver of anger at his behavior, no matter how much he deserved it.

You were so pale, he thought to me. *I thought you were dead.*

I coughed. *I will be if you don't let me breathe.*

Aaron released me, lifting his face in alarm. I smirked at him, then pinched my nose and said out loud, "On second thought . . ."

He gave me a rueful smile. "Everything is a joke to you," he said.

"Not everything. Just most things," I said. I grabbed his now very scruffy beard, running my fingers through it.

Aaron's eyes searched mine for a moment. "I'm sorry, Lina. I didn't mean to hurt you." He meant through our Connection link, but also his behavior before and after.

"I know," I said. "But don't make a habit of it, okay? I would not tolerate that very well. Or at all." He nodded, and then I tugged his beard toward my face, looked him right in the eye, and thought, very clearly, *and I'm not in love with Ward, you moron.*

He glanced back at me, his gaze intense, then he pulled me close and kissed me, gently this time. First my lips, then my cheek, then he hugged me again like he was afraid to let go. Maybe he was. Once he did, we would have to go into the house and possibly find something horrific. That's the thing about pain, though. Sometimes the anticipation is worse than the pain itself, and sometimes anticipation is the only pain, a mountain of your own making.

"You're so fragile," he said.

"Fragile like a bomb."

"What is that?"

I sighed. "Never mind. I'm not sure how those work either." I petted his hair as if I were soothing a child. "We have to go in now, Aaron."

"I know," he said, but he didn't let go.

After a minute, I got up, forcing him to release his hold on me. I peered down at him, waiting, but he still didn't move. He looked so small for someone so big.

"Come on," I said, holding my hand out to him. "We'll go together."

He considered my hand for a moment, then took it, rose, and we walked toward the house.

Chapter Fifteen

Linorra could smell the delicious aroma of rabbit stew hanging within the witch's hearth. This warm, inviting cottage was not what she expected at all. It felt like home.

I feared that when we opened the front door, the smell of decay would hit us in the face, but the house smelled stale, like it had been empty for months. We crept into the front entryway, closing the heavy wooden door behind us. It made a *woomf* as it closed, muffling a chorus of chirping night creatures. The floors creaked under our feet, but otherwise, all was silent and still.

I glanced back at the front door and noticed there was no way to bar it from within. *I know these people have metalworkers*, I thought. *Hasn't anyone ever heard of a door lock?*

Ward saw me staring at the door in confusion and whispered, "Door locks are outlawed here. The magisters—the men who enforce Ministry law—are allowed to enter your home at any time without notice. If they find a locked door, they are authorized to burn your house down."

I looked at him, stunned. "Crazy freaking cult," I mumbled. "That is so messed up."

"It gets worse," he said. "They're allowed to come into your bedroom while you're sleeping and watch you. And if they come upon you having sex with your spouse, they are supposed to ask you for your permit."

"What happens if you don't have one?" I asked.

"They hang you in the pit," he said.

Nothing about that sentence sounded fun. I knew it was bad here, but this was completely out of control. I shook my head. These people had to be stopped.

"Aaron, is he serious?" I asked. Aaron had had multiple locks on his cottage. Then again, he was sort of an outlaw.

"Completely," Aaron murmured. "Let me listen."

We stood in the foyer in the dark while Aaron listened to the house. It opened to what appeared to be one big room, though it was hard for me to see with so little light coming in through the windows. As my eyes adjusted, however, I could make out seating just beyond the foyer to the right, including a green couch with comfortable-looking cushions. I gazed at it longingly.

"I don't hear anything," Ward said after a while.

"Neither do I," said Aaron. "I'll check upstairs."

"Let me do it," said Ward.

I heard no response from Aaron, but after a moment, Ward walked past him, so he must have nodded. I smiled appreciatively. If there were any bodies, it would be better if Ward found them first. I supposed volunteering to take that on was a peace offering of sorts.

Ward walked directly toward the back, all but disappearing into the dark. I heard him climbing what I presumed to be the stairs. I crouched and put my hand on the floor to see if I could feel anything. Apparently, wood flooring doesn't transmit Connection. I stood back up and walked forward until I was next to Aaron.

"What if we don't find anything at all?" I asked.

"My uncle rarely leaves the property, but I suppose it's possible. We could wait, but it might be dangerous. I assume Seleca knew we were headed here. If we find nothing, we'll sleep in the attic in case someone comes in the middle of the night."

I groaned, longing to plop down on that green couch.

"There's a bed up there," Aaron said, smirking.

"Oh, yeah? How big?" I asked, taking his hand to connect. I still felt awkward from our fight, but a little innuendo could be a quick way to get back on track.

Aaron laughed softly. "Big enough," he said. It hadn't exactly been a proposition, but I had vocalized a definite intention to sleep in the same bed with him. Connection let me feel him echo that intention back vehemently.

He was a ball of emotions now. The clearest to my senses was dread at the possibility of finding corpses in the house. Almost as loud was the fear about what might have befallen his family if we didn't find any bodies. Hovering just underneath was the excitement about sleeping next to me and the guilt about letting himself be distracted by it when his family could be dead or in danger.

"So, your uncle lives here with your cousin?" I asked. I let go of his hand, doing a little turn to look around.

"Yes," he said. "There are two rooms upstairs. He's in one; my cousin, Terik, and his bondmate, Farrah, are in the other. They haven't gotten permission to have children yet."

"How long have they been married—bonded—I mean?" I asked.

"Ten years," he said. "And they get frequent nighttime visits."

"Is that normal? Or are they searching for you?"

"A bit of both," said Aaron. "They have been looking for me for quite some time, but Farrah is a sore subject as well."

"Why?" I asked.

"She's a powerful fragmentor, a greater producer, like Jorin, which makes her valuable to bond. She's also . . . quite beautiful," he said, eyeing me. I had let go of his hand too soon. There was more to that story. "Magister Axel wanted her, but she refused to bond to him. She was sixteen and he would have forced her, but Jorin spoke on her behalf. He has influence with the Ministry Council because he produces so many valuable goods. He said that he needed her help with the farm."

"What is a producer exactly?" I asked.

"A grower. Jorin can make anything grow, including livestock. He provides more than half the food in Neesee, no matter what the weather does. Without him, food prices would skyrocket, and people would go hungry. That is also why they leave him alone even though they know he's my uncle. Farrah agreed to bond to my cousin since he will eventually inherit the farm, but Axel has blocked all their birth permit requests and sends his minions to harass them on a monthly basis."

I shook my head again. "We have to stop these people, Aaron. We can't just run away to Earth and leave your family to their fate. The cult that runs this place is ruining lives, killing people. This isn't right."

"It isn't just Eve and Seleca," he said. "Even if we manage to get rid of those two, we'd have to overcome the entire Ministry Council, the magisters, the guild masters, and everyone else who benefits from the system, which includes all those with greater reservoirs to some degree. What could we do against that?"

"We can teach. We can resist. We can fight. If we could figure out how to come and go across the bridge, we could use that as a launching point. People will reject us at first out of fear, but they will be convinced once they see what you have seen."

"And what I've seen," said Ward, appearing out of the dark. Aaron had heard and probably seen him coming, but I hadn't. He still didn't trust Ward but would make an effort at civility for my benefit.

"There's nothing to see up there as far as I can tell," Ward said. "I don't smell a residue either. Whatever the reason your family is missing, it isn't because they were killed. At least not in this house."

Aaron relaxed, but I knew that he would have to see for himself to be sure.

"Thanks, Ward," I said. "Aaron, any chance for me to get cleaned up before we sleep?" I looked down at myself. I was covered in mud and blood again.

"Follow me," Aaron said. "I'll show you."

Aaron lit the oil lamp, then showed me where the bath was. Fortunately, the house had a tiny bathroom on the second floor with archaic but usable plumbing. A footed metal bathtub sat beneath a spigot coming from the ceiling. The tub drained down to a holding tank near a vegetable garden on the side of the house.

The room was barely big enough to fit the tub, and there was no sink or toilet, only a small tiled area in the corner with a grated hole. An empty bucket sat in the tiled area. Aaron explained that the hole was for urine and that you were supposed to fill the bucket with water to help drain it out to the back of the house where the outhouse was located.

I felt very sorry for Farrah. This was not a very female-friendly system. I imagined myself squatting over that hole, stepping on the urine that had splashed from the men. Yikes. Maybe we could bring the young couple back with us. If we found them, that is.

Aaron gave me a dress of Farrah's to wear, heated up my water, then left me to it. The soap smelled like jarring weed, which made for the most relaxing bath I've ever had, but

I also worried that my previous use of jarring weed had contributed to my unintentional astral projection. I didn't want to repeat that experience, nor did I wish to pass out and drown.

I finished washing myself and my clothes, then dried off with what could only loosely be called a towel. It was slightly bigger than a washcloth, thin, and smelled like vinegar. Farrah's dress had clearly been ripped through time out of the Victorian era, navy blue with long sleeves, a high neck, and buttons all the way up the front. It was far too big, scratchy, and completely incongruent with the strange Greek tunic the men wore. It was stupid and I hated it, but I agreed to wear it until my regular clothes finished drying.

While I gallantly risked my life in a hot bath, Aaron carried the dragon corpse to some kind of hut outside the house, butchered it, and created a meal using the meat from that animal, a few jarred and pickled items that he found in the house, and a purple root vegetable from the garden that tasted like spicy parsnips. Maybe it was just that we were all ravenous, but he surprised me again with his ability to create a meal out of thin air.

His remarkable culinary skills made me think of my mother. Was she somewhere crying, worrying about me? I had to get back. I had to, but I also needed to help these people. Plus, they were the key to helping me. The bridge was the answer. If I could only learn how to make one, I could go back to Earth, talk to my parents, and bring back what I needed to support a revolution.

Revolution, I thought. *How do you start a revolution?* I laughed to myself. I should have studied for that stupid history test.

After we ate, I insisted on cleaning the dishes and sent Aaron to the bath. He used the same bathwater I had. Ward refused the bath, saying that he didn't need it when he was a dog, so why would he need it now? It made me realize that I probably could have done a little better job taking care of him. Poor Ward would be sleeping alone tonight anyway, so what did it matter?

I would never tell Aaron, but I would miss my co-sleeping arrangement with Rogue. It had been such a staple of my nighttime routine that if Aaron hadn't been there, I might have continued it with Ward. It was probably better not to think about that in case Aaron plucked the thought from my brain.

The attic was accessible by a ladder from a closet in Jorin's room. The closet door hid behind the false back of a wardrobe, and the wardrobe itself was in the back of another closet. The ladder folded up into the attic through a trapdoor.

Aaron carefully brought the oil lamp up the ladder, then stood at the top to help me. I didn't need it, but I let him help me anyway. Once we were up through the trapdoor, I saw that it had a lock on it. Ward wouldn't come up the ladder and insisted on sleeping on the floor of the closet, so Aaron tossed a bedroll down to him, then closed—and locked—the trapdoor. I didn't blame Ward. I wouldn't want to sleep in the same room with a brand-new couple either—if that's what we were.

The attic was chilly, but not uncomfortable. It had no obvious windows that could be seen from the outside, but there were small viewing panels in the middle of each wall that could be lifted by a latch to peek outside. Aaron peeked out each of the panels while I searched for a place to hang my wet clothes.

Dimly lit by the oil lamp, the well-used space had a vaulted ceiling that sloped low enough on the sides that even I had to crouch near the walls where the trapdoor opened. In one corner of the room, there were two shelves overflowing with books, positioned on either side of a reading chair. I recognized them as the banned books from Aaron's memory.

A wooden counter and a chest much like the one from Aaron's cottage occupied another corner of the attic. I draped my wet clothes over the counter, then continued snooping. The bed, an oardoo-feather mattress on a low platform, was big enough for two very tall people. A little half-sized door that looked like it should lead Alice straight to Wonderland was on the opposite wall, rising to the low end of the vaulted ceiling.

At the peak of the ceiling, a piece of art even more magnificent than the two moons of Monash twisted seamlessly into a dome. A pattern of colorful veneer depicted four jarring weed trees rising from the bottom of the dome to join in a gorgeous violet canopy. Perched on one of those trees, gazing down from near the top of the dome, was a crimson dragon. Bathed in shadows, it looked so real that I did a double take and my heart jumped into my throat before my brain recognized that it was a part of the ceiling. A round window framed by a circle of white marble was set into the dome at the apex.

An oculus, I thought. I'd learned the word during my visit to the Pantheon in Rome a few years ago. I stared in awe.

"My grandfather's work," Aaron said, closing the last viewing panel. "He was a master craftsman in the Woodworkers Guild. He built this house."

"What is this room, Aaron?" I asked.

Aaron glanced around, debating. "It's the guest room," he said. I gave him the *look*, and he smirked. "It's a place to hide people," he said. "Mainly me. And books. Especially *these* books." He pointed a thumb at the bookshelves.

"I see," I said. In other words, it was his bedroom. "Wouldn't someone be able to see this fancy dome from the outside?"

"Once upon a time, yes. But now it's camouflaged by the rain collection cistern and a false roof, and there's another attic we could take them to if they asked to see why the roof is so high, but that's not generally what the magister is searching for."

"Who are these magisters you keep talking about?"

"They work for the Ministry. They're responsible for civil enforcement of Ministry law and have a leadership position in the military legion of each province. Magister Axel has been assigned to Southern Gale for the last twenty years, and he is relentless. That's why I stay away most of the time. If he caught me here, he'd have grounds to destroy my uncle."

"What is he trying to find?"

Aaron looked at me obliquely, then over at the undersized door. "Anything that might get him what he wants."

I narrowed my eyes. "What does he want?"

Aaron rolled his eyes, but he couldn't quite suppress a smile. "You really can't let anything go, can you?"

"I told you. It's my best feature." I batted my eyelashes at him for effect.

Aaron raised one eyebrow at me like he was Spock analyzing an alien lifeform, a comparison that made a lot of sense if you thought about it. "He still wants Farrah," he said, "but he can't just take her because of Jorin's influence."

Ah, right. The incomparable Farrah. How could I forget?

"He's searching for any reason to bring the hammer down on my cousin, which is why he comes so often or sends his minions. Worst case scenario, he would find a reason to execute both my uncle and cousin, and then he could take Farrah and the entire farm. Of course, he wouldn't live long enough to enjoy it."

He dropped his pack beside the bed, then walked over to the trapdoor and opened a small panel that looked down into the closet. Aaron observed Ward for a long moment, then shut the panel again and headed back to the bed. I watched him as he moved around the room, not sure if I should be nervous about the casual way he'd just threatened to murder his enemy. I understood the sentiment, but I'd never heard someone speak that way before. Would I be safer with someone like this?

As long as he was on my side, I decided, *yes. And if he can keep his temper.*

"Is it common to have this kind of place in your house?" I asked, changing the subject.

Aaron shrugged. "I don't know for sure, but I suspect this is not the only one." I wondered how many of these existed in Neesee. I hoped many. If we could find Jorin, I'd ask him if he knew of others who resisted in these small ways. It would be a good place to start with our own resistance.

"What's through there?" I asked, pointing to the little door.

"The escape route. There's a hallway leading to a removable panel with a rope, then another room like this one on the other side, accessible from Terik's room. That's where they go when they want actual privacy. Jorin installed the escape hatch about fifteen years ago when Axel burned down a home near the Moore farm, just southeast of here. Killed two kids." He walked back over to his pack, sat in front of it, and pulled everything out to reorganize.

"Your family are all rebels," I commented, not bothering to hide my admiration.

"No, I'm the only rebel. The rest are silent resisters."

I watched him fastidiously reorganize his pack, glad that I was in his room instead of the other way around. My bedroom was always embarrassingly messy. I had a perpetual basket of clean laundry that I never folded and three years of papers on my desk that I'd been meaning to shred.

Well, that's one problem solved, at least. My bedroom isn't there anymore. I sighed. "I should do that too," I said, motioning to the pack. Aaron smiled, shaking his head. "What?" I asked. "It could happen. Not tonight, though. Maybe tomorrow."

"I'll believe it when I see it," he said, his eyes crinkling at the corners. "You should check in with Spirit before we sleep."

"Okay. I just hope I don't float away with her when she leaves this time."

Aaron considered that for a minute. "Maybe you should sit next to me." His expression remained blank as he said it, but his eyes were searching. He watched me walk toward him like a starving man watching a turkey come out of the oven. I felt a flush creep up my neck as I approached him, though that might have been Farrah's stupid scratchy dress.

"Good idea," I said and plopped down on the bed next to him, setting my pack next to his. "Spirit," I called.

"I'm here," she said. She sounded close, her voice more solid somehow. I turned to see her beside me, lounging on the bed.

"Holy crap! I can see you, Spirit."

She directed a dazzling white smile at me. "I know," she said. She was so stunning I couldn't speak for a moment. She wore one of her usual boho dresses in a midnight blue that made her gray-blue eyes seem like they were glowing. It had a deep V-neck that drew the eyes down before you could stop them. Her white-blond hair was longer than I remembered and flowed around her body as if she posed for Botticelli. I wanted to get her a freaking scallop shell to stand in. I just stared, remembering the last time I had seen her sprawled out on a bed like that. I wondered if I could reach out and touch her.

"You can't," she said.

"Can't what?" I asked.

"Touch me. Or do anything else to me," she said, sitting up. She appeared to sit on the bed, but there was no indentation. The shift in posture drew my attention to the slit in her dress. It was right in the front, went up to mid-thigh, and opened up to show her gorgeously smooth legs.

"Um, wow. That's too bad," I said, glancing at Aaron a little guiltily. Though I knew he couldn't hear Spirit because we weren't connected, he looked at me with that same expression he'd had when Ward appeared. This time, it was probably warranted.

I was glad to see her, but leering was not the best idea. Instead, I leaned my head on Aaron's shoulder to distract myself and hooked my arm in his. Resting my hand on his forearm, our shared mental space opened, and I discovered that he *was* jealous again, but he didn't understand why he needed to be. The man was so perceptive that I knew I would have a hard time hiding my feelings from him the way I had done with everyone since Drew. I tended to keep friends and lovers alike at arm's length, but that might not be possible with Aaron. That fact made me even more nervous than his willingness to kill someone.

I gazed into his eyes and inhaled his amazing scent, which now, after his bath, was a mix of clean soap and a tangy musk. I pulled him into the deeper Connection link so he could hear Spirit. "Any news?" I asked her, not looking away from his eyes.

"Seleca went to the last place she knew Aaron's family to be," Spirit said, "which was an apartment in Seattle, but there was no one there."

Aaron winced at hearing Spirit's voice through Connection. He forced himself to relax then said, "And now there's no one here either."

I sat up straight, my libido momentarily forgotten. "Oh shit. What if your mother knew where Seleca would be ahead of time and evacuated people?"

"Then Seleca might be coming here next," he said, finishing my thought.

"But why would your mother write us a note encouraging us to come here if she knew Seleca might show up?"

He shook his head. "Maybe the two aren't related, or maybe we misread. How would my mother even get here?"

"And wouldn't she have wanted to see you if she had been here?" I asked. *One would hope.*

We stared at each other for a second, then Aaron jumped up to peer through the viewing panels again. "Spirit, can you check again if anyone else is in or around the house?"

She disappeared. When she reappeared a second later, she stood on the other side of the room. "There's no one within ten miles in any direction," she said. Her instantaneous movement across the room was creepy, and I had to look away.

"You were just with Seleca, right?" I asked. "Did you get an idea of what her next move would be?"

"She stole my Precognition reservoir when she murdered me," she said. "I believe she's planning to try to use it, but she'll need to come back to Monash to do that. Earth is blocking her. Even when she gets here, it's going to be harder than she thinks."

I relayed what Spirit said to Aaron. "She'll probably go back to the palace so she can practice in peace," he said.

"Palace? That sounds nice," I said.

"It is," Aaron said. "Eve controls all of the guilds and has hundreds of years' worth of forced labor and theft stored in that palace, including my grandfather's staff."

"Staff?"

"Yes, my mother said it's some kind of focus staff that gives you greater control over a fragment, but she never saw him use it. Now I'll probably never get to see what it does."

"How did Eve and Anick gain so much power?" I asked.

"Projection, seduction, and murder. They've been stealing reservoirs since before my grandfather's time. The history is handwritten in one of those books. It goes all the way back to the pre-Anick era." He pointed to the bookshelf. I looked over, thinking I knew exactly what I would be doing for the next few days.

"Even so," he continued, "some reservoirs are so rare that it took until now for them to be found. The story passed down in our family is that Anick originally had Absorption and Projection. Projection lets you force your own thoughts or perceptions onto others, so he simply convinced people to let him absorb their reservoirs without resisting."

"You can resist?"

"To a degree. You can build a resistance over time and make it harder, but you can't stop it altogether without Protection. Projection can even be used to place a person in a trance, making them act like a puppet with no will of their own. They'll just sit down and starve to death unless they're told to eat. Seleca likes to do that for fun, but I think she finds it easier to just kill people outright, especially if she wants to absorb their reservoir."

Spirit stared at the ground, nodding, her face neutral rather than filled with regret as I would have been. I remembered how nice it had felt when I'd drifted out of my body. I'd always thought death would be a burden, but it's just the opposite. All burdens are lifted in death.

"Spirit, would you please follow her again and let us know if she's coming this way?"

"Sure," she said, her eyes bouncing between me and Aaron, then she disappeared again.

I hoped that if I lay down to sleep that I wouldn't drift out of my body again. I wasn't exactly sure how it worked, but at least I wasn't high as a kite like last time. I was so exhausted now that the risk was worth it. In any case, what was I going to do? Never sleep again?

I leaned over my bag and dug out my toothbrush and water bottle while Aaron finished looking through the panels. After scrubbing my teeth, I finished off the water and pulled out Violet's book, reading the poem again. "I think we're supposed to wait here," I said.

Aaron glanced over at me from the viewing panel. "Do you think that's what the poem means?" he asked.

"That's my guess about this one stanza," I said. "It helps you face your enemy and searches out what seems empty, but if you wait and don't misread, you may avoid a slaughter." I paused to think about the "key" in the poem. "What if Linorra isn't supposed to be me?"

"How could that be?" he asked. "The character's name is too close to yours to be a fluke, and the plot matches. She travels to another world and finds a dragon." He gestured to himself.

I considered that. It made sense that he would be the dragon in the poem, even though I still thought of him as Bear Guy. And I couldn't deny that Linorra and Lina were very similar names. "Okay, maybe she is me, but what if the point of that was to trick Seleca? That's why Seleca didn't know about my Protection because the book keeps saying how Connection is her 'greatest gift.' Maybe that's what she means by 'don't misread'?"

"She probably just needed to buy us time," Aaron said. "Seleca absorbed Precognition from your unfortunate friend, so my mother's reservoir isn't going to help us much anymore, but it bought us time for you to learn how to use Protection."

"But that can't be all," I insisted. "I learned how to make the shield only seconds before I needed it. There must be something else that we're missing."

Aaron closed the last viewing panel and sat down next to me, reading the poem again. "I don't know," he said. "Maybe you're the key in the poem." He looked up sharply, remembering something. "Yes, I remember my mother saying that you were the *key* to helping me find my way back to my family."

"I was definitely covered in mud and blood," I agreed, cringing at how gross I had been. "And I helped you face your enemy earlier today, and then I sent Spirit out to search the empty house."

"But if you wait and don't misread, you may avoid a slaughter," Aaron read. "So, if we wait here, then our families will be safe?"

I reread the poem a few more times, wondering if that was the only part of the book that applied to us. We had come upon an empty house and were trying to decide what to do. I had to think Aaron's mother would have known that.

The rest of the book seemed designed to trick Seleca into thinking I only had a Connection reservoir, but now that she had Precognition, too, I doubted it would work. I worried our previous advantage, foresight, was now a moot point. I hoped that Aaron's mother had a plan for that, but I didn't know how she possibly could. At best, her gift would bring us to a draw. It was up to us now.

I put the book away and lay down on the bed, groaning as I stretched out on my belly. My feet and my back were killing me.

Aaron set the oil lamp down on a little table next to the bed, then sat on the bed next to me.

"Lina," he said.

"Hm?" I was already drifting off. I was so tired I thought I might pass out before he finished his sentence.

"Lina," he said again, a little louder.

I lifted my head, cracking one eye open to look at him. "Yeah?"

"I don't want you to drift out of your body again."

"Neither do I." I set my head down and closed my eyes again. "But I'm hoping that was partly an effect of the jarring weed."

"That may be," he said, "but I think I should sleep in the bed with you so I can stay connected to you and make sure you're still in there."

I suppressed a grin. I'm sure he really was worried about me, but I had already assumed he would sleep in the bed with me. He didn't need an excuse. "That does make sense," I said. "You are very wise."

Chapter Sixteen

Though neither knew it, Linorra and Syndeth had bonded in the way of their ancestors, before the dragons of Hartha had mysteriously disappeared. The more time they spent together, the more their souls intertwined like fibers spun into yarn.

I scooched over to one side of the mattress, then pulled the blanket out from under myself and kicked it down to the bottom of the bed so he could climb in. His warm body slid in next to mine smoothly. There were two other pillows, but they were both flat, so he stacked them behind his head as if he had done it a million times.

When he'd settled himself, he leaned over to place a metal plate on the oil lamp, then pulled the blanket over us as the light dwindled and went out. He stretched his arm behind me, and I turned to lie on my side so I could melt into him, resting my head on his shoulder. His incredible scent made me think about things I could be doing other than sleeping. I placed my hand on his chest, and he curled his warm hand over mine, connecting.

I had thought it would be pitch-black without the lamp, but the two moons shone down through the oculus, casting a pale red spotlight onto the floor next to the bed. There was enough light in the room that I could see Aaron's chest rising and falling. I closed my eyes, wanting to just feel him.

My awareness slid into him easily now, and the moment it happened, I was nearly overwhelmed by how aroused he was. He wanted to suppress it, but his heart raced, and he had to fight to control his breathing. He felt me notice and realized, with embarrassment, that he couldn't suppress anything with me right there in his arms. He was so hard that he would have to go masturbate somewhere or face another night of no sleep.

Sorry, he thought to me. *I can move over to the other side of the bed.*

Don't. It isn't bothering me. I liked it, in fact. I didn't send him that thought directly, but I suspected he knew. What I really wanted to do was run my hand down the length of his body and find out for myself how hard he was. I smiled, pleased that I could make his body react that way.

He took a deep breath in and out, then lifted his head a little to smell my hair.

"You smell so good," he whispered.

"I do?"

"Yes," he said, a little growl in his voice. He took another breath in and out. *It's too bad about the shirt*, he thought. I could feel the heat radiating from him as he thought about me in that shirt. I had to stick one leg out of the blanket to regulate my temperature, and he looked at it, swallowing hard. I resisted the urge to slide my leg on top of him and instead concentrated on relaxing every muscle in my body, one by one.

I closed my eyes and yawned, then remembered that I had done the same thing right before drifting out of my body. Aaron must have remembered, too, because he tensed, then squeezed my hand as if that would keep my spirit tethered to him.

"I can't spend the rest of my life not sleeping," I said, then thought, *It's now or never.*

Aaron stiffened, and I opened my eyes again to look at him, confused.

I meant now or never for sleeping, I thought, laughing a little at the misunderstanding. He'd thought I was telling him to make his move.

Oh, he thought, but he'd already worked himself up.

I knew what was coming, and he knew that I knew, but he needed a minute to think it through. I felt his minty breath on my face as I waited for him. It mixed with his natural scent, plus something flowery from his fresh tunic. The combination was intoxicating. I wanted to pull his tunic up and lick it off his body.

Finally, he repositioned himself on his side so that he faced me. I rolled to my back, opening my eyes again to meet his penetrating gaze. Through our Connection link, his emotions were a jumble of affection, excitement, fear of rejection, and awkwardness. He was still embarrassed at how he'd acted earlier, but his hunger for me outweighed his pride. It burned in his chest, pushing down into his belly and groin almost painfully.

It's because of the Evocation fragment, he thought. *It stirs things.* He leaned down to smell my hair again. *Lots of things.*

That makes sense. My body tensed with anticipation, and I renewed my effort to breathe and relax.

"Lina," Aaron said. "I need to explain something."

I hesitated, sensing that, whatever he was about to say, it would be difficult for him. "I'm listening," I said. I braced myself to hear something soul crushing, like, *Lina, I really want to use you like a blow-up doll but I'm not in a place to make a commitment. Is that okay?*

Aaron closed his eyes for a moment, took a deep breath, and opened them again. "I *feel* so much all the time that sometimes it's like a fire, scarcely contained within a hearth, always threatening to surge out and burn down everything around me. Being around others has always been difficult, but you . . . you're so calm. When that first dragon attacked us, I thought you would collapse from shock, but you just got up and kept going. When Seleca ambushed us, I expected you to run away and leave me to die, but you stood with me to face her. I . . . I am . . ." He closed his eyes, searching for words, then opened them again to gaze down at me. "I felt jealous once before, but it wasn't like this. This was more like rage, like—"

"Like someone burned your house down?" I guessed.

Aaron blew out a breath and sank his head into the pillow. "Yes, exactly. The thought of you with someone else makes me want to commit murder. Also, I'm sorry about your house. I should have said that sooner."

I stared at him, amazed. My soul remained uncrushed, but my heart was having a fit. No one had ever said anything like that to me before. Even after several years together, Drew had been loath to profess her feelings for me. Until it was too late, that is. Now here Aaron was, stating it plainly after two days. His face consumed every inch of my vision, his features in sharp focus despite the dim light.

"I would have been jealous, too," I said, "had I been in your place, but I promise that you don't need to be. Ward will never be anything more than a friend. I don't know exactly what's happening between us, but it's more than friendship."

Aaron caressed my cheek, then leaned down and gently brushed his lips against mine. The sensation made me shiver, and I let out a little sigh. He smiled at my reaction, and I felt his tongue tracing my bottom lip. I opened my mouth in response, and he bit my bottom lip gently, then pressed his mouth firmly onto mine.

This kiss was neither gentle nor patient, nor was it an attempt to simply claim. It was a probing, messy kiss that clearly said, *I want to be inside you*.

I had already decided I wanted him, and the way things were going, I didn't know if I'd get another chance. If Seleca and her Ministry cronies decided to attack us in the middle of the night, this might literally be my last chance with anyone. What can I say? I guess I just wanted to go out with a bang.

On the other hand, on the off chance that we made it through the night, I didn't want to surprise him with my sexual preferences after the fact. If I let my physical guard down too early only to find that I had wasted my time on a bigot, that could get ugly. He sensed my hesitation and pulled away to examine my face, disconnecting.

"Lina."

"Mm?"

"Are you sure you'd rather be up here with me than down there with Ward?"

I rolled my eyes before I could stop myself. "Aaron, there's something we need to discuss. Actually, there's more than one thing." Reluctantly, I pulled away from him and sat up. It had been a long day and my back lodged a complaint, but I needed to explain my situation to him, and I needed to do it without outing Ward before he was ready. I wasn't sure if that was even possible with our mental link, but I would try.

Divide his attention, Evilina suggested.

I unbuttoned the top button of that hateful dress and climbed on top of him. The move startled him, which was kind of the point. His eyes darted all over me, taking in every inch of my body as I settled on his hips, straddling him. His wound had scabbed over and would finish healing in a few days if left alone. I didn't intend to let that happen.

"Okay," I said. "You just bravely shared your feelings with me. Now it's my turn to explain something. First, I don't sleep next to people just to be nice. If I wanted to be down there with Ward, I would be." I unbuttoned another button and then another as he watched. We hadn't reconnected yet, but it wasn't difficult to guess what he felt.

"Is this okay?" I asked, gesturing to my position. He nodded, resting his hands on my thighs. "The second thing," I continued, "is a little harder to explain and a little more awkward, so I need to ask you a question first."

"What?" he asked, his eyes now fixed on my newly exposed cleavage.

"Do you know what the word 'queer' means?" I asked.

He nodded. "Unusual."

That's fair, I guess. "How about the word 'gay'?" I asked.

He nodded. "Yes, of course, it means happy, although it's an old word. What is this about, Lina?"

I groaned. This was not going well. "Okay, how about the word 'homosexual'?"

He stilled, squeezing his eyebrows together. Clearly that word was familiar, too, and he now seemed uneasy about where this conversation was going. I kept unbuttoning and despite his confusion, he dropped his eyes back down to watch my progress intently. The dress was now unbuttoned below the level of my breasts, but I held it closed with my hand.

"Well," I said, "where I come from, those words all mean a similar thing. Gay and homosexual are pretty much the same, but queer is a little broader, and includes people like me." His eyes snapped to mine, and he frowned.

"People like you?"

"Yes," I said. I took his hand and leaned forward so that he had to focus on my face. "I'm bisexual. I am attracted to all kinds of different people, including you. Very strongly to you, but my last serious relationship was with another woman." I let him absorb that for a moment before pushing back into a Connection link. Shocked, he stared into my eyes to see if I was serious.

"I'm serious," I said. "I need to know if it's something that will bother you. If it is, that's fine. I'll button this dress right back up and sleep over there. You should know, though, that it's common on Earth, and fairly well accepted, though not by everyone.

There are still people who think it's an abomination, although I don't think much of those people. I'm guessing that's how it's viewed here, and I'm concerned that, despite your disillusionment with the Ministry and their lies, you might feel the same way."

I took a deep breath, having gotten through the hardest part. "That would be a deal-breaker for me," I said, "because it's who I am. I'm never going to change, and I don't want to hide it from you. If you can accept this about me, we can move forward to the next thing. If you can't, tell me now." I sat up straight and let go of his hand, disconnecting to leave him alone with his decision.

Aaron shook his head a little. "You are sneaky and manipulative," he said.

"I know," I said, unbuttoning another one, then another. His eyes returned to my progress. I only had two buttons left. I tucked my feet underneath his thighs a little.

"I don't understand it," he said, tearing his eyes away from my chest up to my face, "but there are a lot of things I don't understand. You will probably have to be patient with me, but I am willing to listen. *Hard*."

My stomach did a little flip when he said the last word, and I smiled. "Oh, I think you made a joke," I said. "That's a good sign. Okay, I have another question."

He raised his eyebrows.

"Have you ever had sex before?"

He hesitated again, perhaps surprised by my bluntness. He pressed his mouth into a thin line, blinking a few times, but after a moment, he shook his head.

I nodded, my suspicion confirmed. I leaned over him again, pressing my hips gently into his body. The front of my dress was open almost enough to expose my breasts but not quite.

"I have," I said, studying his face. Since he'd excavated memories from my brain, I was sure he already knew that, but I wanted to be clear. If this was an oppressively conservative society, then there was a possibility that my lack of virginity would be a deal-breaker for him. If that was the case, it was better to learn sooner rather than later.

Because that, I thought resolutely, *would just be another form of rejecting my sexuality—something I cannot accept because it's the same as rejecting my humanity.*

Aaron waited for me to say something else, but I didn't. I didn't want to chase him, though I feared it was already too late for that. I hoped by being open and blunt I hadn't broken some kind of unspoken rule that only men and elderly women knew, but if I had, then so be it. I exhaled and lay on top of him, resting my cheek on his chest.

He took in a deep, steadying breath and let it out slowly. He shook a little, but he laid his hands on my back and hugged me to him. "That doesn't matter to me. Goddess, I want you, but I'm not ready to bond you to me, although I wouldn't discount it for the future."

"Bonding is like marriage, right?" I asked, lifting my head to stare at him.

"Yes, 'marriage' is the word my mother used. It's a lifelong commitment."

"That's what I thought," I murmured, nodding absently.

Had he really just said that he could see himself marrying me someday? I searched his eyes for the answer but found none. The reddish moonlight cast a beautifully warm light on the tanned skin of his face, but his expression gave nothing away, so I cheated by reconnecting again. That was exactly what he'd said.

"I'm not ready to bond to you either," I said, trying to keep my voice steady, "but what does that have to do with sex?" I made a face like I was very confused.

He gave me the *look* and said, "Lina, sex causes pregnancy. I wouldn't want you to—"

I laughed under my breath, shaking my head. "I know, Aaron, I was just kidding. But I have an IUD, another one of those Earth inventions. It prevents pregnancy, although normally I would need you to wear a condom anyway. I doubt you have those here and I didn't bring any, so there is some risk involved, but I've been tested for STIs recently, and you're a virgin, so I think we're good."

I was rambling, and he didn't seem like he understood a word of what I had just said. "Anyway, you don't have to worry about getting me pregnant. I swear." I held three fingers up in the Boy Scout salute, not that he knew what that meant, either, and held my breath.

Aaron's brow furrowed, then his expression transformed into something simultaneously enthusiastic and incredulous as he worked through the reasoning. Connection told him that I was truthful, but he still had to weigh the possibility that I might be wrong.

I rested my head against him again and released my breath, feeling his chest rise and fall while he decided. We were only superficially connected, so I didn't hear his thoughts, but I guessed that he asked himself if the pregnancy risk was worth it.

It took for-freaking-ever. As I had noted before, Aaron liked to take his time to think things through. I lay against him as he caressed my hair, thinking. His touch sent electricity straight to my core, and I could feel his erection trapped between us. It was all I could do not to reach down and stroke him.

"Okay," he whispered.

I let him hug me for a moment more, then I pushed myself back and sat up again. "Okay," I repeated, "then touch me." I took his right hand and placed it on my breastbone. His hand was hot, but the room was chilly. I let the heat seep into me, absorbing it like a sponge. The heat filled my chest, pushing down to the base of my spine. I connected to him through the touch and whispered, "Can I come in?"

He let me into a deep connection, and I immediately felt his powerful desire for me. It really wasn't fair, to be honest. There hadn't been much chance that he would say no, though his restraint was impressive given how painfully hard he was just from me sitting on top of him.

I could hear his thoughts now, and they were all variations on the same theme. *Oh, Goddess. This is amazing, but what do I do?* He had only seen breasts once before, and that was by accident when he was a kid.

Just touch me, I thought to him. *Put your mouth on me. Start gentle and end rough.* They were words of a sort, but they were infused with heat and mixed with images of what I wanted him to do to me, where I wanted his hands, his lips, his tongue, his teeth.

I took his other hand and molded his fingers around the fabric of my dress, sending the image of him pulling it open. He complied, pulling the fabric to the side, and I felt his reaction to seeing my breasts for the first time. His lips parted and his breath turned ragged. He was imagining tearing my dress all the way off. I wasn't opposed. I hated that thing.

He slid his hand down to one breast, running his palm lightly over it. The touch sent a shiver through my whole body, and he felt it too. I felt him feeling it, like a feedback loop.

Wow, this is going to be good, I thought and let out a short, breathless laugh.

This clearly broke some kind of spell because he took charge then, lifting my whole body off him as if I were no heavier than a throw pillow. He rolled me to my back so he could hover over me, pressing his mouth back to mine. I spread my knees apart and pulled his hips down. He relaxed against me, his solid form on top of me like a weighted blanket. Despite everything, I had never felt safer than I did right there underneath his body.

"Lina," Aaron whispered. He said my name like a prayer, reverent and suppliant. The sound of it sent an unexpected jolt through me and I moaned a little, grasping at his tunic. His mouth found my neck, then he lifted himself to pull my dress over my head.

My one set of undergarments was washed with my other clothes and laid out to dry. He hadn't known that I wore nothing underneath, and he stopped to stare. I let him stare, then stuck my toes underneath his tunic and ran them from his leg up to his hip, reconnecting, and also learning that he wasn't wearing anything under his tunic either. He reached down and tugged it off, flinging it to the side.

He was leaner than I had imagined. He was naturally a large person and broad, at least by Earth standards, but he wasn't built like a bodybuilder. He looked like a man who had been living off the land, eating just enough to get by and doing lots of manual labor. His chest was lightly covered in black hair, and he had a pronounced farmer's tan, though his palest skin was still darker than mine ever got. He was uncircumcised. I stared openly, wondering how much I could get in my mouth.

Only one way to find out.

He knelt there in front of me while I contemplated that, sending the image to him. He closed his eyes, imagining it, then lay down on top of me, pressing his naked skin against mine. His skin was just short of too hot.

He moved his mouth down to my neck again, then farther down to my breasts and belly. I let my head fall back to bask in the heat of his mouth. He wanted to take his time and worship every inch of my body, doing all the things I had showed him I wanted, but he felt my pleasure too intensely through our link, which made it difficult for him to slow down.

A short little growl escaped his tight control, which made me grin up at the ceiling. *Bear Guy is growling at me*, I thought.

His eyes locked onto mine, one corner of his mouth ticking up. *Bear Guy*, he thought, shaking his head. He moved his mouth back up to mine and settled between my legs, rocking his hips gently back and forth until I ached to push him inside.

Instead, I did something that I belatedly understood he'd been fantasizing about since the first moment he saw me, something that had previously filled him with so much shame that he'd been enraged by it. Despite my disheveled state and his resentment over years of isolation, he had wanted me to touch him so badly that he'd seriously considered leaving me out there in the woods to escape. He was ecstatic that he'd suppressed that impulse.

I slid my hand over his hip, continued down his thigh, then back up between his legs. I stroked him, and he pulled his mouth away and dropped his head back, making a sound like he'd set down something heavy. His voice vibrated through me, and I pulsed with need for him.

Tell me what you want, I thought to him, sending him images of his options.

He gazed into my eyes and thought, *There's time for all those things later. Right now, I just want to be inside you.*

I want that too, I thought to him, relieved.

I stroked him a few more times, then guided him carefully to the correct angle. Once the path was assured, he lowered himself down on top of me, pushing inside me deeply with a loud groan.

I gasped, then I wrapped my legs tightly around him. I closed my eyes and relaxed back, taking in the feeling. He did the same, drinking in the experience of being completely connected to me in mind and body.

He kissed me gently on the lips and neck, barely moving his hips. I glanced up at the healing wound above his eye and decided that now was the time. I sent my intention to him, and he agreed, so I pushed Protection into him, directing it toward that wound again. He moaned loudly, then began thrusting in earnest.

I opened myself up fully to his need, letting him take control. He pinned one of my hands above my head, and I had the other in his hair. It was still damp and fell loosely around his head in dark waves.

I can't believe how good this feels, he thought over and over. *It's so good. It's so good. It's so good.* I felt the sensations of his body as if they were my own, and they were as much a part of my experience as those of my own body.

He closed his eyes and gave in to the pleasure, kissing me as he pressed into me again and again, just as I pressed my energy into him. He held nothing back, and I didn't think it would take either of us long to climax. I suspected that our experiences were so entangled that I would have little choice but to be carried along with the tide.

Unfortunately, his wound chose that moment to finish healing. The scab fell off, landing on my forehead, almost in my eye, which broke my concentration and grossed me out a little. I tensed, unsure what to do. Aaron paused to see what had happened, then he laughed absurdly hard.

"Rude," I said, but he sounded so happy that I couldn't even bring myself to be annoyed. His deep belly laugh was a rare hymn.

"At least it's not pus this time," he responded and broke up again, shaking the whole bed.

"This is quite the romantic start we've got going here," I commented.

He struggled to contain himself, then picked the icky little thing off my face and tossed it off the side of the bed. "Sorry," he said. Then he kissed me again and restarted his rhythm.

"What would happen if I kept pushing Protection into you?" I asked.

"I don't know. Nothing, I think. You can try."

I did. At first, it seemed like he was right. He could feel it, and it still felt incredible, enhancing his pleasure and subsequently my own, but the energy didn't pass through him or come back to me. Instead, it accumulated.

I should stop, I thought.

Not yet.

The unused Protection fragment sought a new target and, not finding one, became a diffuse energy that seeped into every cell of his body. After a minute or two, Aaron glowed with a faintly aqua-colored light. In fact, we were both glowing.

He paused briefly to gaze at his own hand, holding it up to his face just as I had the first time. He let out a short laugh then resumed thrusting. He looked back down at my face and thought to me, *I want to try sending it back to you.*

I nodded and closed my eyes, letting my head rest back again. With a grunt of effort, he pushed Protection back into me from the newly enhanced reservoir that had collected within him, and the feeling was just like what I had experienced in the portal. The pleasure was so intense that I involuntarily cried out. It was as sharp as pain, and I arched my back in response.

He felt it through Connection, just as I had, and it drove him into a frenzy, which was only heightened when the fragment flowed back into him from me a moment later. His speed increased to his maximum, and the room became brighter than day as we continued transferring the Protection fragment back and forth, building with each cycle.

The noise we made when that frag bomb finally detonated was probably heard on Earth. Aaron felt it coming and propped himself up on straight arms for leverage, then threw his head back, his entire body rigid. He was inside me as deeply as he would go, paralyzed by the intensity of his orgasm.

I was dragged willingly into the climax with him, overwhelmed by a feeling of not only pleasure but wholeness. Out of nowhere, my perception of reality bent and twisted, like an intense episode of déjà vu. My awareness expanded, allowing me to see my life as a river. It connected to an extracorporeal part of myself that I instinctively recognized but hadn't been consciously aware of. I felt a Oneness with Aaron that existed in some space outside of physical reality, and for an instant, I caught a glimpse of myself outside of the constraints of time. The moment was over before I could process it, but I was left with the certainty that our paths had not crossed by accident.

Aaron had explained to me that his mother, Violet, predicted our meeting, but I didn't comprehend until that moment the significance of the event. The outcome of our relationship would have momentous consequences not only for us, but also for everyone we knew and loved. If I hadn't been in the middle of a mind-blowing orgasm, I would have been scared shitless.

The Protection fragment surged and subsided, then surged and subsided again, like a pulse. It finished cycling through us one last time, then dissipated. The room dimmed, and we clung to each other for a few more seconds. Aaron slowly pulled out and slid off to the side like a jellyfish, one leg still draped over me. We were both drenched in sweat and breathing hard. We lay there for a long time, panting.

I had never had sex like that before. The use of fragmental energy had turned the experience into something much more profound than just physical gratification. It had been a spiritual experience that had moved me and made me question my entire life's purpose.

"I don't even know what that was," I said, "but it was worth risking the pit for."

Aaron burst out laughing, joy radiating out from him like Evocation heat. "Good?" he asked, though he knew the answer.

I laughed even as tears streamed down my cheeks. "Yes," I said, still catching my breath. "Understatement. Fragment sex. Holy crap. That was just . . ." I shook my head. I couldn't think of a word that described it.

"The very essence of perfection," he said in that deep voice.

I laughed again, almost hysterical. *Jesus, I need to get ahold of myself.* "Yes," I said, "and your memory is too good. I need to watch what I say to you a little better."

"You don't," he said seriously and hugged me to him.

"Good," I said. "I was bluffing anyway. I'm going to fall asleep now. Poke me if I accidentally die."

"That's not funny," he mumbled, "and I already did that. Maybe tomorrow."

I grinned, surprised that he'd made another joke, then snuggled into him and closed my eyes. *You sure did*, I thought.

"I glowed," he said.

I opened one eye and peered up at him. "Yes, and then you actively used Protection. Have you ever done that before?"

"No," he said. "At first, it was similar to when you pulled me into the shield, but then I was able to take control of it, like I do with Evocation."

"I think I gave it to you," I mumbled, closing my eyes again. "Maybe now you'll live forever. You're welcome."

Aaron kissed my forehead and mumbled something, but I was almost asleep and couldn't retain it. I could feel him, though. He was full of wonder, gratitude, and possessiveness. He squeezed me a little and thought, *Mine.*

We'll see, Bear Guy, I thought. *We'll see.*

Chapter Seventeen

Linorra thought about what the witch told her. If what she said was right, then she needed to find her lost love. He was her future husband and would someday give her a son, and then a daughter.

I woke up, which was a relief. Aaron lay next to me, which was also a relief. I had no idea if I had slept an hour or all night, but no light came in through the oculus. I missed my phone.

Aaron had migrated to the other side of the bed, taking the blanket with him. We were both still naked, and the air had cooled to an uncomfortable briskness. I shivered, wondering if I could find something dry to wear in Jorin's closet. I had no intention of putting that weird dress on ever again.

I wondered how Ward was doing and how much apologizing I would have to do about all the noise we'd made the night before.

I sat up, glancing around, but I was nearly blind in the dark room. My regular clothes, I knew, were laid out to dry over the counter, but I couldn't see them.

Aaron stirred next to me and his breathing changed from regular, shallow breaths to ones that were slow and deep, but I couldn't tell if he was awake. *Thank the multiverse he doesn't snore*, I thought, smiling to myself. I was so happy to wake up next to him. I just hoped he would feel the same way.

"He will," Spirit said, startling me. Again, she appeared on the bed in a spotlight, looking as if Heshia and Ishkar shone down from above just for her. She was luminous and beautiful and staring at my naked body with obvious interest.

"Any news?" I asked, finding a bit of blanket. I pulled on it, but Aaron had it tucked underneath him like he was in a cocoon.

"Seleca went back to her mother's palace and went to sleep," she said. "She's still sleeping, and, by the way, she has your phone."

"What?" I asked. I don't know why I was surprised.

"She stole your phone. I'd recognize that ugly orange thing anywhere," she said.

"I'm a Giants fan, so sue me," I said. "Why did she steal my phone? What could she possibly want with it? It doesn't even work here." *And how the hell did she get my password?*

"She looked through your pictures while she waited at your house," she said, "and she figured out how to play *Candy Crush*. Now it's dead, and she has no way of charging it until she goes back to Earth. She got really mad when it died and cracked the screen."

I sighed. *My poor phone.* I shook my fist in the air and whispered, a little too loudly, "I will avenge you, Luigi!"

Aaron repositioned himself in bed.

"That girl needs black tourmaline in the worst way," Spirit said.

"She needs a psychiatrist. And what is that?" I whispered.

"It's a crystal," she said, "a mood stabilizer, and it repels negative energy."

I chuckled. "Spirit, I love you, but that stuff with the crystals is insane."

"Lina, if you would open your mind a little bit, I think they would help both you and Aaron. Especially Aaron," she said. "Besides, a few days ago, you would have said fragments were insane, and now look at you. You're literally talking to a ghost."

She had a point, and Spirit was always smarter than people gave her credit for. In fact, she was brilliant. She had a degree in bioengineering from UC Berkeley and had been accepted into their PhD program. Smart and hot and very dead.

"Okay, what should I do?" I asked.

"Dump your bag out," she said.

"What?" I asked, confused.

"You heard me. Dump your bag out," she repeated.

"Okay, but let me get dressed first, at least." I reached down to my pack, which still sat on the floor on my side of the bed, and fumbled for the flashlight. It wasn't in the little holder where it should be. "Great, now I'll never find it," I said.

"What's wrong?" Aaron asked.

"Sorry, did I wake you?"

He took a breath in and out. "I'm a light sleeper," he said.

That wasn't a no.

"I can't find my flashlight and I don't have your super night vision. I want to get dressed," I said.

"Don't," he said. "Just come back over here with me." He leaned over and took my hand, gently tugging me toward him. I connected to him and immediately knew that he was *up* and ready to try some of those things we'd hastily skipped past the night before.

I seriously considered it. I mean, I was cold, and wouldn't it be great if I could just lie back and spend the whole day fragging Aaron?

Yeah, I said it. It's a word now.

Somehow, I resisted his magnetic pull and said, "Aaron, Spirit is here."

"Oh," he said, letting go of my hand. I heard the rustle of a blanket and guessed he was covering up a growing problem. I couldn't see what he was doing, but I could feel movement in the bed, and then that stupid scratchy dress hit me in the face.

"Um, no," I said. "The only good thing about this dress is how it felt when you ripped it off me. I'm never wearing this thing again." I threw it back at him and missed.

"Wow, you really can't see anything, can you?" he said, chuckling.

Instead of responding, I just sighed melodramatically.

"You could go naked," he continued. "I would be completely fine with that."

"Ha-ha. Ho-ho," I said flatly. "I want my clothes. Are you going to help me or not?"

"Lee, you should really stop wearing those. The pants are too tight. It's indecent."

"You just said I should go naked," I countered. "And did you just call me Lee?"

Aaron grunted, as if that were an informative response. I stood up from the bed and crouched next to where I knew my bag sat. I found the zipper and opened it, deciding to blindly feel around for the flashlight. I heard Aaron get up from the bed and saunter over creaky floorboards to where I knew the counter was located.

"They're still wet," he said.

I sagged a little. "The naked thing sounds fine, I guess. I'm sure Ward will get used to it." I continued searching for the flashlight. My hand found something hard and cylindrical. "Oh, is this it?" I felt for the button and clicked the flashlight on.

"Ha!" I said, standing up, then turning to see that Aaron was unexpectedly right behind me, causing me to jump in surprise. "Ak! Aaron, will you *stop* doing that? I'm going to kill you."

He laughed quietly, wrapped his arms around me, and pulled me into his warm body. It was like stepping into a sauna after a cold swim. I groaned a little and melted into him.

"Ask Spirit to give us some time," he said. "I want to lie in bed with you a little longer. Please, *Lee*." He emphasized what was apparently my new nickname, then he bent down, kissed my neck, and slid his warm hand from the base of my spine up to the back of my neck like he had the first time we'd kissed. The man remembered everything.

I relented. Something about how hot his mouth was made me want to give him whatever he wanted. "Okay. Spirit, did you hear that?"

"Yes," she whispered into Aaron's ear, surprising the crap out of him through our Connection link. He whipped his head around, accidentally pushing me backward. I tripped over my bag and fell onto the bed, laughing.

"Serves you right, you big bully," I said. "Never mess with the ghost whisperer."

His link with me broke when I fell, so he couldn't hear Spirit laughing her head off behind him. She had the cutest little giggly laugh.

"Spirit, will you please give us some time?" I asked. "At least until sunrise. Check the farm for intruders, go check on Ward, then go check on our enemies and report back in a couple hours. Can you do that?"

"Yes," she said, sounding mildly offended. "Although it won't take me more than a second. When you're done *fragging* this one, dump your bag out and look through it." Then she was gone. Had she picked that word out of my head? That was unsettling. Maybe she came up with it on her own. And why the swift change in mood? I decided to set that aside to focus on the naked man stalking toward me.

"You're going to pay for that," he said as he crawled on top of me and pinned me down, beginning an encore of our previous performance, only more elaborate and diverse. It was a rather all-consuming activity, and I forgot about Spirit's directive to go pack spelunking.

We emerged from our shared cocoon a few hours later when sunlight finally lit the room from above. I was nervous to leave the attic and talk to Ward after the obvious kind of night we'd had, but it had to be done.

"What are you worried about?" Aaron asked, sitting up. He watched as I slipped out of bed to pad over to my still-damp clothing.

Somehow, the tables had turned, and I was now the one embarrassed by my overt sexual activity. It was possible that, despite my posturing about not letting society tell me when or with whom to have sex, I was slightly self-conscious about how quickly I had jumped into bed with him.

With no condom. *Jesus.*

I face-palmed before I could stop myself. I worried the whole thing would blow up in my face and I'd be on my own, trying to get home. Or worse, alone in fighting a crazy, house-burning cult.

"I don't want Ward to feel like he's alone while we're up here having the time of our lives," I said, picking up my underwear. It was mostly dry. I decided that I could live with it. I felt strangely bashful as Aaron watched me get dressed.

My response to his question had been a bit misleading. It was true that I worried about Ward's mental health, but I also worried about getting attached to Aaron and then being abandoned. What we'd experienced together the night before had been something extraordinary, but the memory of my déjà vu moment was already fading like a dream. I didn't even know if Aaron had felt the same thing I had.

Don't get me wrong; in theory, I'm fine with being alone. I made my peace with that probability a long time ago, or at least I vowed to make my peace with it, but even someone as independent as me is still vulnerable to the sting of rejection. I knew I could trust Aaron to be upfront and honest. I just didn't know if I could trust myself not to care if he pulled a Drew and decided that I was a stepping stone to better things.

He got out of bed and walked toward me as I slipped my jog bra over my head and pulled it down. His hands brushed down my shoulders and he hugged me from behind, pulling me into a superficial Connection link. Apparently, he could do that now. He was still naked, and his heated skin felt good against my back. I groaned a little, letting my head fall forward. He kissed the back of my head.

"What are you actually worried about?" he asked. I narrowed my eyes and looked over my shoulder at him. He towered over me. I'm not short for an Earth woman. I'm five-eight but, next to him, I could represent the Lollipop Guild.

"Why are you so smart?" I asked. "Why can't you be completely lacking in empathic talent like every other person I've ever . . ." I was about to say "slept with" but caught myself. The last thing I needed right now was to accidentally facilitate the old *How many people have you slept with?* discussion. My number was not small.

"Slept with?" he finished for me anyway.

Dammit.

"And how many of those would there be?" he asked.

Dammit! "I really have to go use the facilities," I said. "Can we talk about this later?"

"Fine. Go water a tree," he said, chuckling. "You're off the hook." He let go, turning to find his own clothes.

I shivered from the loss of his warmth but breathed a sigh of relief and pulled my shirt over my head. I just hung my pants over my shoulder. No time for that nonsense.

I managed to get the trapdoor unlocked, but before I opened it, I paused to regard Aaron.

"Aaron," I said.

"Mm?" He turned back to face me. He'd found a black tunic and donned it. He looked uneasy. I wondered if he thought I was the one abandoning *him*.

"What we did last night . . . that was a first for me. I've never felt anything like that before. I want to do that with you a million more times."

Aaron stilled, his eyes shining. "A million would take a very long time," he said.

I nodded, a smile spreading over my face. "Yes, it would."

Aaron's eyes crinkled at the corners and his mouth twitched. He nodded. "Sounds like a plan."

Yes, I thought, quashing the tremendous joy that threatened to burst out of me like a confetti popper. *It does. Shit. This truly is something real.* I turned back to the trapdoor, carefully lowered the ladder, and gasped as it slid right out of my hand to bang down on the floor with a *crack*. Oops.

"Good morning, Ward," I called. No response. "Ward?" There wasn't enough light for me to see down into the closet.

I tested the stability of the ladder with my bare foot and crept down. I got down to the bottom of the ladder, stepped into the dark closet, and squinted around. I didn't see or hear anything. Aaron came down the ladder after me. He could see just fine. Jerk.

"He's not down here," he said.

That was concerning. What if nighttime visitors had sneaked in and found him? "Maybe we drove him away with our racket."

"Likely," he said, a smug smile on his face. He still didn't know that Ward was gay, and he probably felt a sense of triumph. How would he feel when he found out that the competition was all in his mind? Possibly like he had overvalued my stock.

He cracked the closet door open, stopping to listen as always while I squirmed impatiently behind him. Finally, he opened the door all the way, poking his head out. He had clearly done this many times as he knew exactly how to silently and quickly open and close the hidden closet door within the wardrobe.

We stepped through the outer closet door and into Jorin's bedroom. It was a small space with an extra-long single bed, a desk, and the closet we'd sneaked out of. A large window with white curtains let in dim light. The room was empty of both people and character. I had a feeling that making the bedroom as boring as possible was deliberate.

Aaron stopped to listen for another minute at the bedroom door, then he led me to the tiny bathroom. A chorus of chirping crickets echoed up through the drain I was supposed to squat over, and I imagined one of them jumping up and hitting me right in the crotch. I cringed, but I did what I had to do. Aaron stood guard outside of the door, then told me to wait there while he searched the rest of the house. The feminist in me balked at that directive, but the pragmatist was perfectly happy to wait.

I called for Spirit to search the house too. "Ward's on the downstairs couch," she said.

"Oh, I guess we really did drive him away with our racket," I said. Spirit didn't respond. *Jealous?*

I'm not jealous, she thought to me.

I puffed out a breath. *Spirit, can you hear all my thoughts? Even the ones I don't direct at you?*

Yes, she thought to me.

I gawked. I hadn't expected her to just admit it like that. *Oh, that's just great. I don't get to have private thoughts ever again, I guess.* Then I thought about that for a second. *Wait, can you hear everyone's thoughts or just mine?*

She gave me a sly smile.

Everyone? I guessed, my eyes widening.

She nodded. *FYI, Aaron has a very dirty mind. So does Ward. He got so turned on by the sound of Aaron moaning that he sneaked down to the bathroom and masturbated for the first time in ten years, right into that drain.*

I looked down at my bare feet and cringed again. *Eeew! Why did you tell me that?* I hadn't thought to put my shoes on before I came down the ladder. This world had an extremely irritating learning curve.

Spirit let out one of her delightful little giggles.

Oh, shut up, I thought to her, but couldn't help the smile that spread over my face at the sound of her laugh. It was infectious.

The good news is that he rinsed the drain area afterward, she thought to me. *The bad news is that he feels guilty about wanting to sex up your boyfriend, and the depression is hitting him pretty hard. He's spending a lot of time thinking about how great it was to be dead.*

I was afraid of that. I would need to brainstorm solutions to the Ward problem. At the very least, I needed to counsel him on why gay guilt was unnecessary and pointless. Maybe I could get him back to Earth and set him up with someone. What he really needed, though, was a professional therapist. I probably wouldn't cut it. Actually, we probably both needed a therapist.

Wait, I thought to her again, *you can send thoughts to me from your mind. Could you send other people's thoughts to me so I could hear what they're thinking, directly from them?*

Spirit thought about it. *I'm not sure. Aaron's downstairs berating Ward as we speak. Let's go practice, shall we?* She flashed me those bright white teeth.

I nodded. *Can you check the grounds for intruders again first?*

She blinked out and then back in again. "Nobody's around," she said aloud.

"Okay, let's go."

I came down the stairs to find Aaron speaking quietly with Ward, who lay on the green couch I'd seen on my way in the night before. Ward must have thought the couch seemed as comfortable as I had imagined it to be. A blanket covered him, and he definitely appeared to have slept there.

"You look cozy," I said.

You look like you've been having sex all night, I heard Ward's voice say in my head. I jumped in surprise. The words had been unexpectedly harsh and brimming with jealousy. It was so intense that I reflexively took a step back, unsure how to proceed. He wasn't angry, exactly, but he was definitely upset, and this was more than jealousy over a sexual encounter. This felt more like unrequited love.

Oh no.

I guess it works, Spirit thought to me, smiling.

I didn't share her amusement. Ward had spent quite a bit of time with Aaron as Rogue. He had learned from living with me that being gay wasn't wrong, and then he went to live with Aaron. Beautiful, traditionally masculine Aaron, with his caramel skin and his bright blue eyes and those strong hands that could light the world on fire. I lifted my hand to my mouth to cover my shock. Aaron still spoke to Ward, but Ward wasn't listening. He stared at me with those amber eyes, always so impossibly aware.

Does he know I can hear him? I asked, my heart twisting in my chest.

She narrowed her eyes at Ward as if she wasn't sure, then shook her head. *I don't think so, but he suspects something is amiss.*

I felt my eyebrows climbing up to my hairline. *This might come in handy at some point, but I'm not sure I should be doing it right now.*

Ward's gaze shifted to Aaron as he thought, *I wish I'd been having sex with him all night instead of*... then I saw his memory of what he had done instead, and my hands came up to my face in protest.

Stop, Spirit! I don't want to know any more. Jesus. This is intrusive. I need to not do this to my friend.

The vision disappeared and Spirit burst out into another round of giggles. I gave her a flat stare. As it turned out, there *had* been a competition going on after all, but it had been over Aaron, not me. I had known Ward was gay, but the revelation that he was in love with Aaron was startling. I wasn't sure that covering my face with my hand was enough to cover my shock, so I turned away from them.

"I need to, um, go organize my hiking pack," I said. "I'll let you men hash this out."

I headed back for the stairs, glancing around the great room as I did. The walls were all lined with large, curtainless windows. The morning light streamed in to reveal the same level of craftsmanship I had seen in the attic. There was a long, rather Brobdingnagian table where we'd eaten the night before. It had been like sitting up at a high bar rather than a dinner table.

Though the room was much more understated than the attic had been, it seemed like someone had lovingly applied planks to the floor and walls to create a seamless expanse of rich hardwood. A woodburning stove rose up to the ceiling in the corner with large, cushioned chairs arranged around it. The room was simple yet rich with warmth and practicality. It was as if the love of many generations was infused directly into the fabric of the house. I loved it, but it made me think of my own home, now reduced to ashes.

Mom. Dad. Where are you? Please be safe.

I looked over my shoulder as I trotted up the stairs and said, "Ward, will you spend some time with me today? I need your help with something."

Both men turned to me. Ward said, "Of course." Aaron narrowed his eyes at me and looked back at Ward, pensive.

Wow, I can't even talk to Ward without him getting jealous. Ward is jealous of me. Aaron is jealous of Ward. This is getting out of hand. Spirit, do you have any ideas?

Yeah, dump out your bag, she thought to me.

Oh, yeah, I forgot about that.

Of course, you did, she thought back. *Multiple orgasms will do that.*

It was only two, I thought to her, and then I remembered that two had been the same number she had given me. The memory flashed through my mind before I could stop it, and I thought, *I can't believe I'll never get to do that again.* I knew she heard my thoughts, but she didn't comment. I pushed the thought away. *Okay, I'll go get my bag.*

Chapter Eighteen

And she knew all of Emeris was connected by the threads of creation just as she was connected to Syndeth. She saw the threads with her eyes when she used the key, and with her heart when she flew astride her friend's back.

I made my way to the hidden closet, though I had more trouble opening the door than Aaron had. I climbed up the ladder and into the attic, then reached for my hiking pack. At long last, I sat down and dumped the contents out on the floor into a pile.

An extra pair of socks and underwear landed on my knee, which made me laugh. I also found the bear spray, which I had forgotten about, and which also made me laugh. I attached it to the quick-release strap, where I'd had it for two years. There was a small ziplock bag with cords, one of which had the solar charger and cord that were meant to connect to my phone. The attachment for my watch was also in there. I didn't remember packing that. I found the watch and attached it to the charger, then set it in the little sunny patch in the middle of the floor.

The water bottle was empty, but there were five granola bars left. My keys were in there, a credit card with a twenty-dollar bill wrapped around it and secured with a rubber band, the first aid kit, the useless satellite GPS, extra batteries, the leash and collar, and the book. Still no freaking toothpaste.

I stuck my hand into the bottom of the pack to see if anything was left in there that hadn't fallen out. I wrapped my hand around a piece of cloth and yanked on it, pulling out a windbreaker scrunched up into a ball. It was my waterproof, fleece-lined Columbia jacket.

I could have used this last night. I wish I'd known it was in there.

I poked my nose into the bag again to make sure I hadn't missed anything else, and to my surprise, I found a small survival kit stuffed in the very bottom. It had a lighter, a silver emergency blanket, a windup radio with a compass, an orange whistle, a small bottle of sunscreen, a LifeStraw, and a Leatherman multitool. I didn't remember putting any of that in there either. It was almost as if I hadn't been the one to pack the bag at all.

"What the hell?" I said. "Spirit, are you here?"

"Yeah," she said. She appeared across from the pile of belongings, sitting cross-legged. "So, you finally found the treasure hoard."

"What? You knew this was in here the whole time? Why didn't you tell me?" I asked.

Spirit snort-laughed. "It's your own fault you never listen to me."

"Oh, come on, that's not true. I value your opinion."

Spirit shot me a dubious expression. "No, you don't. You just like me for my body."

I smiled at her. "Can you blame me? You're pretty much the hottest girl I've ever been with. By, like, a lot."

"Really?" she asked, seeming genuinely surprised.

I gave her the *look*. "Are you kidding? Please. You're the hottest girl *anyone* has ever been with. I was so jealous of those Jermez twins that I ran out of the house and jumped into an interdimensional portal."

Spirit grinned. "Not interdimensional. As far as I know, there's only one interdimensional portal around here, and you have to be dead to go through it."

"Right," I said. "The death bridge. That's so interesting. How far away are we from Earth right now?"

Spirit responded in her best McCoy voice: "Dammit, Lina, I'm a ghost, not an astronomer!"

I laughed. "You know, Bones never actually said the word 'damn' on that show, right? That phrase is a myth."

"Okay, Grandma, tell me some more ancient TV trivia."

"I think the word you're looking for is 'classic.' It's *classic* TV trivia," I said.

"Whatever. Unlike you, I was born *this* century. Keep searching through your mess of stuff. There's one more thing under there," she said.

"Oh, the survival kit wasn't the surprise? By the way, how did you know that was in there?" I asked.

Spirit smirked but didn't answer.

"Oh, it's like that? Okay." I didn't see anything, so I picked everything up one more time, shaking it. When I shook the socks, a beaded bracelet fell out. It had a mix of what looked like pea-sized stones. "What's this?" I asked.

"I made that for you, but I wasn't sure why at the time, especially since you don't really wear jewelry. But you know how crazy accurate my intuition has always been. It turns out I had actual magical powers, which I always suspected, of course. So, I made it anyway, and now I think Aaron is the one who needs it. You should give it to him."

"Why?" I asked.

"The stones are mostly Mexican fire agate, the real kind. See the iridescence?"

I nodded, holding the bracelet up to the light. They were a deep orange red, almost brown, with subtle little bubbles of rainbow that shone out when the light reflected off them.

"Fragments are never perfectly contained in a reservoir," Spirit explained. "They have a tendency to bleed out a little. The fire agate will absorb some of the ambient Evocation fragment that's causing Aaron to lose control of his emotions, but he can also pull that back out and use it if he needs to. It's kind of like an external reservoir for him. The blue ones are rough aquamarine," she continued. "Not the clear kind you see in jewelry, but the kind with inclusions, which is why they're more like stones than crystals. Those will bolster his Protection reservoir and calm him down a little."

"Wow, Spirit. This is perfect. Thank you so much." I looked up at her. She wasn't smiling anymore.

"You're welcome," she said, staring down at her hands. I gave her a minute to collect her thoughts.

"What's it like, Spirit?" I asked. "Being dead?"

"It's not that bad," she said, then bit her bottom lip. "It's kind of nice, actually. Sort of worry-free in a way, but instead of feeling things, you have to know things. Knowledge is its own kind of magic, you know. Once you know something, it changes you. Everything you discover while you're on that side will come over with you to this side because it becomes a part of you, a part of your . . . spirit, I guess."

"Knowledge changes your spirit," I repeated. "Like what Aaron learned when he looked into me."

"He looked into you?"

"Oh, so you don't know everything then?"

Spirit smiled. "Of course not. I observe. I listen. I experience, but I am not God, at least not all of God."

"Is there one, Spirit? A god, or maybe a goddess?" I turned back to her in anticipation of some kind of profound knowledge. Spirit had always had a way of dropping truth bombs on me, and it usually left me a better person.

She narrowed her eyes at me, debating. "Yes and no."

I groaned. "Okay, when you paused to think, were you trying to decide what would be the most frustrating answer? Because you nailed it."

She laughed. "Lina, it's not as simple as yes or no. God is an idea born in the minds of humans, as is the idea of the spirit. Are they what people think? Not exactly, except in that the idea itself, which is a form of knowledge or awareness, exists. So, is there something? Sort of, but it's not one thing, or at least not only one thing. It is at once whole and fragmented."

I'm sure I was giving her a blank stare, but I had nothing else to offer to what she'd just said, so that's what I went with. It was a valid choice.

"Look," she continued. "It's not like there's a ghost manual or something, but from what I can tell, your spirit is the part of you that exists over time. It is the you that was, is, and will be. It's like, a person can only die at a single point in time, but existence itself is not a single point in time. It isn't a line or even three-dimensional or four-dimensional."

Four-dimensional? You lost me.

Spirit rolled her eyes, then continued as if she hadn't heard my thoughts. "Existence is infinite. Your spirit stretches into the past and future simultaneously because time isn't linear as we experience it while alive. The spirit isn't time-locked like the body. It is infinite in all directions, just like existence. In fact, from over here, it almost seems like time and existence are the same thing. Therefore, there is a part of you that exists now, but that part is connected to the part that stretches to infinity through time.

"That is what God is too. God is everything that is, has been, will be, could be, and couldn't be. It is all things, all existence at every point in time and outside of it. At least, that's what I think. Like I said, no manual." She sniffed. "I could be wrong, of course."

"Holy shit, Spirit," I said. "You are blowing my mind as always. So unfair that you were both hotter and smarter than me."

"Still am," she said, winking at me.

I laughed. "True, but that's not really much to brag about." I turned back to examining the beaded bracelet.

"Not true," she said. "I think, if I had made it a little further, you and I could have been something."

I slipped the bracelet onto my wrist and turned my full attention to her.

"Me too," I said.

She gave me another sad smile. "The twins were my second choice, you know," she said. "I waited for you, but you had things to do with Drew, so I settled. Even after we left, I still hoped that you would knock on my door."

"I wanted to, believe me," I said. "I didn't even invite her."

"Freaking Marti," Spirit said, and we both laughed.

"That totally sucks they were killed," I said.

Spirit tilted her head, her brows drawn together. "The twins? No, they weren't. They're alive and well and—" Spirit stopped speaking abruptly, her face suddenly stricken. I heard someone squeaking up the ladder and turned.

"Lina?" Ward called out.

"I'm here. Come on up," I said. "Hey, I found the rest of my toothbrush, but no toothpaste." I turned back to Spirit, but she had vanished. *That's weird.*

"Oh, my mother used to use dried mint leaves and salt," Ward said, popping his head up. "She ground them up into a fine powder and mixed a little with water and had us rub it on our teeth. It's not that bad unless you don't grind it well enough."

He crossed the attic and sat in the corner reading chair. He was so tall that he had to hunch over at the slope in the ceiling. I wondered if his thin frame would fill out now that he wasn't stuck in a dog body. It looked like he had transformed back into the body he might have had as a teenager. He had those same beautiful amber eyes, and they roamed all over the room, probably searching for the ghost I'm sure he'd heard me talking to.

"Salt, huh?" I said. I was glad to see him. Now that I could actually talk to him, there was a little more awkwardness, but I still adored him. I opened a granola bar for myself and tossed him one.

"Thanks," he said.

"Did Aaron spank you or what?"

"I wish," Ward said.

I smiled hesitantly. "Yeah, he's pretty, uh—"

"Pretty," Ward finished.

"Yeah."

"That's an understatement," Ward said. "I applaud your restraint."

"My restraint? Is that a joke?"

"Not at all. You waited much longer than I would have. And now you need to break up with him because I saw him first. It's really not fair."

"Sorry, Roogy, but I can't do that. I'm planning to drag him kicking and screaming back to my castle. I'll just have to pay you a wergild or something."

Ward smiled at my use of his nickname, and I relaxed, relieved that he wasn't mad at me. We were still friends. We'd be okay. "What's he doing now?" I asked.

"He went outside. Not sure why. It looks like it might rain." Ward's eyes still bounced around the room.

"She's gone," I said.

"Who?"

"Spirit. She disappeared for some reason. It was kind of weird, actually."

"Oh," he said, visibly relaxing. He didn't ask any follow-up questions about the weirdness with Spirit. As Rogue, he'd always perked up when he saw Spirit, but I guess the whole ghost thing disturbed him. He opened his granola bar and took a bite. The snack was dainty between his thumb and long, thin fingers.

"So, Ward, I was wondering if you would tutor me," I said.

"What do you mean?" he asked, stuffing the rest of the granola bar in his mouth.

"I mean, as a human, it appears that you might be kind of a nerd, and you are the only one in this house who finished fragment school," I said. Ward smiled at that. "I need to know what you know," I continued. "I am going to have to face Seleca again. Maybe soon. And I need to prepare."

"It's not fragment school," Ward said. "It's the School of Noble Arts, or SONA, and they teach everything there, not just fragment theory. What do you want to know?" he asked.

"First, I need you to teach me everything you know about Protection, Absorption, and Connection. I need to learn how to pull up a shield faster. Preferably instantaneously. I need to practice absorbing, and I need to know what things transmit Connection. I know I can connect through dirt, but wood doesn't work."

"Okay," he said. "I can tell you what I know from theory, but I'm not sure it will help you with the shield. That just requires practice. Fragmentation is like a sport. Just because you have the equipment doesn't mean you'll be any good at it."

"Oh, so it's like sex too," I said.

He snorted. "I guess. Anyway, it took me years to fully shift into Rogue. Transforming yourself is much harder than transforming an object. And it's painful too. At first, I could barely make any fur grow. My skin would burn like crazy. I learned how to suppress that and got the fur coat down, then I moved on to reshaping my arms and legs. Believe me, I looked like a crazy mutant for at least two years before I even remotely resembled a dog. Luckily, I already had the amber eyes."

"Why? Can't you transform your eyes?" I asked.

"You can, but if you don't have Protection, which most transformers don't, it's dangerous. If you have Protection, that fragment easily transforms you back to your original self. Otherwise, you have to use Transformation to not only change into something but also to change back. That requires you to visualize and intimately understand the desired form. If you transform your eyes and don't do it correctly, you could end up blind, perhaps permanently. I foolishly tried it once, and never got my eyes back to normal. I still see in the dark, but everything is blurry."

"Maybe you need glasses," I said. "My nerd hypothesis is gaining more and more traction."

Ward ignored the remark. "The same principle applies with the organs, especially the brain. Transforming the brain is nearly impossible anyway, but if you managed to do it, you could easily make yourself too stupid to change back. The heart is also very delicate. When I changed into Rogue, I changed the outer shape, the bones, the shape of my face, and the amount of hair on my skin. My eyes, brain, and organs were all essentially the same, just shifted into different positions. Fitting my brain into that dog skull was the hardest part. It took me three years to figure it out."

"And when you finally did, your reward was imprisonment."

"Yes," he said, "but it was minimum security, and the guards were really nice. They fed me french fries and rubbed my belly."

I smiled. "Oh, it doesn't sound so bad when you put it like that."

"It was hard at first," he said, "but I got used to it. Then I liked it. It was less painful than being at SONA."

"So, just practice, that's all I can do?"

"Practice and read. I recognize a few standard textbooks on the bookshelf. I suggest you start with those. Read as much as you can, and practice as much as you can. I can sit with you and try to answer questions. I can't help you practice Absorption, but you can practice that with Aaron. It will be easier with him, anyway, because you've already done it."

"I have? When?"

"When you made the shield, it seemed like Aaron supported you. Did you see a red-orange color added to your shield?"

"Yes. You couldn't see the colors?" I asked.

"No, you can't see those from outside the shield. It just makes you appear a little distorted, like looking through heated air. I would love to see it, though," he said wistfully.

"I think we can make that happen. I didn't keep Aaron's Evocation, though," I said.

Ward shrugged. "You weren't trying to take it. He gave it to you, but it was still connected to him, so it returned to him when you were finished." He dropped his eyes, frowning. "He probably absorbed some of your reservoir, actually. That happens sometimes when you have a deep Connection link with someone. They call it 'mixing reservoirs.' There's a kind of residue left on both of you from the other. Aaron can probably pull you in with Connection now, and your resonance will increase."

"That's true. He does pull me in now," I said.

Ward leaned over to me and whispered, "Now that you've had sex, you'll be all mixed up, especially if it was as good as *that* sounded."

I cringed. "Sorry, Ward. I know we were kind of loud. I didn't expect it to be so intense."

Ward waved it off. "It's okay. I've been living vicariously through you for years. Do you remember the time you brought home that Lebanese guy?"

"Not really," I said. "Wait, you mean Jasar?"

"I don't know. I wasn't paying attention to his name," Ward said.

"Yeah, I met him at the Kinetic Grand Championship. His sculpture flipped over and sank. I gave him a towel and he was *extremely* grateful. That was a great night."

"I remember," he said, getting up. He crouched in front of the bookshelf and skimmed the titles, his face absurdly close to the spines. So much for Monashi supervision. "Start with this one," he said, pulling a book off the shelf and handing it to me.

I read the cover. "*Beginning Fragment Theory: Uses, Synergy, and Side Effects of the Noble Six*, by Nikos Galanis."

"Yes, that textbook will answer your basic questions about Protection and Connection, which are both Noble. It will also teach you about how to create a blended link, which is the use of multiple fragments together with Connection. You'll need to learn that."

"Why?" I asked.

"Since you have Connection, you can use that fragment to expand the range of your other reservoirs, like expanding your shield farther out from your body, or healing through a Connection substrate, like dirt or water."

"Oh, that sounds useful," I said, a smile settling on my face. The textbook looked handmade and old, as if it had already been through a thousand hands before reaching mine. It had no dust cover, just a cloth-covered binding with yellowing paper and asymmetrically printed block letters. It reminded me of some of the antique books my parents had in their house. My parents loved old books. And old television shows, for that matter. They were the ones to make me sit down and watch the original *Star Trek* episodes.

The smile faded from my lips as I thought about them. I had been dependent upon them for so long. This was the first time I'd ever had to completely figure things out on my own.

I've been so spoiled, I thought. *The people here have to fight to live a normal life. I've just been mooching off my parents, riding around on a pony that my daddy bought me. I spent so much time agonizing over my lack of friends and completely missed how lucky I am to have two stable, loving parents. I need to do better. Give more. If I ever get back, that is.*

"This library is extraordinary," Ward said, pulling me out of my self-flagellation. He squinted as he scanned the books on the shelf, choosing one that looked even older than the one he'd handed me. "*Ascension: Twelve Worlds, Twelve Bridges*, by Gerhelm Meriweather," he read. "Wow, if the Ministry knew this was up here, they would definitely burn this house down. It's forbidden to even talk about the other fragments. They call them the 'Unspeakables,' and they never mention the other worlds at all. I didn't know they existed until Seleca pulled me onto the bridge to Earth."

"Why do you think that is?" I asked.

"I'm not sure," he said, sitting down again in the reading chair, "but it probably has something to do with control. Eve controls everything, down to who gets to mix reservoirs, if you know what I mean." Ward held the book comically close to his face, closing one eye.

I played with the beads on my wrist. The fire agate beads had a slight warmth to them while the aquamarine crystals felt cool.

Spirit?

It took her a moment to appear, but when she did, she had a strange expression on her face.

"What is it?" I asked. Ward looked up from his book and saw I wasn't talking to him. His eyes flicked around the room again, then down at the book.

"You should go outside and find Aaron," Spirit said. "He's out there on a big rock, staring out at the sea."

"Okay. Thank you, Spirit. Will you please go find out what our enemies are doing?" I asked.

Spirit nodded, then blinked out. I felt bad for ordering her around. She was my friend, not my servant, but what else was I supposed to do? She was my top rope, so to speak. I needed her to make sure I didn't fall to my death from this giant cliff I was trying to climb.

I glanced at Ward. He seemed as if he wanted to appear relaxed. I found my socks and shoes and sat to put them on.

"Spirit says Aaron is out by the sea. I didn't even know we were by the sea," I said.

"Yes, the Meriweather Sea. Neesee, the capital of this province, sits on the sea as well, just northwest of here, up the coast."

"Do you want to come with me?"

"No, I'll stay here. This book is all about bridges and their effect on your reservoirs. I think this could be useful. I'll catch up with you later."

"Okay," I said. I finished tying my shoes, but I didn't get up. Was it safe to leave him alone? I sat there, trying to decide whether to press the issue with Ward. He appeared engaged now, not withdrawn, as I'd seen him before.

"I'll be fine," he said, ignoring my stare.

I stood but still didn't move toward the trapdoor. Ward finally looked up from the book, then rose and came over to me, taking my hand. "What is it?" he asked.

I eyed the hand-shaped burn on the left side of his face. I could have lifted my right hand up and fit it right into that handprint. I wondered why it hadn't healed when I brought him back.

"When I drifted out of my body yesterday," I said, "I experienced a feeling of almost giddy well-being. It was really nice, and I didn't want to come back. Now Spirit tells me that being dead is worry-free. I'm just afraid that you might prefer that feeling over being here with me. I hope you know that when I couldn't find you before, I was distraught. You're my family, Ward. I need you here, and I would miss you if you . . . decided to leave again."

Ward pulled me into a hug. My head barely came up to his rib cage, and I could smell his armpits a little, but I didn't care. I clung to him.

"I'm not going anywhere, Lina," he said. "At least not yet. I've decided that I need to search for my brother at some point, but I won't do anything drastic."

"Promise?" I asked, looking up into his face.

"I promise," he said.

I relaxed a little. "Good. I still have your leash and collar, you know."

"Not even a little funny," he said.

"Too soon?"

He smiled at that. "You're not as funny as you think you are, Lina. Most of the time, it's just you laughing at your own jokes."

"Good enough for me," I said, grinning up at him. "I don't need validation. I know I'm hilarious."

He shook his head. "You know what I miss?" he asked.

"What?"

"Our bed."

I nodded. "Yeah, me too," I said. "Don't tell Aaron." I hugged him one more time, then let go and turned around to head toward the trapdoor. "I'm gonna go find him."

"Be careful."

"I will. The last thing I need is a ladder injury. I'd never live that down." I stepped onto the first rung of the ladder, peering down with slight trepidation. I'm only technically an athlete. In real life, I've been known to trip over air. Marti once suggested that I wear a helmet to my ultramarathon.

"No, I mean be careful with Aaron," he clarified.

I stopped, looking back up. "Why?" I asked.

"Fragments all have a downside, Lina," he said. "Some people overcome them, and some don't. I don't know that much about Evocation since it's an Unspeakable, but I have a feeling it might be one of the harder ones to transcend. I think he accidentally Connection-spiked you yesterday. It's something even those with lesser Protection can do. It's basically a recoil from a broken Connection link that flies back and strikes the connector. If you didn't have Protection yourself, it might have killed you. I doubt he knew about it, and I doubt he intends to do it again, but his good intentions won't mean anything when your heart stops and you fall over dead."

Ward lifted his hand to the scars on his face in what I guessed was an unconscious gesture.

"I don't think he can hurt me in that way, Ward. I'm pretty sure I'm impervious to that sort of thing. He'd probably have to cut my head off like a zombie."

Ward didn't smile at my light tone. "I was with him once when two men attacked the cottage. He and I went out for firewood, and when we got back, they were hiding inside. He burned one of the men alive and slit the other one's throat with his heated dagger. It nearly cut the man's head off. They took him by surprise, and he still slaughtered them in under ten seconds. Now, I'm not saying that he would do that to you, I'm just saying that he's capable of extreme violence at a moment's notice. He's dangerous. Beautiful, but dangerous. Just . . . be aware."

I nodded. "Okay, I'll be careful." I climbed down the ladder. I appreciated Ward's warning, but I knew Aaron would be more careful with me now. If we stayed together, he would need time to work through his jealousy, but I was confident he would eventually grow more secure in his attachment. A few more nights like this last one and how could he not? It had felt like he'd connected his very soul to mine.

"Jeez, two days as a man and you're already telling me what to do," I said lightheartedly, knowing it would echo up the ladder to him.

"Once again, not funny," he called after me.

"You never complained before," I called back. I heard a loud sigh, then the squeak of the reading chair. Pretty sure I won that one.

Chapter Nineteen

Linorra saw no people as she flew over the land of dragons. It was a beautiful, tropical paradise with giant flowers in every color. There were trees as tall as the clouds and purple mountains in the distance. It was the most beautiful place Linorra had ever seen. She felt joy in that beauty, but she also felt an ache in her heart for her mother, whom she had left behind.

I walked through the trees that hid the house from view, following the sound of waves. There was a chill in the air and the sky was filled with gray clouds so heavily laden with water that the air itself felt squeezed between the clouds and sea.

I had to walk for a few minutes, but I found Aaron sitting on top of a large boulder marked with an enormous *X*. It rested on the dune like a watchtower, overlooking a beach of black rocks and gray sand, a match to the bleak sky. Here and there lay piles of driftwood, and long lines of brown seaweed had been pushed out by the tide and left behind on the beach. Massive silver and white pelicans nested in one of the larger piles of seaweed, squawking to each other over the wind and waves.

"Do you mind if I join you?" I called up to him, studying the rock.

Aaron glanced over his shoulder at me and shrugged. It was a more lukewarm reception than I'd hoped for, but I took it. A log leaned against one side of the boulder, wedged into a fissure. Cautiously, I scrambled up the log and sat down next to him. He radiated heat, as always, and I sat close to him to use that warmth against the chill. He put his arm over my shoulders, and I leaned into him.

"What's wrong?" I asked, deciding to ask him about the *X*-marked stone later.

Aaron didn't answer right away. He stared out at the sea, which roiled under the gray sky, kicking up a mountain of white foam. I was happy that the fog had lifted, and I could see up the coastline for miles. Somewhere in the distance, I knew, there was a town full of people, living out their lives with no idea that the oppression they experienced wasn't normal.

"When I was seventeen," Aaron said, "my Aunt Clare, my father's sister and Jorin's bondmate, died in a Transmutation explosion. Her reservoir was a secret, like mine. She wanted to turn rocks from this beach into fortite so we could build an arsenal."

"What's fortite?" I asked.

"It's a rare metal. When you mix it with a chalky black substance called durran and heat it up, it becomes durrite, which is what we make weapons out of, among other things. It's hard but pliable. Very useful and extremely valuable. Clare wanted to create a steady supply. Transmutation lets you turn one material into a completely different material, but it's dangerous, and it's impossible to find someone to teach you because it's also one of the Unspeakables."

"It caused an explosion?"

"Yes. We later acquired an old text explaining that you have to go through a series of steps to avoid that. First, you transmute the material to one thing, then to the next thing, and so on, to avoid explosions. Clare knew it could be dangerous to go ahead without knowing what would happen, but she was always stubborn. She thought she could create an army to defeat the Ministry. She was the reason we added the escape hatch. She was the driving force behind a lot of things and Jorin was lost without her for a long time."

I gazed up at Aaron. He lowered his eyes from the sea to my face.

"I feel like that's what we're doing, Lee," he said. "We're messing around with the way the world is structured. Even you and I being out here together is an act of rebellion, and it's dangerous. We don't know what we're doing, and we could get people killed, including ourselves."

I nodded again. "That's true," I said. "We could." I held his eyes. "I am an idealist in many ways, Aaron, but I'm under no illusion that this will be simple or safe. We could get everyone we love killed and still fail. Maybe it's not fair to ask them to make that sacrifice. Then again, are they really any safer if we do nothing?" I shook my head. "I don't know what the right answer is. I just know that this is no way to live, and you and I have a better chance of taking down the Ministry than anyone else. If we leave, eventually they *will* find a way to bring back Anick. Do you want to stand by and let that happen when maybe we could have stopped it?" The question was as much for me as it was for Aaron. My conscience told me that helping was the right thing to do, but Evilina didn't care about helping anyone except herself.

Aaron rested his forehead on mine. "I just found you," he said. I thought he might elaborate on that thought, but he kissed me instead. I leaned into it, letting him pull me against him and into a Connection link. His anxiety was like a weighted vest that he could never shed. He was tired of living every day in fear and just wanted to find his family and have a moment of peace. I couldn't fault him for that. The evoker was burned out.

"I have something for you," I said, pulling back a little. I showed him the bracelet. "Spirit originally made this for me, but now she says I should give it to you. She made it before she died and stuck it in a sock in my bag. It's supposed to act like an external reservoir, absorbing ambient fragment to help you stay in control."

Aaron frowned, but took the bracelet, examining it like it was made of plutonium. He inspected the iridescent stones, then, hesitantly, put it on his right wrist. "I don't feel anything," he said.

I shrugged. "Maybe it takes time."

Aaron considered the bracelet on his wrist, deep in thought for a moment. The edges of his mouth turned up, and he leaned over and kissed me again almost desperately. It felt like he poured his last hope into me, like something in him was unwinding for the first time since he was a child. I kissed him back, knowing that if this thing with him didn't work out that I'd be wrecked by it. In that respect, I poured all my hopes into him as well.

When the kiss ended, Aaron held his forehead to mine again for a moment, catching his breath, then he stood up, offering me his hand. I took it, and he pulled me up next to him. I was shivering anyway and wanted to head back. A drop of rain hit my cheek, and the heaviness in the air weighed on each of my breaths.

"Come on," he said, as he headed back toward the house. I started to follow him, but the hairs on the back of my neck stood up and I whirled around, staring out at the water. A small dock withstood the precarious waves, protected by a rocky outcrop. A skiff was tied to it, nestled between the dock and the rocks. Beyond that, there was nothing except an angry sky dancing atop a restless sea.

After a moment, I relaxed. The sea was dark and full of mysterious depths. Since everything here was supersized, it made me wonder what kinds of monsters might be lurking within that abyss. Perhaps I'd felt a resonance with one, just as Aaron had with the dragon.

Then, as if I had called it with that thought, a great red fin broke the surface a few hundred yards out in the water. It looked like a shark fin, only it was the size of a sailboat. Any creature attached to a colossal fin like that would have to be the size of a blue whale.

"Gah! What the hell is that thing?" I squealed.

Aaron trotted back up to the top of the boulder. "What's wrong?" he asked.

I pointed.

"Oh, that's the Meriweather Monster," Aaron said casually. "It never comes ashore."

I looked at Aaron in dismay. "How would it come ashore? Isn't it a shark or something?"

"Right now, yes," he said. "But it transforms into several creatures, including a blue octopus that turns boats over when they get too close to its territory, a large uncharted island southwest of here. I saw the octopus form once when I was about ten. I was out on Jorin's skiff with him and Terik, rowing to his commercial docks up on the northern beach. I thought it would turn our boat over and eat us, but it just looked at us with one giant black eye, then swam away. It was terrifying, but Jorin said he sees it all the time and it never bothers him. He calls it his friend, Merimo."

I shook my head. "I can't wait to get back to Earth. We don't have any monsters there except the people kind."

"And bears," Aaron said, giving me a playful smile.

"And bears," I agreed. "Small ones." The rain picked up, and we were getting pretty wet now.

"Come on," Aaron said, "you just got those clothes dry." He turned back, making his way down the log again. I followed him but took one last peek over my shoulder at the enormous red fin. It was deeply frightening, and yet I found myself yearning to go out there and see the creature up close, maybe even chase it like Captain Ahab.

"I'd probably just drown," I muttered, dismissing the idea and following Aaron back toward the house.

Chapter Twenty

That night, Linorra had a dream so vivid it hardly seemed like a dream at all. She saw the face of a man in agony.

"Viktor," she said. "Is that you? Where are you?"

The man's eyes lit up with hope when he saw her. "It's me, my love! I'm in Queen Mortier's dungeon. You must find the key and rescue me!"

For the next two months, I woke up every morning thinking *This will be the day Seleca comes to kill us*, but Spirit's daily reports revealed that Seleca struggled to learn how to use her new Precognition fragment. It gave her terrible migraines, and she acted even more insane than usual, ranting about a bearded blond man who haunted her dreams. Everyone feared her. Even Eve kept her distance, disappearing from the palace entirely. Ward said that Seleca's overuse of Projection probably made her more psychologically vulnerable to the side effects of Precognition use.

I spent most of my time preparing for a fight, leaning on Ward to tutor me in beginning fragment theory. I practiced using my reservoirs and read everything I could get my hands on. Ward was correct that Aaron's library was extensive. I finished several textbooks, many of which were antique books written before Anick's rise to power.

Gerhelm Meriweather, one of the more prolific authors, wrote Ward's new favorite, *Ascension: Twelve Worlds, Twelve Bridges*, which included information about all twelve fragments and worlds, including Killmount, the theoretical Conjuration planet that had yet to be discovered. Old Gerhelm even ranked the fragments in order of how painful they are to ascend.

I left that book to Ward to focus on my two priorities for battle, healing and shielding, but he relayed the Teleportation basics. Ascension, he reported, is the linking of an individual's reservoir with a fragment matrix so that a supply of that fragment becomes essentially limitless. This happens through Teleportation over a bridge originating from that world and was exactly what happened to me when Seleca threw me onto the Earth bridge.

Earth sits in a Protection matrix, so that was the fragment that powered the portal. When I traveled over the Protection bridge, I ascended, and the source of that fragment formed a link to me, perhaps in the same way that it links to Earth.

Unfortunately, the process of ascension is unpredictable and possibly fatal to those without Protection. It physically affects a fragmentor's body such that when they directly tap into a matrix, it causes a bizarre glowing and enables the use of that fragment within a shield. It also "raises" lesser reservoirs, expanding their power to a greater level. This explained my multiple greater reservoirs.

After a few weeks, I moved on to advanced texts that focused on the more nuanced qualities of each fragment. I learned about Connection substrates, which transmit the fragment over distances and include earth and water for those with greater Connection, and air for those with ascendent Connection. With practice, Connection can be used in conjunction with other fragments like Evocation—which meant that if Aaron had ascendant Connection, it actually *would* be possible for him to throw fire.

The beaded bracelet didn't solve Aaron's problems, but it took the edge off. I felt for him on that front. Even my own bit of Evocation, acquired from mixing reservoirs with Aaron, flared up my emotions when I attempted to use it. It gave me a better understanding of his struggle, but it wasn't that much worse than a bad case of PMS, perhaps because I barely had enough to reach the level of a lesser reservoir. I couldn't make a log catch fire, but I managed to light the oil lantern. I scorched the tip of my finger, but I did it.

The only break in our daily routine was when Aaron went out to walk the farm. After he watched me push the shield out around both myself and Ward several times, he promptly announced that he needed to search for the oardoo flock. I think he was just stir-crazy and needed alone time. The property was expansive, and Aaron always left before sunrise and came back after dark, reporting that he'd walked around only a portion of Jorin's farm. He always came back looking refreshed.

I used the time to tend the garden and hang out with Ward, who wasn't adjusting well to his new life. Though he put on a brave face, making promises to stay and help me, I recognized the signs of depression from my own experience. He was sad but outwardly calm. He was always tired. He did what was expected of him but nothing more. He read all day, barely eating or sleeping. He made no specific commitments regarding the future.

Worst of all, he spoke longingly of what he remembered about being dead. He went across a bridge, he said, or started to. He didn't remember anything specific about the bridge, only the feeling of wholeness once he stepped upon it. Though he avoided connecting with me, I knew he wanted that peace back more than anything.

He'd lost his home and family. He'd lost his reservoir. Wretched though it was, he'd lost his purpose in life. So, while he didn't outwardly object to becoming my tutor, it was also a reminder that he no longer had the ability to personally use any of his knowledge. In his mind, Seleca had stolen the thing that gave him value. That wasn't true, of course. As far as I was concerned, his value had nothing to do with his reservoir.

Seleca had absorbed his reservoir after he fully shifted into Rogue, and it was supposed to be completely gone, but I had seen his skin ripple just before Seleca threw him onto the Earth bridge. What else could that have been, if not traces of Transformation? But even if he had a small bit of Transformation left, the reservoir would be of the lesser variety, and he wouldn't be able to do anything with it.

Still, I wasn't convinced all hope was lost. Ward himself taught me that one of the most basic principles of fragment theory is the idea of symmetry. Every fragment has a complement. Protection, a force of order, is the complement of Evocation, a force of disorder or change. Connection, a force of pushing or expansion, is the complement of Absorption, a force of pulling or contraction. Therefore, it made sense to me that if a reservoir could be absorbed from someone, then it must also be possible to give a reservoir *to* someone. The raising of lesser reservoirs during ascension was evidence of that, not to mention the fact that Aaron glowed like a radioactive Smurf every time we fragged.

Violet had written in her book that Connection was Linorra's greatest gift. I had assumed she wrote that to throw Seleca off the trail by making her think that Connection was my *only* gift. But after thinking about it, Seleca somehow also knew about my Absorption and Conjuration. Protection was the only reservoir she *hadn't* known about, a fact that still confused me since Eve and Seleca knew about my other reservoirs before Rogue ever came into my life. But if Violet's purpose in writing that in the book wasn't to confuse Seleca, then why did she make that comment about Connection? My intuition told me that Connection had uses I hadn't discovered yet. Perhaps I could use it to help Ward get his mojo back. That would, indeed, be a great gift.

To that end, I asked Ward for another favor, a favor that I knew would make Aaron angry, but that was essential. I wanted to see if I could give Ward a part of my reservoir. I had to be delicate about this because it would require a deep Connection link, and not only was Aaron going to be jealous of any connecting that I did with Ward, but Ward was also actively trying to hide his mental state from me.

I decided to wait until Aaron disappeared on one of his walkabouts. I know, I'm sneaky and manipulative, but there are some instances where it truly is better to beg forgiveness than permission. This way, Aaron wouldn't have to experience the anticipatory anxiety. That's better, right?

Also, he doesn't own me. I would have done it anyway, so why torture the poor guy? I'd planned to tell him afterward. I swear.

It was early morning and the sun had not yet risen, but Aaron was already gone. A light drizzle hit the oculus, and I shivered at the thought of him walking out in the rain, though I knew he'd never be cold. That was a useful side effect of his Evocation, since this part of Monash was even colder than Northern California. Summer was almost over, but the constant rain made it feel more like late fall.

I lay in bed under the oardoo blanket as usual, and the oil lamp threw a lovely orange light over my shoulder that was bright enough to fill the whole room. I had already decided that I liked it better than electric light and would be taking the oil lamp with me to Earth, if that ever happened. In the meantime, I was perfectly content to lounge and read.

I read *The Meriweather Monster and His Kin*, by Marie Faraway, which recounted the tales of sailors who had survived a Merimo attack. The author proposed that the monster was actually a family of creatures whose history extended back thousands of years. I was obsessed and completely engrossed in the book, which is why I practically jumped out of my socks when Ward rapped on the trapdoor.

"Lina?"

"Come on up," I said, trying to sound like I hadn't just had a mini seizure. Ward suppressed a smile, but I ignored it. "It's super early, Ward. Did you sleep at all?"

"A little," he said, shuffling over to collapse into his reading chair. He had somehow managed to claim the cushioned seat as his regular perch despite Aaron's obvious displeasure. "I heard Aaron leave. I figured you were up."

"You know me well," I said.

"You found the monster book, I see," he said, not quite covering his smirk.

"Don't judge me," I said. "It's a real sea monster. I'm part Scottish. I have no control over it. The passion is in my blood."

Ward nodded as if that made complete sense, then picked up his own book to continue reading from where he'd left off. He slouched into the chair as much as his body would allow, curling himself in to drape his long legs over the arm, then brought the book close to his face. He had dark circles under his eyes that deepened day by day.

"Ward," I said.

"Huh?"

"Do you think you'll ever transform again?"

He shook his head, not taking his eyes from the book.

"What would you do if you could?" I asked.

He took a breath in and out, then just shrugged.

I let the silence sit there for a moment, but I knew he could feel me staring at him, waiting. He finally lifted his eyes to mine.

"What?" he said.

I shoved the blanket off and stood. I wore one of Jorin's tunics, which was dark brown and so long that it draped down to my ankles. It was long-sleeved and had a wonderful silkiness. I couldn't understand why the men's fabrics were so comfortable and the women's fabrics were so scratchy. Living on Monash as a woman was like death by a thousand pink paper cuts. I walked over to Ward and knelt in front of his chair. "Ward, can I connect with you?"

He sighed. "I'd rather not."

"I know, but I'm asking anyway. Please. I want to try a sort of reverse Absorption using Connection."

"That's not a thing," he said.

"How do you know?" I asked. "Isn't Seleca the only other greater connector? I'm pretty sure she would never even attempt to give away a reservoir. Please, I want to see if I can give you some of mine. I accidentally gave Aaron lesser Connection, so I think I can do that for you too."

"I'm not having sex with you, Lina," he said, wrinkling his nose.

"I wasn't offering, but wow. You could have said that without looking like someone just offered you a shit sandwich."

Ward laughed. "Aaron won't like it."

"Aaron's not here."

Ward gave me a flat stare. "You were waiting for him to leave," he said. It was a statement, not a question.

"Like I said, you know me well."

"Which one would you give me?" he asked, finally closing his book and giving me his full attention.

I shrugged. "Which one do you want?"

"Protection," he said immediately, "but I don't think it will work. Protection can't be absorbed, so it probably can't be given."

"We'll see," I said, rubbing my palms together.

"And," he continued, closing his eyes for a second, "I'm not sure what you would see in there."

"What do you mean?"

Ward spoke slowly, as if every word needed to be planned. "I'm not right in my head anymore, Lina. I came back . . . different."

I stared at him, bewildered. "Whatever it is, I won't judge. I'll only try to help you. I promise."

He wrinkled his nose again, then sighed. "Okay," he said, though he looked like he wanted to run and hide.

"Good. I've been thinking a lot about how to do this, and I think it would be easier if you were facing away from me. Will you come lie on the bed?"

"Are you insane? What if Aaron walked in? Worst idea ever."

"Fair point," I said, "but I think it might be important for you to be comfortable. I won't lie down with you, I'll just sit next to you, holding your hand."

Ward groaned. "Fine, but if Aaron kills me, I'm not coming back this time."

"If Aaron tries to kill you, you'll protect yourself because this is going to work," I countered. "Come on, it'll be just like old times. Except for the excruciating pain part."

He pinched one side of his mouth. "That sounds exactly like old times," he said. "Get out of the way."

I got up, and he followed me to the bed. Luckily, he'd finally bathed. That was three days ago, but it was better than nothing. I stepped aside, letting him lie down. He sank into the oardoo-feather mattress and released a low groan.

"Oh, it is so not fair that you've been sleeping on this the whole time," he said. "This is incredible."

"See? This was a good idea. Face that way," I said, pointing away from me. He turned on his side, and I sat on the bed behind him, leaning over him to take his hand. It was cool and clammy. "Ready?" I asked.

"I guess," he mumbled. He sounded like he might fall asleep.

I didn't immediately connect with him as I had with Aaron. Because of our mutual attraction, Aaron and I had entered into a superficial Connection link upon the first moment of contact despite our bilateral Protection reservoirs. Ward had only grudgingly agreed to connect with me, so I had to push my way past his reluctance in order to achieve even a faint whiff of Connection. I could feel his exhaustion, and I hesitated.

"Ward, I need you to actively let me in," I said. "I won't force myself on you."

He didn't respond for so long that I thought he must be asleep, but then he drew in a deep breath and let it out slowly. Finally, he let me in. It felt like he drew a curtain aside so I could peer through a doorway that had previously only revealed shadows and silhouettes. The curtain stuck, but he managed to get it halfway open. I closed my eyes and tentatively quested out into the deeper Connection link.

In Ward's mind, I saw a small house, little more than a shack. I knew I still sat on the bed, but it was as if I had been sucked into a dream with him, barely aware of my real body. I stood at the threshold of the house, peeking in. It was dark and smelled stale and smoky. It reminded me of how Jorin's house smelled when we first arrived, combined with the smell of a campfire.

I heard the echo of a dog barking in the backyard. I couldn't tell if that was from Ward's mind or my own memory. It sounded frantic, just like the day of my accident.

Rogue, I thought. *I miss you, my friend. Come home.*

"I'm right here," Ward said.

"Where?" I said, looking all around. I couldn't see a damned thing. Behind me, where a street should have been, there was only emptiness, a vast void that would swallow me whole if I fell backward. I yelped, stepping hastily into the house. It felt so real. The boards creaked under my feet, and I felt a musty draft on my face. "What the hell? Where are we?" I asked.

"This was our home," I heard him say, though he sounded far away. He was a disembodied voice that came from every direction, softly to my ears, yet a little too loudly in my mind.

"Whose home?" I asked.

"My brother and me," he said, "and our mother."

"Why is it so dark?" I asked. "Turn on a light."

"There's no light here anymore," he said. "Not for a long time."

As my eyes adjusted, I noticed that the house wasn't just dark. It was burned to the ground. The minute I noticed this, the smell of burning intensified dramatically and I coughed as if smoke still filled the air.

Exposed wooden posts stood with empty air between them where the walls should have been. Black, scattered piles of what might have been furniture cluttered the floor, and one side of the house had caved in. On the other side, through a large hole in the roof, I saw two moons: one white, one red.

"What happened here?" I asked.

"Fire," he whispered. "Everything in my life has been destroyed by fire. My house. My mother. My face. My whole life."

"Why? How?"

"Seleca," he said. "Once she found out about the strength of my reservoir, she came for me. She was there for *me* the day Aaron escaped. Finding out about his Evocation was just an unfortunate coincidence. After that day, Ellis disappeared, Aaron disappeared, my home and mother disappeared. She took everything and made me believe it was my fault. I had nowhere to turn except to her. She condemned me to Hell and made me believe she was my savior. It was a perfect, beautiful lie, and I didn't realize it until you woke me up that day in the field."

I closed my eyes, feeling Ward's despair in my soul. The pain of it was more than an uncomfortable emotion. It was a physical burden that pressed down on my awareness so hard I fell to my knees. I knew I hadn't actually fallen, but it still hurt when my knees cracked down on the floorboards. For a moment, my mind drifted to the memory of my accident. My lungs were heavy, and I tasted blood in my mouth. *Oh, my friend. I'm here. I'm still here. But where are you?*

I opened my eyes again, but the burned-out house was gone, replaced by my own home in the redwoods. The sun overhead shone brighter than I remembered, but I smelled the sweet and spicy aroma of my favorite place, and for a joyous moment, I thought I had been teleported home. I jumped up, the weight on me abruptly gone. I took off running toward the house, heading for the door to the screened-in porch.

I reached the porch door and yanked on the handle, but it wouldn't open. I pulled on it even harder, confused because the porch door didn't even have a lock. It wasn't locked, though, but frozen, as if it was just a video of a house that had been paused. I turned around, staring at the trees and sky. Everything was still. There was no wind, no birds, no swaying and rustling of branches. The sky was bright blue with no clouds, and there wasn't a lick of fog anywhere. This wasn't right.

Barking still came from somewhere, but it sounded far away. I jogged toward the sound, into the forest.

"Ward?" I called. "Where are you? This is creepy and weird, and I wasn't at all prepared to be sucked into a bright blue nightmare. What in the hell is happening?" I continued jogging toward the sound, which was getting louder and louder. "Ward!"

"Calm down. You're so dramatic," he said.

"Oh, good. You've learned the gaslighter's creed," I said, stopping to glance around. "Do you have a body or am I the only character in this horror movie?"

Then, I heard a growling behind me. I spun to see a white wolf bearing down on me. Its eyes were deep red, and its fangs, which had grown inconceivably long and sharp, dripped with blood. The wolf looked like it might morph into a saber-toothed tiger. I stumbled backward and fell because, ya know, that's what idiots like me do in horror movies. The white wolf jumped clear over me and dashed off into the woods.

I looked over my shoulder in stunned confusion, then got up to follow it because it barreled off in the direction of the barking that I knew must be Rogue.

"Lina, wait," Ward said. "Just let that one go."

"What do you mean?" I asked incredulously. "That was the white wolf that caused my accident. I have to go see what happened."

"Lina, there's nothing for you to see over there. I ran away and hid. That's it. I ran, and then Seleca found me and sent me to lead you toward the bridge. You don't need to see me being a bad friend."

"You're not a bad friend, and you still haven't answered my question about why I can't see you," I said.

"I don't know," he said in a small voice. "Maybe because, in my mind, I'm already gone."

Again, I felt his despair, and again I fell, crushed by the weight of it. I tasted blood in my mouth again as my body and awareness were both pushed down into the dirt so hard that I lost my breath. I had a flash of memory, the hooves of a horse, a crushing pain in my chest. I knew, then, that this trauma might kill me right alongside my friend.

I heard Ward calling in my mind. *Lina, I'm sorry! I can't help it. I've tried. I can't stop!* He was crying again.

I squeezed my eyes closed to avoid getting dirt in them as a force I could feel but not see pressed me deeper and deeper into the ground. *Like a fragment*, I thought.

Though I knew my subconscious mind didn't need to breathe, I nevertheless suffocated under the crushing weight of Ward's anguish and would soon run out of air and die. I was vaguely aware that my real body had slumped over on top of his and was unconscious. It was almost as if I had connected with Ward so deeply that I had left myself behind altogether. If I died here, I didn't know if my body would ever wake up again. I had a strong suspicion that the answer was no for both of us.

I searched for the elusive Conjuration fragment in my mind and found it wisping around in the background as if trying to hide. I reached out for it, but it resisted capture, escaping through cracks in my concentration like smoke.

I would not permit this.

Come! I commanded, then imagined sucking the smoky fragment to myself like a vacuum. *You are mine. Come to me.* It came swiftly now, filling my unconscious body like helium into a balloon. The pressure on me eased, and I breathed easily again.

"What did you do?" Ward asked, sounding relieved.

I shot up from the imaginary ground, filled with inspiration. "Ward, I greatly underestimated the power of Conjuration," I said. "I've barely used it, and only then it was to talk to Spirit. She says that the soul of a person is basically their experience of the past, present, and future. We always assume that the body, or at least the brain, is the thing that makes us think and experience things, but what if there is this thing called a soul that is doing the actual experiencing and the brain is just an interface between that experience and concrete, time-locked reality?"

"Uh, yeah, isn't that what everyone believes?" Ward asked.

"I have no idea. I've always been agnostic, maybe even atheist. I still am, actually. I'm just not an aspiritualist. Is that a word?" I was too excited to analyze the semantics of my idea.

"That's why Spirit can hear people's thoughts—because she is seeing their soul." I ignored Ward's sudden shock at the revelation that Spirit could read his mind. "Conjuration lets me manipulate a soul. Doesn't that mean I can manipulate a person's experience? I could literally undo trauma! I mean, I'm not saying I could unmake the timeline, but maybe I could alter how someone experiences that timeline. Ward, I think I can combine Conjuration with Connection and Protection to not only heal your spirit but to send a reservoir into your soul that will let you heal yourself!"

I spoke rapidly. Rambling, actually. "Best of all, if I could give you greater Protection and we managed to teleport to Earth, we could teleport back to Monash over an Earth bridge, which will ascend your Protection and raise any traces you may have of Transformation back up to the level of a greater reservoir. Then you could travel back to Earth over a Monash bridge and ascend your Transformation. You'd be even more powerful than you were before, Ward. Of course, that will only work if I'm right about the soul being the housing for fragment reservoirs. And if the ascensions don't kill you."

I laughed nervously. It wasn't exactly a foolproof plan. I wasn't sure if I was even coherent at this point. I stopped to look around again as if *this* time, I would find Ward.

"I'm not sure I want it back," he said. "It was a curse."

"Ward, Seleca abused you," I said in the softest voice I could manage. "She fucking abused you from the time you were a child. She is an evil, murderous disease upon this world, and *we* must be the cure. I need you to show yourself to me, Ward. I can't do this without your help. Please."

It's amazing how far the word please will take you sometimes. I heard a scuffling noise behind me and turned to find not Ward but Rogue. He sat still as a statue, gazing up at me the way he used to, his beautiful amber eyes attentive and aware, as always. He was a huge, copper-colored hound with the same handprint-shaped white patch on his face. That patch had a slightly different meaning now, but it was a part of him, and I loved it.

Lina, you're not going to be able to just put your hands on me and fix me. It's not that simple. Even if you heal my spirit, the memories won't go away. I am who I am. Ward sent his thoughts to me, but they were also accompanied by a profound emptiness I knew I wouldn't be able to fill no matter how hard I tried. He would have to do that himself. All I could do was convince him that he wouldn't have to be alone while doing it. I knelt in front of him, which made his dog form slightly taller than me, and I wrapped my arms around his neck.

"I don't want to fix you," I said. "I love who you are, my friend. I always have." I paused for a second. I wanted to get this right. "I just know that when I was alone, I felt hopeless. I felt like I could disappear into the woods and no one would even notice. And sometimes you were the only reason I walked back out again."

Rogue laid his cute canine face on one of my shoulders and a paw on the other, the way he always used to do. I felt a strong surge of love for him, and I sent that feeling into him through our Connection link. He sent it right back to me. For a moment, everything seemed like it would be okay.

"Ready?" I asked.

He made a low doggy groan, and I chuckled. "I'll take that as an 'I guess,'" I said.

I slipped my hand under his paw, touching the pad of his foot, then closed my eyes to concentrate. This would be my first time trying to combine three fragments at once, and it would be tricky because I had to focus on each fragment to manipulate it. I thought it might be best to add one at a time. I was already deeply connected to Ward, so I decided to send Conjuration next.

"I have no idea how this is going to feel," I said. "Brace yourself."

I called to my Conjuration fragment as I had learned I needed to do, and it came to me. I combined it with my Connection fragment into a blended link, and the two energies twisted around each other like colored dyes in water. The stream slid into my friend. When the Conjuration fragment went into him, he shivered violently as if hypothermic. I hung on to him, and the shivering lessened but didn't cease.

I could feel myself getting tired already. I didn't know how long I could keep it up, so I quickly added Protection into the stream. I still had my eyes closed, but I felt Rogue relax and then slump down out of my arms. I hung on to his paw and could feel it transforming into a hand. It was an odd, lumpy process, and a little disturbing, but I hung on. It was working! Conjuration and Protection combined to heal his spirit, and Connection delivered them.

I'm a genius, I thought, feeling extremely pleased with myself. By that time, I really should have known better than to allow myself a moment of smug satisfaction. It's always at those moments that everything goes to hell.

I opened my eyes to find myself back in Aaron's bedroom. Ward still lay on the bed but had slumped onto his stomach, his face smooshed into the pillow. I had fallen on top of him, my left hand still curled over his left hand. God, what would have happened if I had let go? I sat up to hear him moan a little.

"Goddess, that feels good," he mumbled. He lifted his hips a little and reached under himself with his other hand, needing to make a quick adjustment to his anatomy. He pulled his hand back out, thank goodness.

"No comments," he said. "Still not having sex with you."

I snorted in a very unladylike fashion. "Still not offering," I said.

"Well, that's good to hear at least," Aaron said.

Chapter Twenty-one

Linorra slammed the door closed behind Syndeth, panting. He'd barely fit through the door, as large as it was. If it had been any smaller, her friend would have been meat for dwarfs.

"That was too close," Linorra said. "I don't understand why Viktor would send us there, do you? The dwarfs didn't even have the magic sword. It's very odd."

"It's not odd to me," Syndeth said. "If that man is truly your future husband, I suspect you'll have a lot more of these bothersome adventures."

"Aaron, you're back," I said lamely.

"What is he doing in our bed, Lee?" Aaron asked. He was fuming but kept it under control, though I could feel the heat coming off him from across the room. Then, I heard a high-pitched popping noise and we all jumped in surprise. Aaron held the bracelet up to look at it, and one of the little stones fell to the floor, split in half.

Okay, maybe not.

"Aaron, Ward's, um . . . spirit is injured. I needed to heal him."

"In our bed? I know exactly how it feels to be healed, and I know exactly why he lifted his hips up just now. How could you do this? This is too far. How could he possibly be injured enough for you to make this kind of contact with him *in our bed*?"

The way he said *our* bed instead of *my* bed said everything. I had not taken this seriously enough. Aaron considered it to be a sacred space, just for us, and I had laid his competition right down in the center of it. The volume of his voice grew with each word he uttered, and his face took on a deep shade of scarlet.

I stood, inching toward him slowly as if I avoided spooking a frightened cat. "I'm sorry, Aaron. You're right. The bed thing was a terrible idea. Ward tried to tell me, but I wouldn't listen. I'm so sorry. But this is not what you think."

"I want him out," Aaron said. Ward sat up at the side of the bed. He moved as slowly and silently as possible, like he believed Aaron might attack him. I was beginning to think he might be right.

"Fine, I'll send him downstairs."

"No, Lee. I want him out of this house. I don't want him here anymore."

I sucked in a breath. I had badly misjudged the situation. I knew Aaron would be angry about what we were doing, but I had not understood how much.

"Aaron, please listen." I was close to him now, almost touching him. "I need to be able to heal people," I said as quietly as possible. "I'll probably heal a lot of people in the near future. I'm sorry about the bed thing, but there's nothing inappropriate going on here. I swear." I took his hand, connecting. "Are you sure you want to do this?"

I was trying to warn him. I hadn't finished healing Ward, and I wasn't convinced I had actually given him any of my Protection reservoir. Now that I understood the depth of his pain, I couldn't leave him alone. There was no way in hell I would let Ward be banished because of my stupidity and then not go after him.

"I'm sure. The sooner the better," he said.

I just stared at him, shaking my head. I didn't know what else to say. I wasn't going to argue. "Fine," I said, clenching my jaw. I let go of his hand. "I'll get my pack," I said.

"I don't need your pack," Ward said. "I'll go now. It's okay."

"It's not for you," I said. I turned away from Aaron and walked over to the corner of the room where I kept my things. "I'll meet you downstairs, Ward. Don't leave without me because I'll have to follow you, and I'd rather not walk alone." I pulled the pack out and shoved things in.

"Lee," Aaron said. "That's not what I meant."

I didn't answer. I was sick and tired of his temper and jealousy and wanted to be done with it.

Rain tapped on the oculus, and I looked up to see that it was still dark outside. It wouldn't be right to take the oil lamp, but I still had my flashlight and had recently charged my watch. I found the watch and tried to put it on, but my hands shook, and I dropped it. I picked it up again and stuffed it in the pocket of my pants, then continued packing, stuffing in the survival and first aid kits.

It should be light soon, I thought. *I've hiked in the rain before. My feet will be wet, but my coat is waterproof, and my pack has a rain cover. I'll be fine.*

"Lee, please. Calm down," Aaron said.

I snorted derisively but still didn't respond. This was my fault. I'd led Ward astray, and now I had to face the consequences. Ward fled the awkward scene, and I watched him go, but before he descended the ladder, he stopped, his eyes on his feet.

My throat burned and tears blurred my vision as I tore Jorin's tunic off over my head, completely heedless of the fact that I wasn't wearing a bra.

"Lee, what are you doing?" Aaron asked, sounding shocked. He looked over at Ward, who still stood there. He shifted his body to block Ward's view of me. I rolled my eyes.

"He's seen it a thousand times, Aaron," I said.

"And I'm gay," Ward said quietly.

I stopped in my tracks. *Did he just say what I think he said?* Something was different about Ward, but I couldn't put my finger on why at first. Then, he lifted his left hand to his face and I saw it.

"Ward," I said reverently, "your face is healed."

"So are my eyes," he whispered.

I waited for Aaron's reaction, but his attention was on Ward, who still stood, peering down the ladder into the closet. Finally, Ward raised his chin and looked Aaron in the eye.

"I have no romantic interest in Lina or any other woman, Aaron," Ward said. "I'm gay, but I'm still leaving. Lina, you stay. Thanks for trying to protect me. You've been an amazing friend. Far better than I deserve. It's time I returned the favor."

"No," I declared stubbornly. "I'm coming with you." There was no fragging way I would stay here while my friend went out into the cold rain alone. Ward descended the ladder without answering, and Aaron stared after him. I couldn't see Aaron's face and I didn't want to. "Don't leave without me!" I yelled.

I found my jog bra and pulled it on as fast as I could, then threw my original clothes from home back on. Socks, shoes, and jacket went on, then I finished ramming things into my pack and strapped it on.

"Lee, don't go," Aaron said. "At least wait until morning. It's way too late to storm off."

I stared at him, confused, then checked my watch. It said 10:30 p.m. *What the hell?*

"Lina!" Spirit shouted. It startled me, and I glanced up to see that she stood over by the trapdoor as if she'd come through it. She looked panicked.

Ghosts don't panic, I thought.

Aaron's eyes darted around the room as if he'd heard Spirit. Had we mixed our reservoirs so much that he could hear her now?

"Spirit? What's happening?" I asked.

"Seleca ordered Magister Axel to personally come to this house to either find you or wait for you. He's leaving as we speak."

"How long will it take him to get here?" I asked.

"Walking? A couple days," said Aaron. "It's a hundred kilometers by the Caravan Trail."

"He'll be here in one minute, maybe less," Spirit said.

"What?!" Aaron and I both yelled.

"He's a teleporter," Spirit said.

I stared at Spirit, stunned. Then it hit me. "This could be an opportunity," I said. "Maybe I can absorb his reservoir."

"We could go to Earth," Aaron said.

"We could start our revolution," I countered stubbornly. *And I could help Ward.*

Spirit eyed me. *I'll tell you later,* I thought.

She nodded, then looked at Aaron pensively. "You *can* hear me now," she said. Aaron didn't respond, but he glanced in her direction.

"No time for that," I said. "What should we do? Should we try a sneak attack? Wait up here for him to get comfortable, then surprise him?"

"Maybe," Spirit said, "but Axel doesn't seem the type to wait around or do things he doesn't want to do. He may just burn the house down, or he may send in one of his minions."

"We'll have to take our chances if we want to take his reservoir," Aaron said. He still looked stunned, but he was shaking himself loose of it.

I, on the other hand, was panicking. "Do we know if he's protected?" I asked. "I've never killed anyone before. I don't think I could do it."

"You won't have to. I'll do it if it comes to that," Aaron said, marching over to his wooden chest. He wrenched the top all the way off.

"I didn't hear anything about Protection," Spirit said, "and I haven't seen him using it, but maybe it just didn't come up. I'm not sure."

"You can *see* fragments?" I asked. "Like how I see them within the shield?"

Spirit nodded. "Yes, but only when they're actively being used, and I can't sense resonance."

Aaron tore extra knives and bolts out of the chest, then pulled his small crossbow out of the utility vest that he still wore from his hike. He loaded it with five bolts and slipped the remaining weapons into various straps in his vest. I watched his process, mesmerized, then realized that I looked like an idiot standing there. I don't have a process, so maybe I am one. That sentiment gathered more and more evidence as the day wore on.

"We could just run," I said quietly. "We aren't prepared for this. Spirit, can you check on Axel's status, please? Where is he?"

Spirit blinked in and out. "He's out in the yard," Spirit said.

"Too late to run," Aaron said.

"Shit! We need to bring Ward up here!"

"Too late for that too," Spirit said. "He was just leaving the house when Axel showed up. They grabbed him and are holding him down there."

My heart dropped into my stomach. "No. This can't be happening," I said, my hands coming to my head.

"Too late to pretend we're not here," Aaron said. "How many people does he have with him, Spirit?"

"Two holding Ward," she said. "Four more besides, two at the front door with Axel and two at the back. All giant thugs. Actually, they look sort of like giant überzombies."

"They might be thralls trapped in a Projection trance," Aaron said. He appeared as if he might say something else, but we heard a hard banging on the front door.

"Aaron Atticus!" a man shouted. His voice was so piercingly loud that it practically shook the house. "I know you're in there. Come out or I will burn this house to the ground. Bring the girl with you. You have one minute."

"Axel," Aaron hissed, a look of pure hatred on his face.

It's unnerving to experience the beginning of an event knowing that you're about to go through something horrific. It's a bit like driving yourself in for surgery with the knowledge that they won't be using anesthesia. My mind spun, trying to come up with some kind of solution. Could we overpower two überzombies and run out the back? Should we come out shooting? Both of those things could have disastrous consequences for Ward, not to mention the fact that Axel's thralls were probably victims, just like us.

"A shield," Aaron said. "We'll go out the escape hatch with a shield around us and surprise them from the side. That will steal their positional advantage and give us time to negotiate. Come on." Aaron got up and headed for the small door to the secret hallway and unlatched it, swinging it open.

I kept my pack on in case we needed to make a break for it and followed him through the door. Though it irked me to follow commands, Aaron knew the house layout and the enemy better than I did. He was calm, whereas I was a panicky mess, and he had all the weapons.

Wait, why does he have all the weapons?

Aaron didn't give me a chance to question him further. He ducked through the small doorway and into a dark, narrow hallway. I followed him, turning down the hallway to the right. We came to a panel, which Aaron unlatched and removed, placing it to the side. A rope attached to a metal brace jutted out above the panel's frame.

Aaron stuck his head out to look around, then threw the rope down. He held his hand out to me. I stared at it for a second, hesitating, then scooched in close to him without taking his hand. I didn't want to connect if I could help it. He grimaced, then wrapped his arm under my pack and around my waist.

"Start pulling up the shield," he said. "I'll lower us down." I nodded, avoiding his eyes. He leaned out of the panel into the open air, taking me with him. Enormous raindrops slapped my face as I placed my hand on my chest, sending Protection into my own heart. The colorful lights swirled around us like fireflies, interacting with the raindrops and making hissing sounds. I couldn't open the shield wide enough to encompass both of our bodies without pushing the rope outside of the shield, but I held a small sphere ready to expand outward.

Aaron's hand slipped a little on the wet rope and he hugged me to him tightly. It felt good, and I wanted to hug him back, but I reminded myself that we were breaking up. That thought swept me out of my terror and into a desperate anguish.

I had hoped that time with me would give him confidence and security, but it hadn't worked. Sure, he now knew that Ward was gay; though, I still wasn't sure if he fully understood what that meant, but that didn't change the fact that he had attempted to control me and limit the people with whom I interacted. He had intended to isolate me.

Maybe it wasn't his fault, I thought. *I am sneaky and manipulative, it's true, and his Evocation fragment makes emotional regulation challenging and—*

Stop making excuses for him, Spirit snapped, her voice echoing through my head like a bullet. I winced, then spotted her on the ground below, waiting for us to finish our descent. *He's a grown man. I feel bad for him, too, but it's not your job to fix him. Either he's giving you what you need or he isn't, and you deserve to get what you need. If you can't be with me, then at least hold him accountable. You're allowed to have friends, Lina. Now stop thinking about this crap and concentrate.*

I stared down at Spirit as we descended, surprised. *You were never just a friend to me, Spirit*, I thought to her. *You've always been more like a—*

If you put "sister" in that blank, I'm going straight over the death bridge.

Soulmate.

We stared at each other as Aaron and I landed on the ground. There was nothing more to say. We loved each other, but we had missed our chance, and now I had a job to do. I broke eye contact first, swallowing my emotions. They wouldn't do me any good now.

The shield solidified into a transparent barrier with the colored lights flickering within the barrier itself. Aqua, green, blood-red, and magenta were there as before, but with two more colors added. A bright vermilion flame appeared, a result of mixing reservoirs with Aaron, and now, a new fragment that took the form of swirling, molten gold.

Hello, my pretty. Where did you come from?

I heard a tapping noise and looked up to see rain hitting the top of the curved shield and sliding down the side.

Aaron took my hand so we could both be inside the shield, pulling me into a deep Connection link. The uninvited closeness was uncomfortable, but my attention was pulled away from that fact by another *bang, bang, bang* on the front door.

"Aaron Atticus! Last chance! I'm going to burn this place down and then kill your *dog*. Painfully." I cringed, recalling that "dog" was what they called gay people here.

Hurry, Aaron thought. We jogged together toward the front of the house. There was something about the way Axel spoke that made me believe he would not only kill Ward but enjoy it. I hadn't even seen this man yet and I had already reconsidered whether I could murder him. I wondered idly whether I could use Conjuration to rip his soul right out of his body.

Maybe eventually, Spirit thought to me, *but I doubt you're strong enough yet, and I don't think you could absorb his reservoir if you did that. His spirit would depart and take his reservoir with it.*

We slowed to a walk as we reached the corner of the house. Aaron peeked around. *They're all still at the doors*, he thought. *They must be under Projection, otherwise one of those idiots might have thought to check for an escape route.*

They are. I can see it, Spirit thought. *Their spirits have a dark purple haze around them, almost an indigo color. It's strangely hypnotic. It's beautiful.*

"Stay with me, Spirit," I whispered. "Don't go near them. Stay close to me." Spirit didn't look at me, instead drifting toward the überzombies. *Spirit! Stay with me!* I thought to her urgently. She turned her eyes to me. *Focus. I need you to direct Axel's thoughts to me. Tell me what he's thinking.*

Aaron gasped. *What is this? You can read minds now?*

Spirit can, not me.

Spirit shook her head as if to wake herself up, and then I heard Axel's thoughts drifting in. They were audible, as if coming from a radio station with poor reception, but somehow also conveyed context, feelings, and desires. I knew what Axel wanted and what he would do to get it. His voice was Spirit's interpretation, though, and didn't remotely match the voice I heard with my ears, sounding instead like Jafar from Disney's *Aladdin*.

One moment more, Axel thought, *then I get to do my favorite thing.* He gazed down at the torch he held in his hand, entranced. This man loved fire. He itched to burn down the house, regardless of what Aaron did. The only question was who would be inside the house when it burned down and how much the rain would impede his efforts.

Axel glanced over his shoulder at Ward, who lay on the ground, soaked and muddy, but essentially okay. Two men, one with long, dark auburn hair, and one with short, curly black hair, stood on either side of Ward, their dark eyes strangely blank.

A third man, the smallest of the group, stood beside Axel, holding an umbrella. He was really too petite to be called an über-zombie. He was even shorter than Aaron. The last man, much larger than the rest, stood a bit farther away, rocking back and forth as if agitated. Axel didn't notice his distress.

Axel pondered his next move. *Should I throw the dog back in the house? No, I suppose not. We might still need him.* He looked back at the house. *I hope they come out. I want to see this girl the Holy Daughter is so afraid of that she let her linger here for more than two months. It would be a waste to kill her without at least using her first.*

Aaron and I both cringed at the word "using." This man's RTA had officially reached a hundred percent. He intended to rape me right in front of Aaron. To him, that was the most humiliating thing you could do to both a woman and her lover, and he liked doing it almost as much as he liked burning down houses with people inside them. He anticipated doing both today, but I wouldn't be the one burning in the house as he'd been instructed to bring me back to the palace in one piece. He'd opened the front door and left it ajar with the intention of catching me and Aaron in the foyer so he could complete the task. Aaron's plan had saved us from that.

Aaron squeezed my hand so hard I almost pulled it away from him. *Sorry*, he thought, relaxing. He cocked his crossbow, imagining Axel's neck explode.

My attitude toward Aaron softened despite Spirit's chastisement. *Maybe I overreacted*, I thought. I somehow *heard* Spirit roll her eyes.

Aaron turned to me, gazing down into my face. *I won't let him hurt you*, he thought to me. *I love you.*

Aaron's eyes widened as he heard himself think that last part. He hadn't meant to send me that thought. He looked into my eyes, searching for my reaction.

I froze, not knowing how to respond. The sentiment squashed any anger I had left, but it was such awkward timing. Not only were we in danger, but I had literally just recognized that I'd probably been in love with Spirit, or at least had loving feelings toward her. I wasn't even sure what that meant.

Now that my righteous fury had subsided, it was obvious to me that I would have regretted leaving the farm with Ward. I would have missed Aaron's intensity and the way he listened so carefully to everything I said, thoughtfully commenting. Aside from his jealousy, he was very accommodating, tolerating my messiness and my strange Earth ways, and patiently teaching me what I needed to know about surviving life on Monash. I would have missed his beautiful face and his warm hands. I would have missed him terribly, but did that mean I loved him? I didn't know for sure. The question made my stomach twist into knots.

The answer is simple, Spirit thought to me confidentially. *Can you see yourself staying with him forever and having his babies?*

Spirit—

It's okay, she thought. *It's okay to choose him, to trust him. He's kind of an asshole, but he won't do what Drew did to you, Lina. He's all in. That, I know for sure.*

I stared up into Aaron's face and sighed heavily, then nodded. The answer was yes, I could see myself doing those things. *Dammit.*

One corner of Aaron's mouth twitched up, though I knew he wasn't satisfied with that lukewarm answer. Nevertheless, he bent down and kissed me, holding me to him a little too tightly. *Okay*, he thought. *That will suffice for now. Let's go.*

Chapter Twenty-two

"You mustn't give the key to Mortier," said Syndeth. "We would be stuck here in her realm forever while she's out causing havoc and misery throughout all of creation."

"I know," said Linorra, "but I wouldn't be able to live with myself if any harm came to Viktor because of me."

"And what about me?" Syndeth asked.

I dropped my pack at the side of the house, tucked it under a bush, then followed Aaron out into the open. I got a look at Magister Axel for the first time, standing just outside the door. He appeared younger than I had imagined, like a man in his prime who took excellent care of his health. He was tall and slender, statuesque even, and would have been attractive if not for the crazed expression of bloodlust plainly imprinted on his features.

The sleeves of his tunic were rolled up like he was prepared to do heavy work, and his wide-brimmed hat dripped with rainwater despite the umbrella. His tunic was belted with leather, and a matching sheath held a long dagger with an intricately filigreed golden handle.

The petite man had to stretch to hold the umbrella high enough that it didn't catch fire from Axel's torch. Axel gazed at the flames as if they were a precious treasure, then turned to Ward again, spotting us in the process.

"There!" he shouted, pointing a long finger at us. "Get them and bring them to me," Axel said. He sounded thoroughly annoyed.

Calmly, Aaron thought to me, pulling my hand to walk toward Axel.

I'm trying, I responded. I took a deep breath in and out.

The three überzombies who weren't holding the umbrella moved toward us, making Axel scowl deeply. "No, not you, Ellis!" he snapped. "You and you," he said, pointing toward the other two. "Go get them!" He motioned to the man with auburn hair and said, "Ellis, guard the dog."

Jesus. That's Ward's brother, I thought.

I clenched my teeth as we continued to walk toward the magister. Ward lay supine in some muddy grass to the right of Axel, his eyes closed. His newly healed face was covered in blood, his nose misshapen.

I've changed my mind, I thought. *I could easily kill this man.*

The two überzombies strode toward us. As they got closer, I noticed that they were both taller than Aaron, though not as tall as Axel. They had overly pale skin and the same brown eyes and black hair that dominated the region. They appeared unkempt, as if they hadn't changed clothes or brushed their hair or teeth in the past decade. Their knee-length brown tunics were unbelted, more like potato sacks than clothing. They didn't seem to notice the rain, nor did they understand that they couldn't just come and grab us.

The largest of the überzombies approached on the right. He looked as though he could take Aaron in a fight on a good day. He had wide-set, vacant eyes, and a red puffy nose that made me wonder if he was ill. He coughed a few times, then stumbled but didn't fall. This was not a good day for him, it seemed.

The one with short, curly hair approached on the left. He was positively skeletal, and his face and hands were covered in dirt. Both men had bloodshot eyes with dark circles under them. They truly did look like zombies in the sense that they were half dead from exhaustion and neglect.

Save yourself first, Spirit thought. *You can't do anything for these men right now.*

The two überzombies came close and reached for our arms, only to bump up against the shield. They looked at each other in confusion, and then the big one walked behind us and pushed against the shield as if he were trying to push a boulder. It worked. The emaciated one stood to the side, keeping us from veering away.

We got to within ten feet of Axel when he lifted his hand to indicate that we should stop. "That's far enough," he said, overtly leering at my body. The creepy grin on his face sent shivers down my spine and it was all I could do to keep myself from bolting. "Now, release your shield and get down on your knees."

Neither I nor Aaron moved. "No thanks," I said. "I wouldn't want you to get the wrong idea about me."

Don't taunt the psychopath, Aaron thought to me urgently.

Axel narrowed his eyes, his smirk fading, then he turned to Ward. "Ellis, kick the dog." Ellis turned to Ward and viciously kicked him in his side. Ward grunted, opening his eyes for a moment, rolling a little, but then he closed them again, falling unconscious.

"No!" I screamed. "Ellis, he's your brother. Leave him alone!" Ellis stared at me for a moment, confused, then his face went blank again. Like the other two überzombies, Ellis's face was filthy, and he swayed a little, as if he might fall asleep where he stood. His hand was covered in blood, as mangled as Ward's nose.

"Ellis belongs to me," Axel said. "He will do what he's told. Ellis, kick the dog again. Harder this time."

Ellis did what he was told. He kicked Ward so hard that, despite my weak Earth hearing, I heard his ribs crack over the sound of the rain. Ward woke up to whimper, rolled to his side, and spit blood. His breath came in loud wheezes.

I almost went to him, but Aaron pulled me back, tucking me behind him as if to shield me from the sight of Ward's pain. Thunder boomed somewhere in the distance, and the rain seemed to respond to Ward's distress by increasing in intensity. Aaron and I were shielded from it, but the rain that streamed off the side blurred our view. We needed windshield wipers.

"What do you want, Axel?" Aaron demanded.

Axel cackled. "Now we get to it," he said. "First you let your whore speak for you, and finally you step up and speak for yourself. Release your shield and get down on your knees." Axel's body looked relaxed, but his eyes never stopped tracking Aaron's movements.

Still, Aaron and I didn't move. "That's not going to happen, Axel. Instead, you're going to call off your thralls and leave this place."

Axel laughed again. "Tell you what, Aaron. I'm feeling generous today. I will open up a bridge to Earth and send you over there. You leave the dog and the bitch here with me, and we both get what we want."

Aaron was about to respond with an immediate no, but I stopped him. *Wait,* I thought, pulling him to the side, though his eyes remained trained on Axel.

I can protect myself, Aaron. You should take his deal.

What? Aaron's eyes flicked to mine. *Lee, I will not leave you here with this monster. He will kill you.*

I don't think so, I said. *He wants me. I think we could negotiate for Ward. Take him back with you to Earth, and I will go with Axel to the palace with my shield up.*

No, absolutely not, Aaron responded. *I'm not leaving you.*

But, Aaron—

No! Aaron thought to me. The word was absolute. I blinked at the finality of it. *If you want to be rid of me, then I'll leave, but not until you're safe.*

I stared up at him and shook my head, guilt creeping into my mind. *No, I don't.*

"The Holy Daughter was right," Axel said. I turned back to him to see that he'd been watching our interaction closely. "She is a talented connector. She's already mastered internal communication. Interesting. She'd be a very valuable servant. And a healer as well."

His eyes raked over my body again, lingering on my legs. Aaron's warning about the tight pants suddenly made more sense. I would punch this douchebag right in his dick. If I could reach that high.

"Thanks, but I already have a job," I said.

Axel chuckled. "Spirited," he said. "The pit will fix that."

"Your face is a pit," I spat. I don't know where it came from. The rain was pouring down, now, and we were all slowly sinking into the mud. I wasn't so much terrified as I was pissed off. This guy was a lecherous, imbecilic troglodyte, and I wasn't taking any more of his shit.

Lee, don't taunt the psychopath.

Fuck this guy.

Aaron squeezed my hand, pulling me farther behind him so I couldn't interact with Axel directly.

"Ellis, take out your weapon and point it at the dog's head," Axel said. Ellis did as he was told, and my heart skipped a beat. I became aware of the fact that the two überzombies who'd been guarding the back door were now slinking around the house through the dark. These two wore much finer clothes, similar to Axel's, each with a wide hat and golden cloak. They were younger and much less bedraggled than the rest, though their hats didn't save them from the deluge. They moved in to flank us. We were surrounded.

Aaron glanced over his shoulder at the newcomers, then back at Axel and said, calmly, as if he were giving a patient warning to a child, "This will not end well for you, Axel. Hurt him again and you will get to see why nobody has gotten to me all these years, despite their many, many attempts. You only brought six with you, and they all look like they need a hot meal and a week of sleep. That won't be nearly enough to keep me from killing you."

Axel hesitated, then clenched his jaw, his face filling with rage. "How dare you," he growled. "You are a traitor, Aaron Atticus!"

I thought we weren't supposed to piss off the psychopath, I thought, though I was really thinking about what he'd said about their attempts to "get him." Ward had mentioned something about it, but Aaron had never spoken of that to me.

Too late for diplomacy, Aaron thought back.

"Accept my offer," Axel hissed. "You're lucky to be getting any offer at all. I will give you the dog, and I will take the bitch. She can even keep her shield up. I promise not to kill her."

Without warning, Axel's thoughts came to us in a flood through Spirit. *I will make her scream though*, he thought. *First with pain, then with pleasure.*

He was imagining all the things he would do to me, where he would take me, how he would subdue and bind me, and which instruments of torture he would use. He was getting hard just thinking about it.

Axel was an actual sadist, and he had done all these things before, usually to young girls from SONA. Occasionally, he was tasked with subduing the girls who were identified as greater protectors so that they could be inducted into the Rhoyal Healers Guild. They always had Protection; he always succeeded in breaking them. He had one that very minute, a girl of about fourteen, tied up in his manor and ready to deliver to the compound.

He marveled at his luck in getting two protectors so close together. He wondered how long he could keep me before he had to turn me over to Seleca. How many times could he rape me before he had to deliver? Enough to impregnate me? Maybe Seleca would let him keep me if that happened since it was so soon after giving the guild another one. Threats to a baby are always a good way to force a protected woman into staying. That's how the Ministry always did it with the Rhoyal Healers.

He'd always wanted to bond a greater protector who could heal him in his own home every night instead of having to pay for the Ministry-owned healers. He was almost fifty, after all. Time to settle down. I wasn't as exquisite as Farrah, but I was still a very valuable piece of property. He knew at least three others who might want to rent me. Valuable, indeed.

Aaron's rage bubbled up underneath the onslaught of horrific thoughts and images. It nauseated me, making me feel unsteady. I had to rest my forehead on Aaron's back to keep from falling over.

Stop, Spirit! Aaron demanded. *That's enough. We get it. I won't let her go.*

He's pure evil, I thought. *Pure evil. Pure evil.* I shook uncontrollably. Aaron reached his arm back to steady me.

"Well, Aaron?" Axel demanded, his smirk firmly planted on his face again. "What will it be? Go on your way and everyone lives? Or put the dog down?"

Get ready to drop the shield, Lee.

What are we doing? I asked, panicking again.

I'm going to disarm Ellis. You grab Ward and pull the shield back up around all of us. Then we'll leave.

Are you sure?

Yes, he thought, pulling out his own dagger. *I will handle Ellis. You grab Ward.*

Okay, I thought to him uncertainly. It was a simple enough plan, but it didn't feel right. I could hear my own heart pounding.

It wasn't until that moment that I truly grasped that this war with the Ministry would not be an idealist's fantasy. People were going to die. Maybe lots of people. Maybe me. I had known it intellectually before, and I had gotten a taste of it when Seleca attacked us, but I hadn't really believed it. I had believed, deep down, that I would make it home, bring Aaron and Ward back with me, find my parents, and everything would go back to normal.

I had been so naive, but I understood the situation now. Ward was lying on the ground, bleeding again. *Dying* again, at the hands of his own brother, who was in some kind of trance.

These enslaved men could be made to do anything, including ignoring basic needs like eating, sleeping, and bathing. They could be made to kill their own family. It was unthinkable. It was as if their minds were separated from their bodies, like they weren't even aware of what they were experiencing.

Their souls are imprisoned, I thought, *or lured away.*

"By the beautiful light," Spirit said.

Yes. The light. I can't see it, but Spirit can.

That's the Projection trance, Aaron thought. His contribution startled me. I had become so lost in my own thoughts that I had forgotten he could hear them.

Right. Projection. Aaron, what is the complement of Projection?

Transformation, he answered.

My mind raced. An idea had been bouncing around in the back of my head that I hadn't yet acknowledged, and I now had to test it out. My life depended on the answer, but I was willing to take that risk for Ward. I just hoped I wasn't sacrificing Aaron in the process.

Aaron, I need you to trust me, okay? When I let down my shield, let me handle Ellis. You defend us from the others. Do you think you can do that?

Lee, it's too dangerous. Your idea has merit, but we don't know if it will work.

Please, Aaron. I just need a moment. If it doesn't work, I'll pull the shield back up.

Aaron wanted to think about it, as he was inclined to do, but we were out of time. I thought he might give me his absolute *no* again, but he just turned to face me, considering. The rain was now torrential, and in the dark, with the shield around us, I could barely see beyond the transparent barrier. It felt almost private.

Okay, he thought, resting his forehead on mine. *I trust you.* That had cost him something. Giving away trust had been more difficult for him than admitting he loved me. I needed to do a better job of earning that trust.

"Love," Axel sneered. He had to shout over the rain, but his voice was piercing, a disturbing intrusion into our stolen moment. "It's a dangerous thing. It makes you take unnecessary risks to save what isn't worth the mud beneath your boots. Ellis, kill the dog." Then he turned and threw his torch into the open front door.

Chapter Twenty-three

For the first time, Linorra didn't know how to do the right thing. All her options felt wrong. Confusion bubbled up in her mind, threatening to rob her of her resolve.

There was no time to think about saving the house. As soon as I heard Axel's kill order, I dropped the shield and the world transformed into a thunderous waterfall.

Aaron sprang toward the über-zombie holding Axel's umbrella. He slipped a little in the mud, but they must have been expecting Aaron to jump at Ellis first because they were surprised when he instead pushed the umbrella man forcefully into Axel, knocking them both down. Axel squealed like a toddler and landed on his butt in the mud with his servant on top of him. The umbrella flew out of reach, and the rain engulfed them both.

I jumped toward Ellis, who still held a crossbow at Ward's head, his hand shaking. I had a very similar idea to Aaron's, except that I couldn't push Ellis down. He was eight feet tall and had at least sixty pounds on me, but I was able to thrust his arm out of the way so the shot went wide and hit the side of the house. I grabbed his wounded hand and forced Connection into him as deeply as I could, screaming his name through the link.

Ellis! Stop!

Ellis did stop, and his eyes locked with mine. He struggled against me, pulling his hand back. I hung on for dear life, a difficult task given that we were both soaking wet. My link to him told me that he was confused and desperate and that his hand was broken and in excruciating pain.

Somewhere in his mind, he must have known that he'd been ordered to murder his own brother. His grip on the crossbow was shaky, as if he tried to make himself drop it. Perhaps he fought to take back control and was making progress, but it wasn't quickly enough.

Ellis! Listen to me! I'm trying to help you!

Ellis wrenched his hand away, but his feet slipped in the mud and he fell backward, taking me with him. I landed on top of him, trying desperately to hang on. It would be mere moments before his superior strength overcame my efforts. Then he would kill me.

Aaron was busy with the other four überzombies and couldn't help. He'd managed to shoot three of them in the upper thigh, downing them neatly, but the fourth über-zombie, the largest, was on top of him. He had gotten his hands around Aaron's throat.

Axel shouted behind me, but I couldn't hear what he said over the storm. I wanted to get through to Ellis first, but it wasn't working. Desperate now, I rammed Protection into him as fast as I could, focusing on his broken hand.

This healing was nothing like that first time I'd healed Aaron. I had been weak and unpracticed then. I hadn't known how to quickly mobilize the fragment and direct it with precision. I still had a long way to go, especially with flow regulation, but I had been using the Protection fragment daily for the better part of two months and was now stronger and more skilled.

I was still ignorant as a baby, though. I hadn't understood how much the mutual attraction between Aaron and me had influenced how Protection actually manifested for us. The pleasure of it was always intensely sexual in nature. Even Ward, who had been *expecting* Protection to feel like sex because that's what he was always told, had experienced it that way.

It isn't that way for everyone, though. Ellis, for example, was vehemently opposed to any kind of forced sexual encounter due to his time spent with Axel. So, for him, Protection felt more like getting jabbed with a syringe full of narcotics. And while Aaron had grown accustomed to receiving the Protection fragment and had built up a tolerance, Ellis had no such defenses. He immediately let out a brief, high-pitched wail, then went rigid with what looked like a seizure but probably felt more like an overdose of heroin. His eyes rolled back in his head, and he dropped the crossbow into the mud.

Oops. That might have been a bit much. Sorry, Ellis. That's two fragments. Halfway there. Don't let go!

I called to the Conjuration fragment from the reservoir I knew to be lurking in the back of my head. It filled my body with its misty presence, and I sent it into the stream of fragments flowing into Ellis. His body stopped convulsing and tensed, then shivered violently as Conjuration caused my blended fragment link to latch on to his very soul. His mouth opened in a silent scream, letting water pour in from the sky. He choked and coughed violently, nearly throwing me off.

Shit. That's three. Here comes the tricky part.

I had been right about Ward. He did, indeed, have a bit of his Transformation reservoir left in him, and he had donated some to me when I was sucked into his nightmare. Its golden light had appeared within my shield like a beacon of hope. My consciousness had delved so deep inside of him that we had literally intertwined our spirits. In doing so, we had mixed reservoirs, and I had come out with the exact thing I needed to break his brother free. That is, if I could figure out how to use it.

Ward told me once that Transformation was a fragment that could bring your body into alignment with your spirit. It brought your physical being closer to how you envisioned yourself. Ward had imagined himself to be a dog. Ellis had envisioned a future in the Metalworkers Guild. Aaron had seen himself as a dragon, lurking in the mountains. But what was I?

"A warrior," Spirit said.

What? No, I'm not! I'm a freaking office manager, a clumsy jackass who cries and falls down.

"You," Spirit said sternly, "are the woman who was thrown onto an alien planet and within a day outwitted an enemy that had a hundred years of experience. You're the woman who, within a summer, read nearly an entire library and learned skills it should take decades to master. You're the woman who convinced a dragon to abandon his dream and help you fight a war against an oppressive theocracy. You're the woman who puts one blistered foot in front of the other and keeps fucking going. You're a warrior, Lina!"

Her words stunned me. I had never heard Spirit speak like that before. She said "fuck" and everything. And it was all true. I had done all those things.

"I *am* a warrior," I said to myself.

Axel shouted directions at the one minion he had left as Aaron wrestled the giant überzombie. Though he'd gotten out of the chokehold, he was still occupied. I had seconds before Axel came for me.

I reached for Transformation, imagining myself as a warrior. The only thing I could think of was *Xena: Warrior Princess*, which I had loved as a kid.

"I'm a warrior!" I screeched to no one. I solidified that image in my brain, and it glowed with a radiant golden light. I imagined myself scooping up that golden light with my hands, and when I did, it injected a feeling of pure exhilarated inspiration into my body.

The world became a glorious city of gold, ripe for the taking. I could do anything I set my mind to. I was a goddess. I was invincible. *Forget Xena*, I thought, *I'm freaking Captain Marvel!* I didn't want to let the feeling go, but I had a goal, and I had no doubt whatsoever that I would be successful. *I* was the key to unlocking Ellis's mind.

My Transformation reservoir was sparse, and I had trouble grabbing it, but I added the meager amount of fragment I could manipulate into the stream flowing into Ellis. My Connection carried it the rest of the way for me. His eyes flew open, and he screamed in agony, shocking me out of my manic confidence. I'd felt so good that I hadn't considered that forcing Transformation into another person might be painful.

I gripped Ellis's hands as he squirmed away from me with everything he had. His wet hands slipped out of my grip, and he finally bucked me off. I landed on my back in the mud, right at Axel's feet.

"Enough!" Axel bellowed. He held the umbrella over himself now.

I froze. Axel brandished his golden dagger, shoved it at my throat, and pressed down. It broke my skin with a sharp sting. Drenched and muddy, Axel leaned in close enough that I could clearly feel a familiar resonance. He was protected.

The rain had lessened a bit but still came down steadily around the perimeter of the umbrella.

I glanced in Aaron's direction to see him standing over the prostrate body of the giant über-zombie. The unconscious man's face was covered in burns, his brown potato-sack tunic smoldering.

Aaron's tunic had been torn almost off and was only held in place by his belt. He'd lost his crossbow somewhere as well as his vest. It looked like the other three had gotten back up to fight him at some point, but they now lay around him, unconscious, faces bloodied. One of the men had a bolt sticking out of his left shoulder, and he panted like a dog.

Axel glared at Aaron with unrestrained hatred. Aaron stared right back.

"Take one step and I will slide this dagger so far into her neck that no amount of Protection will save her," Axel growled.

"Do that," Aaron responded, "and I will kill you before you have the chance to pull it out again. I told you six wasn't enough. You should have fled while you had the chance." His voice was steady, controlled, but little wisps of steam fluttered off his bare chest and shoulders. His bracelet was gone. He looked like a man about to commit murder for sport. He was terrifying, and I saw that terror reflected in Axel's eyes.

Ellis rolled over and sat up. He looked around, then spotted his crossbow lying on the ground. With some effort, he got to his feet and retrieved it from the mud.

Axel watched Ellis retrieve the weapon and he visibly relaxed, his face regaining that crazed expression. It was more clenched teeth than smile. He spoke directly to me for the first time. "You see, you ignorant child? Ellis is mine. Did you really think you could heal the Projection fragment out of him? It doesn't work like that. All you did was strengthen him so he could hold you down while I teach you your first lesson."

Axel tossed the umbrella aside and grabbed a fistful of my hair. The rain had turned to sleet, and it pelted my face and stung my eyes. He pulled my face up to his mouth with gleeful malice. I winced but ground my teeth against the pain of ripping hair. "The first lesson is always the hardest," he purred, "and the most fun." He sensuously tipped his head and took my earlobe into his mouth, a low sigh of pleasure in his chest. Then he bit down and ripped my earring out with his teeth, tearing through my earlobe.

I screamed, instinctively grabbing Axel's hand to pull it away from my throat, but he was too strong. I used the contact to push Protection into him even harder than I had for Ellis. Nothing happened. He spit my own blood back into my face.

Aaron moved toward us, but Axel drew his dagger tightly against my throat, slicing into me.

"Don't move, traitor!" Axel screamed at Aaron. He held me by my hair, squeezing so hard that I thought he would pull my scalp clean off. I cried out again as the blood streamed out of the wound in my neck, mingling with rain and blood from my ripped earlobe and spilling onto my wet clothing. I shook from the stress, the pain, and the cold sleet.

"I will kill her," Axel said. "I swear it. I only need one of them and I already have the dog, so you'll either watch me take her or you'll watch her die. Your choice. Ellis, point your crossbow at the traitor."

Ellis didn't move. He blinked a few times, then lifted a hand to wipe mud off his face.

Spirit! What do I do?

"Ellis!" yelled Axel again, his voice cracking. His dagger shook when he spoke, digging deeper into my neck.

I squeezed my eyes shut. *Spirit! Help me!*

"You've already beaten him," Spirit said calmly. Her voice cut through the storm as if it were directed into my ears through earbuds. "He just doesn't know it yet."

Axel's eyebrows knit together, realizing he'd missed something. "Ellis, kill the traitor!" he shrieked.

Ellis no longer appeared confused. He lifted his eyes to meet Axel's gaze, and they glowed brightly with that same beautiful amber color Ward's had. That's how I could see, even in the darkness, that Spirit was right. He had come back to himself, and he had only one thing on his mind: revenge.

Ellis lifted his crossbow to Axel's chest and pulled the trigger twice.

The impact knocked Axel back a few feet and onto his back with a *squish*. The dagger flung away from my neck, slicing me again in the process.

"Lee!" Aaron yelled. He ran to me and held his hand to my neck to apply pressure. "Hang on, I've got you," he said. I bled profusely and the whole world spun around me, but I could already feel Protection healing my wounds. Now that I had a sense of it, I could push it along to speed up the process.

"I'll be okay," I rasped. "Help me over to Axel before he dies and we lose our chance." My teeth chattered and my words slurred.

"I'm more worried about losing you," he said. "Your lips are blue."

"I'll be okay," I insisted. I tasted blood in my mouth, but I would not be distracted. "Help me."

Aaron picked me up and carried me over to Axel. He held me against his bare chest, and I soaked in his body heat like a sponge. The sleet, which had briefly fallen with a painful vengeance, had become a soft, quietly drifting snow.

Axel stared up at the sky, stunned. His reflective eyes blinked against the snowflakes that caught in his eyelashes. He held his hands up as we approached him, as if he could push us away. He was already weak, though, and his arms were floppy and uncoordinated. His beautiful golden dagger lay several feet away.

"Heal me," he mumbled. "Heal me. I'll help you fight her. I'll help you." He exhaled and closed his eyes as his arms dropped to the ground.

Aaron cautiously set me down next to Axel but stayed pressed up against my back for warmth. Blood, black in the dim light, spurted around one of the bolts in Axel's chest in rhythmic pulses. It had hit him just above his heart, entering between the ribs. He'd be dead in seconds.

Must have been lesser Protection, I thought.

I stared down at him, watching his lifeblood drain from his body. I could have healed him then and saved his life. I could've said that I didn't want to be like Eve and Seleca, that I wanted to do something different, to be a good person and not let someone die who I had the ability to save. But the truth is, Evilina isn't some demon trapped inside of me.

She's me.

I wrapped my trembling hand around Axel's neck and delved into him, searching for his Teleportation reservoir. It was there, hovering around his solar plexus. I couldn't see it, exactly, but I could feel the Absorption fragment within me trying to stick to it like Velcro.

I let it happen. His Protection reservoir was still there, too, but strained in trying to save him from death. I pushed Absorption past Axel's weakened barrier and wrapped it around his reservoir like a mother swaddling a newborn.

I couldn't see his soul leave his body. Perhaps, I speculated, it was because I hadn't yet ascended my Conjuration. Or maybe I didn't want to see the ghost of a man I'd let die so I could steal his reservoir.

I could feel it, though, the way you feel a change in air pressure. I couldn't sense his soul with any of the five basic senses, but there was something in my brain that actively pinged like sonar. I shivered as his spirit fled, and I felt the Teleportation reservoir pull away from me. I hung on and visualized pulling that reservoir out of Axel's chest into my own. It tugged, then came loose.

I had it.

Then, it had me. The instant the Teleportation reservoir snapped free from Axel, it surged into me just as I'd surged back into my body after drifting out, or maybe like Ward when his soul had rushed back into his body, pulling my Protection fragment with it. It felt like the Connection spike, but instead of pain, I was hit with extreme vertigo reminiscent of the feeling you get on a roller coaster rocketing downhill.

I gasped and almost fell, but Aaron caught me. I felt his warm embrace and let him support me entirely, closing my eyes against the dizzying sensation. The vertigo dissipated, only to be replaced by an exhaustion so heavy that it brought to mind my experience in the hospital when they'd pumped me full of drugs. I opened my eyes again, struggling to stay awake, but blackness crept into the corners of my vision.

"Aaron," I muttered, "I'm so tired."

I heard Ellis talking to Aaron, but I couldn't make it out. Aaron responded, "Absorption fatigue" and then something about reliving bad memories.

Great. Thanks for the heads-up.

Chapter Twenty-four

Linorra left Syndeth perched on the lowest bough of an ironwood tree at the edge of the forest, looking out upon Queen Mortier's dark castle. The witch's directions had been true, and she found the secret entrance to the dungeon without incident, then crept down as quickly and silently as she could, nearly slipping on the wet stairs. There were no torches to light the black walkway or cells. She held the glowing sword out in front of her as a light, gripping it tightly. Her hands shook with fright.

When I was a kid, we lived in Eureka, California, close to the Sequoia Park Zoo. It was an older neighborhood with beautiful mature redwood trees and small, well-maintained homes. Back then, it was still safe. I used to walk to and from school every day by myself.

One day, when I was nine, I walked home behind a group of three girls, all a couple of years older than me. I didn't want to join their group. Being alone was so much easier back then. I just trailed at a safe distance, pretending not to see them.

One of the girls turned around to stare at me, then giggled at the other two girls. There was something about my pink *Powerpuff Girls* shirt that they thought was funny. After a minute, that same girl turned around, looked at me again, then stopped to wait. The other two girls followed suit.

Ugh. They're going to say something mean and I'm going to cry again.

"Lina!" the girl called. She knew my name somehow, but I didn't know hers. She was taller than the other two girls and had short, mousy brown hair. She wasn't particularly pretty. I mean, she wasn't ugly, but both of her friends were definitely prettier than her, and I'm thinking that didn't sit well.

"I like your shirt," she said. The other two girls smirked. I'm not always great with social cues, but even I knew she was making fun of me.

"Thanks," I said, then sped up and passed the girls.

As I passed, Mousehead said, "And your backpack!" Then they all tittered. My backpack was purple and had *Xena: Warrior Princess* on it. Okay, maybe the shirt was a little babyish, but my backpack was badass. I turned around and gave her a look like she was crazy.

"Thanks," I said again, obviously sarcastic this time.

"No," said Mousehead. "I really like it. Can I see it?"

"I can't. I gotta get home," I said, then sped up to a jog. This was turning into a bad situation.

"Don't be a baby. Just let me see it," she called after me. She jogged to catch up to me and grabbed the loop on my bag, forcing me to a sudden stop and pulling me onto the ground. One of the other girls came up behind her, helping her rip the bag off me. I sat on the ground staring up at them in disbelief.

"Give it back!" I yelled. Then I remembered that my art project was in there. It was a little clay bowl I'd shaped and painted with a pink heart on the bottom. It was nothing special, but I'd planned to give it to my mom. I cried, of course. After all, I am the girl who cries and falls down.

"Why are you crying, little baby?" Mousehead taunted. "It's not like I hurt you."

"Give me my backpack, you stupid *mouse head*!" I yelled. It wasn't the smartest idea, I'll admit, but I was a pissed-off nine-year-old. I had no sense of diplomacy back then. Or ever.

Mousehead glared like she was about to kick me, but I heard a car coming down the road. She looked up, standing back from me. "You want it back?" she asked. "Go get it."

Then, just as the car drove by, she threw the bag into the road under the tires. The car screeched to a halt just after its front tire crunched over the bag. I screamed, tears running down my face, but there was nothing to be done.

It wasn't until then that I heard my mom's shar-pei, Molly, barking furiously from the back seat and noticed that it was my dad's car. A surge of vengeful hope filled me. Mousehead would get it now. My dad looked over at us calmly, then got out of his car and ambled over. I still sat on the ground, crying. He knew exactly what had happened, he told me later, but he pretended to be confused.

"What is going on?" he asked in his adorable accent. "Someone attacked me and Molly with a purple missile."

Mousehead pointed at me while the other two girls just kept their heads down. It seemed to me that their expressions of guilt should have been obvious to anyone.

"I see," he said. "Well, let's see what we can do." He walked over to the car and bent down to retrieve the backpack from behind the right front tire. My dad pulled the bag out and brushed it off. It was dirty, but it seemed okay.

"It had my present in it," I said, then cried even harder.

"Oh, no!" he said, opening the bag to peek inside. I knew what he saw in there. It was crushed, like my little heart.

My dad eyed the girls one by one, then said, "Girls, go on home." Mousehead smirked, knowing she had gotten away with her evil crime, and they continued down the street.

I stared after them incredulously, then up at my dad.

"Get in the car, Lina," he said.

"No!" I snapped. "I don't want to get in the car with you. They pushed me down and ruined my present, and you just let them go. You don't even care about me!" The tears made trails down my dusty face. Molly whined from the back seat and scratched at the window.

He's even worse than Mousehead, I thought.

My dad gazed down at me with compassion, then squatted next to me and rubbed my back. The sun gleamed off the top of his bald pate.

"Lina, you're gonna learn that, while there is a time and a place for punishing evildoers, most of the time they hang themselves. That tall girl thought she got away with it, but did you see the other two girls?"

I shook my head.

"They looked mighty anxious. They weren't smiling at all, especially that girl on the left. I think she was pretty upset. I think she might be wondering if it's a good idea to be friends with a bully who pushes people down and gets her in trouble. If you wait, you might see that the tall girl gets exactly what's coming to her and you didn't need to lift a finger."

I crossed my arms and pouted, refusing to get up. I wanted justice. I wanted Mouse-head's mousy head on a platter. With chips!

"Lina, a lot of times you have no choice but to fight, but there are always consequences to that route. When you can, it's better to step away and let people suffer the consequences of their own bad choices. It gets you into less trouble and teaches them a lesson that fighting never could."

He was right. That girl on the left, Emily, told her parents what happened, and they forbade her from being friends with Mousehead. Then the other girl, Jess, chose Emily over Mousehead, and she also abandoned her. Then, those two girls called her "Mouse-head" in school, and the name stuck.

She had that name until I moved away a year later, and probably beyond. I actually felt kind of bad for her, though not really because she blamed me for the whole thing. Maybe he wasn't entirely right about the lesson part.

The wave of exhaustion passed, and I opened my eyes again to see Axel's corpse. In death, his eyes had fallen open just a crack, staring at nothing, his pupils huge and black. I looked away, not wanting to see the ugly result of my work. I had fallen asleep just long enough to dream about my first enemy, Mousehead, the one I'd destroyed with words and patience. That was the beginning, and now here I was at the inevitable progression of my corruption. My first kill.

I told myself that it wasn't *I* who'd pulled the trigger, but I couldn't escape the fact that I could have saved Axel and chose not to. He was dead because I wanted him that way. Period. Did he deserve it? Probably. He was a murderer himself, wasn't he? He was a rapist and a sadist and a child killer. I couldn't think of someone who deserved it more, yet it left me feeling empty, like I'd just lost a part of myself that I could never recover.

Aaron crouched behind me, still holding me up, waiting for me to finish mourning my lost innocence. The only light had come from the fire in the doorway, but it was out now. The rain had flooded into the entryway and put the torch out before it could do anything more than make a black circle on the wood floors. Lucky.

Aaron picked me all the way up and held me in his arms like a baby. His zombie opponents had landed a few good hits on him. He had a goose egg forming on his left temple. There were fingernail scratches on his forehead that trailed toward his right eye, but his eyes were clear and bright.

"I let him die," I said, staring into his shadowed face.

"Yes," he said, "but don't take responsibility for it. He did that to himself. What you have to decide is if you can stomach it again because if we stay here and fight, this will not be the last death you witness. It will only get worse, and they won't all be pure evil like Axel."

I mulled that over for a moment. I didn't know what I was supposed to feel. I was glad the man was dead. He was an evildoer, as my dad would say. But who was I to decide his fate?

"Put me down," I murmured. "I can stand now."

Aaron set me on my feet and rubbed my back. I was still bone-tired and overwhelmed by a deep longing for home. *I need to learn how to use this Teleportation fragment as soon as possible.*

Spirit appeared in front of me. *Well, that was super creepy. Are you aware that you just ripped up a person's soul?*

I gave Spirit a flat stare. *A ghost is calling* me *creepy. I've hit a new low. Wait, Aaron can't hear when you send thoughts to me, can he?*

"They're all thoughts, sort of," she said aloud, "just projected differently, but no, thoughts go to one person. Words go to all." Aaron glanced in Spirit's direction, then squinted as if struggling to see something far away.

He's starting to see me, Spirit thought to me, grinning. *That will be fun.*

I decided to change the subject. "Axel has a girl tied up in his house," I said. "A kid. We have to save her."

"Cobb took my brother too," Ellis said, walking toward us. "Back over a bridge to Neesee. It doesn't matter that Axel is dead, Cobb will do whatever he was told."

Ellis picked up the umbrella and brought it over to us. He handed it to Aaron, who held it over me. His Protection reservoir had grown significantly since we met, and his wounds healed in front of my eyes.

"Thanks," I said, leaning into Aaron.

Ellis was covered head to toe in mud, but he was full of life now, unlike when he'd arrived. I really *had* strengthened him. A little too hard, perhaps. I felt my cheeks heat up, and I looked away from him.

Then, my stupid brain processed what he'd said. I spun around. Cobb, the umbrella-toting not-quite-über-zombie, was gone, and so was Ward.

"Dammit!" I exclaimed. I spun around again, still not convinced, but I had to grab Aaron again to steady myself. "Axel must have sent them back while I was . . ." my voice trailed off. Best not to discuss what I had done to Ellis.

Aaron looked back toward the house, then gave the other überzombies a once-over. They were all still on the ground but were stirring. The skeletal man was trying to roll over. Man, that bony guy was persistent.

"Can you heal them like you did Ellis?" Aaron asked.

I nodded, giving Ellis a sideways glance. "You'll have to hold them down," I said.

"I can help," Ellis said, grimacing. I wondered how many girls Axel had made him hold down. More than one, I'd bet.

"Okay," I said.

One by one, I broke their Projection trances with Transformation, combined with Connection, Protection, and Conjuration. The skeletal man, Shane Smite, was the easiest to heal. He had no strength left in him. His older brother, Fitch Smite, the large man, was also easy to heal but much harder to hold down. I was as weak as a kitten, so had to rely on the men for that.

Shane and Fitch hadn't eaten in almost three weeks. Once they were released from their trance, however, they were mostly concerned with saving their other brother, Cobb, who was still enthralled.

The other two men, Markinius and Falondeitric Eboros, were also brothers and the sons of one of Axel's political enemies, Regalinius Eboros. They'd been kidnapped two days prior. They hadn't eaten in that time, either, but were in much better shape. They appeared to be in their late teens, younger than I'd thought when they were a towering presence behind our earlier defensive position. They both had the same black hair and pale skin as the Smite brothers.

"Seleca could send someone to follow up at any time," Aaron said. He glanced up at the sky, then into the distance. Snow covered the ground in a fine powder and cast a peculiar beauty over an otherwise gruesome tableau.

"She'll send more than a handful the next time," Ellis said.

"We need to feed these men and let them sleep," I said, shivering again. "We can leave in the morning. Let's go in. I'm fa-freezing."

"I can stand guard," Ellis said, hugging his own shoulders.

"We'll rotate," Aaron said. "Lina is right. You need to sleep first, Ellis."

"I feel fine," Ellis said. "Great, actually." Ellis smiled, but it didn't reach his eyes, which darted to me for an instant, then looked away. He turned and headed for the house. Aaron watched him go, then narrowed his eyes at me.

I coughed. "I need to grab my pack," I said, then turned and stumbled back toward the side of the house.

Chapter Twenty-five

"Viktor?" Linorra called. There was no answer. There were no guards anywhere. The cells were all empty. The sound of a door slamming at the top of the dungeon stairs sent a spike of dread into her heart and she nearly toppled over with fear. Then the bolt turned, and a muffled laugh floated down to her like poison gas from a troll spider's bog.

Aaron moved Axel's body while I retrieved my bag. He found the man's golden dagger and strapped it to his own belt. Then he walked me up to the tiny bathroom, grabbing the lantern along the way for my weak eyes. He left Ellis to guard the front door while Shane and Fitch guarded the back. Spirit opted to follow Seleca's spiritual stench back to her palace full of stolen heirlooms to make sure that she wasn't headed our way.

Aaron stood guard at my bathroom door while I got cleaned up. He didn't trust the Eboros brothers and wanted to make sure there weren't any "misunderstandings" while I was in there.

When I finished, he bathed himself, then he drained the filthy water and refilled the tub with clean water for the other men, providing them with dry clothes from Terik's and Jorin's closets. None of the men had bathed during their captivity and were grateful.

I helped Aaron prepare a meal for everyone from an oardoo he'd killed and brought back from his walkabout. Over the last two months, he'd taught me the cooking techniques he'd learned from his aunt, Clare, and I was finally becoming semi-useful. I'd never learned to cook as my mother had always dominated the kitchen, but Aaron said I had a knack for it.

"I found the flock down at the southern edge of the property," he said once we'd sat down to eat. "They'd been intentionally penned there. Jorin and Terik probably went to the Moore farm to help them in some way. He does that on rare occasion, and the flock follows him."

"Where is that?" I asked.

"It's just southeast of here, down the coast. He may have gone to Seagral as well, which is a village just on the other side of the farm. That's the only explanation for why the flock would be down there. I would have gone to search, but I didn't want to leave you here by yourself overnight."

"Good choice," I said.

"I didn't think so at first, but now I'm glad," Aaron said.

I didn't respond to his jab. I focused on my food, pushing it around my plate. It was just after midnight, and I was too exhausted to be hungry. The fire crackled in the hearth behind me, and I wanted to curl up next to it on the thick braided rug and fall asleep.

"What did you do with Axel's body?" I asked.

"It's too cold and wet out for a pyre right now," he said. "I hung him in the butcher shed. The body will freeze tonight, but it'll be fine. I'll take care of it tomorrow."

"I've never known it to snow this early in the season," Ellis said. "The Harvest Festival isn't for another couple of days."

Aaron shook his head. "It is strange." He eyed the men as they ate. The oardoo tasted like turkey, except its body was roughly ten times the size and had to be cooked in filets within the hearth. The men would likely finish every bite of it. "You all like the meal, I see."

"I had no idea food could taste this good," Shane said with his mouth full. Wrapped in Terik's hat and coat, he was like a new man. He was still skeletal, but with a clean face, he looked like a human instead of a zombie. They all did.

I noticed for the first time that none of the men had beards. I doubted they'd had access to a razor during their thralldom, revealing that Aaron was the only one who could grow one. That was odd.

"Yes, thank you for your hospitality, Aaron," Fitch said. This was the first time I'd heard him speak, and his voice was rougher than a pack-a-day smoker. He sounded like he chewed up his words before he spit them out. "We won't forget it. I've never eaten oardoo before." He paused, then added, "And thank you for saving us."

He hadn't said it so much *to* me as *near* me. His words floated in the air like an unfinished sentence. Perhaps one that ended with "instead of killing us."

"You're welcome," Aaron said. He turned to me and said quietly, "Oardoo is a delicacy here. We rarely butcher it for meat. The feathers are too valuable."

Ellis knit his brows together as Aaron explained, glanced at me, then back down at his plate again. None of the other men met my eyes.

I reached over and rested my fingers on Aaron's forearm to connect. He'd found his belongings and had donned his bracelet again, though a few of the stones were missing. I slid my hand underneath the bracelet, toying with it idly.

Are they allowed to talk to me? I asked. *I was the one who released them from that awful trance, and no one has acknowledged my presence except Ellis.*

They're embarrassed, Aaron thought to me. *Don't you remember how I was when we first met? You healed them even more quickly than you did me.*

I know, but it wasn't the same as when I healed you. I don't think it felt like sex to them, more like a massive dose of jarring weed.

That may be, but healing usually takes place in private. It's—

Frowned upon, I know. I don't suppose I can show them why it's okay in exactly the same way I showed you.

Aaron snorted. I smiled at him, remembering that glorious event. Everyone looked up from their plates, then down at Aaron's arm where I touched him, then at each other, then back down to their plates.

What's going to happen when they see us heading toward the same bedroom?

Aaron glanced at me, sighed, then said aloud, "You're right. We should address that." The men all looked up expectantly.

"Okay," Aaron said. "I'm sure you've all noticed that Lina is not from around here. She's a greater connector and protector, and she has three other reservoirs as well."

"Four," I corrected him. They all glanced at me, their eyes narrowed, then back at Aaron. My Protection reservoir was actually ascendant, not greater, but it was probably best not to dwell on that. I supposed that the only other people they knew about with so many reservoirs were their dear leaders, Eve and Seleca. It wasn't exactly a welcome comparison.

"Right. Four now." Aaron paused, gazing down at me, then said, "She's also my beloved. I will defend her from *anyone* who tries to harm her."

I gaped at Aaron. I hadn't known the men might need that kind of warning. He'd made a public declaration of his love for me, even though I hadn't technically said it back to him.

I opened my mouth to speak but nothing came out. We stared at each other for a moment.

Finally, Aaron's eyes drifted back to the men. "I also warn you that she's dangerous in her own right and could kill any one of you." He sniffed, then said casually, "Ask your questions."

After a short, awkward silence, Ellis asked, "Who are you?"

I took a deep, steadying breath and said, "My name is Avelina Silva. I'm from Earth." The Eboros brothers finally looked at me, their eyes wide. Falondeitric dropped his fork on the floor. I raised one eyebrow at him. "Ever heard of it?"

"It's real? How did you get here?" Falondeitric asked. Though he was slightly taller than the rest, he seemed young, maybe eighteen or nineteen. Markinius couldn't have been more than a year or two older than that.

I glanced at Aaron. *The Eboros brothers know about Earth*, I thought to him. Aaron shrugged.

"Seleca picked me up and threw me onto a bridge like a fish at market," I said. The Smite brothers nodded, clearly familiar with the concept.

"Where is Earth?" asked Ellis, who sat to my left.

"You mean, like, directionally speaking?" I asked, turning to him. "I have no idea. I don't even know how far away it is. It's another planet."

The Smite brothers looked up with roughly the same expression the Eboros brothers had a moment ago.

"You mean metaphorically?" Shane asked with his mouth still full of oardoo.

I shook my head.

"It's true," Aaron said. "Bridges don't just take you across the province. They can take you to other worlds."

"Is that how your family escaped?" Falondeitric asked.

Aaron narrowed his eyes. That information was supposed to be a secret too. Falondeitric wilted before Aaron's intense regard, dropping his gaze back down to his plate. "My father told me," he said softly. Markinius glared at his brother, pinching one side of his mouth.

Falondeitric appeared as though he might say something else, but Markinius interrupted him. "Stop talking, Falon," he said. "Aaron, we're glad you set us free, but that doesn't change the fact that you're a criminal. We can't help you. If you go to the dirt planet, we'll keep our mouths shut, but that's the most we can do."

"They saved your life, Markus," Ellis snapped, his top lip curling. Apparently, Ellis knew Markinius well enough to use his nickname, a detail I hadn't previously recognized. "You owe them more than that."

"I don't owe them anything," Markinius sneered. "Axel wouldn't have killed us. He planned to trade us back in exchange for mining rights. We would've been back in two days at most. It will take longer than that for us to get back now. I doubt this *healer* can use the Teleportation fragment she absorbed." He'd said the word "healer" as if it were a great insult.

Aaron's chair made a sudden scraping sound as he stood to face Markinius, who sat across from me. Aaron had been sitting at the end of the table, between us. He glared as if he were about to make Markinius into our next meal.

I laughed. It was an odd reaction, I admit, but the whole thing was ridiculous. "Healer? Does that mean prostitute in this stupid world? Jesus, the misogyny here is even worse than on my planet. How could you have so much women-hating when you have a fake goddess in charge?"

Everyone stopped to stare at me. Markinius's face turned bright red. I wondered if he had a fancy gold dagger like Axel's that he might pull out and use to stab me.

"What did you say, *girl*?"

I didn't flinch. I was at least five years older than this brat, and with Aaron right there, I felt pretty brave. I leaned forward and stared Markinius down.

"Fake. Goddess," I said, pronouncing each word distinctly. "She's fake. She's phony. She's false. She's a liar. It's not true. She is *not* a goddess. She's nothing but an evil reservoir thief with a giant ego and a stupid daughter with stupid yellow pants. She's fake! And I'm here to make sure everyone knows it. That's who I am, *boy*," I said and leaned back again. I turned to Ellis, mimicking Aaron's casual tone. "Any more questions?"

Nobody said anything for a moment. Markinius's eyes looked like they were about to pop out of his head, and the only thing keeping him from climbing over the table to kill me was Aaron's looming presence. Falondeitric seemed shocked, too, but not angry. It was more like he'd just had his worst fears realized.

"Her pants *are* stupid," Fitch rasped. Shane chuckled in a higher, almost melodic voice. They had turned back to their food to eat as if nothing out of the ordinary were happening.

"I'm in," Ellis said. He sat between me and Fitch. He stared at his plate like he'd forgotten it was there.

"Ellis!" Markinius sputtered, his eyes wide.

"Seleca murdered my mother, Markus!" Ellis shouted. His face turned red, and bits of spit flicked out of his mouth as he spoke. "She burned down my house and enslaved me and my brother. They made me . . ." Ellis's voice broke. He heaved a breath, then continued. "Eve is no purified goddess. She's a monster. I don't care what you think. I don't care what anyone thinks. I killed Axel, and I would do it again. The bastard deserved it, and so does she. If I can make that happen, I will. I'm in."

The silence stretched out over us, and I shivered as I recognized that our situation had just fundamentally changed. I had openly declared war for the first time, and now I'd gained allies.

"That reminds me," Aaron said, pulling Axel's filigreed dagger out of his belt. "This is yours." He pushed the dagger over to Ellis.

Ellis took the dagger, gripping the handle so tightly that his knuckles were white. Then he glanced up at Aaron and nodded. "Thanks," he said and tucked the dagger into his own belt.

"No, thank you," Aaron replied. "You saved Lina's life."

"Yes, thank you, Ellis," I said.

Ellis met my eyes for a brief moment, then looked away again. "You saved Ward from *me*," he said. "I won't forget that."

And through the rubble and debris, I thought. The men were all brothers, grouped into twos and threes. It was happening. *Too late to back out now.*

"I'm in too," Fitch said.

"Me too," said Shane.

We all turned to the Eboros brothers.

Falondeitric closed his eyes, his brow furrowed, then took a deep breath. "I'm in too," he murmured.

"Falon!" Markinius stammered. "How could you? She gave our family everything we have."

"Well, maybe she shouldn't have, Markus," he snapped. "And Seleca was the one who trapped us in a Projection trance. You don't know that she would have let us out. Look at Shane!" Falondeitric pointed at the bony man. "They were gonna let him starve to death. He used to be your friend until you got too important for him. I guess now that you're Father's right hand, things like that don't matter to you anymore."

Markinius glanced at Shane, then back at his brother with an expression of outrage. "That could be me or you," Falondeitric continued, heedless of his brother's ire. "I'm in. With or without you."

The two brothers stared each other down, and my opinion of Falondeitric, which had teetered on the edge of contempt, rose considerably. He still hadn't thanked me for setting him free, but he'd come close. He was reasonable, at least, which was more than I could say for Markinius.

Markinius threw his fork on his plate and rose from his chair, sliding it back so hard that it tipped over onto the floor with a *crack*. He stalked around the table in the opposite direction of Aaron. He had some sense, at least. He stomped to the front door, pushed it open, then stopped in his tracks.

The scene outside had transformed from a cold, wet night, to a complete whiteout. Snow had begun to fall more heavily sometime in the last hour and had already stacked two inches deep against the indentation made by the opening of the door. Falondeitric followed his brother to the door with Aaron on his heels. The rest of us trailed behind Aaron.

Markinius cried out in surprise, then bolted out into the snow.

"Markus!" Falondeitric howled at the empty doorway.

Aaron jumped to catch Falondeitric, forcibly holding him back. I came up behind them to peer out of the door, but Aaron held me back too.

Out in the snowstorm, a few dozen yards from the door, stood Seleca. She didn't move when she saw us. She just stared, the snow swirling around her in an unnatural funnel. The flakes collected in her black hair, but she hardly seemed to notice.

Axel's corpse was draped stiffly over her shoulder, and her clothes were disheveled, like she had been awakened from sleep.

Markinius forged a path through the clean snow and threw himself down in front of Seleca. He knelt before her, his head bowed, his hair and tunic thrown out sideways by the strange wind. Seleca grasped the front of his head, I presumed, to connect to him and learn what our group had just discussed.

Her eyes narrowed, and her hand clenched Markinius's head. He cried out in pain, struggled against her in vain, then fell limp into the snow. Markinius had literally thrown himself at her feet and she had used him, then disposed of him like garbage.

"Markus!" Falondeitric screamed. He flailed, trying to escape Aaron's grip.

"I can go," I said. "I'll put my shield up."

"No, Lee," Aaron said. "You're too tired. You could pass out in the snow and your shield would come down. It's too dangerous."

I wanted to argue, but he was right. It had happened before, and I was dead tired.

"Fine, what then?"

"Just wait," he said.

Spirit! I called. Why hadn't she warned us that Seleca was coming? Where was she?

"I'm here," she said. She appeared behind us, within the house. I turned to her, but she wasn't as solid as usual. It was like the image of her was pixelated, and some of the pixels were burned out. "I'm sorry, Lina, I couldn't come."

"What do you mean? Why not? What happened, Spirit?"

"Seleca has Conjuration, like you. She's had another ghost helping her this whole time and knew that I spied on her. That's also how she knew about your reservoirs to begin with, but she kept me from reading that in her thoughts. I don't know how. And this time she bound me, keeping me from coming to warn you. I couldn't come until you called me directly."

"But . . ." I began, but I didn't need to ask why. I knew. I spun back to see Seleca smiling.

Seleca must have seen what we were going to do with her newly acquired Precognition. She'd waited for me to mix reservoirs with Ward. While he gave some of his Transformation to me, I had probably given him a little of all my reservoirs as well.

A rare combination of reservoirs, I thought. That's what Ward had said. And now he had that combination too. My stomach dropped and suddenly I thought I might throw up. She had beaten me.

Seleca's smile widened as she watched me figure out what had happened. "I told you he was my most useful asset," she said, her face alight with triumph. "I finally have everything I need, and I have you to thank for it. Unlike this one"—Seleca chuckled as she patted the corpse she carried—"a *living* body that's empty but still spirit-linked is necessary to let in the possessing soul, but that only happens if the body's original owner had Conjuration. We almost had *your* body that first week when you let yourself drift out, but alas, we'll have to go with plan B."

"If you hurt Ward, I'll kill you," I said softly, knowing she would hear me.

Seleca laughed. "You've never played Daggers and Dragons before, have you?" she asked. Her reflective monster eyes shone a bright blue green in the darkness. "Let me give you a little tip. It's nothing like chess." She laughed again at that, then turned away and stalked into the swirling snow, disappearing onto a bridge beyond the view of my weak Earth eyes.

I cried out as if I had been slapped. My vision narrowed and I dropped to my knees in the blackened entryway. *Oh, Ward, my friend. I'm so sorry. I've killed you. I've killed another one.*

Chapter Twenty-six

Though she had narrowly escaped Queen Mortier's trap, Linorra knew that she was not yet safe for she had lost the key. Nevertheless, her bond with Syndeth remained true and brought her great comfort. This connection would be their strength in the coming days. With Syndeth's help, Linorra vowed to find the key and her lost love, then they would fly out to meet their destiny.

Fitch and Falondeitric dragged Markinius back into the house, pulling him up beside me. Seleca had dug her thumb right through his forehead. Blood spurted from the wound disturbingly fast. He looked like someone had dumped a bucket of blood on his head. His face and chest were completely covered.

"Avelina, please, can you help him?" Falondeitric cried desperately. He was hysterical, sputtering and hyperventilating, but I couldn't remember what to do about it. My head hurt, and my mind was full of helium.

Fitch reached for Falondeitric and held him like a weeping child. It was distracting, and I winced at the sound of it, but at least he didn't throw himself on top of his brother.

It's not over, Lina, Spirit thought. *You're still a warrior. You said it yourself, remember?*

Spirit was always right, wasn't she? No. This time she must be wrong. I wasn't a warrior. I was just a self-deluded idealist. I doubted I would ever beat Seleca, but my own grief was no excuse for letting Markinius die. If I did that, then it needed to be a conscious, well-considered choice, not a result of numb indecision.

I shook myself, then reached over and grasped his hand, easily pushing into a Connection link. He was alive, but not for long. He had no thoughts at all. His forehead and upper skull had been crushed. The base of his brain was okay and kept his body alive for now, but blood gushed into cavities in the skull where it should not be. It would be mere moments before his soul drifted out of his body.

Holy shit. How strong do you have to be to crush someone's skull with your bare hands? What the hell am I even doing here?

"Focus, Lina," Spirit said.

Right, sorry. I sent Protection into Markinius at a steady rate, trying to regulate the flow so that it was constant but not overwhelmingly strong. I focused on his head injury, spreading my awareness into his brain but also reaching out for his mind.

He didn't respond at first, but then I felt an abrupt halting of the hemorrhaging that was killing him. The artery in the front of his head that had burst steadily repaired itself, and the blood was reabsorbed. The immense swelling that had impaired his consciousness subsided, and his mind reemerged.

Wake up, Markinius, I thought to him gently. *You're going to be okay. Wake up.* His eyes fluttered but didn't open. Then he released a pornographic moan.

Falondeitric stared at his brother, eyes wide, then wiped the tears from his face. Fitch raised one eyebrow, glanced at me, then released the stunned Falondeitric and stood to get some distance from the embarrassing noise. Aaron knelt next to me, ready to pounce.

Markinius grasped my hand tightly and pulled it down toward his groin, at which point Aaron promptly intervened, ripping our hands apart. I hadn't expected that response from Markinius since I had been fairly certain about my hypothesis on Protection. Healing was highly pleasurable but not necessarily sexual, and Markinius hadn't done that the first time I'd healed him.

I sighed, giving up my effort to understand for now. There was still so much to learn. Every time I thought I had a handle on my reservoirs, I was promptly shown otherwise.

I let Aaron pull me into his arms. "We'll get him back," he whispered, holding me tight. I felt so defeated that I didn't even respond. I just sniffed and wiped my eyes with my sleeve, drained of both energy and willpower.

Markinius mumbled something, but I couldn't understand him.

"What, Markus?" Falondeitric asked, leaning over his brother. "What'd you say?"

Markinius opened his eyes, wiped his bloody face with his hand, then examined his red fingers and palm. "I'm in too," he croaked. He sat up, but he didn't look at me. He took a deep breath and let it out again as if bracing himself. "You've saved me twice now, Avelina Silva. I'm sorry I didn't say it before. Thank you."

I smiled. *Well, that's one way to gain an ally.* I glanced at Falondeitric. He breathed easier, but his face was tense, like he still couldn't believe his brother would be all right. His gaze shifted to mine, but his expression of awe made me uncomfortable, so I avoided it by focusing on Markus.

"We're all friends here, Markus," I said with a nervous laugh. "Call me Lina." I hoped that meant I could call the Eboros brothers by their nicknames since their full names sounded needlessly pretentious. I wondered if that had anything to do with their social status in Neesee.

"Friends," Markus repeated, glancing up at Aaron warily. "I've never been friends with a girl before."

"Well, you can't say that anymore, can you?" I observed. His comment struck me as strange. He must have gone to SONA like the rest of them. Hadn't he made a single female friend the entire time? So odd. "A lot of things will change around here if we have our way. That's the least of them."

"What do you mean?" he asked doubtfully.

Aaron nodded at me. *Go ahead.*

Not that I needed his permission to speak, but I valued his judgment to guide me through the social sand traps of this strange world.

"No more burning down people's houses, for one," I said. "No more enslaving people with Projection. No more begging for a permit to fall in love, bond, and have children. No more illegal reservoirs or hiding who you are. And most of all, no more worshipping of murderers and thieves. I'm sure there will be more, but that's a good start."

"That all sounds great," Markus said, "but so far Seleca's beaten you pretty easily."

"She's had an advantage, it's true," Aaron said. "We need to find my mother. I think she's the only one who would know how to counteract that advantage. To do that, Lina needs to learn how to use the Teleportation fragment. There are two books in the library that I know of that discuss it. In the meantime, we'll take Jorin's skiff up to the commercial docks and borrow a larger boat to sail up the coast to Neesee."

"To save my brother," Ellis said.

"Ours too," said Shane.

"And the girl," I added. "Seleca will know we're coming."

Aaron nodded. "Yes. We'll figure it out. We need to save them."

We probably didn't *need* to save Ward from Aaron's perspective, but he knew what it meant to me. I hugged him tightly.

"She took Axel's body," Ellis said. "Why would she do that?"

I looked up into Aaron's face. *Can we trust them?*

I think it's all or nothing, Aaron thought. *We can't do this alone. Trust may be the most dangerous thing we can do, but without it, we risk losing everything.*

I gave him a small smile. "That does make sense. You are very wise."

Aaron reflected my expression back at me, a heat growing in his eyes. That's what I had said to him just before we slept together for the first time. I knew he remembered. Aaron never forgot anything. He lifted one hand to rub his thumb over my one dimple, a gesture I had learned signaled his desire for me. I wasn't sure we'd be able to scratch that itch under the circumstances.

Suppressing a groan, I got to my feet and faced "the crew," as I'd begun to think of them. "You all know that I have multiple greater reservoirs, but I haven't told you what they are. Two are Noble and three are Unspeakable. Among those, the rarest is Conjuration." I searched the crew's expressions for signs of recognition. I didn't have to wait long for an answer. Falon and Markus looked at each other meaningfully.

"Are you saying you talk to ghosts?" Falon asked doubtfully.

"You don't believe me? Come here," I demanded, exasperated. I held out my hand. Falon hesitated to meet my request, instead helping his brother up from the floor. His eyes flicked up to Aaron for an instant, then back down to me. I sighed, then stepped close to them both and grasped Falon's forearm, connecting to him brusquely. He jumped at the sudden sensation and then stilled, gazing down at me intently. His boyish face relaxed to a bland expression, but through our link I could feel his keen interest. This was not a man accustomed to being grabbed by girls, and he liked it. What's more, he knew I could feel how much he liked it, and he made no attempt to hide it. He inhaled slowly through his nose, taking in my scent.

Startled, I took a half step back but didn't let go. I hadn't meant to attract that kind of interest, I just wanted to prove a point, though I'd forgotten what that point was for the moment. I was surprised not only by Falon's obvious attraction to me, but also by the boldness with which he conveyed this through my own Connection.

In a flash of insight, I realized I had misjudged his age. He was older than he looked, and as he was also more than two feet taller than me, I now felt like a silly child trying to get a grown-up's attention by pulling on his sleeve. I averted my gaze, but I could feel my face flush. I swallowed, then I grabbed Markus's forearm and said, "The rest, too, if you would. I want to show you all."

Ellis, Fitch, and Shane shot nervous looks over my shoulder at Aaron, who must have nodded because they gathered in reluctantly to lay a finger on the top of my hand or wrist. I pushed Connection into the group with some effort. I hadn't attempted such a wide link before. It was a bit like trying to blow out candles on opposite sides of a birthday cake without turning your head. It was harder than I thought, but I did it.

Aaron sighed heavily, then positioned himself closer behind me as if he might need to quickly pull me away again. I wasn't sure if he noticed Falon's reaction to my touch, but it was clear that he considered something like that a possibility from at least one of these men.

"Spirit," I said, trying to shake off my anxiety. "Say hello to the crew."

"Hello, crew!" Spirit yelled needlessly loud. Everyone jerked, tugging their hands away from me like they'd been burned. Aaron laughed, and Spirit joined him, giggling in her girly way.

"Jarring, isn't it?" Aaron commented.

"Who the Rhoya was that?" Shane asked.

"That was my friend, Spirit. Seleca murdered her. Now she's helping me. Us, I should say."

Us, I repeated to myself. There's an *us* now.

"You have a ghost following you around?" Markus asked, his face pinched.

"Yes," I said, "but that's not all you can do with Conjuration. If you have someone's body, there's a way to bring them back. I'm not sure how long the body is good for, if there's a sort of expiration date, so to speak. God, I hope so."

"The term über-zombie just took on new meaning," Spirit commented, still giggling.

"Anyway," I continued. "Seleca has Conjuration, too, so she can probably bring Axel back. You need Protection for that, which Seleca doesn't have, but she can probably use someone else's." Ellis stilled, staring at me hard. The rest of the crew fell silent, their eyes wide.

"And," Aaron added, "there's someone else she might be able to bring back as well."

"Anick," Fitch guessed. His gravelly voice somehow mirrored the roughness I think we all felt. I nodded, surprised a little. Fitch didn't say much, but what he did say was spot on.

"That's why she took my brother?" Ellis asked. "To use his body?"

I nodded again. "So, you see now why we must fight them. If Anick comes back using Ward's body, there will be nowhere to run and nowhere to hide." I turned to Aaron. "Even Earth isn't safe. We have no choice. We have to stop Seleca before it's too late."

Aaron and I stared at each other for a long moment. We took a breath together, and I turned around, keeping one of his arms around my shoulders. Let Falon take that as a clear message.

"You've all said you're in," Aaron said. "Can we count on you?" He looked at each of the men in turn, making eye contact with every face.

The Smite brothers nodded right away, as did Ellis. They all had family to rescue. The Eboros brothers glanced at each other first, took a breath, then nodded more reluctantly. They had less to gain and more to lose. Falon's eyes met my own, then he looked at Aaron, then back at me, his eyes searching. One corner of his mouth twitched, and Spirit started laughing again.

"I think someone likes a challenge," she commented aloud.

Seriously, Spirit. If you must comment, could you keep it between us? I stole a peek at Aaron, knowing he'd heard what Spirit had said. He returned the look, his brow furrowed. I rolled my eyes and shook my head in the universal gesture that meant *never mind*, then resolved not to meet Falon's gaze again.

"Okay," Aaron said. "We'll leave in the morning, after we've gotten a few hours of sleep."

"Why not now?" Ellis asked. "Ward can't wait for us to take a nap."

"Neither can Cobb," added Shane.

Oh, interesting, Spirit thought to me. *Here's something we should keep between us.*

What?

Cobb's a woman who's been disguised as a boy her whole life.

"Skiffing isn't safe in this weather," Aaron said, oblivious to my conversation with Spirit, "at least not in the dark. Besides, you're all dead on your feet, especially Lina. You won't be any good to anyone if you're too exhausted to hold an oar."

Why is she disguised? I asked Spirit.

I'm not sure. The Smite brothers aren't thinking about why, they're only worried that someone will find out while Cobb's enthralled. That would significantly worsen her current situation. It's a miracle that it hasn't happened yet.

"And we need to make a basic plan, at the very least," Fitch said sensibly. "I don't want to botch the rescue."

Aaron nodded. I could tell those two would get along nicely. "And if your brother took Ward back to Axel's home," Aaron added, "which is not definite, then we don't know who could be there. We'll most likely only get one chance to rescue them."

Ellis and Shane both frowned but yielded to the logic of Aaron's argument.

I'm guessing this is related to why there are so few girls around, Spirit thought.

Yeah, I agreed, *I haven't met one since I've been here.*

Aaron turned to me. "Let's show them the library," he said, and thought to me, *and go to bed.*

Our bed, I thought back, yawning. "That sounds great."

He smiled, taking my hand. *Our bed, yes. But this?* He squeezed my hand a little to indicate that he meant me. *This is mine.*

With that, he pulled me past the crew toward the stairs. I didn't know if the timing of his declaration was significant, but I very carefully avoided Falon's eyes as we passed him.

We told our new crew everything that night. Spirit volunteered to patrol the grounds while we educated them on the reality of what the Ministry actually was and what they wanted. Namely, power. That was always the motivation behind the Ministry's plan to resurrect Anick, the so-called Holy Father. If they knew him like I do now, they would have run away screaming. He was not who they believed him to be. Violet Atticus knew, though. She knew everything.

Fitch, Shane, and Ellis looked through the forbidden books with reverence as if they were finally discovering the answers to a great mystery. Falon and Markus already had many of the same books in their own private library at the Eboros estate in Neesee.

We learned a great deal as well. Shane and Fitch were lesser transformers but had no greater reservoirs. The Eboros brothers were both greater transmuters, a family secret that Markus was loath to reveal. Transmutation ran in their family much like Evocation ran in Aaron's family. Their father owned all the most important durran and fortite mines on Monash, but those mines didn't produce nearly as much as they claimed. Instead, the family secretly specialized in transmuting stone into the two substances and then selling those products to the Metalworkers Guild and the Caravan Traders.

No wonder Markus and Falon acted like spoiled rich kids. That's exactly what they were. Falon slightly less so, thanks to his mother's influence. Spirit was right about that guy, though. He did love a challenge.

Ellis had been trapped in Projection the entire time Aaron was in hiding. He was lucky to be alive, let alone sane. If it hadn't been for my method of healing using a blended Connection link with Conjuration and Protection, he probably wouldn't have been. Even so, the Ellis who emerged from long-term captivity was not the same one Aaron knew. Aaron later told me this new version was more like a reflection of his friend and former roommate, one who looked the same but was empty behind that facade.

I think Ellis was trapped in a well of darkness. He was free of his Projection trance but not of the memories he made there. Not only had Ellis been made to hold girls down for Axel, he'd also been forced to attempt the impregnation himself on more than one occasion. Entranced, he'd had no ability to prevent those encounters, but he carried the guilt all the same.

He thought he might have a daughter, Willette. The girl was four years old and had auburn hair just like his. She lived with her mother in the Rhoyal Healers Guild. That revelation gave me a new perspective on his conflicted reaction to me force-healing him. I wonder sometimes if Ellis was hoping Axel would be resurrected just so he could kill him a second time.

Our plan was to pack up in the morning and pile into the skiff at first light. Hopefully, no one would be at Jorin's commercial docks because those docks were there for the trading vessels that transported Jorin's harvest up to the Neesee Harvest Festival. There, most of those goods would be sold or traded, minus the tithe to the Ministry. Shockingly,

Jorin hadn't planted this year, so there was no reason for those ships to come in, but Jorin kept his own sailboat there to transport the most valuable of his goods, the oardoo feathers.

Once we obtained the sailboat, it was on to Neesee, where we would split into two groups to search for Ward and Cobb, one group to Axel's estate, and one to Seleca's palace. It was ungodly late by the time we all lay down to sleep. Ellis crashed in Ward's reading chair, looking so much like his brother that I could almost pretend Ward was there, safe and reading in his spot as always.

Falon and Markus fell asleep on the braided rug next to Ellis. Shane and Fitch migrated over to the secret room across the secret hallway and fell asleep in the secret bed. We didn't tell them that it was Terik and Farrah's secret sex bed.

Aaron was going to stay up to keep watch, but Spirit convinced him that she would be enough, and he and I fell asleep in our own secret sex bed. Nobody said a word about it.

Epilogue

Linorra watched a small whiff of smoke escape Syndeth's nostrils and knew that he was very serious. "What do you mean by belong?" she asked.

"Just what I said," he answered. "Belong."

It's strange to think back on those first months in Jorin's farmhouse and recall how they ended so abruptly. At the time, I thought of myself as oppressed. Hunted, even. In reality, those were the best days of my life. Ward was safe. Everything with Aaron was so pure and uncomplicated.

I was still innocent.

There's a reason why they say reservoirs aren't just something you *have*, but something you fundamentally *are*. I didn't realize until much later that because a reservoir is attached to the soul, maybe even located inside the soul, when you absorb someone else's, you rip off and integrate a tiny piece of their spirit as well. It's like mixing reservoirs, but in reverse and to the benefit, or in my case detriment, of one person. It has been one of the biggest regrets of my seemingly endless existence.

In retrospect, things didn't really start to go downhill until after I absorbed Axel's reservoir. His soul was an unwholesome thing, and I gobbled it up like a vampire. That is, essentially, what absorbers are. We're vampires. Once you taste the blood, you are well and truly turned.

Zig often laments that he didn't meet me until after I consumed Axel because he could have warned me that you must be exceedingly selective about who you absorb. I know, I haven't gotten to Zig yet. I will. He's important.

I wonder how different my life would be if he'd found me before Aaron. Then again, Violet never would have let that happen. She always cared more about saving the people she loved than saving the universe. That's one of the few things we always agreed on.

After all, would it be so bad if the fragments of creation collapsed back into the Oneness? If that meant the end of the universe, so be it. Of course, that's what Anick's been trying to tell me for the last thousand years. He is, I admit, the most persuasive man I know.

Thank you for reading!

I depend on reviews from readers like you. It would mean the world to me if you left a review on Amazon or the platform of your choice. To authors like me, leaving a review is like leaving a tip. It makes all this work worthwhile!

Wanna keep going?

Sign up for my newsletter and I'll send you the first three chapters of *The Wisdom of Dishonor*, the second book in *The Cult of Anick* series, due out Thanksgiving 2024. I also like to send out updates on new releases, interviews, and book signings. Subscribers will get the first notice when I'm recruiting ARC readers for future novels. Unsubscribe at any time. Go to www.brooksbooks.net/newsletter or scan this QR code:

Acknowledgments

First and foremost, I want to thank Chris Brooks, who is such a great support and alpha reader. You get the worst version of me and keep going.

Thanks so much to my amazing editors, Becky Wallace, Jennifer Cappello, and Laura LaTulipe. I learned so much from you gals and I'm truly grateful for your patience and guidance. I also need to thank Rebecca Frank and Leo Hartas for your incredible artwork. And to my talented friend Mary Evans, who is the best beta reader ever, and who also agreed to record my audiobook on consignment because she's just a big heart smothered in sarcasm.

Also, thank you to Heidi Cox, who graciously agreed to be my cover model for this series. You're a good friend and the prettiest person I know in real life. Thank you so much to my other friends, family, and beta readers whose encouragement has kept me going, but especially my sister, Jennifer, who gives brutally honest comments that give me heartburn but make my writing so much better. Lastly, thanks to everyone who contributed to my Kickstarter so I could afford to do this thing.

Writing this acknowledgment section is so humbling because it brings to mind all the people who have supported me for absolutely no reason that I can think of. If ever I'm feeling down, I'll just come read this again. Thank you.

About the Author

L. E. Brooks is an indie author, RN, musician, bad feminist, worse LGBTIQA+ fringe member, and reader of all genres. She has been writing songs, poetry, and short stories for more than two decades, and is the author of two novels, *Avelina* and its sequel, *The Wisdom of Dishonor*. She lives in the Midwest with her husband, two kids, and a ferocious pack of hell hounds.

Follow her on Instagram and Facebook, or go to www.brooksbooks.net.

@AUTHOR.BROOKSBOOKS

Made in the USA
Monee, IL
23 July 2024